COLOMBO
HEAT

Christopher Hudson

MACMILLAN
LONDON

by the same author

The Killing Fields
The Final Act
Insider Out

First published 1986 by
MACMILLAN LONDON LIMITED
4 Little Essex Street London WC2R 3LF
and Basingstoke

Associated companies in Auckland, Delhi, Dublin, Gaborone,
Hamburg, Harare, Hong Kong, Johannesburg, Kuala Lumpur,
Lagos, Manzini, Melbourne, Mexico City, Nairobi, New York,
Singapore and Tokyo

British Library Cataloguing in Publication Data

Hudson, Christopher
Colombo heat.
I. Title
823'.914 [F]   PR6058.U313

ISBN 0-333-42824-2

Filmset in Palatino by Filmtype Services Limited,
Scarborough, North Yorkshire.
Printed in Great Britain by
Anchor Brendon Limited, Tiptree

*for two generations
of the McLeod family*

ONE

AFTER three hundred years as gentleman farmers the Tancreds became accident-prone. A streak of stubbornness, inbred from centuries of harrowing the Devon clay either side of the Rubble, was very probably to blame.

George Tancred, Guy's grandfather, went bankrupt in 1890, having spent all his money attempting to perfect a potato harvester which never did succeed in separating potatoes from clods of earth and stones. His son Reginald was attempting to recover the family fortunes in the City when the Great War came. Convinced that it would consist of prolonged cavalry skirmishes he invested all his capital in leather and saddlery, and was caught short by the combustion engine.

Harry Tancred, Reginald's elder son, looked set to suffer the same fate. Leaving Oxford rather abruptly he turned his hand to rubber-planting in Ceylon, just before the Depression sent rubber prices tumbling to an all-time low. It was left to Harry's brother Guy, ten years younger, to repair the Tancred fortunes. With a foresight unapparent in the rest of his family he studied economics at Oxford and left knowing more about money than most of his richer friends who took it for granted. After three illustrious years in Lazards he was invited to join the finance department at Dunlop Orient with a view to a directorship in six or seven years' time. Intrigued as much by the coincidence as by the challenge – Dunlop Orient owned his brother's rubber estate – Guy accepted the position.

Confident and quick-witted, he rapidly got to grips with the intricacies of the international rubber trade. Then war broke out. Rubber stocks dwindled. Dunlop determined to send him East, in the autumn of 1941, to keep an eye on the market and gather intelligence on rubber output.

At the age of twenty-eight, darkly good-looking, urbane, something of a social butterfly, Guy found himself in a situation he for once had not anticipated. He knew nothing about the East. He was an investment adviser, not a rubber expert. The potato

1

harvester rattled in his dreams. He thought of resigning to join his uncle's regiment, the Devonshires; but the Dunlop Orient job for some inscrutable reason turned out to qualify as vital war work. Duty was invoked, patriotism. Even Lydia waved the flag. Accepting his fate with a good grace, he wrote to Harry in Ceylon. On the long voyage he took out his brother's reply more than once and read it over with a faint unease.

> Kelani Lodge,
> Kelani Rubber Estate
>
> Dear Guy,
>
> Thank you for your letter and Mother's enclosed. It came airmail. Mine will have to wait its turn for the Bombay packet. Of course you must come and stay, for as long as you like. You will be company for Jill. And it will be fun to talk about "old times" to someone who does not smother them with nostalgia like most of the professional expatriates I run into here. Not that you may remember the "old times", I suppose.
>
> You intimate that Dunlop Orient are worried about the Yanks siphoning off rubber from Ceylon for the US Rubber Reserve. I wouldn't know about that. But I warn you, rubber planters are a proud bunch, and they don't much care to be told how to behave, particularly with the market just starting to pick up after the Slump. We can talk about all that over a split when you arrive in November. Jill will consult the sailing schedule and we'll be at the harbour to meet you.
>
> > Yours affectionately
> > HARRY
>
> PS. Try to keep fit on the voyage. If you lack for reading matter, let me commend to you Mr Leonard Woolf's book about Ceylon, *The Village in the Jungle*. It is an education. Mr Woolf understands the Jungle that is in all of us.

Guy landed in Colombo in his pale cream suit. The light still hurt his eyes. In the imperial gloom of the Customs House a woman he hardly recognised, honey-brown with a freckled smile, took him by the hand. She led him out past tiled godowns; past cliffs of stencilled tea-chests awaiting shipment and bales of copra that gave off the nutty, sweet smell of drying coconut. Wiry brown men in grubby white banyans and sarongs ran across his path, shouting and hauling barrow-loads of luggage, before disappearing between the cliffs of tea. Ropes snaked on the dockside, between the drums of copra and coconut oil. He stepped over them carefully.

"Did Harry come?" he asked, shading his eyes.

"He couldn't get away. His *Sina Dorai* is down with malaria."

Her Australian vowel-flatness removed any doubts that this was Jill Tancred. The only other time they'd met had been in London five years ago when Harry had brought her over on leave shortly after their marriage. Guy had felt sorry for both of them: Harry with his stilted courtesies, Jill nervously conscious of seeming out of place with her sun-tan and provincial manners, as vulgarly Australian as a sunflower in a bed of madonna lilies. Talking to his cousin Lydia about the two of them, he'd been ashamed to find himself on the defensive, describing them as exotics, creatures of the heat and light. After they'd met, for tea at his mother's flat in Cheyne Gardens, Lydia had made a little *moue* with her mauve lips – "I'm terribly sorry, darling, she's not an exotic, she's a *colonial*. Never mind."

By now Lydia would have swooned in the heat and been carried back in a launch to the boat by dashing army officers. Jill seemed not to notice it. She had organised the stowing of his luggage in the black Morris 8 and was propelling him into the back seat.

"Now, Guy, you must tell me what's *really* happening," she said.

"I shouldn't think there's much I can tell you."

"What do you mean? *Everybody* knows more about the war than we do out here." She must have caught his glance, because she cried, "My wretched impatience! Here you are, fresh off the boat, and I don't even give you time to look around!"

As it happened, Colombo harbour was not so different from Bombay – the same hot, throaty smell of pepper and cinnamon and monsoon drains, the same hullaballoo of shouting brats, bicycle bells, car horns, the clatter of rickshaws over the loose chippings. With a bang, the Morris boot slammed shut. Twisting round, Guy saw through the rear window a brown face inches from his own. A long narrow face with full lips, a straight nose broadening at the nostrils, brown eyes, as bright as an animal's, staring boldly back at him through the glass. The boy was probably in his middle twenties, a few years younger than him, it was hard to tell.

"Let's go, Michael," Jill was calling. "Let's not waste time."

The head vanished, to reappear in the front seat. "You're safe with Michael Kandasala," Jill announced as they drove away

3

from the Customs warehouses. "He's a better driver than most Sinhalese who drive like Italians or worse. Are you really out here on business?"

"I'm very grateful, you know."

"What for?"

"Letting me stay with you. Especially at a time like this."

"Oh, what English politeness! Just like Harry. It's you who's doing us a favour, honestly. All our young men being shipped off to the war, we're relying on you to restore the balance."

Guy shifted uncomfortably on the cloth-covered seat. This wife of Harry's couldn't be all that much older than him, certainly not old enough to taunt him with such a disinterested smile. But Jill was in her element, he mustn't forget. In her flowered sundress she was a creature of the heat and light, as he'd said to Lydia back in Civilisation.

He smiled and blinked in the glare, looking round with a boyish delight. The car leapt forward into the afternoon, scattering rickshaws and leaving in its wake a patter of small boys. Down a wide street lined with rain trees and dazzling white government offices, a bronze viceroy on horseback shimmered uncertainly in the fearsome heat.

Jill leant across him and pointed up at a lofty *palazzo* facing on to the harbour. "That's the Grand Oriental Hotel. It's where Harry and I met – would you believe? – at the Clarkes' wedding. Ten years she's had of him, poor girl."

It occurred to him that Jill must have been having a fling with his brother all through Guy's time at Oxford. Yet the first any of them heard about it was when a mutual friend came to see Mother after stopping off in Ceylon on a world cruise, and talked about Harry and Jill as if they were man and wife.

That was when Mother had sold the house and burrowed into the little Cheyne Gardens flat. Rebuffed in her tenderest affections, she felt wounded, diminished. "Reginald would have gone out and told him a thing or two," she used to say through pursed lips; but she never did go out herself.

He phrased it carefully. "How long were you together before the wedding?"

"You know your brother." Jill smiled. "Harry likes to deliberate about things. And why not? He was about the most eligible planter in Ceylon, what with the Kelani estate being so close to Colombo; and I was this Australian girl Jill MacAlister from the back of beyond, tongue-tied, hair in a bun. Nothing going for me except my smart little nurse's uniform. For a convent-educated child like me, sex was something the dogs did before the gardener kicked them apart."

"Harry must have taught you a lot."

"Do you think so?"

He laughed and brushed his hand through his hair. Were they all so direct out here? Perhaps it was the East: perhaps it liberated people. Squinting happily through the window, he saw they were crossing a canal and leaving the wide, swept streets of the European quarter behind them. "Where are we?" he asked.

Jill's answer was swallowed up in a roaring dusty confusion of noise and milling brown bodies. The car slowed to walking pace. Jostling salesmen pressed against his window. A big Moor in a black fez elbowed through and held up a length of scarlet cloth –

"Here is big chance, lady!" he cried through discoloured teeth. "In shop, three rupees a yard! Here, one rupee fifty! Big bargain, lady!"

The Morris surged forward once more. Moor and scarlet cloth were lost in the hubbub of other pavement bargains – baskets, cooking pots, silver bangles – along the arcaded thoroughfare. Stallholders spat betel-juice and peddled their wares.

"This is the Pettah!" Jill shouted. "The native market. It's where the Dutch lived, two hundred years ago. That belfry you see used to summon them to Lutheran prayer on top of Wolfendahl hill. Some of the houses above these boutiques are quite fine."

"What happened?" he shouted.

"They moved south, to Colpetty and Cinnamon Gardens. The old Town Hall's full of mangoes, chillis, lady's fingers, bananas and dried fish. How am I doing as a tourist guide?"

A greybeard waved at them from the doorway of a rickety Jewellery And Curious bazaar. A man in a white dhoti picked up a betel-leaf. Dipping it into the little saucer of juice on the betel-seller's tray, he folded over the leaf as if he was rolling a cigarette, and put it in his mouth to chew. Guy smiled at his sister-in-law, exhilarated despite himself. Really it was quite picturesque if you were a connoisseur of street scenes. There was – he searched for the word – a *voluptuousness* about it all which was charming to observe, if not to smell. . . . Over the blare of horns, the rattling of trams and the creaking of covered bullock-wagons he could distinctly hear a dance tune. It came from a wheezy gramophone in the dark recesses of what may well have been a hardware shop.

5

He sat back and took a deep breath. "All this," he said with a laugh. "It's all so public, don't you find? It's like small children. I mean, as if you can see right into their lives!"

He had spoken without thinking. The glossy black head in the driver's seat turned slightly, and nodded, as if passing a private comment. "Metaphorically speaking," Guy added.

The market noise fell away behind them as they came out of Layards Broadway and crossed the tramlines into Prince of Wales Avenue. Each new street name rang out more imperially than the last, but the houses on either side had plainly given up the unequal battle. Humbly they backed away from the pavement, shielding their flaking plaster behind large, cursive signs – *Paradaise Textiles, Saree Printers, Come Eat Your Full at the Shangrilla Restnt.*

They crossed the railway line and a low bridge over a wide, muddy river which the road then followed towards the hills. A sudden greenness enveloped him: the emerald green of paddy-fields, the darker green of palm trees shadowing the dusty macadam; and on the verge vivid scarlet chillis laid out in the sun like a road accident. Jill wanted to talk about the war: but what did he know about Rommel and Rudolf Hess, the British defeats in the Baltic and the German advance upon Moscow, that she couldn't read for herself every morning in the Colombo Daily Whatever?

Something fretted at his thoughts. He said, with more abruptness than he intended, "I haven't seen old Harry much, you know?"

Jill waited. He hurried on with a laugh. "It's a funny thing, isn't it, I suppose? Older brothers and all that nonsense. I was ten when Harry went off to be a planter. He's been back three times since then. The first time, there were stamps for my stamp collection and these extraordinary boys' magazine tales, I'm sure you've heard them. Hunting for elk by moonlight in the coastal jungles. Lying awake in his lonely up-country bungalow listening to the rat-snakes in the rafters and the screams which came out of the snake's belly as the rats were swallowed head first. All good fun, but you know. . . ." He paused, fanning himself with his hat.

"Yes?"

"I was doing my finals during his next leave, and he had reasons for not wanting to come up and see me in Oxford. And the one after that, of course, he came over with you and quite rightly took you off round the place. . . ."

"You joined his company."

"That was coincidence."

"Was it?" Jill gripped the leather door-strap as the car swerved round a rocky outcrop, sending up a cloud of red dust. "I can understand you not knowing what to expect," she said, choosing her words deliberately. "Remember, Harry's been out here a long time. Actually, he's very proud of you, Guy. He's always saying he's the black sheep of the family, the last of the great Tancred nonconformists, and you're the one who's made a success of things."

Guy looked down at his expensive tussore silk suit, the trouser-creases put in by the ship's laundry already flattening in the heat. "Is that his idea of himself?"

"Why not?" The chin tilted. "Do you think I'd have gone for him if he'd been one of the usual stick-in-the-muds you find out here?"

Without warning the paddy-fields and shadowing jungle fell away, to be replaced by rank upon silent rank of slender grey-limbed trees rising arrow-straight into a darkness of green foliage. They might have been a vast plantation of silver birches except for the tell-tale cicatrice in the bark which bled milky droplets into the half-shell of coconut suspended underneath.

Jill sighed. "On the radio the other day someone said our rubber pays for Britain's breakfast once a week. I suppose you Head Office people know about things like that."

"I suppose so," said Guy, who hadn't the faintest idea. The absurdity of his situation struck him more forcibly than ever. His natural habitat was the City of London, not this tropical wonderland. He was qualified to list the performance of rubber shares on the London market. He could give an instant summary of the cost per ton in pounds and dollars of Malayan, Netherlands East Indies and Ceylon rubber, and details of their price fluctuations over the past decade. He understood the workings of the International Rubber Regulations Committee – so expertly that he could usually predict what production quotas it was going to set. What did it matter to him how the blessed product came to exist in the first place?

It occurred to him, as they motored through the silent army of rubber trees, that he was getting deeper and deeper into things he knew less and less about. He had been despatched into the unknown, for reasons which were at best ambiguous. And at the end of the road was a long-lost brother of whom the most his wife would say was that he had been out East for a long time. . . .

7

They passed a clearing in the plantation. Guy caught a glimpse of corrugated-iron hangars, before the driver turned up a narrower dirt road which climbed off the valley floor. The rubber trees stood back. Green lawns opened up. In the middle of them, its red-tiled Dutch eaves sloping steeply to shrubs bright pink with hibiscus and bougainvillaea blossom, lay Kelani Lodge.

His brother's home was bigger than he'd expected. A sprawling wooden two-storey bungalow, its shuttered rooms opened on to wide, elevated verandahs which ran round all four sides. "It's a palace!" he exclaimed.

Jill smiled. "You've been at sea a long time," she said.

As the car drew up under the pillared porch, Michael sprang out and opened Jill's door. He gave rapid instructions to two lighter-skinned Tamil houseboys in white jackets and sarongs who came barefoot down the steps.

"Guy, is that you?"

Guy looked up. He took an involuntary step backwards. Harry Tancred stood at the top of the steps. He was naked except for a white sarong wrapped around his waist and a heavy moonstone ring on his middle finger. His face and torso were thinner than Guy had visualised; his blue eyes had retreated behind the strong forehead and prominent cheekbones giving him a severe, rather ascetic appearance – like a fakir, thought Guy uneasily, if fakirs could be pink-skinned.

His embrace, fortunately, smelt of nothing more exotic than Wright's Coal Tar Soap. "You look whacked," he said gruffly. "Michael will take you to your room and draw your bath. Dinner's at eight, so we'll have time for a drink. Off you go."

Guy's room was white and high-ceilinged. The fan turned indolently beside a bunched mosquito net. On his bedside table stood a jug of filtered water with a beaded cover to keep off the insects. His suitcases had already been opened; one of the boys was putting his clothes in the wardrobe. Guy said sharply, "Thank you, I'll do my own unpacking."

"I am hanging them for you, sir."

A voice spoke in Sinhalese from the door. As the houseboy salaamed to Guy and left the room, Michael Kandasala walked over to the window and closed the shutters. He had taken off his buttoned jacket and was wearing a loose white shirt over his sarong.

"Will I run your bath, sir, now?" he enquired in perfect English. "Or will you like to do your own?"

Left to himself, Guy folded away his clothes and put on the silk

8

dressing gown Mother had chosen for him as a farewell present. If Harry wanted to go native that was his prerogative. To his mind, it reeked of old-fashioned paternalism. The world had moved on since the days when big white chiefs assumed native dress as a token of empathy with their subjects. What had been carried off with effortless superiority in the glory days of Empire now struck him disagreeably as a manifestation of weakness, conciliation, a kind of inverted snobbism. It invited the sort of impertinence he had just had from Michael.

The bathwater was tepid. It had the brownish tinge of weak tea. As he began to relax, a gecko scuttled out from behind the geyser and stared at him fixedly. In its jaws it held a fat brown moth; Guy could distinctly hear its thin scream. With a casual flick of its head the gecko beat it against the damp-mottled plaster and then vanished with it into a crack in the wall.

Guy got out, shivering in the warm air, dressed and went to join the others.

Night in the tropics fell as suddenly as a blindfold. Harry, now respectably English in a jacket and tie, sat in one of the wooden reclining chairs on the verandah. He was looking out on the black lawns encircled by a deeper blackness where the rubber trees began. On a low tray-table beside him stood glasses, a soda siphon and two bottles of White Horse whisky. Guy took the other chair; his brother pushed one of the bottles across.

"Help yourself, old man. You'll find a glass-rest on the arm of your chair. Jill sends her apologies, by the way. She's got a bit of a headache, she might join us after the meal. There's ice on your left. That's it." He waited until Guy had poured his drink, then raised his glass to him. "Ayubowan!"

"I beg your pardon?"

"Your very good health. It's splendid to see you, Guy. Now, let's have it. How was the trip out? No Boche trying to blow you out of the water?"

Over more whisky, and a simple supper of grilled fish and potatoes, Guy was led to talk about the war. The drink and the strangeness of his surroundings loosened his tongue; he unburdened himself as he had never done at home. While the owls hooted, and the bats swooped among the swinging verandah lamps to gorge upon the insects drawn to the light, he talked about smoke and brick-dust, about the strange blurred softness of fallen buildings and the blackened limbs he had seen hosed out of them by firemen clambering in the smoke, and about the

9

blessed rain which washed the black dirt off his hands and face and blotted out the bombers' moon.

One hundred-pounder had gone straight through the hatch and into the cellar of the Three Tuns at the bottom of his street . . . but Harry was nodding through it all with a polite concern, as if he was listening for Guy's sake, as if the war itself, looked at from eight thousand miles away, was no more material than devils dancing on the head of a pin. As Guy faltered, the older man pushed away the fruit he'd been peeling and put the tips of his fingers together.

"What, in your view, is the purpose of this war?" he asked. "What good will come?"

"None if we lose."

"And if the Allies win?"

Guy frowned. "It's self-evident. We save the world from the tyranny of Adolf Hitler. We save England from Nazi dictatorship—"

"At the cost of how many hundreds of thousands of young men killed? How many millions maimed and wounded? I'm not being perverse, Guy. I was sixteen when the other war ended. When I went up to Oxford there were hundreds of men up, still, who had fought in the trenches. Been through the Somme and Passchendaele to gain a few hundred yards of mud and craters. Do you think they didn't ask themselves what the point had been? They'd seen their friends blown to shreds; they were haunted by nightmares, you could hear them on the staircase. . . ." He fell silent, staring out across the verandah to where the crickets were shrieking in the grass.

Guy felt himself reddening. "Are you saying we should let Hitler walk over us? Is that what you're saying?"

Harry seemed not to have heard him. "War is Hell without the prior grace of Judgement," he quoted, half to himself. "Max Fremantle always used to say that: War is Hell without the prior grace of Judgement."

"Who is Max Fremantle?"

"One of the chaps who had nightmares." In the look he gave Guy there was something proud and shy at the same time. "Did Mother ever tell you why I was sent down from Oxford?"

"You were sent down?" Guy was appalled. "She never told me that! She said you left because you weren't happy at university, you found it too constricting."

"That's not untrue. Damned humiliating to be a fresh-faced schoolboy among all those warriors. Trying to get wise from

10

books when they had the real knowledge, the *deep* knowledge. Most of the fellows in my year couldn't handle being with the veterans. I was different. I suppose I wanted to share the pain."

He paused. Guy had the feeling that the cavernous eyes were looking through him towards the invisible, bleeding trees. "Max was at the battle of Arras in 1917. Don't know if you've heard about it? Lloyd George had put that Frenchman, Nivelle, in overall command. His dodge was a big push to take the Germans by surprise. You can guess what happened. His generals, French and British, squabbled over the tactics for so long that the Germans had time to dig the Hindenburg Line right where the surprise attack was coming. Max said that going over the top was like trying to stay dry in a downpour by dodging between the raindrops. He actually was luckier than 142,000 of the people with him at Arras; he was just badly wounded. Think of it Guy. Most of an entire division and all but one of his fellow-officers killed inside of six days, and here was Max doing Greats at New College and taking tea on the Master's lawn. Have some more whisky."

"Not for me."

"Go on, we're celebrating! I got to know Max pretty well. Spent a lot of time with him. He had a lady-love, a very pretty, clever girl called Violet, one of the first degree-course girls they accepted. Nihilism was fashionable then – always is after a war – and she was fascinated by Max, this girl. Didn't see the danger signals. So when Max bought an open-top sports job, and drove at seventy miles an hour off a bridge on the Aylesbury road . . . I had to pick up the pieces, you might say. She was pregnant, you see. Discovered it a week after Max's suicide. I made her say it was me had got her in the club."

"You!"

Harry lit a cheroot and offered the box to Guy who shook his head. "Not for her sake, of course. For Max's. He'd suffered enough, without this posthumous disgrace. Vi saw that too. Wasn't an undergraduette for nothing."

"What happened?"

"She miscarried at five months. I came out here. What's Mother's story?"

"She said you always wanted to be a rubber planter. I just accepted it."

"Call of the East, is that it? 'The mysterious East, perfumed like a flower, silent like death, dark like a grave. . . .'"

Harry smiled up into the brackish cloud of cheroot smoke that

11

hung between them in the lamp-light. Guy, more than a little giddy with drink and tiredness, told himself he had not crossed two oceans to sit and be patronised. He burst out with heavy sarcasm, "Conrad, am I right? I suppose you fellows out here get time for reading, more than us Londoners do in the blackout."

"Is that your impression of us?" Harry, still smiling, appealed to someone behind him. Guy turned to see Jill standing in the doorway in a long blue robe, her hair loose about her shoulders. "What do you say, my dear? Guy thinks time lies heavy on my hands. Shall I take him out on morning muster?"

"He's tired. Let him sleep—"

"It means getting up at five a.m. Can you manage that?"

Guy felt that somewhere along the line he had been out-manoeuvred.

Guy was roused briefly by some small animal visiting the drain outside for water. He listened out for air-raid sirens, for the rumble of omnibuses past his bedroom window and all the muffled, bustling sounds of waking London magnified in the pitch dark of the blackout –

> *Everybody do the "Blackout Stroll"*
> *Laugh and drive your cares right up the pole*

– and what came back at him was a silence so deep he could hear the blood pulsing in his ear-drums, a thick, blind, suffocating tropical silence, broken once or twice by jungle screeches that cut out as suddenly as they'd begun. . . .

"Master! Master!"

A brown hand was on Guy's shoulder. He sat up in the darkness and covered his eyes from the stabbing of the candle-flame. His head was throbbing.

"What's the bloody time?" he asked hoarsely.

"It is five o'clock in the morning, Master."

"Very well. You can turn on the light."

"No light, Master." The boy handed him the candle. "Electricity is on the blink."

By candlelight, half-conscious, Guy bathed his face in cold water. By candlelight he shaved and threw on a shirt and trousers. Guided by the glow of a solitary paraffin lamp he stumbled out on to the verandah. Harry was waiting for him, a

12

pair of half-boots in his hand. His dark hair, combed back flat and glistening against his pink cranium, smelled of Brylcreem.

"There's your early tea," Harry said, pointing to a glutinous brownish liquid in a tall glass on the butler's tray. "Drink it up, old chap. Then we'll try on these chukka boots. There's a lot of dew, and your brogues are worth looking after." He watched while Guy drank, and chuckled at his grimace of disgust. "Raw eggs and Worcester sauce. It's called a prairie oyster. Does wonders for the stomach."

"I don't see yours."

"Not me. I don't drink. Didn't you notice? Last night, while you were downing whiskies, I was on ginger beer."

He waited for Guy to struggle into his boots. Still smiling with satisfaction, he picked up the paraffin lamp.

Guy followed him out across the lawn and into the rubber plantation. The thin creaking of cicadas ceased instantly. The silence was broken by faint but sharply distinct cracks all around as if they were under fire from snipers in the trees.

"Rubber fruit bursting," Harry explained. "The seeds produce oil if you process them, but it's only good for varnishes. Jack Lubbock, up the valley, has his weeders pick 'em up and sort them, then he sends them for export as heads for hatpins. But I expect you know all this without me telling you."

Other lights were flitting like glow-worms through the trees. Shapes of men hurried past, all headed in the same direction. As the sky began to lighten, the ghostly silence of their tread was explained. Underfoot lay bare earth, soft, crumbly, scoured of every growing thing.

The break in the plantation came without warning. Guy found himself in an open space the length of three football pitches, bordered on the far side by narrow, whitewashed buildings roofed with corrugated iron. Tamil women in bright purple and scarlet saris prepared food: husking rice, grinding millet and scraping coconuts for the midday curry. In front of them their sons and husbands waited in long columns. Some were still chewing the last of their breakfast; some yawned and scratched, others stood stiffly to attention as if on military parade, their white singlets hanging over sarongs tucked up between their legs.

The dawn broke as abruptly as dusk had fallen. A ground cuckoo began singing. Harry turned out the paraffin lamp. "That chap taking names, he's the *kangani*, my divisional overseer," he said. "The one beside him is the dresser. He checks up on the coolies missing from the roll-call, to see if they're playing possum or if they're really sorry for themselves, in which case he might have to cart them off to hospital in Hanwella. We had a few problems with dysentery a couple of years back. Half the labour force started inventing tummy complaints after that. I installed a new drainage system in the Lines and that put paid to the shirkers."

"The Lines?"

Harry shot him a quizzical glance. "They don't teach you these things in London?" He pointed to the whitewashed blockhouses. "Those are the Lines. That's where the plantation coolies live."

Guy must have frowned, because his brother gave him a long stare. "It may look pretty basic to you, Guy, but I'll tell you something. My rubber workers live as well as any in Ceylon. When I came here first as assistant manager, Dunlop Orient had just taken over the estate. The Lines had no proper sanitation. No running water except for an outdoor tap set in concrete every hundred yards or so. Men and women were segregated in long dormitories with triple-tiered bunks; it smelt like the hold of a slave-ship. You can imagine the consequences."

"Riots?"

"No. Low productivity. You can't pen people up like that and expect optimum efficiency. I rebuilt the Lines and the investment paid for itself in five years. You can tell that to your bosses in London."

Guy moved away to hide his exasperation. He was here in Kelani as a guest not as a supervisor. Obviously it appealed to some sense of gloomy irony in Harry to cast himself in the role of an inferior: the elder brother eclipsed by the younger's success. It enabled him to score points, like the one this morning over the whisky and the ginger beer.

Guy was struck by the thought that Harry had been putting this on from the first moment they'd met, when Harry had advanced half-naked down the steps to receive him. The sooner he found his own lodgings in Colombo, the better. The man to help him was Major Rawling, the Estates Agent in Colombo whose job it was to oversee the day-to-day business affairs of Dunlop Orient's Ceylon rubber estates.

The Tamil workers had begun to disperse into the rubber plantation. Many of them carried little buckets, like children going down on the sands. "They have to move fast," said Harry. "The latex coagulates in the heat, as you possibly know—"

"I do—"

"And that gives them a maximum of three and a half to four hours to tap the bark before the latex ceases to flow. It's as delicate and skilful a process as shaving with a cut-throat razor—"

"So I've heard—"

"If you try to rush it, you damage the tree." Harry's eyes were boring into him. "And if you tap too heavily, to get maximum yield, it is irresponsible, criminally stupid, because you exhaust the tree quicker than you can grow a new tree to take its place. That's what you've got to remember."

Guy nodded. His brother's face softened. "Come on, I'll take you to the factory," he said. "Let you see what you're dealing with."

Harry led the way back into the plantation. As far as Guy could see, there was nobody working on the trees at all. Instead, white-saronged figures crawled about on the floor of the forest, some on their hands and knees, some bent forward and moving at a snail's pace, their eyes fixed on the ground. At regular intervals one of them would swoop and pluck out some offending scrap of green, which went into the canvas bag over his shoulder.

"My weeders." Harry spoke curtly. "Too much undergrowth and the trees get root fungus. Donald Fraser will tell you."

They were joined by a ginger-cropped young Scotsman with freckles across his pale, bony face and khaki shorts which flapped against pale, bonier knees. He did, in fact, look unusually pallid for the tropics. Guy decided that this must be Harry's *Sina Dorai*, his chief assistant, whose sickness yesterday had been the reason for Harry's absence at the dockside.

Ill or not, the youngster struggled gamely to impress them with his expertise. In a broad Glasgow accent he explained that the section they were in had been tapped yesterday and would therefore not be tapped again for a couple of days. He pointed to the thin white diagonal grooves in the tree-bark and described how they were shaved a little further each tapping, a cut no bigger than the paring of a toe-nail. He showed Guy the metal spout attached to the lowest groove on the bark and the half-coconut shell beneath into which the milky secretion of latex fell slowly, one drop at a time.

Standing in that dark wood, Guy had a vision of car tyres and tank treads, barrage balloons, rubber dinghies, rubber life-jackets. . . . The war came beating through the ranks of trees in a chaos of screeching wheel-tracks, and departed as suddenly, leaving the pure white drop to bleed into the shell and find its way to Europe.

Harry's eyes had been darting around while Donald held forth. Now he gave a muttered exclamation of disgust, and took Guy by the arm. "You see this?" he asked, pointing to a tree.

Guy could see only the oblique white grooves on the bark. He peered closer. A greenish deposit had formed on the lowest groove.

"The tapper has cut too deep," Harry told him. "See here. He's sliced through all the levels of the bark. The tree has had to heal itself, which impedes the flow. And the damned idiot has left bark shavings in the shell. Donald, find out who was tapping this row, will you?"

The young assistant blushed with mortification. Guy felt sorry for him. "Bad luck, probably," he suggested. "Man's knife must have slipped."

"There is no such thing as luck," replied his brother. "Only carelessness."

They walked for another half-mile through the plantation, and came out to the corrugated-iron hangars which Guy had glimpsed from the road the day before. Two of the women he had seen at muster were bringing out large buckets with a detachable sieve clipped to their rims. Nearby stood a weighing machine.

"I pay the tappers by results, it's the only way," said Harry. "The latex gets weighed and filtered out here, so they don't track dirt inside the factory. Any dirt in the process, like those shavings you saw in the coconut shell, and quality goes to pot. That's why I run regular hygiene checks on the factory coolies."

The next half-hour brought vividly to life the dry pages of the manual Guy had read on the boat coming over. He saw how the dry rubber residue of the latex was transferred to large metal tanks and solidified by adding acetic acid. He watched the rubber, recognisable now, taken out in sheets and passed through a mangle to wash out the acidic water (useful for flushing down drains because no mosquitoes could breed in it). He was taken up wooden stairs to a loft to see a coolie turning over the sheets that hung suspended in the wood smoke from a furnace-room below – the last and longest process before the rubber was packed up in crates to be sent to Dunlop Orient's godowns beside Colombo harbour.

Finding Guy a ready listener, Harry shed his defensiveness. He spoke with barely concealed ardour which encompassed every level of the operation, from what kind of fuel best suited his machinery to his long years of learning how weather patterns affected the final product – a process of understanding in which

16

the only way to mastery was through surrender. He spoke like a man who in one area of his life had discovered something perfectible, which it lay in his own power to perfect.

Back outside the factory, with the sun now appreciably warm above the forest, Guy got a sideways glance from his brother. "I suppose you must wonder what I see in all this."

"I would feel the same way."

Harry gave a bark of laughter. "Forgive me, but you wouldn't. Your life is dealing with people. That's why they sent you out here, isn't it, Guy? I'm not like you. I find people unreliable. I've learnt to put my trust in what I can control, nothing else. You've seen this estate. It runs like a Swiss watch. Rawling will bear me out. I've got eight hundred acres here, and I know the yield I expect on every one. My trees aren't going to get drunk; they're not going to walk off; they're not going to fight; they're not going to cheat me. Nor are my coolies, if they know what's good for them. Acre for acre, Kelani is the most productive rubber estate in Ceylon. You may not see the beauty of that. But when I look around and see the mess the world's in . . . well, by God, it means a lot to me."

There was a hoarseness in Harry's voice; a brightness in his eyes. Guy felt a stab of mingled fear and pity. Was this what happened with age? That your horizons narrowed, that you crawled back like a snail into its shell? Or was it a Tancred thing, a throwback to centuries of farming a patch of Devon valley and not daring to raise your eyes from the clay?

"There's a wider obligation," he said, more roughly than he'd intended. "We're at war. Here as much as anywhere. We sink or swim together. It's the wrong time for individual feelings, it's all hands to the plough."

Harry Tancred did not reply directly. He put his hand on Guy's shoulder and pointed towards the road, where Michael Kandasala was waiting in his buttoned jacket. "Come home and have some breakfast," he said.

Not until they were in the car did he return to the subject. "Did you study those grooves in the bark the tapper makes?"

"Yes."

"Cut a fraction too deep and you wound the tree. A fraction too light and you won't get the yield. That's a fact, and no talk of patriotic duty's going to make any difference. Thank God, the war hasn't been invented that can change nature."

As if that settled the matter, he leant forward and tapped Michael on the shoulder. "Is the power restored?"

17

"Electricity is back, sir."

"There you are, Guy. You can have eggs and bacon, toast and marmalade, fish-cakes. Porridge too, if you like. So you see," he smiled, "we're not completely cut off from the things that matter."

The Morris rounded a steep bend. Guy saw, for the first time, Kelani Lodge in the sunlight, festooned in morning-glory, brown-shadowed in its pool of green; behind it another lawn hedged by flowering shrubs, a tennis-court, and a screen of low trees shielding the servants' quarters, before the ground rose steeply upward in a tangle of long grass and shrub to a bare boulder-strewn hillside.

"You seem to have achieved most of the things that matter," he was prompted to say.

"Ah!" Harry's silence might have been of unspoken thoughts; he dismissed them with a laugh. "Wait till you see what Cook does with your eggs and bacon!"

The Tamil boys, Rasani and Kelamuttu, served them breakfast. Guy, who was starving, had put away grilled kidneys on toast and dark pulpy red tree tomatoes alongside the eggs and bacon. Harry avoided all the cooked food. Limiting himself to papaya fruit and toast, he listened with an obliging smile to Guy's sardonic character-sketches of his fellow-passengers on SS *Burdwan*. As soon as he'd swallowed his tea he excused himself and drove back to the factory.

Guy didn't sound so funny to himself, alone with Jill. "It's so quiet," he complained, after the boys had cleared the table. "After Colombo, I mean. Just the clock ticking. Don't you find it quiet? What do you do all the day?"

"Do? What a question! First thing every morning I have to add up what Cook's spent and give him money for lunch and dinner. Then there are two boys, Michael, the dhobi-man and the garden coolie to organise and set to work. I garden. I sketch. How can you ask me what I do?"

"Don't you miss the city? Social life?"

"Colombo." Jill scratched at a spot on the tablecloth with her fingernail. "You won't find it any different in Colombo. Liz Donaldson plays the piano and does charity work and has a dangerously pretty daughter. Ottoline Hoathly does work for the Ladies' League. Kitty Clarke embroiders cushion-covers. They play tennis and golf and bridge and go to church on Sundays.

What did you expect?" She laughed. "Come on. I'll show you round the palace."

The sitting room, dark, cool, smelt of furniture-polish, a mixture of beeswax and paraffin. Enormous armchairs squatted like tanks on the polished teak floor. Against one wall stood a bulky G & C radiogram marked "Made for the Tropics". Teak bookcases on either side of the imitation fireplace held faded detective stories, book-club novels, Sir Edwin Arnold's *The Light of Asia*, E.J. Thomas's *The History of Buddhist Thought*. There were framed photographs around the walls and on the elephant table; Jill pointed them out to him.

"Lionel Wendt took these," she said with a note of pride. "Have you heard of him? He's got an international reputation, I believe."

Guy had not heard of Lionel Wendt. The photographs – artistic compositions of native fishermen, palm trees, folk-dancers and watery landscapes – did not impress him. He was overwhelmed by a desolate intimation of the gaucheness of Ceylon, a place where small talents made large reputations, a paradise of the banal.

"Not bad," he said with a shrug. "I suppose antiquities is the thing here, isn't it?"

As if on cue, an elderly coughing noise could be heard some distance away. It hoarsened into a low, lazy buzz, which rapidly grew noisier. With a cry Jill ran outside on to the lawn. Guy followed her.

Three dumpy biplanes with RAF flashes trundled out of the blue sky, flying low over Kelani Lodge. They were early 1930s Westland Wapitis: Guy could see the uncowled engine, and the Lewis gun mounted in the rear cockpit. He looked at them in disbelief; he almost burst out laughing.

"It's 60 squadron!" Jill was waving at the pilots and cheering. "Liz Donaldson told us 60 Squadron was coming over from India!"

Guy watched the little planes sputter on towards the hill country. He exclaimed, "*Wapitis!*"

"What's so funny? They can carry a bomb beneath the fuselage, didn't you know? I'd like to see anyone attack Ceylon with them in the air!"

Guy was silent. The war had found him. It had sent him a message. It gave him the excuse he'd been looking for.

"Guy? Is anything wrong?"

"I must get hold of Major Rawling," he said.

19

4 April 1942.   3 a.m. Koggala Lagoon.

In the jungle there is no dead of night; but it is pitch-dark when the three men in oil-stained overalls set off down the muddy track that leads from their cadjan huts to the Lagoon. They shield their flash-lights with their hands, looking out for kraits in their path. Ahead of them, their shapes almost invisible under the camouflage netting and the canopy of Salvinia weed strung between the mangrove trees at the water's edge, lie the six bulky Catalina flying boats.

The ground crew are making for the newest arrival in Koggala Lagoon. Flying boat QL.A, piloted by Squadron-Leader L.J. Birchall from St John's, New Brunswick, flew from England via Gibraltar, Cairo and Karachi and arrived less than forty-eight hours ago. Since a Dutch crew has refused to go out, QL.A has to be made ready for its unexpected dawn patrol.

The men climb on the wings and remove the camouflage netting, piece by piece. They check the batteries. They prime the engines by hand-turning the two propellers round three complete rotations, which on these Cats is no easy task. They give QL.A a maximum fuel load so that when it returns to Ceylon it can circle until daylight on the following day. Birchall and his crew have hardly settled in, let alone had time to practise night landings on Koggala Lagoon.

Overnight rain has not dispersed the thunderclouds. There is moisture in the air as Birchall and his crew of eight assemble in front of the mess tent at 0345 hours. Since the canteen is not manned at this hour, they have had to make do with a few slices of bread and butter. Their orders are: to patrol the seas through an area of 250 miles south-east of Ceylon and report on all ships sighted, hostile or friendly. All they have been allowed to know is that the British navy is patrolling somewhere in the waters off Ceylon.

Squadron-Leader Birchall and his co-pilot Flying Officer Kenny clamber in through the door at the rear of the fuselage and take their seats in the cockpit. Sergeant Henzell has crawled ahead of them, under the

21

console, to man the front turret machine-gun. Immediately above him as he lies cramped in the nose of the plane is the emergency hatch. Once QL.A is forced down on the water, and begins to sink, this will be their only means of escape.

Sharing the flight deck with the pilots is the navigator, Warrant Officer Bart Onyette, another Canadian. Behind them are the Wireless Operator, Sergeant Phillips, and his two assistants who double as blister gunners, Sergeants Calorossi and Davidson. Sergeant Cook, another air gunner, has taken his place in the rear turret, under the tail fin.

Last is Sergeant Catlin, the engineer, who squeezes up to his seat in the narrow pylon which joins the fuselage to the wings. As the pilots begin flicking on the master switches on the cockpit windscreen sill, the dials in front of Catlin come to life. Batteries, fuel tanks right and left, oil pressure, gyro compass – the engineer checks them and gives Birchall the all-clear.

The pilots have made their own checks. The radios are operating. After Catlin comes through on his headphones, Birchall switches on the magnetos and presses the starter motor.

A choking cough like a camel's, a few wisps of white smoke, and the engines begin to whirr. Birchall pushes the throttles full forward and taxies to the head of the only stretch of clear water in Koggala Lagoon. At V-1 he pulls the stick back and lifts the heavy aircraft into the grey, cloudy sky. Behind them lies a very small island. Ahead roll thousands of square miles of ocean, stretching uninterruptedly to the South Pole.

The checks have proved what they anticipated. Since landing, QL.A has been quietly and comprehensively stripped by base personnel at Koggala. Over the intercom they assess the damage. Worst is the apparent removal of all their tracer ammunition for the Vickers guns. Birchall speaks into their headphones.

"Nothing we can do about it. We'll inspect the ammo pans when we get back. I'm going to raise hell about this."

Flying at a steady 90 knots, QL.A reaches its allotted patrol area just after sunrise, and begins the 400-mile zig-zag reconnaissance pattern which has been mapped out for it. Like all parasol aircraft, its wings high-set above the fuselage, it flies slightly nose-down so from the cockpit there is a good view through the high, narrow windscreen. On this mission, for hour after hour, there is nothing to look at but empty sea.

It makes Onyette's task as navigator a hard one. The sun by itself is no help in confirming QL.A's position, nor are the compasses and artificial horizon dial in the cockpit. Onyette has to rely on dead reckoning all day. Not until the moon rises, about two hours before their daylight patrol is due to finish, is Onyette able to use astro-navigation to get a fix on their position. It places them at the very southernmost point of their pattern, almost 350 miles south-south-east of Ceylon, well out-side the ambit of a likely enemy approach.

They begin to work out a course back to base. At 1730 hours, Onyette goes to the galley and begins to make himself a bully-beef sandwich from the rations they picked up at RCAF HQ in London. It is then that one of the rear gunners notices a black speck on the extreme southern horizon.

They are in a no-man's land, well clear of shipping lanes. Birchall speaks to Catlin who rechecks the fuel. In their long-range transatlantic tanks they have enough to keep them airborne until the following morn-ing. Birchall turns south to investigate.

They descend to 2000 feet and fly towards the ship. As they close with it they see more ships, and more beyond. A great armada of vessels lie spread out before them – battleships, carriers, destroyers, supply ships –

They have chanced upon the enemy fleet.

Squadron-Leader Birchall stamps hard on the rudder pedals. As QL.A turns for home, Sergeant Phillips begins tapping out his first sighting report giving (a) the position, (b) the course, (c) the speed of the fleet. He follows it with details of the fleet's composition, tapping out the code letters for the different types of ship, with the number in each class. He has got away his first message and begun the second of the three required by naval regulations, when the six Japanese Zero fighters come up astern.

There is no cloud cover. The maximum speed of the Catalina at full boost is 180 m.p.h., half the speed of which the Zeros are capable. Even so, the end of QL.A comes faster than its crew could have expected. Japan bought some Catalinas from the US Air Force before Pearl Harbor. The Zero pilots know where to aim. Before Sergeant Phillips is halfway through his third transmission, his wireless equipment is smashed to bits and he himself is wounded.

Sergeants Calorossi and Davidson, on their tramline seats in the middle of the aircraft, swivel their machine-guns and fire through QL.A's cupola-shaped gun-turrets either side of the fuselage. No tracer ammo, but it makes little difference. The Zero is armed not only with .303-inch machine-guns but with two 20 mm cannon which fire explosive shells. These rip through the Catalina with terrible effect, shattering Sergeant Calorossi's leg and sending splinters into the engineer, Catlin, wedged in the pylon under the wings.

Birchall, a bullet in his leg, takes what evasive action he can with the lumbering plane. Internal fuel tanks in the Catalina begin to blaze. The crew put them out with fire extinguishers. As the Zeros press home their strafing attacks, the fire starts again. The Catalina begins to break up in the air. Flaming gasoline pours on to the hull from the fuel tanks under the wings. They are low above the sea: too low to bail out with para-

23

chutes. Struggling with the controls, Birchall manages to get the plane down on the water seconds before the tail falls off.

There is no let-up from the Zeros. Several of QL.A's crew are hit; two are badly injured. Birchall, Kenny and Onyette manage to get most of them into Mae Wests, and throw them out of the plane. Two cannot be saved; the others swim for their lives, knowing that the Catalina carries depth charges pre-set to explode at sixty feet. Still the Zeros come in firing, one behind the other. The men dive, swimming with all their strength away from the burning gasoline on the water. Sergeant Davidson, in a fully inflated life-jacket, cannot dive. He is hit by several bullets. He dies instantly.

Six men are left alive, three of them severely wounded. They are picked up by the Japanese destroyer Isokaze *after thirty minutes in the sea. Darkness is falling. On board, the injured men are beaten repeatedly and asked the same question over and over again.*

Did you send any messages?

"No time to send a message," lies Squadron-Leader Birchall.

A LIFETIME of service to the Crown had taught Sir Oliver Prescott two or three lessons of which the most axiomatic was that the day started as it meant to go on and it therefore tempted fate to forgo a proper breakfast. Thus to be confronted, on this of all mornings, with a bowlful of disgusting orange jelly in place of his chunky Cooper's Oxford Marmalade disturbed the Governor's peace of mind and filled him with uneasy forebodings.

The explanation for the jelly was close at hand. All he had to do was turn in his high-backed chair and look out across Gordon Gardens, at the merchant ships riding at anchor in the roadstead. The Colombo harbour strike he himself had settled yesterday by intervening between the dock coolies and the harbour management, but it would take days to clear the congestion and land his Frank Cooper's; days of jelly tasting of citrus-flavoured sugar, days of irritability and indigestion.

He rang for the boys to clear the table and rose slowly to his feet, a sacred white elephant among scurrying mahouts. His study was down a corridor the length and width of two cricket pitches. He trod past the ballroom, the billiard-room, the gun-room (his aide's office) and the secretaries' pool where young poppets in patterned frocks sat elbow to sunburnt elbow in front of elderly typewriters. The tapping keys sounded in his ears, as he passed, like the crackle of dead leaves in a winter garden.

Mollie had brought such life to the Governor's mansion. She had filled it with voices and scampering feet and tubs of flowering bougainvillaea. Now she was dead, the sheer size of the place vexed him with its pretensions to a grandeur it could no longer justify.

Its imperial halls reminded him of the draughty pomp of his father's vicarage in Hertfordshire. As a child he used to scuttle like a church mouse through high, damp-smelling, Gothic-windowed rooms which Church of England stipends were too meagre to keep aired. There were rooms like that in Queen's House, rooms he had never penetrated . . . he imagined them to

25

be occupied by snake-charmers, scriveners, bookkeepers telling the beads of their abacuses, boot-blacks, beggars, notaries – all of them the fathers, brothers, sons and cousins of the servants who silently attended him on the upper floors.

With a nod to the turbaned boy who clicked his heels by the door, Sir Oliver let himself into his office. It, too, was a tropical version of his father's old study, with its broad mahogany desk, its uncomfortable chairs and its tall glass-fronted bookcases jammed with important, unreadable volumes. He had served Caesar for forty years, as diligently as his father had served God, and his material rewards – there was no doubt about it – had been correspondingly the greater. But what was it all worth, if one ended up administering a small island, six thousand miles from home, where one couldn't obtain so much as a decent breakfast?

The ceiling fan ruffled what remained of his hair as he bent over his desk. Long-sighted, he took out his reading spectacles and perused the memo his staff had left for him. It read, in full –

1045 hrs   Major Rawling. German nationals.
1200 hrs   Vice-Adm. Sir Thomas Phillips in *Prince of Wales* docking in the Harbour.
1215 hrs   Mr Oliver Goonetilleke, State Council. Constitutional discussion (see attached position paper).
1245 hrs   Lunch, private dining room, Lady Lusted (opening of Girl Guides HQ).
1500 hrs   You piped aboard *P of W* (dress uniform).
1900 hrs   Reception here for Vice-Adm. Phillips. Evening dress. See attached guest list.
War update   Auchinleck said to be making headway at Tobruk. Unconfirmed report that the German Army Group Centre, advancing on Moscow, are in hand-to-hand fighting with Russian troops around perimeter of city.
Ceylon Daily News   Do we take action on their published appeal by Gandhi for Indian independence – e.g., bad for morale?
NB Have managed to locate suitable kilt for Caledonian Society Ball tomorrow.

The Caledonian Society Ball. . . . The Governor sighed, and summoned in Simon House, his ADC, from the adjoining office.

The morning was predictably bad for his constitution. For security reasons the reception had to be kept hush-hush, with guests invited over the telephone and the guest of honour's name kept "a surprise". Needless to say, several telephones were out of order, and his staff were kept busy ferrying messages round Colombo. Then Major Rawling (another of the crosses he had to bear) wanted to talk about Japanese nationals, not Germans at all.

"Hideki Ono, for example."

"Who?"

"Ono & Company's retail and wholesale dry goods trade here is substantial. Ono speaks fluent Sinhalese. He could be a major intelligence risk. We have reason to think he's been gathering information about our defences on the island. One of his sons was spied last week taking photographs of our anti-aircraft emplacements on Galle Face Green."

Sir Oliver recollected the two 25-pounder museum pieces on the sea-front which constituted Ceylon's defence against enemy attack. "Hold on a jiffy. We're not at war with Japan," he protested. Rawling's bland round pink face always made one uneasy, one could never tell what the fellow was thinking behind those pebble-glasses – not that one ever could with these intelligence types. . . .

"Not at war yet, Sir Oliver," Rawling was saying. "But in my view it's only a matter of time. Weeks, or even days. We underestimated how hysterical the Japanese would be about Roosevelt freezing their American assets and embargoing US trade with Tokyo, especially after Churchill followed suit. We thought they'd back down on those naval bases they went and took in Indo-China. Fact is, they can't survive without oil and iron ore. Instead they've put their War Minister in overall charge, this man Tojo who's a bloodthirsty little number by all accounts. And frankly, sir, with things the way they are, there's not a great deal we could put up against the Japs if they do decide to get involved—"

"That's where I have to disagree."

"I beg your pardon, Your Excellency?"

The Governor had looked at his pocket-watch during Rawling's little lecture. Now, he beckoned him over to the window and opened the blind.

There she was!

Dead on time the pride of England's navy, her newest and fastest battleship, was poised on the flat blue seaway, her long curved bow and the bristling turrets of her superstructure as sharply framed and insubstantial as a paper transfer pasted on the glass.

"The Prince of Wales!" Sir Oliver announced, in the vibrant baritone of a toastmaster. The venomous beauty of her lines brought tears of pride to his eyes. Involuntarily he fingered his toothbrush moustache, the phrases of his latest sonnet already forming – *Through distant seas it drives to daunt the foe, Its purpose deadly as its course is true. . . .*

"One swallow doesn't make a summer," said Rawling.

With a snort the Governor shut the blind. To get Rawling off his back – really the man was a complete Cassandra where the Japanese were concerned – he promised to give urgent attention to whatever sanctions the Major thought necessary, so long as they did not unduly antagonise Colombo's Japanese traders. This concession understood for what it was worth – precisely nothing – he ushered Rawling to the door.

The meeting with Oliver Goonetilleke went smoothly. The man was reasonable – trained in the Inner Temple – and understood that the vexed question of devolving power to the Ceylonese must wait until the war was won. With the Nazis knocking the Russians for six and Rommel rampaging through North Africa, this was hardly the time for debating how many Tamils would get a seat in the State Assembly.

The trouble with a lot of these chaps, in Sir Oliver's view, was that the Platonic idea of independence, the *noumenon* of it, dazzled them. The very word, Independence, bandied about, acted on their systems like adrenalin. It made them lose sight of the detailed, laborious process by which independence had to be achieved. Goonetilleke wasn't like that. He didn't overstay his welcome. He understood the principle that *Natura non facit saltum*. In fact it was high time Goonetilleke was found a serious job in the Administration.

An agreeable lunch in the small dining room with Lady Lusted and Simon House was clouded for Sir Oliver by the thought of the reception ahead for Sir Tom Phillips. When Mollie had been around, to host them and talk to the wives, they had been – though one said it oneself – rather splendiferous occasions. With amazing tact Mollie used to siphon off the prigs and the viragos and let him circulate among fellows who had something to say worth saying.

These days one was stranded. Vulnerable. A sitting duck for the bores in their Red Sea rig who wanted to tell one about the 150-pound sambhur they'd bagged on the Horton Plains, and the wives who . . . well, the wives were the worst.

Across the calamander dining table, left by the Dutch when

they fled the island, he glanced uneasily at Deirdre Lusted. A bust like an aircraft-carrier, and three strings of fat pearls which couldn't disguise the pockets of fallen skin. She had started asking him about his health and his diet, always a dangerous sign. Wherever one went in Colombo these days, society was booby-trapped with women of a certain age who cast themselves in the role of the damsel rescuing St Oliver from the dragon of widowerhood. Like Deirdre, baring her teeth across the table.

And all the time, like the sweet, rotten taste of the tropical durian fruit, his young poppets down the corridor sat golden-curled at their typewriters, sweating very faintly into their underwear. . . .

A cube of tinned pear lodged in the Governor's windpipe. He recovered before the Lady President of the Girl Guides could offer her services as his night nurse. "It's a dashed nuisance," he told Deirdre Lusted, with a happy frown, "but I'm going to have to be rude, if you'll excuse me, and leave you and Simon to your coffee. I've got to put my gold braid on and go and inspect a warship. Wish I could tell you which one, but I'm not allowed to spill the beans, or Simon will report me to the Admiralty, eh?"

"It can't be *Repulse* because she's been here for a week," he heard Lady Lusted say as he left the room. "It must be *Prince of Wales*."

Which just went to show, as the Governor was to remind himself two weeks later, how impossible it was any longer to send capital ships across the oceans of the world without their movements becoming public knowledge. *Bismarck* had learnt this lesson as soon as she'd emerged into the Denmark Strait. As he looked across that afternoon from the main deck of HMS *Prince of Wales* at the native dockers and the harbour officials gawping and cheering on the jetty, he reflected that any one of them with a rough idea of geography would know where she was headed.

"A warm reception," he remarked to Vice-Admiral Sir Tom Phillips. "I hope you get the same in Singapore."

A fish-eagle screamed above them and plummeted out of the sky, its claws opening on something in the water. Phillips, his sharp little bull terrier's face almost as pale as his white dress uniform, nodded without speaking. He had been abstracted throughout the formal visit which protocol demanded, despite Sir Oliver Prescott's efforts to display interest and appreciation.

Had he not been at pains to admire the speed with which gangways had been rigged and green awnings spread by the ship's mostly young, inexperienced crew? Had he not been ostentatiously impressed by the unprecedented quadruple turret of 14-inch guns fore and aft (capable of firing from Dover to Boulogne, he was told) with another two-gun turret superfiring forward; and quite bowled over by the secondary armament of sixteen 5.25-inch guns which could pot enemy aircraft out of the sky as easily as ships out of the water? Had he not sympathetically deplored the appalling ventilation below decks (no doubt a result of the impregnable armour plating) which had so far put thirty ratings into the infirmary with heat exhaustion? When he ran out of compliments about the battleship, had he not extolled the beauties of Colombo harbour itself – fully one square mile of sheltered anchorage, as he explained, enclosed by a 4,000-foot breakwater of which King Edward VIII had laid, so to speak, the first stone?

Tom Phillips had nodded, and drawn on his cigarette.

Holding his plumed hat under his arm, the Governor now tried a different tack. "I gather you're taking over the command of the Far East Fleet from Geoffrey Layton in Singapore?"

"Layton is stepping down to be my Number Two."

"I've met him once or twice" – and disliked his arrogance, Sir Oliver was tempted to add. "Plays a useful game of tennis, I believe."

"Oh, really? That comes as news to me."

Again Phillips let the conversation die. The man was of course rumoured to be "brilliant", and one never could be sure of one's ground with fellows like that. Moreover this was his first time in command of a fleet, despite having been Vice-Chief of the Naval Staff. Probably felt he had something to prove to himself; people did in these situations. It might be best to overlook the taciturnity. Sir Oliver cleared his throat and said, "You've chosen absolutely the best time to come out here, you know."

"Have I?"

"Good heavens, yes. November, December, you've missed the monsoon. It's not too hot, not too rainy. Give your young chaps a chance to adjust to the tropics!"

"What luck."

"Not that you'll have much to do, I should hope. Unless the Japs suddenly run amok and invade Malaya, hah!"

Admiral Sir Tom Phillips was gazing across the water at the First World War battle-cruiser *Repulse*, his only other support in Malay waters apart from four elderly destroyers and a few obsolescent Brewster Buffalo biplanes. With a slight shock the

Governor realised that what he had taken for rudeness was in fact profound nervous exhaustion. The man was grey with fatigue.

"We've got the resources," he heard Phillips say. "If the Japanese chance their arm, we'll steam up the coast and cut off their beachheads." He turned back, with the first suspicion of a smile.

"So you see," he observed, "you have no cause for alarm here, Sir Oliver."

The reception in Queen's House was to begin at 7 p.m. – or, as Simon House persisted in calling it, 1900 hours. Six-thirty found the Governor at his dressing-room mirror, exchanging one set of high-necked gold braid for another. This reception tonight; the Caledonian Society Ball tomorrow; the levee for the King's Birthday the week after next, followed by his Address to the State Council – why was it that the more elevated one's rank the more uncomfortable the clothes one had to wear?

A passing resemblance to Donald Wolfit had made Sir Oliver realise what other colonial governors must have discovered before him, that one's role in life was closest to that of actor-manager of a touring rep. Half one's day was spent ensuring that the show went on; the other half between dressing room and stage making up to play the lead. Even then, one could never read the expressions on the dark faces beyond the footlights, or catch more than a rustle of applause. He wanted – to spin the metaphor out while he fumbled with this damned slippery collar-stud – like Prospero he wanted to break his staff, to hand over the show and the theatre itself and say to the people in the penny seats, "Take it: it's all yours, do with it what you will."

But his touring company were not yet ready to follow him this far. There were too many careers and too much sentiment at stake. Not to mention the take at the box-office.

His costume finally in place, Sir Oliver plucked the guest list off the table. Apart from some of the deck officers off *Repulse* and *Prince of Wales*, he knew all the names. Between the froth of visiting bigwigs and the deposit of Colombo worthies it was pretty small beer. There was Petty from the Admiralty and Smythson from the Ministry of Food and a man from Wavell's staff who'd been scouting around. The Dutch consul-general was down to come, and the shipping agent Howard Cotton who represented American interests on the island. Sir Frederick Underhill was coming in from Kandy. Deirdre Lusted was bringing

31

her nephew – or was it cousin? – Charles Bilbow who was "slumming it", she'd said, as a naval rating.

After that, it was Colombo Society, the gentlemen traders in whose company Sir Oliver had spent more of his life than he cared to contemplate. Ruddy-jowled, pipe-smoking, ex-minor public school men whose taciturnity stemmed from never having very much to say; "damn good sports" whose long years of honest toil under a foreign sun had been deservedly rewarded with the Secretaryship of the Golf Club or the Vice-Presidency of the Chamber of Commerce; honourable, decent, boring men with wives who'd "stuck by them" and children who were packed off at the earliest opportunity to shiver at one of the South Coast prep schools strung out like Siberian prison camps between Worthing and Bexhill-on-Sea; men who had spent their lives as comfortable drudges in the common rooms of Empire, rarely looking back at the lights in the Headmaster's Lodge: these were his guests tonight.

Their favourite watering hole – not his – was the Colombo Club, housed in a beautiful gabled nineteenth-century Dutch mansion on Galle Face Green. Here they raised the barricades which enabled them to replenish their self-respect: barricades against the Ceylonese (except waiters), against women (apart from the occasional weekend dinner-dance), against the young, against the ill-bred, against the unconnected.

The Colombo Club had once been exclusive enough that the proudest boast of its octogenarian members was to have rejected Sir Thomas Lipton when he paid a visit to his estates in Ceylon. Nowadays they would have welcomed him with open arms, the Governor reflected, as he ran a silver-backed brush over his thinning hair. He himself was an ex-officio member, though he'd hardly been to a dinner there while his wife was alive.

On his last visit, walking along a corridor to the Club lavatories, he had come to a wall-cupboard stocked from top shelf to bottom with bottles and bottles of Andrews Liver Salts. From somewhere he had distinctly heard Mollie's gentle, bubbly laugh at the thought of old buffers who couldn't hold their liquor.

He hadn't been back.

Buttoned, buckled and belted, Sir Oliver pocketed his spectacles and strode down to his reception. With half an ear he listened to Simon House reminding him which encounters to encourage, which to avoid. The disquiet which had arrived with his morning marmalade-substitute still weevilled away a couple of inches under his cummerbund. All the newspapers declared that

Japan was exhausted after four years of war with China and wouldn't have the energy left to take on the West. If that was true, why was Rawling so mysterious? Why was Tom Phillips so reticent? And, given the chronic weakness of British air and naval support in Malaya, what was the Vice-Admiral doing out here with the best new battleship in the Royal Navy? Good God, Rawling seemed to know what was going on much better than he did himself. Was London deliberately keeping him in the dark?

These anxieties evidently sank into Sir Oliver's subconscious because later that evening, to an uninterested question from Tom Phillips about the Gordon who gave his name to Gordon Gardens, he blurted out – "That's the chap! Head chopped off and stuck on a pole, let's hope it won't be my turn next, what?"

His joke fell flat. Deirdre Lusted looked at him as if ready to launch Spitfires off her aircraft-carrier bust. Damn lucky that her straw-haired young nephew Bilbow had the wit to put his oar in.

"General Gordon didn't have fourteen-inch guns, Your Excellency. Now they would have taught the Mahdi a thing or two!"

Sir Oliver led the chuckles. Even Tom Phillips smiled, though with the sadness in his face of one who caught in these ringing tones of proud enthusiasm an echo of himself when young. "Which is your ship, young man?" he asked.

"Sir, *Dorsetshire*. I join her in twelve days' time."

"*Dorsetshire*. That's John Agar's ship. You'll be in good hands."

Charles Bilbow's pink cheeks burnt deeper pink with pleasure at being addressed by the Commander of the Fleet. "Yes, sir. Thank you, sir."

Tom Phillips was drinking boiled water out of a wine-glass. The Governor suspected he was taking pills to keep going; he still looked in the grip of profound fatigue. Gently he took the Admiral's arm to introduce him to some of the local crowd. Sebastian Clarke, Deputy Financial Secretary, was nearby, but so was his wife Kitty. The Governor, who had a horror of women who drank like men, steered his guest past them into the middle of the room.

"Admiral, I should like you to meet one of the doyens of Colombo society, Mr Ingram Bywater. He founded Coir Products (Ceylon) Ltd in 1919 – the oldest-established company of its kind, I.B., I believe?"

Ingram Bywater, the Treasurer of the Colombo Club, had a fierce little pixie face, veined and rheumy-eyed, with tufts of grey hair starting out of his ears and nostrils. Leaning on a stick to rest

33

his crippled leg – the result of a groin injury received, he claimed, in India during the Great War, though the Governor had heard a less salubrious story – he nodded to Phillips with a touch of condescension.

"Done an A-1 business exporting coir prayer mats to the Japanese," he remarked. "Bring 'em to their knees, what?"

The bull terrier showed his teeth in a smile. "I trust our prohibition on trade with Tokyo isn't doing the same to you," said Admiral Phillips.

Sir Oliver tactfully retreated and gazed around for other suitable introductions. George Donaldson, his top man in the Secretariat, was the safest bet. Elizabeth, his wife, would steer the conversation away from the war. Frankly, this constant talk about the Japanese was making him queasy. They were all at it, as if they knew something. . . . Here was Percy Buller, Chairman of the Orient Star Line, holding forth in his high, affectedly precise voice to Ingram Bywater's wife—

"Can't see in the dark, y'know. Blind as bats."

"Surely, I mean, they must have some—"

"No. Not at all. It's an established fact. The Nips don't have night vision. It's why they can't fly planes at night. Did you ever meet Hideki Ono? He runs a chain of stores. That jeweller's down Bambalapitya. . . ."

Mrs Ingram Bywater, a grave, rather beautiful woman in a black lace evening dress, had a cosseted complexion and thickly waved grey hair. She shook her head decisively at the idea of knowing by name any shopkeeper, let alone a foreign one.

"Tiny eyes," continued Percy Buller. "Sunk in rolls of fat. Not that they have many airworthy planes, so I hear. Or ships, come to that. Or tanks. A very primitive manufacturing capacity. Sir Oliver will bear me out. The reason why in China they go to war on bicycles, Sir Oliver, am I not right?"

"I'm afraid you have me on the bicycles," admitted the Governor, knitting his brows. Where had Buller got his information from? Rawling? They all knew more than him. Not that he'd ever cared much for Percy Buller. The man smoked Abdullah cigarettes. He gave song recitals. He was, very possibly, a bugger.

Buggery was a vice indulged as much by the Sinhalese as by the British. There was that case – Sir Oliver had happened to be thinking of it the day his posting to Ceylon came through – that case in 1903 of Major-General Sir Hector Macdonald, the hero of Omdurman, who shot himself dead in a Paris hotel after having been discovered – *in flagrante* they said – with

34

four Ceylon schoolboys in a train. . . .

"In China," Buller was saying, "the Nips went to war against the Chinese on bicycles. Carrying umbrellas." He took off his spectacles and polished them with podgy fingers which trembled at the tips. "A queer lot, if you ask me."

Nobody was willing to deny that the Japanese were a queer lot. In the momentary lull, Sir Tom Phillips's unmistakable tones could be heard raised in disputation.

"Aircraft be damned!" exclaimed the Commander of HMS *Prince of Wales*. "There's nothing can sink a battleship if she's fought properly except another capital ship of her size. I've said it to Churchill and I've said it to Smuts. Well-trained gun crews and good high-angle cannon can match anything in the air—"

Conversation drowned the rest of his speech. When Sir Oliver was to recall his words, after the sinking of Sir Tom's flagship, it was with a vivid image of the doomed Admiral, small and belligerent in his white dress uniform at the reception, opening his mouth and swallowing gulp after gulp of water.

Right now, however, the Governor had a lump in his throat. The C-in-C was here, here in Queen's House, and a damned good show had been put on to welcome him. For these brief hours, Ceylon was the hub of British power in the Far East. It made one feel dead at the centre of things again.

Unbidden, new lines for his sonnet made music in his brain. As soon as his guests had departed – diminutive Tom Phillips clasping his hand at the last and wishing him a warm goodnight – Sir Oliver hurried up to his private quarters, and got out paper and fountain pen –

Through distant seas it drives to daunt the foe,
Its purpose deadly as its course is true,
Its aim as straight, whatever winds may blow,
As loyal, brave and chivalrous its crew.
A prince in name, a prince in deeds of war,
A greater prince it serves – the Prince of Peace
Whose Christian message sounds from shore to shore
That final Victory comes when all wars cease.
Till then, as knights in shining armour tread
The field of battle, swords unsheathed and keen
To slay the enemy, strike the dragon dead,
Defend the Church, the Empire, King and Queen,
It plows across the ocean to Malaya
Urged on by all our hopes and all our prayer.

Well satisfied, the Governor read it through four times and added the title BATTLESHIP and at the bottom his initials A.C. – an unhazardous modesty since the sonnets were always posted on Queen's House embossed writing paper. Though, really . . . this one was almost too accomplished for a parochial readership. Should he not send it to the London *Times*?

For a minute, Sir Oliver Prescott sat gazing into space, the down-draught from the ceiling-fan softly caressing his scalp like sprigs of laurel. The tradition was there, of course, from the Great War. Newbolt, Henley, Herbert Asquith – immortal hymns to an imperishable glory. . . .

Alas. He knew old Mayne at the Colonial Office, the cutting remarks he would make about inessential communications being air-freighted to London at a time like this. *Patriotism is the last refuge of a versifier* – he could hear the Minister now.

With a sigh, the Governor slipped his poem into a buff envelope and addressed it in a bold, nay a commanding, hand to the Editor of the *Ceylon Daily News*.

In the savage midday heat butterflies trembled over the bursting yellow fruit of the guava tree. A column of ants danced along the whitewashed window-sill, swaying under the colossal carcass of a beetle. Michael stood still in his quarters in Kelani, barefoot on the red cement floor, staring at the monstrous apparition in the mirror.

It wore baggy cavalry twill trousers . . . a waistcoat in a similar brown fustian, buttoned over a creamy white shirt with a clip-on bow tie . . . a greenish-brown Norfolk jacket that was awkwardly bunched at the shoulders as if cut for a man of broader build. A triangle of handkerchief poked jauntily out of the breast pocket.

This vision in the mirror in impeccably fogyish taste, impervious to its surroundings, had all the hallmarks of the well-bred Englishman. All that was wrong was the face above the costume. It was dark, almost black. Its expression was one of mingled misery and loathing.

Self-loathing. Michael Kandasala stared at his image in the rust-spotted glass and hated whatever it was in himself that had impelled him to this insult to his race, his pride, his dignity. What made it so much worse was that the togs belonged to Sylvia Donaldson's brother.

If Sylvia ever found out . . . he could see her as bang in front of him as if she was standing there in the mirror: her Reckitts-blue eyes widening, then her pretty, pouting face crinkling into hopeless giggles. The laughs were on him, of course. The laughs had always been on him.

Why had Mrs Donaldson given William's old Going Home clothes to him? Only one explanation made sense. After all this time Mrs Donaldson still wanted to put him in his place. When his mother was employed as Sylvia's ayah, and he and Sylvia had played together, black and white, Mrs Donaldson had made a big show of not minding. Little ones cannot get up to much mischief, she used to say with a little frown at the corner of her smile.

37

But little children get bigger. Their games get more curious. Mrs Donaldson had never forgiven him for what had happened.

Sylvia had been told to keep her distance from the servants' quarters. He himself had been polished off to a posh native school up-country with a whole lot of Tamils. He was there when his mother died, in the malaria epidemic. When he came back, to the only home he knew, Sylvia had gone to school in England. He was passed over to Uncle Albert, the Donaldsons' head boy, to be groomed to take over from him one day. But before Sylvia came back from school, all airs and graces, he had been transferred to the Tancred master and lady in Kelani Lodge.

A trickle of music floated across the back verandah and through the curtain of wooden fretwork screens that hid the servants' quarters. Afternoon rest was ending. Michael had drawn himself up to his full height, when he noticed that something peculiar was happening.

William's togs seemed magically to be fitting themselves to his person. The trousers falling with an unbroken crease. The shirt unwrinkling. Even this strange half-belted jacket no longer sagged if he drew back his shoulders, puffed out his chest, hitched his thumbs under the lapels—

"No!"

His cry startled black crows off the almond tree, and set up a muttering between the two Tamil boys in the next room. Before Kelamuttu could wrap a dhoti round his waist and go and investigate, Michael had torn off the Englishman. Panting, mother-naked except for the crucifix round his neck, he stood before the mirror. The spell was broken. Sylvia would not dare laugh at him now. She would cover her face in confusion, peep through her fingers at his manhood as she'd done once before. . . .

To his dismay he saw that another monster was rising from his loins at the thought of this. Looking over his shoulder, he pulled William's shirt on to cover it. Kelamuttu tapped on the door. At the same instant the house-bell rang. In the turmoil of his thoughts he recollected that Lady was needing the motor-car. She was having dinner in Colombo, with the Donaldsons.

In December, two days after the Japanese bombed Pearl Harbor, Guy Tancred moved down to Colombo, to the Metropole Hotel.

It was a small room he had taken, overlooking Queen Street and the old lighthouse. The tap-water dribbled brown every morning and the bed had creaky springs and a concave mattress. Nevertheless it was clean, and if Guy leant far enough over his balcony he could see a square yard of staggeringly blue sea. The Estates Agent for Dunlop, Major Rawling, had fixed it up for him. Rawling could fix most things in Colombo, as Guy was beginning to find out.

The last of the year's monsoon storms broke just as he set off on foot to the Dunlop Orient offices in Chatham Street. As he clambered into a rickshaw, heavy drops of water bounced on the pavement in little puffs of dust; in a moment, curtains of water shut him off from the outside world. The casual violence of it disheartened him: how could people learn to become civilised in countries where Nature set such a savage example? He tried to imagine himself home in London, strolling in St James's Park with Lydia and watching her elegant, slim fingers as she tossed broken biscuit to the pampered ducks; but the monsoon storm kept returning his thoughts to his approaching interview with Rawling. On the telephone to Kelani Lodge the Major had kept postponing his descent on Colombo, until Guy had begun to wonder if he was unwelcome.

The sun came out just as the rickshaw splashed to a stop in Chatham Street. By the time Guy had walked up to the first-floor landing of Dunlop Orient's palatial offices, a rainbow was arching brilliantly over the harbour. On the steaming pavements, red, blue, green and gold umbrellas were being lowered and shaken. With a nonchalance that had impressed him Colombo had ridden out rainfall so intense it would have brought half of London to a halt for flood repairs. In a few minutes only the monsoon drains would register that there had been a storm at all.

A dry cough behind him made Guy wheel round from the

window. The elderly Sinhalese clerk, dapper in a white drill suit, took a step backwards as if expecting a reprimand.

"I am sorry, I am Edward," he said rapidly. "Are you Mr Tancred to see Major Rawling? Please to come with me."

Guy followed Edward up into what must once have been a merchant prince's spacious drawing room. It was now rudely broken up by jak-wood and frosted-glass partitions, creating two narrow, box-like offices either side of the main window. Four desks, piled high with ledgers, bills and shipping manifests, took up most of the remaining space. On the walls blown-up aerial photographs of rubber plantations hung on the walls either side of a hand-coloured poster luridly illustrating the blights, cankers, rots and mildews which *Hevea brasiliensis* was heir to.

Edward's desk stood in the middle by the window, the impress of his narrow shanks still on the chair-cushion. The clerk dithered for a moment outside Rawling's office. Then he stooped forward from the waist and opened the door a few inches, inserting his bald head like a lizard through the narrow gap. With his free hand he beckoned Guy to approach.

"You are expected, please. This way," he said in a low voice.

Rawling was on the phone. Guy found himself face to face with a heavily built man in a white shirt and khaki shorts. Probably in his fifties or late forties (about his exact age, as about so much else, he was never to know with the Major), he had an enormous balding, shiny head on which an incongruously small face had been kneaded as an afterthought. Round and chubby, it was dominated by a fleshy, bulbous nose on which perched small, round, thick-lensed spectacles. In one pink hand the Estates Agent held a stumpy briar pipe. He waved it in greeting to Guy as he went on talking down the line.

To conceal his interest in Rawling's conversation, which appeared to be about exchanging his Straits dollars for sterling and moving them out of Singapore, Guy made a show of looking around. The office, with its overstuffed filing cabinets, and maps with coloured pins hung slightly askew on the partitions, had an air of hectic abandon, the HQ of an army command that had gone down fighting.

"Confounded accountants," complained Rawling, as he put the phone down. For such a bulky man he had a surprisingly light, even voice – champagne out of a Toby-jug. "Exchanging currencies in wartime is a darn sight trickier than exchanging prisoners, if you were to ask me. Rawling, by the way," he added, rising from his chair to give Guy a clumsy handshake.

"Welcome to Ceylon, Tancred. It calls for a minor celebration. Whisky and fizz?"

"I thought the Straits dollar was a strong currency," Guy volunteered, once Edward had been despatched for the soda-water.

The Major paused for an instant, then clapped his hand to his forehead. "Of course, you're an accountant yourself. Of a sort. How rude of me."

"An investment adviser, as a matter—"

"That's right, dear me. Loss of memory is something you'll have to forgive me for." There was a suspiciously bland smile on Rawling's face. "For instance, I've forgotten who it was at Dunlop Orient you had your interview with before coming out."

"J. S. Brooke."

"Ah, yes."

"To be frank with you, sir, he left it rather vague what I'd be doing, how I'd be helping you. This is much more your line of country: talking to planters, co-ordinating their production. He was unable to explain how I could be of much use to you."

Rawling seemed in no hurry to enlighten him. Out of his desk drawer he took a small round tin and carried it to the window. Raising the venetian blinds a couple of inches, he dusted the window-ledge with a white powder.

"Bugs are a damned pest at this time of year," he remarked. "Bugs everywhere in Colombo, especially after rain. Tell me, are your people in England?"

"My mother, yes. My father died in 1916."

"The Western Front?"

"No, actually not." Guy scratched his ear. "Piles. He was working in the City, had a bad case of burst piles. I gather he died of loss of blood."

"I seem to have heard about that. Your brother must have told me. How is Harry by the way? Is he better?"

Guy paused. Edward had entered with the drinks, bending to a stoop as he came in to the sanctuary.

"Better? He's fine, so far as I know. They both send their regards."

"Jolly good." Rawling let the blind drop and came and clapped Guy on the shoulder, as if to congratulate him on passing some mysterious test. "Welcome to your new horse-box," he said with a chuckle, gesturing round the room.

"What?"

"Didn't you know? This is now your office. You'll be standing in for me. Acting as my eyes and ears, so as to speak."

41

"From here? Where will you be?"

"Next door. In the other horse-box. I'll move some of this paraphernalia out of your way...." He indicated an upended steamer trunk in the corner. A round wooden wireless with a zig-zag grille balanced dangerously on top of it. The drawers of the trunk bulged open with files marked "Personal".

Guy ran his hand through his hair. What had old Brooke been thinking of? With a note of desperation in his voice he asked, "If it isn't a rude question, sir – what will you be doing?"

"I?" Major Rawling took his time answering. He sat down and with a matchstick dug out his pipe dottle into a huge Bakelite ashtray. "I'll be around to give you the gen on our planters. Lend a hand, of course, if any ticklish problems arise. I've got a lot on my plate at the moment, Tancred, what with the war, and the United States Rubber Reserve people going straight to planters to get source-of-supply prices. D'you know how much natural rubber the US Reserve had stockpiled at the end of last year?"

"Approximately 130,000 tons."

"Good. And you know what their latest stockpile estimate is for this year?"

"Before I sailed it was upwards of 350 thou—"

"500,000 tons. That's an increase of 370,000 tons in ten months. They had a Presidential committee declare that lack of rubber constitutes the greatest threat to the safety of the US. It's sent the Americans into a buying panic. They've been buying rubber sight-unseen all over South-East Asia and Ceylon, dis-regarding the fact that it's us who are doing the fighting."

"Not just us any longer, sir, surely? Not since the Pearl Harbor raid. Besides, doesn't Dunlop Orient take the view that there's enough rubber to go round?"

Rawling blew noisily through the pipe and began to search in his pockets for tobacco. "There's something you haven't gras-ped, Tancred," he said in his mild voice. "The reason I asked for you to be sent out in the first place. Armies cannot fight without rubber, and Singapore still controls the world's rubber market. The Japanese have cottoned on to this. Keep it under your hat for the moment, but twenty-four hours ago the Japs managed to establish a beachhead in Kelantan, east coast of Malaya. A place called Kota Bharu. If we were to be denied Malayan rubber—"

"That's impossible!"

Rawling had plugged his pipe. He lit a match and held it over the bowl. "Perhaps," he admitted. "But in the meantime we have to protect our own sources, and look out for trouble."

42

"What sort of trouble?"

"There are cowboys about, Tancred. Ugly customers. Out to make what the Yanks call a fast buck. Down on the docks the other day I came across a whole lorry-load of amber crêpe, marked for export to San Francisco. No paperwork. Nothing to show it had gone through the weekly rubber market at the Chamber of Commerce. Turned out to be an out-station dealer, getting US prices and paying half the extra profit straight back to the planter."

"What did you do?"

The Major sucked on his briar and looked at Guy through little round eyes that gave nothing away. "Bloke responsible must have got homesick," he said in mock puzzlement. "He sailed so fast for London that he left his rubber on the quayside!"

Guy got to his feet. He took his whisky-glass to the window and opened the blind, crinkling his eyes in the glare. Along the hot, white pavement coolies jogged, carrying on their heads wooden trays piled high with curry lunches in tiffin-tins for busy office clerks. A bullock stood patiently, steaming in the sun, between the yokes of an empty cart.

"Major Rawling, I am not a policeman," he said.

"The strong-arm stuff we leave to others." Rawling's voice sounded mocking, though Guy could not see him until his eyes had readjusted to the room's shadow. "It's intelligence work I need you for, Tancred. Requiring a bit of background knowledge, a quick mind and common sense. I hope you aren't going to let me down on the common sense." He went on without waiting for an answer. "I've got you here in the nick of time. We're going to fix the sale price of Ceylon rubber and make sure nobody gets paid over the odds. And we're going to drive up production quotas on the plantations. That's where you come in. You can go and talk to them. You've just come out from England: you can tell them how bad things are. They'll listen to you."

Guy essayed one last objection. "Sir, you're the expert. And the planters, they don't know me. They know you."

"That's right." Rawling gave an unexpected chuckle. "They know me and they don't trust me an inch. Quite right too."

Standing on the Governor's lawn in his light-grey Palm Beach suit, George Donaldson raised his tumbler. "God save the King," he declared, and sipped the export gin. His immediate circle echoed the loyal toast.

"And send him victorious," added Guy for good measure.

It had been at Rawling's insistence that, the day after he arrived in Colombo, Guy should attend the Governor's levee in honour of King George VI's birthday – "My dear Tancred, these rituals *matter*." It had meant hiring Palm Beach suiting from F. X. Pereira and turning out at 8 a.m. to watch the combined units of the Ceylon Defence Force parade in a straggle across Galle Face Green, while a brace of light cruisers in the harbour fired off their guns in salute. Then to Queen's House for the levee, for which Guy had obediently applied in advance to the Governor's ADC, a moon-faced Old Harrovian known behind his back as Bungalow, allegedly because he had so little upstairs.

While boys brandished punkahs in their faces (refrigerators going full blast to cool the drinks meant the electric ceiling-fans were slowed to 16 r.p.m.), Colombo society, giving off a faint odour of mothballs, formed a queue that stretched through the ballroom, out of the french doors and down the croquet lawn to a trestle table laden with toasted cheese bits, cashew nuts in glass bowls, curry puffs, little sausages on sticks and devils-on-horseback.

Rawling had already gone through into Gordon Gardens. Guy, who had supposed that "Major" was some sort of honorific, was startled to see him resplendent in a singular grey-green uniform adorned with shoulder-strap, epaulettes and lapel-flashes: although what regiment, indeed what armed service of what country, he could not immediately identify.

As he came up, Rawling was holding forth to a tall, handsome woman in her late forties. She had thick brown hair Marcel-waved around her high forehead and pale blue eyes whose melancholy gaze made a nonsense of the polite smile on her lips.

"I can only tell you what Roosevelt is getting from his operatives in the field," Rawling was confiding gravely. "The Japanese may – I stress may – have perfected a high-powered radio signal which can effectively jam all local radar communication. That's the only explanation for the way the Yanks were taken by surprise at Pearl Harbor. . . ."

He broke off when he saw Guy and waved him over. "I want you to meet Mrs Donaldson," he said. "She's been grilling me about you. Haven't you, Elizabeth?"

The serious eyes appraised Guy as they shook hands. "How do you do, Mr Tancred? Jill has been telling me all sorts of things about you. But she didn't tell me you were good-looking as well."

Guy bridled. "She mentioned you too, Mrs Donaldson. She

said you had a perfect garden and a beautiful daughter and that you played the piano and went to church on Sundays."

"Dear Harry!" Mrs Donaldson gave a little laugh. "It's him, you know. I'm sure he's given Jill a complex. He thinks we women are like his precious latex: we coagulate in the heat. What do you think, Major? Do you think there's any hope for us?"

"It depends how quickly we can get reinforcements to the Malay States."

"I mean for us women out here?"

"Ah." Rawling clicked his heels together in anticipation of the gallantry he was about to deliver. "Let me just say this: that without the fairer sex it is us men there would be no hope for, no hope at all!"

Simon House trotted over to them and whispered in the Major's ear. Rawling excused himself and hurried back with the ADC into Queen's House. A charming face appeared round Elizabeth Donaldson's shoulder.

"Mummy, go and get another drink; I want to talk to this gentleman," it said.

With her golden hair cut in bangs across her forehead, her cornflower-blue eyes, tip-tilted nose and pouting mouth, Sylvia Donaldson was undeniably pretty. She was also coquettish in a jejune, provincial way which Guy thought rather charming. Introducing herself, she extended her arm stiffly from the shoulder as they taught in finishing schools.

"You're Guy Tancred, you *must* be. I'm thrilled to meet you. There hasn't been anyone new in Colombo for *ages*. Everybody's leaving, you know. Even Charlie, and he's only just got here...." Her voice trailed off, but she recovered instantly. "But now you're here, we're not going to let you go! Where are you staying? Don't be cross if I tell you you don't look in the *least* like Mr Tancred. Aren't you supposed to be related?"

"Yes. He's my brother."

Sylvia's mouth opened in a pretty O of pretend-amazement. "But Harry Tancred's so...." She paused.

"He's so what?"

"Well, I s'pose Piggy and I are perfectly different too, that's what everyone says. Piggy's my brother William. He's square-bashing at a camp in England. Catterick or some dire place. They make him march when it's snowing! Poor Piggy, he sends us postcards saying he's in the sick-bay with flu; Mummy goes potty worrying about him."

By the time she had led him across to meet her friend Charlie,

45

Guy knew all he thought he could want to know about the Donaldsons: how you could always see when Daddy was upset because he took his spectacles off and cleaned them and there had been a terrific lot of spectacle-cleaning in the last couple of days because as Civil Defence Commissioner instead of Daddy they'd appointed a Sinhalese – "Goon-something" – despite all Daddy's years of service to the Crown . . . and how dire it was for Mummy's migraine, what with Piggy coming up for his posting overseas, and you could tell when she had an attack coming on because she'd shut herself away in her music-room and play the Appassionata, that sort of thing, on the piano at which point Daddy would stomp off to the Club . . . and how they all felt ghastly about poor Kitty Clarke but Guy really must be careful and not let anything slip—

"About what?"

Sylvia sighed patiently. "About Sebastian, of course! He's her husband, the Deputy Financial Secretary. He has *affairs*. Everyone knows, and Kitty knows, but she will keep on about what a terrific person Sebastian is. Urgh! If I had a husband like that I'd. . . ."

"You'd what?"

"I wouldn't let him fool around," she finished primly. "Now. Come and meet Charlie. His father's Sir Edward Bilbow the famous QC who's Mummy's brother's brother-in-law so I suppose he's a sort of cousin, but he's more closely related to Lady Lusted, worse luck for him, but he's staying with us because who would want to stay with her?"

Guy had already noticed Sylvia exchange a long glance with the good-looking naval rating who now came up to them. Hardly out of his teens, he had the sort of soft, milky-pink English face which emerges unblemished from an expensive private education. The type was familiar to Guy from the bright-eyed public-school rowdies who would motor up in a team to London at half-term and swagger from the Café Royal to a night-club where they'd dare each other to challenge the women who brushed past their table on the way to more rewarding customers. But there was an attractive deference about the way Bilbow greeted him.

"Are you on shore leave?" he asked.

"Sort of. My ship's HMS *Dorsetshire*, a County-class cruiser. I board when she berths here in a few days' time. Can't wait, really!"

"Is it your first commission?"

"Charlie's signing on as an ordinary seaman," broke in Sylvia, pride in her voice. "He couldn't wait to get a commission, he wanted to go and fight, didn't you, Charlie?"

"Starting at the bottom," agreed Charlie. "Learn the ropes."

"He gave up a terrific job selling something in the City. Didn't you, Charlie?"

"We've all had to make career sacrifices for the war," Guy reminded her sharply. Still, it took spirit to give Dartmouth a miss and sign up as an ordinary seaman. He smiled encouragingly at young Bilbow. "Perhaps you'll get a transfer to *Prince of Wales*."

"Golly, yes. D'you know, I actually jawed with Sir Tom Phillips at the Governor's reception? He asked me what ship I was joining. And I saw *Prince of Wales* in dock. Did you? She's the most beautiful ship-of-the-line ever, don't you think?"

A white-jacketed boy brought round a tray of sausage rolls. Sylvia bit into one, and brushed a flake of pastry off her perfect chin. "I was telling Guy about Sebastian Clarke and poor Kitty. You don't think we'd ever become like that, do you, Charlie?"

"I don't know what you mean," said Charles Bilbow with a shocked glance at Guy.

"Oh, Charlie! Tell him the story about the Archdeacon's flowers, it's so funny, Guy. According to Maria de Vos – who *never* tells a lie – Kitty Clarke rang up old Eric Hoathly the Archdeacon last week, quite early in the morning, to complain about his mean-spirited congregation putting artificial flowers on the graves of their dear departed. So old Hoathly says," Sylvia giggled, "'But Mrs Clarke, real flowers just wither in this heat.' To which Kitty replied down the telephone, 'Death is a nashural process, Vicar, above all in the cemetery'!"

Their peals of laughter brought disapproving looks from the more crustacean guests at the Governor's levee. But it was a warm day with a light breeze that made it more like an English summer's day than a Colombo December, and the Sinhalese boys with betel-stained grins had been liberal with the gin and the whisky splits. Birds sang, and the bougainvillaea bobbed its purple bells in the breeze, and when Charles Bilbow spilt a little whisky and Sylvia put her handkerchief to her lips and wiped it off his uniform, Guy knew that no war could touch them.

Even the Deputy Financial Secretary, a couple of drinks later, could not spoil his mood. A tall, spindly man of thirty-eight with a few strands of red hair combed across his pink scalp and a long nose that gave him a supercilious air, Sebastian Clarke had failed to pass into the Indian Civil Service and had settled for an Eastern

Cadetship in Ceylon. Like all bachelor cadets in the 1930s he had been sent home at twenty-seven and given four months' leave to find a wife. It coincided with his mother's last illness; Kitty Clarke had been a nurse at the teaching hospital where she died. That was ten years ago and Clarke looked as though he had let no other emotional impulse affect his judgement since.

"I hope you aren't going to stonewall us on rubber," he said almost at once, with a thin smile, to Guy.

"What does that mean?"

"I know how solicitous Dunlop Orient are of their planters. They might try to give us a hard time when we want to step up production. Am I right?"

"We're dealing with finite resources," returned Guy, confused. Was Clarke trying to trap him, or did the Trade people out here really not know that Dunlop Orient was on their side over production quotas. Or – for God's sake – was it Rawling on his own initiative who was about to demand the slaughter-tapping? Who was the Estates Agent working for: Dunlop or the British government?

Sebastian Clarke looked at him down his nose, quizzically. Floundering, Guy said, "At a time like this everyone has to do the best they can."

"And what would you say was a fair target? 220,000 pounds?"

"It depends upon the conditions. Disease . . . weather. . . ."

"Talking shop again, sweetie?"

Kitty Clarke had come to Guy's rescue. High heels pocking the croquet lawn, she still only came up to his chest – a bird-like woman with bright eyes made brighter by gin, a pill-box hat skewered to her black curls, and a purple dress whose flounces at the shoulder and hem made her look like a walking bougain-villaea blossom.

"My husband is inveterate when he's talking shop." She pronounced each word distinctly. "Only last night when I was going through his shirts, I reminded him that the Governor's levee was an occasion for social small-talk. And do you know what? I've just caught him in a corner with Howard Cotton talking about importing wheat from America? Am I right, sweetie?"

She clasped her husband's arm, which hung limply by his side. Sebastian Clarke's face had gone a dull red. "I hope Mr Tancred didn't find my conversation intolerable—" he began.

"Oh, you're Harry Tancred's brother!" Kitty Clarke sipped her gin and bitters and took a step back, the better to get him into focus. "Are you a Buddhist, like Harry? You look quite normal to me."

"Kitty. . . ."

"My brother's not a Buddhist, Mrs Clarke. Good Lord," Guy laughed, "he's far too busy on the plantation for all that nonsense!"

At the same time he could not help feeling, on this sunny morning, a little cold shiver run up his back. Those Buddhist titles he'd seen in the teak bookshelves in Kelani Lodge. And of course Rawling asking – he'd let it go at the time – if Harry was . . . *better*.

"Quite right, I'm sure," the Clarke woman pronounced as she focused up at him. "I mean you can't say the Buddhists are peaceful, you can't, can you? I mean, look at the *Japanese!*"

As she hissed this last word a Chinese gong was struck, with a long, low, moaning vibration. Party-talk stopped dead. The faces that looked up were anxious, startled, frightened, some angry: as if this uncivilised sound had momentarily bypassed their defences and summoned up fears they none of them admitted, even to themselves.

Sir Oliver Prescott stood on the ballroom steps. In his shaking hand he held a piece of paper.

"I'm afraid I have to interrupt our festivities with some bad news," he said in a high voice which carried across the Gardens. "I say bad news: it is, in truth, shocking news. Our two great capital ships in these waters, *Prince of Wales* and *Repulse*, have been attacked and sunk by Japanese aircraft off the coast of Malaya. Thanks to prompt and courageous action by other ships in the vicinity, most of their crew were saved and will live to fight another day. We shall, of course, give details as they emerge. Meanwhile, I hope you will carry on enjoying yourselves here, in a spirit of resolution and loyalty."

After the first groans of horror, a hush descended which lasted for some seconds after the Governor turned and went inside. Then a woman began laughing hysterically. She had to be helped away. In spite of Sir Oliver Prescott's patriotic appeal there began a general drift towards the exit gates.

"I shall be needed," observed Sebastian Clarke. He set off in the direction of the ballroom, Kitty scuttling in his wake. As Guy looked round for Charlie and Sylvia, Major Rawling strode down the lawn.

"Did you hear the news?" demanded Guy, unable at that moment to think of a more intelligent question.

Rawling paused, and spoke in a low voice without looking at him. "It's worse than it sounds. Technically, yes, most of the crews were picked up yesterday. But we've lost Sir Tom Phillips, forty-six officers and eight hundred men. Total enemy losses, nil."

Rawling marched on his way. Guy stared after him. Almost all the Governor's guests had now departed, including Mr Fernando de Mel, the celebrated baritone, who had been due to sing for them "The Road to Mandalay". The croquet lawn was deserted – unless one counted the white-jacketed Sinhalese servants who, left to themselves, began chattering and quietly laughing as though nothing had happened. Animatedly they moved back and forth, picking empty glasses out of the grass and collecting all the short-eats that lay uneaten on their doilies on the trestle table. Almost under Guy's nose one of these servants, carrying back a tray, unobtrusively picked out a curry puff, popped it in his mouth, and began chewing it with every sign of satisfaction.

4 April 1942.   6.30 p.m. Addu Atoll.

The Wireless Operator who takes down the message from the Naval Office in Colombo doesn't wait to make a copy. Clattering up the gangway he runs to find Admiral Sir James Somerville on the armoured deck of Warspite, *waiting to welcome aboard his flagship the captains and flag officers of his Eastern Fleet.*

As the motor-boats converge on his battleship, Somerville glances at the hastily scribbled message. It was received, twenty minutes ago, from a Catalina flying boat, now presumably shot down over the Indian Ocean. It reads: "Large enemy surface force sighted 360 miles SSE of Dondra Head. Heading NNW. Exact composition unknown."

As he records in his diary, Somerville has been putting a brave face on the British naval position in the East, laughing and joking with his men and doing his best to keep up morale. Nevertheless the situation now uncovered by Catalina QL.A's sighting report is almost enough to make him despair. Believing that the intelligence report one week ago predicting a Japanese carrier-borne air attack on Ceylon must be inaccurate, and that the enemy must have postponed or cancelled its attack, he has taken a step he is now bitterly regretting. He has dispersed his fleet.

Many of his ships were in need of refuelling. Others – the four R-class battleships under the command of Vice-Admiral Willis – were running out of fresh water. Somerville has therefore taken the larger part of his Eastern Fleet to replenish here at the secret Maldives naval base of Addu Atoll, 600 miles south-west of Colombo. At the same time, he has sent two of his fast, modern cruisers, Dorsetshire *and* Cornwall, *back to Colombo harbour,* Dorsetshire *to continue her interrupted refit and* Cornwall *to take over escort duties for an Australian troop convoy. The aircraft-carrier* Hermes *and its attendant destroyer* Vampire *he has despatched to Trincomalee, on the other side of the island, to begin preparations for the forthcoming assault on Madagascar.*

The result is that the Eastern Fleet is stranded well to the west of the enemy's approach line, its fast division in the middle of refuelling, its

51

slow division not ready for sea until the following day, and two of its best ships-of-the-line dangerously isolated in Colombo, in the path of the enemy.

The Admiral makes his most urgent decisions before the flag officers board his ship. Dorsetshire *and* Cornwall *are to be instructed to make ready and put to sea in the direction of Addu Atoll.* Hermes *is to be told to sail from Trincomalee and keep clear to the north-east.*

Throughout the late afternoon and evening, as the blistering heat subsides and the tankers and water-boats bustle from ship to ship, Admiral Sir James Somerville consults his flag officers and ponders his tactics. On paper, his fleet is impressively large. It consists of three aircraft-carriers, five battleships and an adequate number of cruisers and destroyers. In practice, it is a different story. The Fighting Admiral, who commanded the navy's celebrated Task Force F on exploits that ranged from hunting Bismarck *to bombarding the French warships at Oran, has been stranded without a proper fighting fleet.*

All five battleships are of Great War vintage. His own battle-scarred old flagship Warspite, *a veteran of Jutland, has been modernised and could perhaps engage the Japanese Kongo-class ships on something approaching equal terms. The four R-class battleships have not been modernised. "Coffin ships", as Churchill called them, they can manage an absolute maximum of eighteen knots through the water. They need constant refuelling. Built for warfare in the North Sea, their thin steel sides burn to the touch in these tropics. They cannot distil fresh water fast enough to replace boiler losses; their sweltering crews are forced to go without baths or clean clothing.*

Of the two aircraft-carriers currently at Addu Atoll, only one, Indomitable, *is fully worked up. Between them they carry forty-four torpedo aircraft and thirty-seven fighters – Fulmars, Sea Hurricanes and Martlet IIs. Somerville still has no information about the quality of the Japanese Zero fighter plane; but he is well aware that his torpedo aircraft – Albacore biplanes modelled on the antiquated Swordfish, already obsolescent before the war – will be no match for the Japanese fleet in daytime operations.*

"So this is the Eastern Fleet!" he greeted Vice-Admiral Willis with a rueful smile when he first rendezvoused with the four "coffin ships". "Never mind, many a good tune is played on an old fiddle." At the same time he complained to his diary – "I hear a lot of blah about how everything now depends on our maintaining control of the Indian Ocean. That's poor bloody me and I wonder how the devil it's to be accomplished. My old battle-boats are in various states of disrepair and there's not a ship at present that approaches what I should call a proper standard of fighting efficiency. . . . To be frank, I feel that whilst my brother commanders-in-

chief are riding comfortably in their Rolls-Royces I am pushing a broken-down Ford with a flat tyre."

Ill-trained and poorly equipped, the raggle-taggle armada now assembled around him are no match for Nagumo's Carrier Force, almost certainly the same fleet which attacked Pearl Harbor. And yet it is these ships, all that can be spared after Britain's two and a half years of world-wide struggle to keep the seas open, which have the responsibility not only of sharing in the defence of India and Ceylon but also of maintaining the security of Britain's sea communications to Suez and the Middle East, northwards to Asia and the Persian Gulf, and from the Cape eastwards to Australia. It is an enormous task, as wise old Smuts in Cape Town was the first to see. Shaking his head over the division of Allied strength between Hawaii and Singapore into two fleets, each separately inferior to the Japanese navy, the Field-Marshal cabled Churchill after meeting Somerville that if the Japanese were really quick off the mark there would be an opening for a first-class disaster.

Somerville's overriding strategic imperative, therefore, is to avoid closing with the Japanese and risking the possible annihilation of his fleet. As the sun sets on the desolate ring of barren islets which surround Addu Atoll lagoon ("Scapa Flow with bleeding palm trees", his sailors call it), he comes to his decision. It has little to do with logic. It is an instinctive response. It is based on 350 years of naval supremacy which scorns all the evidence that a new generation of carrier-borne bombers has rendered naval battles obsolete.

His decision is to collect his "scattered and untrained boys" and sail towards the enemy.

Signalling his intentions to Colombo, Admiral Sir James Somerville orders refuelling to proceed with all possible speed. As soon as this is completed, around 1 a.m. on Easter Sunday, the faster ships of his fleet will head back towards Ceylon, making a rendezvous with **Dorsetshire** and **Cornwall** on the way. The slower division, led by Willis's four ancient battleships, will follow when they are ready and keep at a supporting distance from his battle squadron.

Somerville is not hoping to intercept the enemy fleet before it launches its attack on Colombo. But he has been practising night operations with his Albacores. With any luck he will be able to manoeuvre into a position to launch night attacks on the Japanese aircraft-carriers as they retire south afterwards.

The broken-down Ford with the flat tyre is cranking on to the warpath.

HOT days slipped into warm nights. The newspaper that brought stories of distant major victories and distant minor defeats lay neatly folded beside the fresh papaya on the breakfast table. *To fight England is like fighting fate*, wrote Lord Dunsany to *The Times*. This analogy was generally agreed in Colombo to be spot on.

Meanwhile the GOC, Ceylon, prickling pinkly under his sunhelmet, gave an audience to gentlemen of the press. There was absolutely no need for panic or alarm. Jitterbugs, or rumourmongers, or indeed any persons attempting orally or otherwise to influence the buoyant level of public morale should at once be reported to the authorities from the nearest telephone, post office or railway station, whereupon they would be dealt with in summary fashion.

The gentlemen of the press bent submissively over their notebooks. The headlines of the Ceylon newspapers that evening blazoned ABSOLUTELY NO NEED FOR ANY PANIC, and stirred the first ripples of disquiet.

Bugs of a different kind disturbed Guy's slumbers. In the ceiling above the almirah (as he now learnt to call a wardrobe) he could hear an unmistakable munching sound, as of somebody masticating very deliberately on dry paper. He presumed, at first, that it was cockroaches. But the noise seemed to come from one spot; worse, it appeared to be working its way round the edge of the ceiling towards his bed.

He summoned the manager of the Metropole, an Italian known as Smith.

"It sounds like jaws, chewing," Guy told him.

The manager nodded.

"Well? What is it?"

"Jaws, Mr Tancred. Is what it is. Jaws. We have here big poochies. Snap, snap." Smith demonstrated the pincer movement of beetles with a nicotine-stained thumb and forefinger.

"Eating paper?"

54

"No. No paper. Wood. Dry wood."

"Are you telling me they're eating the *joists*?"

Thumb and forefinger opened a millimetre. "Nothing. Tiny, tiny bits on the edge. And very slowly. There is, please, no need to be alarmed, Mr Tancred. It is OK."

"Can't you put down a powder, or something?"

Under Mr Smith's flourishing black moustache spread a furtive smile. "Yes. We put down a powder. They eat the powder."

"Oh."

In the periods between his poochie-haunted sleep, Guy worked his way through Rawling's backlog of Dunlop correspondence. For the time being he resisted the Major's pressure to have it out with the planters about slaughter-tapping their rubber trees. He intended first to have every detail of his arguments ready. He had not come out to Ceylon to act as a whipping-boy, either for Orient or for Rawling. He had his future to think about: his career. Besides, he had more immediate problems, like coping with the consequences of a mysterious fire which broke out on the Harbour-Lake Canal and destroyed two godowns holding Dunlop Orient rubber before it was brought under control. Look out for trouble, Rawling had warned him. Arson was the kind of trouble Guy had not been anticipating.

He attended every week at the rubber market in the Chamber of Commerce to keep track of the movement of prices. He began visiting some of the low-country rubber planters, in an old Wolseley Rawling had found for him. It had wide running-boards, on which he scraped the red mud off his shoes after each duty tour of a rubber estate.

He went with Rawling to lunch at the Colombo Club overlooking Galle Face Green. The cavernous smoking room had crossed elephant tusks above the mock fireplace. Prosperous men in shorts and long socks stretched over bulky calves flicked through copies of *Country Life* and the *Tatler*, looking at south-facing villas for sale in Bath or Bournemouth or even Tunbridge Wells. In the furthest corner an elderly planter, brown and shrivelled, lay insensible in a deep armchair, his breath feebly stirring the hairs on his upper lip.

Rawling had no sooner ordered their drinks than a stout ruddy-faced man loomed towards them through the cigar smoke. He nodded curtly at Rawling and stuck out a pudgy hand for Guy to shake.

"Buller, Percy. George Donaldson tells me you're Harry Tancred's brother. Working for our friend the Major here. Come and join us, I'll introduce you. Just been saying, Major, it's a confounded disgrace."

"What is?" enquired Rawling.

"Naked females. Practically naked. I've just been down to the beach at Mount Lavinia. Official business. Place was full of young popsies cavorting in skimpy bathing costumes. I was saying to Sandy – hardly big enough to keep 'em from being tanned where they ought to be, what? Some of 'em in the Naval Reserve, too. I've a good mind to write to the paper about it."

"It's the war," said Rawling, mildly. "It lowers the moral tone."

"What's that? What did you say?" A thin, tall, elderly man with streaky white hair and eyes of an intense blue stared in the Major's direction. Rawling repeated his remark. The man exposed discoloured teeth in a sarcastic smile. "Moral tone, hah! Not much moral tone to lower hereabouts, eh, Percy?"

"Sandy, this is the Major's guest, Guy Tancred," said Percy Buller quickly. "Sandy Duncannon plants tea up Badulla way. He doesn't come down much to Colombo any longer. Do you, Sandy?" he shouted.

"It's the food," replied Duncannon, staring hard at Guy. Decades of isolation had preserved his Scots accent undiluted. "Is this your first meal at the Club, laddie? You'll find it's not quite the Savoy Grill."

"It makes a change from all those curries you must get, Sandy!" bellowed Buller, making a joke Guy did not understand.

A few other men joined them. Guy noticed how they all – with the exception of Sandy Duncannon – treated Rawling with the respectful but wary caution one might pay to an outsider who has to be reckoned with. Which was odd, because it seemed to him that Rawling fitted in with this crowd as to the manner born, making the same sort of jokes and uttering the same grave, oracular pomposities as he smoked on his briar pipe. Only occasionally did he dart a quizzical look at Guy through his little round spectacles.

Guy let his eyes wander round the room, and was fixed by the glassy stare of an antlered head protruding above a doorway. This must be a sambur, the Indian variety of elk which was hunted on the Horton Plains. Its lip was drawn back in a snarl, exposing yellowing teeth like Sandy Duncannon's. All it needed was Rawling's briar pipe in its mouth. . . .

As he pondered the mystery of Rawling's apartness – admittedly the Major had never been known to play rugger or golf, which out here was regarded as a criminal offence in someone who had the use of all his limbs – a wizened little man came out of the next room, leaning heavily on a cue.

Billiards: that would explain the regular clicking noise as of badly fitted false teeth. Percy Buller at once broke off his conversation to introduce Guy to Ingram Bywater, Club Treasurer. The billiard-player looked him up and down with a fierce expression.

"Don't I know that tie? Oundle, is it?"

"I was at Westminster, sir. This is an Oxford tie. The Peel Society."

"Peel? Good fellow! We can do with a few more horsemen now the young chaps are going. Sandy, what was the name of that chestnut young Johnson had to leave on the Horton Plains?"

Guy regretted the moment of weakness that had made him put on this approximation to an old school tie before coming to the Colombo Club.

"It's Sir Robert Peel," he began. "Not John—"

"Time for lunch, I think," said Rawling with a bland smile. He waved a boy over and signed the chit for their drinks. "Tancred, do you want to come along?"

Lunch was bubble and squeak on a long table in the Club's small dining room. On the way in Guy had imagined it to be kedgeree because of an unpleasant smell of fish, which grew stronger as the meal continued. Ingram Bywater signalled to one of the white-coated boys to close the windows.

"It's the factories on Slave Island," Buller explained to Guy. "Established fact. Damn fish start rotting and we get the benefit whenever the wind's off the lake behind us. We've petitioned to let the natives go down and pick the fish up for free, but I'll be blowed if Prescott's lifted a finger so far."

"Were they Ceylonese slaves? On Slave Island?"

Guy's question was met with chuckles. "The British never enslaved the Ceylonese," said Buller, leaning back so that his plate could be removed. "I'm told we once kept fuzzy-wuzzies in that part. Am I right, Major?"

"Kaffirs," said Rawling. "Kaffir slaves who'd been brought here in 1840 murdered a Sinhalese family and were imprisoned over there."

"Fuzzy-wuzzies, I told you so!" exclaimed Buller, draining his whisky and water.

While white-gloved hands offered ice-cream and tinned pears round the table, the conversation turned to jungle tales – told largely to impress the newcomer, Guy suspected. Ingram Bywater described how in his younger days he had once gone stalking with a tracker behind a trained buffalo. All the big game of the forest, leopard, elephant, bear, had not vanished, as they would have at the sound or scent of man. They had scented the buffalo, heard the familiar noise of it crashing through the undergrowth, and had stayed where they were, until I. B. had sighted them down the barrel of his gun.

"That's a trick old John Still used," observed Sandy Duncannon. "Best white tracker there's ever been in Ceylon, though he wasn't one for killing. He taught your brother one or two things, Tancred. Like how to tame a wild cobra with your forefinger."

"What's wrong with a forked stick?" asked Guy, fascinated and appalled at the same time.

"Some men don't do things the easy way," replied Duncannon. "Actually it was a little dodge that Still picked up from the gypsy snake-charmers, the Kuravar – although *they* used a piece of root, as something for their magic to be seen to belong in. He would, very slowly, bring his finger down towards the cobra's hood, at an angle of about sixty degrees. It's the angle that's important. That and never varying the speed of your approach – until eventually his finger would be touching the top of the cobra's head. With his hand he'd then push the snake's head flat on the ground, grab its neck in one hand, its coils in the other, and shove it in his basket. It's a sort of hypnosis, he used to say."

"Sandy, didn't you go travelling the elephant roads with him once?" shouted Ingram Bywater. "Or was it the monkey trails?"

This started Duncannon on another jungle anecdote, in which he was quickly interrupted by Percy Buller, anxious to drag the conversation back to the human animals around them.

"Monkeys!" he suddenly burst out, his high-pitched voice yapping the word. "That's all the Nips are! It's no good beating about the bush. I've seen 'em on my packet boats, scuttling down the hatches. And they're Germans who fly their planes, because I'm blowed if I'll believe the Nips can bloody well handle aircraft, what?"

The violent tone of this speech took the others aback.

"What about the Zero?" asked Guy. "Technically that's a pretty good fighter plane, isn't it?" He looked at Rawling, who nodded and was about to speak. Ingram Bywater pounded the table.

"I'll tell you what I hear. The designs were drawn up by the United States and rejected. The Japs can copy, but they can't invent. Cheap toys is all they're good at. Cheap toys and umbrellas. The British have seen off better fighters by far – and we've got Lutyens's Victory Column out there on the Green to prove it! Eh?"

"And Churchill," added Buller. "Don't forget what Churchill said. 'We have no need to doubt the justice of our cause, or the fact that our strength and willpower will be sufficient to sustain it. We have four-fifths of the population of the world on our side!' "

He sat back with a look of satisfaction, as quiet Hear, hears! ejaculated round the room. Rawling seemed to be calculating.

"Four-fifths," he remarked. "That must include an awful lot of wogs and fuzzy-wuzzies. I do hope Winston's right."

In the evenings and at weekends Guy stepped out briskly into local society. The partial blackout, imposed by Sir Oliver Prescott the day after Pearl Harbor, had actually accelerated the tempo of Colombo's social life. People came in from up-country. Everybody said it was like August week. As the island's eligible young men were shipped off to Europe, or Malaya, Guy found that the calling cards he left in the little wooden boxes outside the best houses in Cinnamon Gardens were taken up with an indecent alacrity.

In no time at all Guy had met Fiona who was fat and noisily cheerful; Angela who was also large, with black bangs and the beginnings of a small moustache; Monica who beat him at tennis which was the end of Monica; Audrey who had learnt passages of Byron's *Don Juan* by heart but had a phobia about exposing any part of her body to direct sunlight; and Patricia whose mother put him off the idea of any closer acquaintance.

What these perfectly mannered colonial girls had in common, he quickly decided, were parents who had taught them an impenetrable indifference to politics, literature, music, painting or any intellectual hobby. 'Talk about Expressionism and they think it's a new game of pulling faces,' he wrote irritably to Lydia in London. "Auden is 'one of those new-fangled poet chappies' and Dylan Thomas is absolutely totally unheard of. Does he still come in to Broadcasting House, by the way? I do envy your access to people of real talent like that."

He persevered. He had nothing better to do. He played tennis on Sunday mornings at the Garden Club. He went swimming at the new Swimming Club after work. He swung a badminton racket on the Donaldsons' lawn. He was invited back to homes in Edinburgh Crescent, Guildford Crescent, Maitland Crescent; Barnes Place, Horton Place, Ward Place, Torrington Place, Rockwood Place; and all the avenues that marched left and right off Colpetty, the main road south between Cinnamon Gardens and the sea.

Cinnamon Gardens! Where blond children in Clarks' sandals played tag behind leafy hedges of hibiscus and crotons; where the nearest approximation to gunfire was the crack of willow against leather in Victoria Park or the rattle of traps on the Racecourse starting-boxes; where the Labrador dozed with its tongue out on the sweet-smelling verandah while the boy tiptoed past with the tray of drinks. Spacious bungalows, clustered in rows but casually at an angle to each other, they were bowered in flame-of-the-forest trees and bordered with glowing beds of cannas, flocks and bougainvillaea. Inside, the blinds shut down behind furniture knocked up by local carpenters out of Heal's catalogues, and roast chicken was placed in front of Master to carve and pass with the fried onions round the table.

Guy ate a whole battery of roasted chickens. He spooned his way through a tankful of tinned fruit salad. He went to an air carnival; he went to a Ceylon Planters' Rifle Corps dance where he taught a plain girl called Millicent how to begin the béguine. At the pressing invitation of Lady Lusted, Charles Bilbow's aunt by marriage, he looked in at the Silver Wings Charity Whist and Mah-Jong Drive held at the Colombo Town Hall, and left without entering the competition for prizes of a half-bottle of whisky and an iced sponge-cake baked in the shape of a Lancaster bomber.

The climax of the season arrived with Sylvia Donaldson's twenty-first birthday party. It was just before Christmas. Sylvia, who must have thought it jolly boring of Jesus to steal her thunder, had banned streamers, crackers, Christmas cards, mistletoe, sprayed flowers and plastic holly from the big verandah room. The tone this year was to be sophisticated, cosmopolitan and romantic, with just a dash of the unpretentious elegance she had seen the week before last in *The Philadelphia Story* at the Regal.

Guy arrived after dinner in Red Sea rig, as he now knew to call evening dress, to find the Donaldsons' garden moonbeamed with fairy lights strung in the frangipani trees. In the blacked-out upstairs verandah room of the superb old Dutch bungalow the lighting was subdued. Cane tables and chairs had been pushed back to make a dance-floor. Between the silver salvers piled with mangoes, plums, pawpaws, loquats, pineapples and lady's-finger plantains squatted bowls of fresh cashew nuts and little

60

saucers of dark Jaggery fudge made from palm sugar and coconut bits. Up at the far end, in a jungle of anthuriums and maidenhair fern Felice's Blue Star Band from the Grand Oriental Hotel had launched into a treacly Neapolitan rendering of "Smoke Gets In Your Eyes".

The trifling melody drowned Guy in a sudden penetrating nostalgia. It was what the band had played at the Trocadero the night before he sailed from Tilbury. He had danced with Lydia, and she had wept a few tears on his shoulder, and apologised, and wept again.

"It'll be all right," he had told her. "You're the one in more danger than I'll be."

"What—" she had blinked back her tears, "do you mean, from a broken heart?"

It was most un-Lydia-like, this whole conversation. He had wondered about cancelling his passage. But there were more important things in life for a Tancred, he had told himself, than attachments of the heart. There were worlds to be conquered, challenges to be overcome, ambitions to fulfil. Vital war work awaited him. He had danced with Lydia until dawn; then he had put her in a taxi.

> *They asked me how I knew*
> *My true love was true –*
> *I of course replied*
> *Something here inside*
> *Cannot be denied.*

He made his way over to the bar where the Donaldsons' elderly head boy Albert, his watery eyes straining in the gloom, ladled ice into tumblers of fruit juice, gin and limes and whisky splits. Guy had a glass of bottled passion-fruit, drank it down, and had another. He watched the dancers with a sudden feeling of oppression, of deep and unhappy bewilderment, as if he had no right to be here, witnessing a happiness he could not share.

It was evident to him that he had somehow wandered out of the war into a place where war had no meaning. Those two over there, dancing with a maraschino cherry held between their noses, had never seen blood spilled, or heard an ARP warden's rattle, or smelt the stink that rose in the morning from rubble and charred timbers before the fire and ambulance crews started work. It was he, Guy, who knew all about that, and who bore the knowledge of it, here and everywhere in this unscarred island, like a leprosy which kept him in perpetual quarantine.

> They said Someday you'll find
> All who love are blind.
> When your heart's on fire,
> You must realise
> Smoke gets in your eyes.

What had Lydia said, between her tears? *I won't know you any more.* But what could make the slightest alteration to him in this pampered colonial backwater, where losing face was the ultimate humiliation? In wartime London you had no room for prissy morality. You lived and loved. Out here he wasn't doing much of either. He resolved there and then to follow up Rawling's suggestion and take what he delicately called a "rickshaw girl". He had no time to waste trying to come to terms with the East. The East would have to come to terms with him.

Sylvia came up to him. She planted a wet kiss on his cheek. "I'm the birthday girl. I can kiss anyone," she said with a bright despairing smile. Guy's heart went out to her. Charles Bilbow, he knew, was due to sail out of Colombo in HMS *Dorsetshire* the next day.

"You look beautiful, and very chic," he told her – and indeed she did, in a dark red evening dress made of some shot silk material which shimmered in the dim lights of the verandah room.

"Charles goes to sea tomorrow," she said.

"I know."

"And you know what? I join the RNVR as a cipherette!"

"Is Ceylon in that much danger?"

"Don't be horrid, Guy!" Sylvia giggled and poked him in the ribs. "You're jolly lucky you weren't here for my birthday party last year, which was fancy-dress. I'd have made you come as Dracula!"

"With fangs." He bared his teeth and feinted at her white neck. Sylvia gave a delighted shudder. "Would I have won?" he asked.

"Not if I bled to death. You beast."

"Who did win?"

"What?" She looked disappointed he hadn't pressed home his attack. "Oh, actually it was rather fun in a silly sort of way. Piggy was all blacked up in a loincloth as the King of the Zulus. Mr Buller came as Churchill, of course. Mr and Mrs Clarke came as

Rudy Valentino and Clara Bow, can you imagine? Daddy was Old Father Time, yawn, yawn. Archdeacon Hoathly got first prize. He was all dolled up in baby clothes as Life Begins at Forty. And David was there!"

She beckoned over a tall serious-looking man in his early twenties. Wavy brown hair and a prominent nose gave him a faintly Grecian look. "David, what were you last year? At my fancy-dress party?"

The young man smiled. "I honourable Emperor Hirohito," he replied with a low bow.

"In black pyjamas, that's right! And we all thought you were Fu Manchu! Guy, do you know David Gifford? He was at school with Charlie."

So this was the airman who had flown over Kelani Lodge. Guy said politely, "I believe you know my sister-in-law, Jill Tancred."

"Yes. I mean, I've met her."

"Actually," Sylvia whispered. "I think David's a bit in love with her."

"What rot!" David Gifford blushed. "I met her exactly twice, staying here with you before I was sent to India. Sylvia, you do say the most wicked things!"

"Is she coming tonight?" Guy asked.

"Who?"

"Jill."

"She should be here." Sylvia drew herself up to her full five foot one and craned her neck. "I wish you'd get your brother out of Kelani sometimes, Guy," she added. "He's an absolute hermit."

Guy had moved on to whisky and water. He felt perfectly composed. The verandah room was beginning to fill with people. David Gifford left to talk to a sloe-eyed beauty with the slight, athletic body of a dancer and lustrous black hair (Eurasian?), who was standing by herself nervously clutching an empty glass. Sylvia had rushed off to comfort some friend called Juliet who was in floods because one of her ponies had broken into the hayloft and died of overeating, up in Nuwara Eliya (Newraylia, he was told to pronounce it; it sounded like a thermal resort version of Cinnamon Gardens). Elizabeth Donaldson, her face flushed, circulated with a tray of stuffed chillies and curry puffs. She was followed by Albert, carrying another tray. The bank played selections from "In the Mood".

A hand tapped him on the shoulder. It was George Donaldson. "D'you know Tony Apple?" he asked, awkwardly abrupt

63

even at introductions. "Tony, this is Harry's brother you were asking about."

Guy restrained his impatience, and shook the ringed hand held out to him. Gold cuff-links, greying hair, a surprisingly young, unlined face that would have been strikingly handsome if it wasn't for the first signs of jowliness around the sensuous mouth – Sylvia's dismissive phrase about him being a rich bachelor with a stable of women and horses seemed to sum up Tony Apple pretty well.

"You know my brother?" he asked.

"We smoked opium together."

"You did what!"

"Before he married dear Jill, of course. Are you an opium man?"

"No. But—"

"Pity. How about polo?"

"Not my game. But—"

"Pity. They're shipping Johnnie Ross out next week. Tripoli or somewhere. At this rate we won't be able to get together a five-a-side."

Guy was silent. Tony Apple changed tack. "I say, you weren't at the Races today, were you? I lost a bomb. Bet on a filly in the three o'clock that beat Silver Hackle by yards in the Champion Stakes, and the wretched nag loses by three lengths to an outsider. I try to recoup on a promising Arab in the Mysore Plate and it breaks a bloody leg. How long have you been here?"

"About half an hour."

"No. I mean in Ceylon. Serendib. Pearl of the East. Otherwise known as a tear fallen off the cheek of India, or a dressed ham hanging from the rafters. I prefer my ham undressed, you've probably been told. Terrible puritans, these Scots, except in private."

"I didn't know Harry smoked opium."

"He introduced me to it." Tony Apple's eyes sidled over Guy's shoulder. He drew out his wallet. "Interesting man, your bro. Look, Tancred. Here's my card. I keep a set of rooms at the Swimming Club, the annexe. If you want any help," he drawled the words, "finding your way around, give me a tinkle."

He was gone. When Guy turned round, Sebastian Clarke was advancing on him. His heart sank. With a guilty wave of acknowledgement he spun on his heel and hurried out to the balcony.

People looking for air had gathered in small knots on the Donaldsons' lawn. Under the fairy lights white shirts and white

64

dresses gleamed with a ghostly pallor. He saw Jill. She stood alone, under a frangipani tree. She was wearing a simple grey-and-green dress nipped in at the waist and ruffed at the shoulders. Her hair, brushed straight back, broke out in curls down the back of her chiffon stole.

When Guy came up, she greeted him with a sombre smile, pulling her stole closer round her shoulders. Neither of them spoke for a second. Things shrilled in the frangipani-scented darkness.

"Did Harry not come?" he asked.

"No." She looked away. "Isn't this a lovely garden? Liz has done it beautifully. I'm surprised she can get away with the fairy lights, though. In the blackout."

"They're under the official limit for voltage."

"Ah."

It seemed they had nothing more to say to each other. He commented politely, "You look marvellous in dark green. It suits your complexion."

"You mean because I'm so sunburnt?" She gave a nervous laugh. "Oh dear. We Australians have got such vulgar skin. Do you know what Sylvia's old ayah once told me? That if Melbourne was as hot as I said, we ought all to be as black as she was!"

"Australia. Yes." He plunged his hands into his pockets and gazed around. Felice's Blue Star Band had been persuaded to tackle a rumba: from inside came a confusion of laughter and pounding feet. He burst out, "Don't you wonder, often, what you're doing here?"

"You're trying to keep control. That's what we're all doing, all the time. Coolies, rubber trees, insects, the house, the garden . . . it's what Harry would call a holding operation."

"For what, though?"

"Isn't that a silly question?"

"I'm not talking about the economic rationale. I mean you, Jill Tancred. What are you doing it for?"

They were walking past a flowerbed. Jill bent down and tugged out a weed. She was frowning. "Why do you ask?"

He shrugged. "Curiosity."

"Is that it? Curiosity?" She turned to face him, planting her feet squarely on the ground. "Guy. I know you're Harry's brother. But that doesn't give you the right to pry into my feelings. I'm sure you think I'm some sort of bored, frustrated creature who can't wait to pour out her miseries into the first sympathetic ear—"

"No, I don't!"

"In actual fact I enjoy my life here. I make the best of what I have, even if it does seem stultifying to you. In your London circles I'm sure women are fascinating and beautiful and read all the latest books. We memsahibs must be a big disappointment to you."

"That's not what I meant, believe me! Besides, London women aren't a bit glamorous these days. They all work in munitions factories."

"And here I am, going out to parties," she retorted, torn between anger and laughter. "Guy, I gave up trying to change the world a long time ago. You do what you like. Go back to England to fight, if you can't bear it here. But don't take it out on me."

They had reached the verandah steps. Up above there was a loud scream. A tray of glasses crashed on the parquet floor. The verandah-room doors opened in a shaft of light; Sylvia and Charlie came out on to the balcony, hand in hand. Guy and Jill drew back into the shadows.

"Come on, everybody!" Sylvia cried. "We're going for a midnight swim!" She caught sight of Guy. "Come on, Guy! You too!"

He turned round. Jill had vanished. For a moment he stood there, undecided. Sylvia was halfway down the steps towards him.

He raised his arms, in mock surrender.

WITH much shouting and giggling and popping of fizzy-drink stoppers her party piled into three elderly cars and rattled down Reid Avenue to the coastal highway to Mount Lavinia. Sylvia squeezed herself between Juliet, still wittering on about her pony, and Stuart Fraser who was in the next Ceylon consignment for north Africa and had drunk himself into a disgusting stupor. Guy Tancred sat in front, next to darling Charlie who drove the Hillman as if death held no fears for him.

A bottle of whisky was passed round; they all took swigs. Charlie had just had his naval haircut: the back of his neck, all white and hollowed out, made him look like a young schoolboy. Overcome with emotion Sylvia leant forward and flung her arms round his neck, spilling half her drink down his shirtfront. The Hillman swerved and nearly ran down a native at the side of the road; they saw his terrified eyes and a flash of white sarong as Charlie skidded back on to the highway.

"I say, steady on, little goose!" he cried. "Give a chap a bit of warning, eh? I've got a boat to catch!"

"Oh, Charlie, take me with you," whispered Sylvia. She buried her face in the whiteness of his neck. But Charlie was busy telling Guy Tancred about HMS *Dorsetshire*: how she had been in the Invergordon Mutiny in 1931 and the entire ship's company, officers and men, had spent the whole time amicably watching films together in the ship's cinema; and the famous story of how, earlier in this year of 1941, *Dorsetshire* had fired the three torpedoes which finally sunk *Bismarck*, and then had closed in to pick up German survivors struggling in the water.

Sylvia had been told this story several times already, but she wanted the others to hear it. She shushed Juliet and sat back with a brave little smile such as she had seen on her mother's face when Piggy went off to war. She had pictured in her mind the dramatic farewell scene with Charlie, even to the place on the docks where they would kiss for the last time, creating a small island of grief and tenderness amid the swirling, heedless crowd.

Yesterday she had wandered through the men's department at Millers, looking for his farewell present. The counters were stacked with Christmas trinkets, more suitable for a Somerset Maugham play than for a man going off to fight. A silver-plated cocktail-shaker? A "presentation box" of imitation onyx shirt-studs and cuff-links? She had stopped in front of a red silk dressing gown and fallen into a protracted daydream of Charlie wearing it, until a shop assistant with a nasty Liverpudlian accent asked if madam wanted it wrapped. Finally she settled on something practical: a leather-cased brandy-flask with a silver stopper. Even more prudently she had filled it last night with her father's Napoleon Cognac.

"What's *Dorsetshire* been doing recently?" Guy Tancred asked Charlie.

"Nothing special. No great adventures. Hunting German commerce raiders. Escorting troop-carriers from Durban to Singapore with reinforcements to fight the Japs. I should think they'll have landed enough by now. It can't take that many divisions to push the Japs back into the sea. Can it?"

"Rule Britannia!" shouted Stuart Fraser, suddenly waking up and waving the empty whisky-bottle. "Here's to Admiral Charlie Bilbow! Hip! Hip!"

"Hooray!"

They all piled out of the cars at Mount Lavinia, and ran down beside the magnificent old hotel to the long strip of sandy beach which curved round the side of the promontory. The ocean was darkly phosphorescent, its slow surges lipped with spectral white. On the still-warm sand, scattered with coconut husks, they stripped off shirts and dresses, trousers and petticoats, and ran half-naked, screaming, into the water. Sylvia stood apart from the others, thigh deep, tolerating the Indian Ocean curling up between her legs. Her head thrown back, she gazed up at the stars, a moistened goddess waiting to be swept off her feet. Charlie came plunging to her side and crouched before her.

"On my back, little goose," he panted. "I'll take you riding."

This was a game which dated back to their childhood. Clambering on his back, she used to lie across him and let herself be towed out to sea, his powerful strokes (Charlie was the best swimmer of any of them) buoying her along as though she was riding a dolphin. But that was a long time ago. Tonight Sylvia felt sophisticated, cosmopolitan, romantic. She did not want to be called little goose any longer, or play childhood games. Anyway, there were sharks out there, beyond the reef. With a light laugh she dipped her hands in the water and splashed Charlie's face. Then she ran back to the beach, leaving him spluttering.

Malcolm Pennycook, one of the north African consignment with Stuart Fraser, had bought a gas-mask from Millers who were selling them in the sports department. He was pretending to use it as a snorkel, blowing huge bubbles in the water to shrieks of laughter from Juliet and some of her silly friends. Higher up the beach, under the palm trees, an illegal bonfire of driftwood and coconut husks had been started. Somebody had brought a gramophone; a crackly tune danced out of the warm darkness. Feeling drowsy, and a little bit maudlin as the effect of the champagne wore off, Sylvia picked up her clothes and went and sat with her back against a catamaran beached by one of the fishermen, using her green dress as a neck-pillow.

People came and went by the bonfire, talking in low voices. A couple were dancing to the music, so close that they appeared as a single silhouette, turning slowly. Sylvia sighed and closed her eyes. Romance became so difficult as one grew older.

As a child she had sat and daydreamed, like a princess at the high tower window listening for the hoofbeats of her own true knight to tell her when to let down her blonde hair. In those days they had been real knights, in their fabulous armour of greaves and cuirasses, although when they raised their visors she could never quite decide what she wanted them to look like. In silly adolescence, of course, they were the drumming hoofs of Errol Flynn and Douglas Fairbanks who would sweep her into their arms and hold her, light as a feather, while they spurred into a forest glade and laid her on the greensward, their murmured words of tenderness belied by the ravenous gleam in their eyes.

Now she was a middle-aged woman in her twenties, Sylvia had grown out of all that. Going to school at Cheltenham, and staying with her aunt in London during the winter holidays, she had quickly realised that her favourite novels had it all wrong about romance. It wasn't anything to do with starlit nights on a tropical beach, like now. Where you were didn't make any difference: it was who you were with that counted. Not until she'd left England and come back here to live with her parents had she discovered just how full of boring men Ceylon was. Quite honestly, there was no one out here with enough imagination to know what romance was. Even devoted old Charlie – and she loved him dearly – didn't have much clue how to make a girl feel special.

Why should she delude herself? She knew exactly what was

making her feel this way. Two days ago, while her parents were out to dinner, she had given Charlie a farewell present of a different sort. That wasn't how she had put it, but they both knew what it meant. Charlie was going to sea; she was going into the Naval Office. Their lives were changing. They felt lonely and solemn, and a little frightened.

She had wanted Charlie to carry her into the bedroom and make passionate love to her, but it hadn't happened like that. She'd had to lead him into the bedroom, and he turned out to be as inexperienced as she was, all fingers and thumbs and slobbery kisses, and the thing itself was over so quickly that there was nothing for her to enjoy at all. Then he hugged her in his arms so tightly she thought she was going to suffocate, and she'd had to pull away from him and go into the bathroom to hide her tears of disappointment. What made it even more hurtful was that Charlie's attitude to her afterwards didn't change at all. He still called her his little goose, and ruffled her hair. There had been nothing electric in the atmosphere at the breakfast table. . . .

Low laughter and scuffling of feet in the sand made her open her eyes. Maria de Vos stood by the bonfire in a red swimming costume. She must have come straight out of the sea, because she was shaking the water out of her long black hair and towelling her face. David Gifford was talking to her, and every now and then Maria would stop and glance up at him with pretend shyness through her wet hair and put her hand on his arm, in a manner that was quite unlike her and rather brazen in Sylvia's private opinion.

The other beastly thing was David addressing her like an equal. It wasn't – she didn't mean – because Maria was a Burgher, of mixed blood, and therefore not in the same social bracket. Not at all. Maria was a friend of hers. But David seemed to be talking to her quite unself-consciously and with more animation than Sylvia ever got out of him. Quite honestly David Gifford tended to make her feel a bit of an idiot: perhaps because he was so grave and intense, a bit like Laurence Olivier as Darcy (*Pride and Prejudice* had just been on at the Majestic) except more darkly handsome, so that Sylvia never knew quite what to say to him.

At least once recently she had woken up in the middle of the night repeating the polished ripostes she could have made to David instead of the dumb remarks that dropped out one after the other every time she opened her mouth. Even earlier tonight, dancing with him, while Angela and Juliet who fancied him like mad stood by the silver salvers with sour expressions on their faces, she'd found she had nothing intelligent to say and he'd had to make all the running, and it was almost with relief that she'd finally excused herself to go and dance with Charlie again because it was his last night in Colombo.

It was too bad that he should open up to Maria. What did she have to talk to him about? The two of them had absolutely nothing in common. Yawning and stretching, as if she had just woken from a snooze, Sylvia got up and walked over to the fire.

"Silly me, I didn't bring a towel!" she said to Maria with a laugh. "May I borrow yours a moment? My legs are absolutely sticky with sand."

Bending over, she carefully brushed the sand off one bare leg and then off the other. Maria and David seemed to have lost the thread of their conversation. When she looked up she caught David's eye. Although the fire by now was burning merrily, a little cold shiver ran through her.

At that moment Charlie came bounding up the beach, looking like a puppy dog wagging his tail, and enfolded Sylvia in a dripping wet embrace. She screamed.

"Come on, little goose," shouted Charlie. "Time to go home."

The next morning Sylvia stopped off at Mademoiselle Orliga's Dance School. The door was open. She called up to Maria. When there was no answer, she went on up the stairs. They had not been swept. One of the children had left a paper bag on the landing with the remains of sticky sherbet that had been sucked out with a liquorice straw. On the powdery walls hung framed "photographs" of famous ballet dancers (some of them obviously cut straight out of *Dancing Times* and the *Illustrated London News*). A notice on the door at the top, written in a flamboyant hand, said "Come In And Don't Forget To Wipe Your Feet!!"

Mademoiselle Orliga's office was empty. The open window looked out over the rain trees along Colpetty. Pinned among the dance schedules on the noticeboard were Christmas cards: a bulldog standing on a Union Jack; a cottage garden scene in the Cotswolds entitled "England, Home and Beauty"; a lively one from Kitty Clarke's little girl of three owls with red, white and blue bows on their necks inscribed "Knock Us Off Our Perch – Not Likely!"

There were sounds from the salon. Sylvia walked down the short corridor. She stopped. In the wall-length mirror, which usually reflected the pink and straining faces of little girls on their

71

points at the barre, she could see Maria de Vos. In the middle of
Mademoiselle Orliga's parquet floor, scuffed by a thousand tiny
feet, Maria was dancing, in graceful solitude, humming the melody of "Smoke Gets In Your Eyes". Backwards and forwards,
sideways and round she danced in her silver ballet pumps, her
arms outstretched to hug an absent partner. She was like a
gazelle with her long legs, her soft, brown face. A faint shadow
crossed Sylvia's face as she watched this vision.

"*They asked me how I knew My true love was true—*"

"I've brought your towel back."

"Oh! Oh, Sylvia."

"I didn't mean to interrupt."

"No, no. I don't know what I think I'm doing. I've got the
Clarke and Hoathly children arriving any second. I should be
looking out their music and choreography." Maria rushed over
to the piano stool and began rummaging in it to cover her embarrassment. "You know, the dress rehearsal for *Cinderella* is tomorrow, and they still haven't got the Russian Peasant Dance right."

"Really? I didn't know there was a Russian Peasant Dance in
Cinderella."

"It's Orliga, the old bat. You know what she's like, telling
everyone she's related to Diaghilev and using it as an excuse to
raise the fees. She wants the Peasant Dance as the Brownies'
showpiece. I told her that little girls might not have the strength
and the balance, but she just says," Maria mimicked, "'Little girls
can do anyzink. Vee muss give zair parents value for zair
money!'"

"How dire!"

"You should see her demonstrating it." Maria proceeded to
give an imitation of the portly Mademoiselle Orliga doing the
Russian Peasant Dance, throwing back invisible scarves over her
shoulder, flinging her arms wide and kicking her legs out in front
of her while dropping her bottom lower and lower towards the
floor. Sylvia rocked with laughter. Maria joined in.

"I haven't thanked you for a wonderful party last night," said
Maria then, suddenly solemn.

"You looked as if you were having fun."

"Yes. Oh, yes. I never met that new friend of your parents,
what's his name?"

"Guy Tancred."

"Yes. He looked very nice."

"What about David?"

"David?"

72

"David Gifford."

"Oh." Not looking at her friend, Maria walked over to the window. She stared out over the hot shimmering street, brushing her lips with the sheet music. "You noticed, then," she said. "Sylvia.... I know it's stupid. I just can't get him out of my head."

"David?"

"Yes." Maria sat on the window-sill. "Don't be hard on me. I know you must think I'm mad. We went out into your garden. He told me all about flying his Wapiti biplane down from Bombay to join 60 Squadron at Ratmalana. He looks like – I don't know. Did you see Laurence Olivier in *Pride and Prejudice* last week?"

"Oh, for heaven's sake—"

"And look at me! I'm a mess. I haven't got your lovely porcelain colours. My ears are too big. My feet are too big. My nose ... oh, Sylvia!"

This cry from the heart touched Sylvia. She ran across and hugged the beautiful, desolate figure at the window. "Did David drive you home?" she asked carefully.

"No. After you and Charlie left, we all went off for bacon and eggs at Princes Club. They've got a rule about Burghers, so I just said I didn't want breakfast, and walked home."

"Charlie thinks he's ace."

"Does he? Does he? Oh, Sylvia, and Charlie's going away tonight, I'm so sorry! But does he really think so? I wish you'd tell me about him. He stayed with you, didn't he? Before he was sent to Bombay?"

"David only stayed a few days. He never told *me* anything. I know he was at Marlborough, with Charlie. He told me how poor Charlie used to be ragged because he had a stutter."

"Marlborough?"

"It's a school. In England." Sylvia was tempted to add that David Gifford had told her last night he was probably going to be posted home to England to train as a Hurricane pilot. But she saw no reason to disillusion Maria. The poor girl was probably imagining him in his aeroplane somewhere overhead, practising wingflips and dives and daring turns on to the enemy's tail. Whereas at this very moment he could just as easily be sitting in a mess at Ratmalana bragging about the sweet little chi-chi girl he had at his heels. Men were like that.

There were footsteps on the stairs. Sylvia recognised the heavy tread of women after a morning's shopping in the heat. She yawned, and caught herself thinking that twenty-one was too old to be up all night. *Quelle bêtise!* Next she'd be worrying she was on the shelf.

"You take the kids," she said, going back to the office as plump Iris Hoathly and the other two seven-year-olds burst into the room. "I'll give them coffee, just to help you out. I'm sure Orliga wants her paying customers kept happy."

Ottoline Hoathly, the Archdeacon's wife, was a tall, red-faced woman with broad shoulders, prominent teeth and red hair drawn back in a bun. She was carrying sheet music and wearing – of all things in this beastly heat – a raincoat. Seeing her with Kitty Clarke, Sylvia could not avoid thinking of Laurel and Hardy because really Kitty could not be more different with her diminutive birdlike appearance and birdlike manner too, chir-ruping away and darting beady looks to check that she had not committed a *faux pas*.

"Well, I won't say no," she chirped, taking a cup of coffee from Sylvia and carrying on to describe what it was like to be pregnant with your third child and sit resting your legs in Millers, only to have a woman walk straight in front of her and snap up the doll she wanted for Penny, her daughter.

"My dear, I saw hundreds of dolls in Millers," Ottoline Hoath-ly objected.

"Cheap ones, Tillie. Just a cotton frock and bonnet. The nice ones had a white lace gown, silk lingerie . . . twenty-three rupees but *so* pretty. And what with the war on there isn't a thing to be had that's decent any more, I don't know why we bother with Christmas, especially when you've got to do it all yourself."

Sylvia felt another yawn coming and turned it into a polite laugh. She felt sorry for Kitty Clarke; she knew the malicious things people said about her behind her back: that she used to be a Nippy in Lyons Corner House, or else she'd worked behind the hosiery counter at Whiteaway Laidlaw (so Mrs Ingram Bywater had claimed). But Sebastian Clarke was such a beast, having all those affairs – some said with married women – and Kitty stayed so loyal to him always. Why did men have to be such rotters?

She heard strains of the Russian Peasant Dance coming from the salon where poor Maria was striving to turn those little round pumpkins into carriages. But the noise coming from the other side, from Colpetty, drowned the music. Putting down her coffee she went to the window.

"What is it, dear?" asked the Archdeacon's wife.

A convoy of lorries (evidently requisitioned, they still had ONO & OC painted on the side) moved slowly south down the coast road. Sitting in them were rows of bearded, khaki-clad Punjabi troops, among them several Sikhs in white turbans. Excitedly they waved and cheered at the passers-by (not that the Sinhalese in the street took a blind bit of notice).

Looming behind Sylvia at the window, Ottoline Hoathly declared, "If they're going to Malaya, they're going the wrong way."

"What about the News?" exclaimed Kitty Clarke, clasping her hands over her stomach at the sight of so many Indians in uniform. "Sylvia, be a dear and switch the radio on."

It was not the announcer they heard but an unfamiliar voice which seemed to come from a great distance, weary, fragile.

"We stand by the ship. From the sands of Egypt to the snows of the Antarctic, the British Empire looks to us – no, not only the British Empire, but all people who love freedom, justice, truth and fair dealing. Let us then steel ourselves to endure. We have had some shocks – we expect more – but Singapore must not fall. It shall not fall."

The voice was extinguished. The announcer came on in brisk, almost cheery tones –

"That was Sir Shenton Thomas, Governor of Malaya, addressing the people of the Straits Settlements. Latest reports from Malaya indicate that the Nipponese Army is being given the rope it needs to hang itself with. Orderly evacuation from Jitra, Kuantan and Penang has enabled our British lads to fall back to more advantageous ground for defensive operations. Nippon is being drawn down into a trap, and our crack troops under the command of General Percival just can't wait to turn on those yellow monkeys and give them a taste of their own medicine."

Domestic news followed: a sailing race off Trincomalee; preparations for the Silver Wings Carnival, with aerial joyrides on Tata Air Lines and dinner-dance-cabaret in a Balinese setting. Sylvia turned off the radio. Nobody spoke for a moment.

"Poor old Hong Kong, too, from what one gathers," said Ottoline Hoathly eventually, pulling the collar of her raincoat up.

"Hong Kong was much more exposed," shot back Kitty Clarke with surprising decisiveness. "Sebastian says it's much more exposed. He says we should have evacuated Hong Kong as soon as Japan came into the war, and moved all those troops across to Malaya instead of leaving them to the mercy of the Japs. Sebastian thinks everyone underestimates the Japanese. He thinks we're in for a long fight in Malaya." She added, "Did you see that from tomorrow Elephant House is making only one delivery a day?"

"Millers too, dear," returned Mrs Hoathly. "And nothing at

all on Sundays. Still, one shouldn't complain. As I said to Eric, what are refrigerators for? And if you think of those poor boys in north Africa, in all that heat, I feel so sorry for them. Has your mother mentioned our Victory Shop, Sylvia dear? Elizabeth and I have been thinking of starting up a Victory Shop for the refugees. I've been knitting fit to bust. Scarves, socks, balaclavas. . . ."

Kitty Clarke nodded. "I'm told Lady Lusted is embroidering cushions with her own hands."

As they contemplated how both High and Low were pulling together for the war effort, in pounded Iris, pink from her exertions on the dance-floor.

"Maria says it's your turn, Mummy," she panted.

"Good-oh." Ottoline Hoathly took off her raincoat. Sylvia's mouth fell open. Underneath she was wearing a chocolate-brown leotard spotted with white paint and a green tutu made of some transparent gauze material; nothing else.

"Oh dear," said Kitty Clarke involuntarily. "Cinderella?"

The Archdeacon's wife nodded. She flourished her music. "Interlude: Faun Dance," she explained, and pranced down the corridor.

The momentary silence which followed gave Sylvia her opportunity to escape. Mummy was giving Charlie a farewell lunch which was going to be an absolutely dire occasion, she was sure of it, with everyone sniffing over their curry and sambals. Then she'd help Charlie pack, and iron her RNVR uniform for the morning, and after that they'd take a rickshaw to the docks. She would give dear darling Charlie the silver brandy-flask and tell him to keep it in his breast pocket, over his heart, to protect him from shrapnel (did ordinary seamen *have* breast pockets?).

As she walked back through Cinnamon Gardens the thought that her own dearest Charlie might be going away to sea without so much as a breast pocket made the tears start to her eyes and flow down her cheeks, quite unchecked by the fleeting thought that the war seemed to be bringing into Colombo as many young men as it took away. Charlie was, after all, a great support in her life; someone to rely on, and to confide in, and to turn to for comfort when everyone was on at her to do things and Mummy was in one of her impossible moods, mooning over Piggy's snapshots in the music-room.

Wednesday and Saturday were going to be her only days off from the Naval Office this week. On Wednesday she had to take tea with her godmother, Miss Utteridge, in the Pagoda Tea

Rooms to discuss organising what the old lady called a "Cinnamon Gardens party" expedition to an ancient statue of Buddha which had just become accessible by road. On Saturday she had already promised to help her parents give a reception for the new Civil Defence Commissioner, Oliver Goonetilleke. Was this what fate had in store for her? She envisioned herself as an old maid: busy on social errands and at cultural evenings; presiding over her aged parents' dinner parties and church bring-and-buy sales; reading the latest Daphne du Maurier novel as it came in; developing a passionate interest in the world refugee problem.

"Sylvia. Sylvia!"

A horn tooted. Hastily she brushed her cheeks and turned. Guy Tancred, in a rather nice-looking car with proper running boards, leant across and pushed open the passenger door.

"Can I give you a lift somewhere?" he asked.

"Oh, gosh. That's frightfully sweet of you. I was just walking home, actually."

"Jump in. I'll take you."

Bending gracefully, Sylvia got in. A slight flush had crept into her cheeks. "It was so nice that you could come, last night," she said at once. "Colombo's becoming such a jolly place now, don't you think?"

4 April 1942.   7.15 p.m. Indian Ocean.

As night falls, the six survivors from Catalina QL.A are transferred to the aircraft-carrier Akagi, *the flagship of Vice-Admiral Chuichi Nagumo. Nagumo himself has no wish to interrogate them. He already knows that the Catalina crew were lying: his Wireless Operator has intercepted Colombo's request for a repetition and clarification of the message received. This is a pity. It means that tomorrow's air strike will meet with retaliation from Ceylon's air defences, estimated by his intelligence at a strength of some 300 aeroplanes. It makes no difference: the British fleet will not have time to get away.*

Nagumo has been thinking of advancing the operation and carrying out a night raid. After all he is used to night engagements; he used to specialise in night warfare. But that was naval manoeuvres in the cruiser Takao, *back in 1933–4. Air raids are a different matter.*

He has no air background, no real experience of naval warfare; unlike his relentlessly successful lieutenant in Takao, *Mitsuo Fuchida, who led the raid on Pearl Harbor and is now in* Akagi *as Commander of the First Fleet's Air Group. The Admiral has no intention of asking Fuchida, and his Air Operations Officer Minoru Genda, what they think about a night raid. He knows that they already think him indecisive, lacking in confidence, too ready to accept their advice. On the upper bridge he stops pacing and stands quite still, a stocky figure, staring fiercely ahead as* Akagi *drives through the seas at nearly thirty knots towards Ceylon.*

"Daiboju!" he can hear the voice of Kusaka his Chief of Staff in his ear, "Don't worry!" But that's not all. He has other things on his mind. One of them is Admiral Yamamoto, Commander-in-Chief of the Combined Fleet.

Yamamoto is a clever tactician, there is no question of that. He has always excelled in fleet exercises. Yet because of his celebrated successes with carrier-borne aircraft, Yamamoto has become obsessed by them. He insisted on the Pearl Harbor raid, despite Nagumo's objections that the Striking Force would be laying itself open to American land-based air

79

attack from Hawaii. When, owing to the element of surprise, the initial raid on Pearl Harbor proved successful, Yamamoto criticised Nagumo's decision not to authorise a further attack on Oahu in the hope of finding US aircraft-carriers to destroy. Yamamoto, the brilliant C-in-C, ignored the radio intercepts which had revealed the existence of about fifty enemy aircraft still operational. He paid no attention to the fact that Nagumo's striking force no longer enjoyed the advantage of surprise.

Now Yamamoto is saying that the First Fleet should not extend its conquests in the East; that it should double back into the Pacific to hunt down the American aircraft-carriers it failed to destroy at Pearl Harbor! In this, Yamamoto appears to ally himself with the hated Imperial Army Staff who constantly block the navy's plans, who lack any conception of grand strategy, whose attention as always is focused narrowly on its old enemy the Soviet Union (despite the fact that the army itself is already fighting as far west as Burma and is expecting Nagumo's force to safeguard its advance!).

These rival strategies are wasteful. When action is joined, the correct place to issue orders is from the bridge of the Admiral's flagship. In Nagumo's opinion, it is not yet time for the Imperial Navy to consolidate its strength. The whole Imperial war plan depends on a swift victory. What is the point of advancing in order to turn back? The Admiral is descended from a long line of Samurai ancestors. Honour does not permit the Samurai warrior to expose his men to battles which are not worth fighting.

Since Pearl Harbor, his Kido Butai or Carrier Striking Force has had an uninterrupted string of victories – at Rabaul, at Darwin, at Tjilatjap in Java. Malaya has fallen. Sumatra has fallen. The Andamans and Nicobar Islands have dropped into their hands as sweetly as plums from a tree. If Ceylon and the Eastern Fleet can be picked off with as much ease, it would be fruitless to stop here and not continue westwards and link up with the German armies in the Middle East or southern Russia.

Nagumo has heard that the new tripartite Axis military agreement makes no reference to a joint German–Japanese offensive. This is disappointing. It provides ammunition for Yamamoto, not to mention Fuchida and Genda who are also eager, he knows, to return to the Pacific. But the momentum of Japan's westward advance cannot be checked now. Even Hitler must recognise it. And if Hitler were to react to the conquest of the Indian Ocean by pressing for a joint offensive, the Imperial Army would hardly be in a position to deny the conqueror of Russia. . . .

On the upper bridge, the pacing resumes. Captain Taijiro Aoki and the Fleet Navigator Commander Gishiro Migura (in his carpet-slippers, as always) exchange glances. But Admiral Nagumo has relaxed his fierce expression. He can feel around him the inexorable forward thrust of his

great Striking Force – four other aircraft-carriers, four fast battleships,
three cruisers, nine destroyers, 105 fighter planes, 237 bombers – and he
knows in his blood that no power on the open seas can check its irresistible
advance.

EMERGING from his study, Sir Oliver Prescott almost collided with the fellow. A dark-skinned Ceylonese, he carried a bag of tools in one hand and a bucket in the other. With a salaam and a graceful side-step he avoided the Governor and sauntered on down the high-arched corridor cheekily whistling a tune.

Sir Oliver contemplated his retreating back. A plumber, he was probably on his way to unblock a sink. He understood exactly where he was going and what he had to do. When the pipes were fixed, he would pack his tools and go on to the next job. The plumber's life was bounded by certainties as profound as those of the boy with bucket and spade who dug in the sand to reach water: and in the eyes of the Governor of Ceylon, as he gazed after him, there was a momentary longing.

What certainties there had been in Sir Oliver's life were slipping away from him. Mollie was dead: that was the loss of the greatest certainty he had ever been fortunate enough to possess. Physically he was not in A-1 shape. He had tension pains in his left shoulder. His digestion had started playing up, usually at the most confounded awkward moments.

Worst of all, the Empire he had devoted his life to serving was under siege. In the last twenty-three days, the achievements of his twenty-three years in the Malay States had been laid waste by the Japanese army. In India, Nehru made unfriendly speeches. The wretched Chandra Bose was raising Indian militia to fight alongside the Japs, and had the nerve to call one of them the Gandhi Brigade. Here in Ceylon, among the gentlest and most civilised people one could ever wish to govern, a violent independence movement, led by British-educated revolutionaries, was busy setting fire to warehouses and generally raising Cain.

Taken all in all December had been a deplorable month. His levee for the King's birthday had been ruined by the sinking of *Repulse* and *Prince of Wales*. Percival was making an utter ass of himself in Malaya. His own successor as Governor of Hong Kong, Sir Mark Young, had been forced to surrender the Crown

Colony last week to a Jap general called Saki, after holding out with six battalions against half the Nipponese army attacking through China.

Right at this moment Young was probably languishing in Stanley Gaol on a diet of half-cooked rice, which would play havoc with his teeth. If Shenton Thomas in Singapore went the same way, which God forbid, it would leave him, Oliver Prescott, as the sole remaining colonial governor in the East, apart from some chap whose name he couldn't remember in British Borneo, itself being evacuated at top speed.

One's personal tribulations were immaterial in the light of all this, of course. It had nevertheless to be put on record that his devoted housekeeper had chosen this of all months to return to England, and he had found no one suitable to take her place.

For the first time in his long career, Sir Oliver had found himself having to buy his own Christmas presents. He had mingled with the sweltering crowds in Main Street and pondered what to buy his secretaries. In Cargills he had lingered over silk stockings which came in shades of Capri, Tingle, Passion Flower, Caress and Honeysuckle; but what he bought were presentation boxes of Sugar Kreem Toffees. Entering into the spirit of the occasion – why had one never done this with Mollie? – he got hold of a large sack, filled it with his presents and handed them out to each poppet in turn, offering his cheek for a sedate kiss.

Most of the girls vanished up-country for the Christmas weekend – sleeping, he knew, often in the same bedroom together, piling into the same big bed in a tousle of blonde hair on the pillows and a profusion of bare arms and legs, bare midriffs, often bare all over, one wouldn't wonder, if it was a hot night, as frequently happened even in Nuwara Eliya at this time of year, and they had thrown off the coverings. . . .

Which left him in Queen's House, all alone except for a retinue of servants, and plumbers trudging hither and thither, and that unseen, unmentioned colony of hangers-on whose agitated whisperings and scurryings sometimes reached his ears from the basement rooms.

A dinner party with yule logs, mince pies, and crackers most of his guests were too elderly to pull apart constituted the main excitement of his Christmas. That, and going to *Cinderella* at the Regal Theatre, where he watched little girls in clogs and knickerbockers, his ADC and William Steuart primping as Hitler and Hirohito the Ugly Sisters, and the Vicar's wife unveiling her not-so-young limbs in a Faun Dance (Hind-dance would have been more anatomically appropriate).

Add to these the usual round of functions in which he appeared ex officio, armed with a speech and a pair of scissors to cut the tape. Opening the Printer's Pie Carnival, in aid of Tank Week, he was handed one of the few presents that anybody thought to give him this Christmas – a Genoese layer cake with red, white and blue fondant icing in the shape of a victory "V". This he took back with him to Queen's House, where it melted.

What most depressed him during this wretched December was London's disinclination to believe that one was pulling one's weight. This was admittedly his own fault, and it all boiled down to his State Address.

He had burnt the midnight oil over the address to the State Council. By the time he had it ready it was, in his humble submission, as stirring in its cadences as any of the sonnets he sent off to the *Ceylon Daily News*.

He had burnt the midnight oil over the address to the State Council. By the time he had it ready it was, in his humble sub-discussions over the loosening of Ceylon's ties with the United Kingdom. On a rising note (he could see Senanayake and Goonetilleke shifting in their seats) he declared that the atmosphere in which such discussions would eventually take place was growing warmer year by year, and there was the greatest degree of confidence, in London, that their successful conclusion would lead to the setting up of a commission, or conference, in which the whole issue of constitutional reform for Ceylon would be ventilated at the highest level, and with a keen awareness of the urgency with which the State Council would be awaiting its successful outcome.

With morale in the Chamber undoubtedly boosted by this candid summary of the constitutional position, Sir Oliver had gone on to explain the exceptional steps he was taking to strengthen the defences of Ceylon against the common enemy and to ensure the safety of all her citizens. These steps had ineluctably compelled him to assume special gubernatorial powers – including the setting up of a War Council which left the elected body to which he was speaking with no decision-making capacity of any kind – but he was confident, as he stood there before them, that they all understood how such matters as civil defence, food rationing, military camps and a hundred and one other things were best dealt with at a speed which did not admit of prolonged consultation.

After much thought, Sir Oliver had decided to bring his peroration to a close not with a long roll on the drums but with a few high, clear trumpet notes, whose echoes would linger in the Chamber and carry across the seas to Whitehall. "I am not come, this afternoon, to indulge in rhetoric about the cause for which we fight, or our determination to see it through to victory. These are things that lie too near the heart for words.... Let me leave them, rather, to the eloquence of our War Fund and our War Loan subscription lists, which continue to manifest the strength of our common aim. Thank you."

This State Address he had delivered on 17 December. He had sent the manuscript of it to Lord Moyne in London. One week later, receiving a somewhat testy query from the Colonial Secretary, he was mortified to discover that the sole copy in his possession had been sent to London by sea mail.

He cabled Moyne. He assured him that the Address, when it arrived (probably next March), would testify to his unceasing activity and enhance his reputation for sustaining morale. The response from London was cool. Sir Oliver felt increasingly isolated. It would have been so much easier if Ceylon wasn't so far away ... if one was better acquainted with Moyne ... if one was able to address Moyne by his nickname as he knew Leo Amery did. If you could call a man by his nickname there wasn't much he could do to you.

In the meantime, Sir Oliver threw himself with ever-increasing vigour into the mobilisation of Ceylon. The problem, the Governor found, was that the Colonial Office and the War Office displayed embarrassingly little sensitivity for the feelings of the Ceylonese. His constant missives to London begging for caution, circumspection, tact, were filtered through the usual assistant principal secretaries who undoubtedly wrote their pedantic little memos to each other on the bottom of them – "Can we go along with this? H.G.V.", "R.M. to see and pass to S.G.B. for comments, then N. St J.P. to file" – like a parlour game of Consequences which moved a stage further from reality with each annotation.

The refugees, who had begun to arrive in dribs and drabs from Singapore, were being fed, clothed and housed by Colombo's voluntary services. These came under the overall command of Mrs Ingram Bywater, who instilled in them an awesome efficiency shared by no other organisation in Ceylon. Refugees were not a worry to the Governor. His worst headache, aggravated by a stream of cables from London that alternated between the ignorant and the hectoring, remained civil defence.

By now there was very little that Sir Oliver did not know about civil defence. Manuals had been pressed into his hand. Experts flown in from London had lectured him at length and in astonishing detail about gas respirators, Air Raid Precaution shelters, wells, slit trenches, incendiary-bomb scoops, tin hats and first-aid posts. Since a slide-show put on for him in Queen's House by his ARP Controller and Deputy Controller, he had become an authority on trench shelter angles and the minimum protective thickness of walls.

At this point of absolute theoretical readiness a few practical snags began to surface. For one thing there were only four stirrup-pumps on the entire island. Hardly any steel helmets had arrived. Ceylon's negligible stock of gas masks had long since been exhausted, and no supplies were due from London. A shortage of metal made it impossible to reinforce surface air-raid shelters to the proper specifications. And Colombo's high water-table meant that when Sir Oliver persuaded his gardener to dig a slit trench by the oleander hedge facing the croquet lawn it immediately filled with a slurry of mud.

The simulacrum of a civil defence force was established, even so. First-aid posts were set up (with a surfeit of steel stretchers). Goonetilleke divided Colombo neatly into nine areas, each with its hierarchy of ARP officers. Dressed in white socks, brown shoes, pointed stars on their white drill tunics and different widths of blue ribbon on their white armbands, they practised before admiring onlookers the full repertoire of the advice they could give – IN THE EVENT OF AN AIR RAID, TAKE COVER.

Putting the best face on things he could, Sir Oliver ended a cable to London: "I may add that, at Queen's House, tubs of sand, buckets of water and other such remedies necessary to deal with incendiary bombs are ready on the roof and in the passages."

His own civic example signally failed to impress the Tamil population of Ceylon. Over the Christmas break, and again at the New Year, thousands of Tamils queued in lines at Colombo's railway stations for tickets back to India across the Palk Strait. Uneasily aware that the justification for British rule anywhere lay in the maintenance of public order, the Governor called in Sebastian Clarke.

"It's a bad show," he told him. "We've lost seven thousand Tamils in the last four weeks. At this rate we'll start running short of dockside labour."

"I'm afraid, sir, it's going to get worse before it gets better."

"How's that?"

"Tomorrow, sir, if you remember, we start issuing the rice coupon books. Rice rationing is going to hit them where it hurts, in their bellies. It's the sense of repletion they get from their all-rice meal—"

"I know about rice, Sebastian. There won't be any more rice for them in India. It's fear I'm worried about. It can snowball into panic. If there's an air raid on Colombo I could have a mass exodus on my hands."

"Could we not recruit a new lot of harbour coolies back from India?"

"No. They're jittery. They're all jittery, Sinhalese as well. People have started withdrawing their savings. The one thing we don't need at the moment is a run on the banks."

"No."

Leaning at an angle sideways in his chair, Sebastian Clarke pondered the matter, thin strands of red hair falling over his hooded eyes. Sir Oliver looked at him hopefully. His Deputy Financial Secretary had some batty ideas – his obsession with spending money on what he called "aid projects" for one – but he beavered away dashed efficiently, and had been known to come up with some surprisingly bright answers.

Sebastian Clarke thought aloud. "You can't double the rice ration for the dock labour force because everyone else would start claiming it. However, we could put your propaganda team on to creating a whole new diet for them. . . . Sorghum . . . coconut. . . ."

"I've thought of that. PWD has kitchens and canteens under construction. I'm down to eat the first meal in one next month. It doesn't solve the problem of fright."

"Draft in prisoners?"

"Lighterage work is semi-skilled. And the Prison Department tells me they would all get seasick in monsoon swells."

"Ah. Well, then. We could bring in a system of permits to board ships in harbour and ferries across the Palk Strait."

"Yes. That's worth thinking about."

"Other than that, sir, I'm afraid it's down to persuading the Tamils that they've got nothing to fear from air raids. And that is a civil defence problem."

The two men stared at each other across the desk. Each knew what the other was thinking. Civil defence was not a problem. Civil defence was a nightmare.

*

It was a couple of days after this exchange that the Governor left Queen's House to inaugurate the new grandstand at the Racecourse. As always, on the first afternoon of the New Year Race Meet half of Colombo was marooned in a long and deafening traffic jam down Colpetty. Even in his informal dress of white shorts, white shirt and khaki hose, Sir Oliver found himself bathed in sweat. He sat back, grasping his hat, shifted uncomfortably at the stickiness of the moist leather through the cotton seat-cover of the Sunbeam Talbot. He felt distinctly ill.

He knew why. After a light lunch, he had eaten a durian. What it was that drew him to this repulsive fruit, with its corrupt smell and its taste like sweetish creamy Gorgonzola, he preferred not to ask himself. He never used to eat the things when Mollie was alive: she wouldn't have them in the house. His native boys in Malaya used to prize the durian's white custard as an aphrodisiac. On him it had the opposite effect. It satiated unnameable desires that nowadays came over him without warning and sometimes quite frankly reached the verge of overwhelming his self-control. Like all perversions, at least the minor ones, there was a price to pay for its indulgence. In Sir Oliver's case, the price was indigestion.

He released a loud fart, coughing to cover the noise. The chauffeur in front nodded approvingly. Jack Phillips, his own chauffeur, had reported sick with a heat rash; this was a Sinhalese substitute. Not for the first time, the Governor experienced a twinge of anxiety. His white staff were deserting him. Native Ceylonese seemed to be appropriating his domestic arrangements. His housekeeper; now his chauffeur; his major-domo; the unseen creatures in the basement.... And wherever he went in Queen's House nowadays, in the corridors and on the stairs, these mysterious men carrying what looked like plumber's bags.

Rawling, this morning, had not helped with all his talk of spies. Now that Hideki Ono and the other Japanese nationals were out of harm's way that should have been an end to it, but Rawling remained convinced that the Japs were akin to an elemental force of evil and cunning. A Mephistophelean enemy, he once declared, with his bland smile, needed a Faust to combat it. Sir Oliver had agreed, until something one day had led him to look up Faust in *Brewer's Dictionary of Phrase and Fable*. Evidently what Rawling had meant was that he'd sacrifice his principles to beat the Japs at their own game. It made you wonder about the man.

Vigilance was the Major's keyword. If there were no more Japanese on the island it could only mean one thing: they had left their agents here to do their dirty work for them. According to Rawling it was quite probable that Nippon had 'sleepers' in Ceylon – Buddhist monks, for example – sent here some years before the war to remain dormant until activated by wireless instruction from Imperial High Command. He requested permission to put up a broadsheet in every post office in Ceylon offering a 5000-rupee reward for a tip-off leading to the capture of an enemy agent.

Grudgingly Sir Oliver had given his approval. "But no harassment of Buddhist monks," he warned. "If we antagonise the Buddhists there'll be hell to pay. Besides," he added, "the main threat, surely, comes from the Sama Samajists?"

"Possibly. But not necessarily."

"What about the Canal fire? The godowns reduced to ashes?"

"That was the snag, Sir Oliver. Ashes. We'd like to pin it on the communists but I'm afraid we're short of evidence. However, there are still these insurrectionary pamphlets. They're being circulated to cinema queues, Christmas shoppers, racegoers, political meetings. You might care to know that I now employ a force of five men to go round printers' shops in the Pettah and read pamphlets upside down."

"Upside down?"

"Yes. That way my men don't draw attention to themselves. They proceed to shadow individuals who turn up at the shops which carry Sama Samaj material. Unobtrusively, I need hardly tell you. We've got three distributors in the bag so far." Rawling leant back heavily in the chair and put the tips of his fingers together, as the Governor was accustomed to do. "Basically it is a question of vigilance—"

"I agree—"

"Of the sort that has been sadly lacking in Malaya. The Japs haven't once used the deep jungle so far. They've been advancing through the rubber estates as if they were born on them. They must have had every one of them carefully mapped out before the war by spies disguised as estate workers, botanists, amateur photographers, brothel keepers, even monks."

"Really?"

"Prepared to the last detail. Devilish clever. We can't let that happen in Ceylon."

"No, indeed."

As frequently happened in these meetings, the Governor was

left feeling inadequate. Conceivably it dated from that occasion a couple of years ago when Mollie had asked the Major (ostensibly just Dunlop Orient's Estates Agent then) to make up her four at bridge. Full of jokes and little gallant asides, he had nevertheless amassed more points on the scorecard than any of them had seen before or since.

Then and there, in his office, Sir Oliver had decided not to bother Rawling with his suspicions about the Queen's House "plumbers". He put young Simon House on to it instead.

The traffic on Colpetty had begun to crawl forward. His Sinhalese chauffeur, flashing the trafficator, turned up Green Path, along Flower Road and Racecourse Avenue. The access lane to the new Grandstand entrance took them through throngs of Ceylonese who parted like the Red Sea at the sight of the Union Jack fluttering on the long black bonnet. A reception committee waited under a yellow awning to greet him: William Steuart, chairman of the Turf Club, Peter de Souza, Tony Apple, John Kotelawala and Percy Buller. A slight, bespectacled, dark-featured man with an anxious expression was introduced to him as J. P. Kandasala.

"Hot, eh?" said the Governor, who was not feeling any better.

"If you would care to give your address in approximately half an hour, Sir Oliver," said the Jockey Club chairman. "That's after the Kandy Plate, over seven furlongs. I think we should give the crowd time to get into the spirit of the occasion, don't you?"

The Governor concentrated on climbing the stairs.

"'Fraid we've got a slight diversion," Steuart went on. "Seems your ARP people are holding some sort of exercise. Planes flying over the Racecourse, not my idea. Mr Kandasala here has something to say."

"With your permission, Excellency." Smiling fixedly, the Sinhalese civil servant who had followed them up into the Royal Box conferred upon him a typed sheet of paper. Sir Oliver realised why Kandasala had looked familiar: the man had projected the slide-show at Queen's House about air-raid shelters. He sat down, with an involuntary belch, and took out his spectacles.

"You want me to read this out?" he enquired.

J. P. Kandasala shook his head. "Yes, if I may make so bold, Your Excellency. It is best if we do these exercises while we have all our eggs in one basket. Aircraft will be overhead" – he consulted a pocket watch on a gold chain across his grey waistcoat – "in thirty-seven or thirty-eight minutes' time. I am obliged by your kind participation. Goodbye, Excellency."

After shaking hands with each Jockey Club member in turn, Kandasala climbed higher up the Grandstand, presumably to monitor the success of his exercise. From where Sir Oliver sat, the Racecourse crowd did disturbingly resemble Easter eggs in a basket. They were packed into a smaller grandstand on the far side, into a two-rupee enclosure beside the bend leading into the home straight, and into what was known as the gandhi-enclosure in the centre of the Racecourse, where the poorest natives stood in a splash of brightly coloured sunshades.

The Ceylonese, he knew, loved above all things to gamble. There must have been three or four thousand people around the track; the bookies' voices were high-pitched with urgency. There was a rumble of excitement as the horses were led out of the paddock for the first race of the afternoon. Tony Apple leant towards him, smelling of gin.

"Look out for the navy blue and maroon strip, sir," he murmured. "That's Stargazer, he's a better weight than he's been all year. With Jim Butler up, he should get his nose in front of Intolerant at the post. He ran Intolerant to a neck over a mile last month in Galle, and seven furlongs is his pet distance."

Sir Oliver Prescott hardly heard him. Sitting with his hat on his lap and his knees apart to ease his tummy ache, he reflected sombrely on the multitude of His Majesty's subjects below. At the latest estimate there were six million souls in Ceylon. That was equivalent to the population of Greater London: and responsibility for their safety resided in him.

Tradition held that it was easier to govern an island. Ever since Clive, India had unsettled her British administrators with her numberless hordes and illimitable horizons. But when external danger threatened, there was no question, islands had the worst time of it. Ceylon was like Hong Kong. There was nowhere to retreat gracefully; no refuge. One stayed with one's ship. Like Tom Phillips.

The starting pistol fired; the crowd roared; the ropes around the gandhi-enclosure strained to snapping point. The Raj could not long outlast the war; Sir Oliver was convinced of it. Daily news of the British retreating and retreating in Malaya would not be forgotten, or forgiven. There was something in the air – he could sense it, perched up here – an intimation of disrespect, a hint of *How are the mighty fallen!* Things had slipped a long way since that famous Coronation Durbar of Edward VII, held in New Delhi forty years ago, when the Viceroy, Lord Curzon, refused to permit the playing of the hymn "Onward, Christian Soldiers".

It contained the lines "Thrones and Crowns may perish, King-
doms rise and wane" – not ours, admonished Curzon.

Blasphemy! So his father would have replied, knitting his
bushy eyebrows like the famous picture of Jehovah in his *Cassell's
Child's Bible*. But when Oliver Prescott was a boy of eighteen, and
Kitchener had returned in triumph with the Boers' surrender,
were there many Englishmen who would have disagreed with
Curzon? Forty years it had taken, to see that *imperium* as one with
Nineveh and Tyre. Forty years to arrive at poor old Shenton
Thomas blustering on about the British Empire stretching from
the sands of Egypt to the snows of Antarctica while all the time,
thanks to the incompetence of Malaya Command, his own
fortress city of Singapore was shaking on its foundations, its
women and children evacuated at such speed that this very
week, so he'd heard, British soldiers had been rounded up to
play the fairies in *Iolanthe* at the Alhambra. . . .

Around and below him the cheers had reached a crescendo.
Four horses were rounding the last bend and racing neck and
neck down the home straight. One of their jockeys wore the navy
blue and maroon strip.

Sir Oliver peered at Tony Apple. Six months ago in Nuwara
Eliya he had presented Tony with the Federation Tennis Challenge Cup. Now the man looked as if he hadn't stopped celebrating since. His face was puffy, his eyes bloodshot; his tennis must
have gone to pieces. Percy Buller, alongside him, looked equally
the worse for wear.

He should have expected it. They were businessmen, after all.
Like a hundred other businessmen in Colombo they had witnessed their investments in Hong Kong vanish overnight, and
their investments in the Malay States go plummeting. There was
little any of them could do to get their Straits dollars out of Singapore. More than a few would be left penniless, bankrupt, by the
time the war was over.

Sunk in these gloomy reflections, Sir Oliver did not realise that
the Kandy Plate was over until the horses were leaving the
racetrack and he heard the first fruity strains of "When the Saints
Go Marching In" from the Police Band strutting around the
gandhi-enclosure. He rose to his feet and sat down again.
J. P. Kandasala slipped into the Royal Box. Without speaking to
the Governor, he tactfully tapped the microphone as if to make
sure the public address system was working, and left as incon-
spicuously as he had come.

The Police Band eventually lowered their tubas. The horses for the Perth Plate were already out on the track, cantering in a leisurely fashion towards the starting boxes. Sir Oliver stood up, switched on the microphones and cleared his throat with a sound like gunfire.

"If God in his wisdom will forgive me," he began in a jocular tone, "I am going to register a minor disagreement with something that we read in the Bible. Ecclesiastes it is who tells us that the race is not to the swift, nor the battle to the strong. In our personal lives this happily is often borne out. Here at the Racecourse, however, you don't need the bookmakers to tell you it's a fair bet that the race is always to the swift, ha! In the wider world just now, I have equal confidence in telling you that the battle will be to the strong. . . ."

In the silence, he could hear the jockeys urging their mounts into the starting boxes. He left out the next two sheets and hurried on. "In these circumstances it gives me great pleasure, at this first meet of the New Year, to inaugurate this splendid new Grandstand, and to express the appreciation you all feel to the contractors, Weaver & Gittings, and to the Jockey Club whose good husbandry has meant that the sum raised by the Appeal could be matched out of Club funds."

Was that an angry murmur from the crowd? Or – great heavens – the aeroplanes on their way? "You are about to participate in an Air Raid Precaution exercise!" he shouted. "When the aircraft come over the Racecourse" – he consulted Kandasala's note – "the correct procedure is to lie prostrate on the ground." Good God, he could see the planes. "Take out your handkerchief and clench it between your teeth! Rest your face on your forearms! Wait until —"

The rest was lost in a thunderous buzz. Three RAF Vildebeeste biplanes dipped down over the far grandstand, roared low over the racetrack, and out over the heads of the two-rupee enclosure.

The gandhi-enclosure fell prostrate, like a field of vividly dyed washing blown by a gust of wind. The grandstands were a bedlam of flailing limbs and shouts of pain as spectators struggled to get out their handkerchiefs and take cover simultaneously. As Sir Oliver lifted his head from between his legs, where a final explosion of wind had surely carried him over his indigestion, he was in time to see the beginning and end of the Perth Plate.

The field had bolted in whinnying fright as the Vildebeestes flew overhead. A few jockeys were up: a couple were being dragged in the reins; the rest were on the starting line shaking their fists in fury. The gandhi-enclosure rose with cries of outrage and surged across the track to corner the bookies and get their money back. In the midst of the uproar, J. P. Kandasala reappeared in the Royal Box, his face now bright with gratification. He shook the Governor by the hand.

"In my opinion, Excellency, it is awfully much better to be safe than sorry," he said.

Sir Oliver departed shortly thereafter. He felt no small apprehension that the race crowd might blame him for the wrecking of the Perth Plate, and vent their feelings on his 4-litre Sunbeam Talbot limousine. In the event, the only casualty was his hat-brim, on which, having no handkerchief, he had deemed it necessary to clench his teeth, *pour encourager les autres*.

As the chauffeur drove home, he examined the hat with a frown. He took it with him on most outdoor occasions; his predecessor in the 1920s, Sir Hugh Clifford, had become unhinged after refusing to wear headgear in the Ceylon sun. Was the same thing happening to him? Had he been imagining all these natives traipsing around Queen's House with large bags – *portmanteaux*, not to mince words – quite capacious enough to smuggle in weapons?

Incarceration of the Sama Samajist leaders had not put a stop to fifth-column activity. That was a fact. Rawling admitted as much. And nothing was simpler – he'd watched from his window – than to get past the police guards on one pretext or another. But so many? Were they reconnoitring the place? It took only one fanatic with a pistol. . . .

The realisation came with a jolt that rocked him back on the seat. The basement rooms! What better place for a rebel armoury or explosives hoard than right under the noses of the chief officers of state! And tomorrow morning there was a full meeting of the War Council in the Queen's House conference chamber. . . .

The car drew up outside Queen's House. Grabbing his hat, Sir Oliver moved agilely up the steps. There was no time to acknowledge the salutes of the tasselled guards either side of the entrance doors. His private secretary was waiting in the hall.

"Where's Simon?" demanded the Governor.

"Upstairs, sir. In your office."

Breathing heavily he climbed the stairs. The door to his secretaries' pool was open, letting out a fragrance of Elizabeth Arden lavender water. His step did not falter. He was in a minefield. Every pot of anthuriums, every bucket of sand in a passageway, seemed to carry the invisible warning – *Danger: Unexploded Bomb.*

"Well?" he barked to his ADC.

"Well what, sir?" Simon House's moon face had gone blanker than usual.

"Don't be a fool, Simon. The plumbers. What did you find out about the plumbers?"

"Oh, I see. Well, they are plumbers. They are definitely plumbers."

"You think so! If they are plumbers, what the devil are they doing? And why are there so many of them?"

"I gather . . . I gather you were saying, sir, before Christmas, about the new lavatories. That they were too small. Built for Indian posteriors, you said. And that the water pressure was too low. It has apparently been a major plumbing operation, sir."

Sir Oliver sat down. It was true that he had been complaining. The effect of the uncomfortable seats, and then of having to nudge through his excrement by hand, had been to give him constipation that lasted right through the Christmas period. But he remained gravely concerned. There was something too neatly plausible in this excuse. What would Rawling have said? Vigilance. That was the key.

He said, "Simon, I want you to come with me."

"Where to, sir?"

"You'll find out."

He picked up his hat. With the ADC at his heels, he strode along the corridor until he came to the back stairs. He stepped down them cautiously, passing several of the Ceylonese servants who shrank back against the stairwell.

As he had expected, these steps continued on down, below the Queen's House kitchens. As they arrived at the basement, a low, uneasy murmuring could be heard. Simon House switched on the light.

A long passageway, smelling of damp plaster, stretched the length of the building. Cockroaches scuttled ahead of them as they started down it, their shoes ringing on the concrete floor.

The Governor threw open a door. It squeaked on its hinges. The room it revealed, large and cellar-cool, was windowless except for a small fan-light set high in the far wall. A stack of roof-tiles had been piled carelessly underneath it. Nearby, a grand piano, rotten, worm-eaten, grey with dust and cobwebs, lay propped against the wall, its four legs unscrewed and set neatly beside it.

Sir Oliver advanced down the passageway, flinging open door after door. In one room, they found three tall wine-racks, full of bottles which had the dust of generations upon them – although when Simon House pulled some of the bottles out they found them uncorked and empty; only the blurred trace of fingerprints around the neck showed how stealthily they had been enjoyed. Another room, a rusty padlock hanging on its door, contained wooden filing cabinets and empty tea-chests stencilled with the warning: "Secret: Classified". It must have been used as a repository for state papers during some period of political crisis – probably the riots of 1915.

"This is all part of the Security Officer's round, I believe," ventured Simon House. Sir Oliver paid him no attention. The murmuring had risen now to a sullen chatter. His joke to Tom Phillips about General Gordon speared at Khartoum came back to him; this time it was no laughing matter. Summoning his courage, he turned the handle on the last door, and pushed it open.

A blast of hot air made him recoil. In the gloom it was Siva the Hindu god of destruction, a giant many-limbed form that towered above him. From its copper joints came a hissing, a clattering, a furious barracking as if the entire Ceylonese State Council had risen as one body to heckle his State Address.

In silence Sir Oliver Prescott contemplated the ancient boiler. In silence he retreated, closing the door and leaving the machinery to shake and rattle at his back. As he retired down the passageway with the ADC a man came towards them, an elderly barefoot Tamil in a white loincloth, sweeping the puddles with a broom. When he saw the Governor, he brought his wrinkled hands together in a salute and bowed low.

"Good afternoon," said Sir Oliver Prescott with dignity, inclining his head.

WITH the help of the faithful Edward in Chatham Street, Guy rapidly mastered the Dunlop Orient books and ledgers. In the horse-box opposite, surrounded by maps, telephones and files marked "Personal", Rawling talked in low tones to mysterious visitors. The Major these days was rarely out of his smart, enigmatic uniform. His new quarters were far busier than his old ones could ever have been. On the stairs Guy would frequently pass anonymous-looking Europeans who appeared to have stepped straight out of E. Phillips Oppenheim: silent men, presumably recruited from the better class of tradesmen, who never removed their hats indoors even to acknowledge Guy's salutation.

It was hard to know where Dunlop Orient stopped and Rawling's private war began. Guy had written confidentially to J. S. Brooke at Head Office to request confirmation that Rawling's instructions about slaughter-tapping were Dunlop Orient policy. He had had no reply. This added to his sense of isolation, his feeling that he had nobody to turn to. He paid several visits to the Colombo Art Gallery, where an exhibition of Lionel Wendt photographs was being held, in the hope of running into Jill. But she never put in an appearance. He heard from Mrs Donaldson that she had gone to spend some time up-country, on the estate of her uncle Bruce MacAlister.

He was in the middle of composing a letter to MacAlister, one of Dunlop Orient's more cantankerous rubber planters, when one of the Ceylonese office girls, in a demure short-sleeved frock, brought some papers in. As Guy glanced up from signing them, he caught her large, liquidly clear brown eyes fixed upon him. He smiled at her. She ducked her head and hurried away.

It set him thinking sombrely about Sandy Duncannon. Rawling had told him the story after lunch at the Colombo Club. The truth of it was that Duncannon, a pillar of planter society, had lived with a Sinhalese woman out in Badulla district for the last thirty years. It was common practice in the old days, when a newcomer to an estate had settled in, for a good-caste villager

97

with daughters on his hands to pay a visit to his bungalow. He would discuss a domestic arrangement with the young planter, and would reappear the following day with his selection of two or three possible concubines – "sleeping dictionaries" as they were known in planter circles.

The arrangement hardly ever varied. As and when the planter got to the end of his sleeping dictionary, a generous settlement would be made on her and another willing young Sinhalese daughter would be brought along. Sandy Duncannon was one of a number of Europeans in Ceylon who found these girls sufficiently captivating never to have married one of his own kind. He was now on his third native concubine, and paying alimony to her predecessors and their offspring – one reason why he could not afford to pack his bags and retire Home.

Guy recalled the lank-haired, stooping figure with the sarcastic mouth, and heard again Percy Buller's wounding riposte about all the curries he ate. Poor Duncannon. He had survived into a purse-lipped era in which miscegenation was no longer the behaviour of a pukka sahib. He drank heavily: his digestion was now apparently too whisky-impaired to stomach beer. Repeated doses of quinine taken as a prophylactic (his idea, to stop his mistress conceiving additional burdens on his salary) had made him hard of hearing. No wonder he rarely made the journey to Colombo. All that remained to him was his domestic privacy, in which whatever was left of love or soft dependency in his nature could be displayed out of earshot of prurient fellow-countrymen.

Guy pushed back his chair with a clatter against the partition. He stuck his head out of the window and drew in deep breaths of the muggy air. Across the street a fine-boned beauty of a young Sinhalese girl walked demurely by. Her short cotton *choli* and bare midriff, the way in which her close-fitting sari displayed the sensuous movement of her hips, held out the promise of sexual delights much sweeter than the unripe fruit of Cinnamon Gardens.

What, after all, did they matter, the reproachful looks, the disapproving voices? Harry had paid them no heed. Twenty-year-olds from Ceylon were being shipped off to die in the desert who had never made love to their favourite girl because it wasn't the done thing. Any day now, out of the tropical sunset, a Japanese fighter squadron might dive and blow them all to pieces. Then it would be too late.

Guy blurted out something along these lines to George Donaldson, when they invited him to dinner in their Dutch bungalow. He'd misread the invitation and arrived early. Elizabeth Donaldson was still dressing. Her husband, a shy-mannered man, his thick black hair streaked with silver, waved away his apologies and took him over to the drinks cabinet.

"Are you happy with life at Dunlop Orient?" he enquired, carefully measuring out two whisky splits. "Is everything going according to plan?"

Guy glanced at him sharply. As always George Donaldson's hooded eyes, his sad, imperturbable face, gave nothing away. Only the dissatisfied lines around his mouth suggested an acute mind hidden somewhere behind the conventional social phrases. It was a different kind of loneliness to his.

He said, "The work's fine. Whether I'm happy doing it . . . does it matter? It seems to me happiness is a luxury these days."

"Ah."

"I imagine, sir, that when one's settled, with a family, it's easier to take happiness for granted. Until coming out here, I must say, I'd never given much thought to the value of companionship."

"Ah, yes, family life." Donaldson nodded. "Of course, there are some men with families who would tell you that happiness only comes with peace and solitude. Do you know the D. A. O'Briens?"

Guy shook his head. This was getting nowhere. Why had he brought up the subject? He said flatly, wanting to change the subject, "I would think that solitude as an absence of company and solitude as an absence of love are quite different things."

George Donaldson looked down at his glass, swilling the whisky in it. "Seven-fifteen," he observed. "Tancred, we have a little time before the others arrive. Would you care to cast your eye over the newest acquisition to my family?"

Puzzled, Guy followed him up the wide stairs. Donaldson crossed the landing, threw open the door to a back verandah room and switched on the light. Laid out on an enormous hardboard table-top on trestles in the middle of the room was an elaborate model railway. Engines, coaches, goods wagons, all perfectly to scale, stood on a gleaming '0'-gauge track in the shape of a side-joined figure of eight. The track had points and signals; around it had been set a goods yard, a railway crossing, a water-pump and an imposing train station with two platforms and the name COLOMBO FORT hanging from the arcade. Everywhere little people, also to scale, waited on the platforms or at the railway crossing, wheeling luggage, taking tickets, sweeping beside the track.

"I've never seen a train set with people before," exclaimed Guy. He picked up a tiny wooden guard with a red flag in one hand and a green flag in the other. Its arms moved up and down. "They're beautiful. Incredibly well made!"

"The people, yes, they're made for me by a little man in Wellawatte. No, this is what I want to show you."

Putting on a pair of half-moon spectacles, George Donaldson opened a leather case. With both hands he lifted out a chocolate-brown locomotive complete with its tender. "It's the 'Princess Elizabeth'," he said. "Went into production three years ago, it's the finest thing Frank Hornby's ever built. Look at the workmanship. Outside cylinders, six-coupled driving wheels, chromium-plated handrails. All the joints soldered of course. Look at these fire-boxes inside the cab... every last detail. Lamps. Hooter. Isn't she a beauty? Automatic reversing, too."

"It's electric, then?"

"Of course it's an electric railway. My dear chap, I wouldn't be playing around with clockwork at my age. She's got a twenty-volt engine inside there. I'll show you."

He brought out two coaches in the same brown livery and set them down on the track by the station platform. Their spotless, beautifully furnished interiors were empty, nor did any of the wooden Ceylonese passengers on the platform look as if they expected to be let in. Donaldson switched on the electricity, picked up a black control box and pressed a button. Gently the "Princess Elizabeth" reversed on to her coaches. As she coupled with them the carriage lights went on.

Guy looked at his host. The remoteness had gone; his eyes were intent and sparkling, his lips were parted, he had lost years from his face. With the little black box he was able to control everything – the points, the signals, a goods train which came to life with a little jump and set off on a separate line pulling a cattle truck, a tank wagon and a brake van. Only the little people didn't respond.

"So, this is the newest member of your family," said Guy.

George Donaldson seemed to collect himself. He took off his spectacles and looked at Guy. "It's something I wanted you to see, before I say what I'm about to say. I don't expect you to believe me, but you're a lucky man, Tancred. You have everything in front of you. Courtship. Marriage. Children. Elizabeth and I, you know, have been married for twenty-four years. We gave all our love to our children. Now William has gone away to fight, goodness knows when we'll see him again. Sylvia's going

100

to leave home and get married. If not to Bilbow, then to someone else. You say there are different sorts of solitude, Tancred, but I'll tell you this. When you lose your children, you lose love and companionship both at the same time."

Guy didn't know what to say. He looked down at the "Princess Elizabeth", clattering around the outside track, flashing helter-skelter past the unmoving passengers in Colombo Fort. Donaldson's finger was still on the control.

"Work remains," he ventured finally. "Your administrative work for the colony must be a great consolation, I would think."

"Here in Ceylon?" The downward lines reappeared around Donaldson's mouth, giving him the ironic expression of one accustomed to making the best of a bad job. "I've learnt a few lessons recently, Tancred. You can care for people and educate 'em and bring 'em to maturity and you think they owe you something but they don't. I fought to keep William with us in Ceylon. I got him a job on the Governor's staff that would have qualified as war work. But you can't keep people if they want to go. You're in trust over them, that's all. I've worked like a black to make this island governable. And one day soon they'll come to me and they'll say, 'All right, Donaldson, you've done a good job; we'll take over now.' So they pack you off home to England, and you look back, and you watch – and bit by bit it starts crumbling. All you've built, it starts falling to pieces. The railways stop running on time. The drains start overflowing. The police force gets out of hand. It's happened before, Tancred. Read Tacitus. Read Gibbon. It's all there. . . ."

Guy stepped forward. George Donaldson's knuckles had whitened round the controller. The "Princess Elizabeth" was positively racing round the Hornby solid steel track; its coaches rocked dangerously from side to side as it careered round the bends. It whooshed so fast through Colombo Fort that the little brown guard with the red flag fell flat on his back.

"I say—" began Guy.

"What? Good heavens, yes. Can't be setting a bad example." With a sad smile, Donaldson brought the "Princess Elizabeth" to a halt. He uncoupled her and placed her gently back in the presentation case and closed the lid.

"Not the sort of thing you can leave out in the sun," he said.

The other guests had arrived when they came downstairs. Jill Tancred was there, wearing – inappropriately, Guy thought – the

101

same ruffed grey-and-green dress she had worn to Sylvia's party. Sylvia herself and Charlie Bilbow (on shore leave from HMS *Dorsetshire*) were making Albert stand with a heavy tray of glasses while Tony Apple explained at length which drinks were the most alcoholic.

Jill inclined her cheek coolly for Guy's kiss. "Here I am, you see, I do get out of the house occasionally," she said.

"And Harry?"

"Harry couldn't get away, I'm afraid. He's had a great deal of reorganising to do since your letter about slaughter-tapping arrived."

"Oh. Has he?"

"You surely know what's involved. You're the one asking for it."

"Me? Oh, well, I see what you mean. It's not my idea actually, it was Major Rawling's. That's to say Dunlop Orient's."

"Yes. Well – it arrived on a very appropriate day. December the twenty-eighth, the Killing of the Innocents."

"Oh, is it? Well," he said, floundering unhappily, "there's a lot of that going on."

He was saved by Mrs Donaldson. "I gather George has been introducing you to 'Princess Elizabeth'," she remarked.

"The prize of his collection, yes."

"Does George collect princesses upstairs?" asked Jill.

"Ha, ha! Kidnap!" Elizabeth Donaldson's eyes flickered anxiously towards the kitchen quarters from which an enticing curry smell had escaped. "Ha, ha! No, George has been showing off his train set again, it always gets introduced to people before I do. Albert? Are we ready to eat?"

Guy was placed opposite Jill at the dinner-table. In the candlelight her features were softer than when she'd confronted him. The curry was hot; he drank glass after glass of beer, and found himself being uncommonly amusing.

He talked about the poochie in the ceiling of his room at the Metropole: "I mentioned it to Major Rawling, who's susceptible to bugs. He instantly suspected sabotage and sent round a coolie to prise up the floorboards above. The idiot arrived with a jemmy and a sledgehammer; I bribed him to go away quietly before Generalissimo Smith called the police!"

"A rum old bird, Rawling," remarked Tony Apple when their laughter died down. "Not much of a conversationalist, but by God those little round eyes take it all in."

"We get on famously," said Guy. He smiled at Jill. "I'm like

Harry, I'm afraid I have a Tancred mind. It's happiest with patterns that can be plotted, schedules which fall into place. My father was like that, I'm told. Rawling's the same."

The houseboys cleared the plates away. Jill lit a cigarette. "I remember the second time I went out with Harry," she said. "He'd booked a table at the Grand Oriental for six-thirty sharp, because he had to be up before dawn the next morning. I was on duty at the Pasteur Institute; I'd put on my best dress under my nurse's coat so I could go straight over when my shift finished. A patient threw up all over me and some got down inside and ruined my good dress, so I went home and changed. When I got to the GOH, Harry was sitting at the table. The place was laid in front of my chair, and on the plate was his watch. I was fifteen minutes late and this *watch*, in the middle of my plate. . . ."

"What did you do?" Guy interrupted. "Ask whether it came with vegetables?"

"Of course not. I launched into my excuse, thinking that was the end of dinner, the end of everything, and just as I was finishing, the waiters came up to the table with heaps of delicious lobster and a vase of yellow zinnias which Harry knew were my favourite flowers. And Harry forgave me and I forgave Harry, though I don't remember ever being late again."

"I don't think of Harry as being romantic," said Guy.

"He used to be," Jill replied.

"Used to be?"

But Jill had turned her head away, to listen to Elizabeth Donaldson down the table. "Men are all like that," she was saying. "They never associate romance with marriage, it's always part of the mating dance. The idea that wives might enjoy being courted occasionally never occurs to them."

George Donaldson laughed and patted his face with his napkin. Sylvia pulled a face at Charlie and whispered something in his ear, at which the poor boy went scarlet and gazed anxiously round in case anyone else had heard. Tony Apple's pale eyes flickered up the table, resting for a moment on Guy and Jill.

"But, darling Elizabeth, wives do go on being courted," he drawled. "Not by their husbands, I agree. That would be too boring. But if their husbands lose interest in them, why shouldn't they find other men attractive?"

Guy laughed. He was about to defend Tony Apple against George Donaldson's expostulations when something made him look at Jill. She was blushing furiously. The words died in his throat. Seeing his gaze, Jill leant across and stamped out her half-smoked cigarette.

"If you're such an expert on adultery, Tony, how is it that none of the marriages we know about has been breaking up?"

"D. A. O'Brien and his wife have separated," said George Donaldson. "Do you know the O'Briens?"

"There's no need, Jill," Tony Apple replied. "What woman with a steady lover and a devoted husband wants to change her life?"

Jill shrugged. She took out another cigarette. Guy reached for a candle and tipped the flame towards her. She leant her face forward. The flame highlighted her wide cheekbones and lit sparks in her yellow-green eyes. Hot wax dripped on to the polished table. Guy sprang up with a cry of apology.

"Albert!" called Mrs Donaldson.

"*I* would. I'd change a steady husband and a devoted lover for two devoted lovers," exclaimed Sylvia with a giggle, fluttering her eyelids at Charlie. But her father had evidently had enough of this conversation. Clearing his throat, he addressed Tony Apple.

"Are you putting your boat into the Trincomalee regatta next week, Tony?" he enquired.

"I would do, but my crew has just gone off to fight for King and Country. Tancred, don't suppose you sail, do you?"

"Not an awful lot."

"Pity."

Mrs Donaldson ushered them into the music-room for coffee. She took Guy's arm. "It can be a bit wretched, being on your own," she said to him. "Please feel that you can come and visit us any time you like. George might be at work, but I'm always here."

"That's very kind of you." Guy had noticed, on top of the piano, a glass vase full of zinnias. "Excuse me," he muttered, pulling away from Elizabeth in his eagerness. He walked over and plucked out a single stem. Shaking off the water on to the carpet, he took it over to where Jill was sitting and placed the orange-yellow zinnia in her lap.

"I'm making up for my brother," he declared with a loud laugh.

There was a second's silence before everybody joined in the merriment. Tony Apple said something witty about romance. Sylvia slapped Charlie on the hand for not thinking of it himself. Jill laughed shortly and bit her lip, lowering her head to wipe the droplets of water off her green dress.

When coffee was served, the brandies poured and the boys gone away to the kitchen, they talked about the war. Nobody could understand why Malaya Command had let the Japs come so far south, even though, as George Donaldson declared, they were now up against bone.

"It's all very well, George, but the Japs are making us look silly asses!" Tony Apple burst out. "You read what happened yesterday. They flew right over the Singapore Golf Course, cool as cucumber, and bombed whacking great divots out of the greens. How can we hold our heads up here when that sort of thing gets in the public prints?"

"That's right," said Elizabeth Donaldson. "More coffee, anybody? Darling, can't we keep these details out of the papers? It doesn't do us any good, you know."

"Well, we do keep quite a lot out," returned her husband after a pause. "But perhaps we should take another look. I do agree that the Singapore Golf Course is a case where discretion might have been the better part of candour."

This brought the conversation round to Messrs Gandhi and Nehru and their seditious calls for independence from Britain which the authorities (and George Donaldson smilingly accepted some of the blame) were allowing to be reported in the *Ceylon Daily News*. By common consent it was then time to prevail upon Elizabeth Donaldson to perform. Their hostess went graciously to the piano and played the slow movement of Beethoven's Sonata in E Flat, "Les Adieux", her head dreamily raised and her eyes gazing ahead, focusing on nothing unless it was the vase of zinnias.

Jill had to get back to Kelani. Charlie was staying over. Guy offered Tony Apple a lift back to the Swimming Club in his elderly white Wolseley. In a chorus of leave-taking they went out into the warm, thick night. The Wolseley was waiting in the porch. Of Jill's car there was no sign. Michael Kandasala came plunging out of the darkness. He ran up the steps, his eyes wide with indignation.

"Lady! Lady, someone has pinched the battery," he gasped. "They have cleanly swiped it from under the bonnet. The car can't budge without battery!"

There was a moment's consternation. "You must stay overnight, Jill," said Elizabeth firmly. "Albert will get one of the boys to make up a bed."

"No, no." Jill was frowning. "Thank you, Liz, I must get back tonight. Would you be very kind and order me a taxi? Michael

105

will get a new battery fitted and bring the car back in the morning."

"Yes, Lady."

"Hang on." Guy stepped forward. "Jill, I'll take you back to Kelani. It couldn't be simpler. I'll drop Tony off at the Swimming Club and then take you home."

"A taxi's fine. Liz, may I telephone for one?"

"I insist." Guy appealed to Mrs Donaldson. "It's absurd to put Jill in a taxi all the way to Kelani at this time of night!"

Elizabeth Donaldson nodded. "I'll telephone ahead to Harry."

Acknowledging defeat, Jill went reluctantly down the steps. Guy held the car door open.

"After all, what's a brother-in-law for?" he grinned, swaying slightly.

She didn't answer.

Tony Apple, who had drunk even more than Guy, was noisily asleep before they had motored the half-mile to the Colombo Swimming Club. Guy woke him up and directed him through the doorway of the annexe. Returning, he revved the engine rather too loudly and drove back through Cinnamon Gardens towards the Kelani road.

"What's so absurd about me taking a taxi?" asked Jill.

"We're in the middle of a war. You have to be careful."

"You call this a war? There's not even a proper blackout."

"There will be, very soon."

The shadowy figure beside him seemed to be brooding on this. "Is Singapore going to fall?" she asked abruptly.

"No. I should think it's the most impregnable fortress east of Berlin." He couldn't resist adding, "According to Rawling, who knows about these things, there are thousands of Australians in Singapore. Australians are an obstinate crowd; they've a tradition of resisting until they're forced to surrender. Isn't that so?"

"I don't know."

"As at Gallipoli. So I'm told."

"I don't know. Guy, it's sweet of you to be taking me back. But I'm very tired. Do you mind if I try to get some sleep?"

"Oh, no. No. Not if you want to."

Jill folded her stole over the top of the curved leather seat and laid her cheek against it. He could smell her closeness to him: not a perfume so much as a natural fragrance he associated with her skin and hair. He had never properly looked at her. Now that she was invisible to him, it was as if he saw her for the first time – her classical wide brow and short straight nose, and the sensuous, mobile mouth which subverted them. For the first time too, he saw, behind her strength of character, a vulnerability.

As he drove slowly along the moonlit road, the dipped head-lamps lighting an area no bigger than a cowcatcher in which small animals started up and bicycle wheels wobbled to safety, it began to occur to Guy that every mile that brought him closer to his brother widened the gulf between them. Why this was he couldn't explain, not even to himself. But it had to have some-thing to do with the sleeping, trusting figure in the seat beside him.

As he turned off the main road, the moon went behind clouds. Hunched over the steering wheel, driving at a snail's pace, Guy negotiated the dirt roads through the darkness of the rubber trees. The track dipped down. The trees retreated to make way for the blacker blackness of Kelani Lodge.

He stopped under the porch and took Jill's hand, pressing it to rouse her. She woke with a start.

"It's pretty late," he said. "Harry will be in bed."

"I don't think so."

"Why?"

"You see that light?" – and now indeed he saw the faint but steady glow coming from behind the sitting-room blinds – "That's Harry's light, the one by his armchair. There must be something wrong."

She got out of the Wolseley and hurried up the steps. Guy followed her, stumbling in the darkness. There was an odd smell in the house, something sweet and strong. Jill pushed open the sitting-room door. Harry was sitting by himself, at the edge of a pool of light, staring into the empty fireplace. Three clay pipes lay on the arm of his chair. Guy realised, with a shock, that his brother had been smoking opium.

Jill tugged Guy's arm. "Come away, leave him," she whis-pered. It was too late. Harry had recognised them.

"Come in," he commanded. "Come and speak to me, little brother. You can't bring me worse news than you have already. Jill, give him light."

Guy stood blinking in the middle of the room. "If you mean the slaughter-tapping—" he began.

"No need to defend yourself. You were, as they say, carrying out orders. On the contrary, I should be thanking you. You have schooled me in humility." In a voice that rang through the sleeping house he bellowed, "Kelamuttu! Another pipe!", then added, more softly, "Come and sit over here."

Jill sounded frightened. "Please, Harry. No more tonight. You promised me."

"Nothing in excess. That is what I promised. Guy will look after me. Guy will tell me when I am being excessive. Won't you, Guy?"

Sullenly, Guy sat down in the deep armchair on the other side of the hearth. Whenever he thought he was getting to know him, his brother had a way of transforming himself into someone different, like a genie in a fairy-tale. Even so he thought he recognised a familiar mocking tone in Harry's voice, and resented it. He had had enough of Harry's veiled mockery. He looked at Jill and spread his hands, drawing her into the conspiracy of his exasperation. Jill shook her head.

"I'm going to bed," she told them. "Guy, you must stay the night. Kelamuttu will show you where your room is."

She went out, and shut the door. Guy stared across at his rubber-planter brother, escaping into opium dreams, and where he might have felt pity he felt anger. The Tancreds had been brought close to ruin by the dreamers in the family. Over the past fifty years – really it had taken no more than that – they had contrived to disinherit him from a fortune he could have multiplied, and an ancestral estate, Rubble House, which he could have turned into one of the finest in Devon.

"You have nothing to thank me for," he said bitterly.

"I think I do. You have reminded me that none of us is master of his fate. I aimed too high. I thought I was overlord on this plantation. I had it under absolute control. I drove down to my factory through the rubber trees like a general through the ranks of his silver infantrymen, who bled for him, it's true, but never died or suffered. But I didn't escape far enough from the old world, did I, Guy? You brought it here, with all its destructiveness, its power to make people fight and die and still learn nothing, so their children end up fighting and dying in turn."

"Like dragon's teeth," said Guy.

Harry stood up with a gesture of impatience. He put out a hand to the big bookcase to steady himself. At that moment Kelamuttu came in with a fresh opium pipe, already lit. Harry offered it first to his younger brother. Guy shook his head.

"I'm from the old world," he remarked when the houseboy had gone. "We may be destructive, but we try to keep things in perspective."

"I'm not attacking you. I'm trying to make you understand. What your world does, your *Christian* world," he pronounced the word with distaste, "is to make it easy for people to pretend they can get rid of evil through prayer. I was eleven when you were born, Guy. The Great War didn't exist for you. I watched you grow up into an England which was busy tidying away all that pain and death. *Nice to see you up here at Oxford, Mr Fremantle, do you take milk and sugar?* Stiff upper lip be damned. It was a conscious decision to forget: the same way I watched Mother make a conscious decision to forget how our father died, in all that pain and humiliation. And I knew – even before they hauled Max Fremantle's body out of the river, I knew – that a world which could so quickly dismiss the agonies of one war would be condemned to another war before long."

"I see. So you escaped to somewhere you could control good and evil—"

"Rubbish. I came out East to be among sane-minded people. People who know, because it's part of their religion, that when a dreadful horror is perpetrated it doesn't suddenly stop existing. Sooner or later it's going to have to be expiated – if not by them, by their children. So they live peaceably, as much as they can. They carry a sense of responsibility to the past as well as to the future."

The smoke from Harry's pipe was rising in wisps towards the ceiling. Guy leant forward. He hissed, "Before you come up with any more fine phrases – you could have had some of that responsibility towards the past, has it occurred to you? You didn't have to come out here. You could have stayed, and helped Mother get over things when she most needed you. You were head of the family; I was only ten or eleven. You did your duty by Max Fremantle. What about us?"

Harry threw back his head in a silent laugh. "Very good, Guy. I wondered what I had done to deserve your letter and now you tell me – although I can't say I feel much guilt about it. Mother had the means to lead a very good life. But there you are. Retribution has arrived – and delivered by the hand of my own brother, could anything be neater? Thus the whirligig of time brings in his revenges."

"I'm glad you can be so philosophical. Mother still thinks you ran away."

In the silence that followed Guy began to feel ashamed of this rejoinder. Harry had closed his eyes. Just as Guy was about to speak again the door was flung open. Jill stood in a white night-dress in the doorway, her hair loose, a paraffin lamp in her hand.

"It's past two," she said. "I have sent Kelamuttu off to his quarters. Is he the only one with work to do in the morning?"

Harry did not look up. "You two go off to bed," he said. "I'll stay here a while. I won't be long."

Guy woke up with a dry mouth. His clothes smelt of opium. It was late: Harry would have gone down to the factory hours ago. He looked out of the window. Three little half-naked Sinhalese boys were washing his car in the driveway, watched by Rasani with folded arms. On the lawn beyond, a gust of wind shook the feathery leaves of a magnificent flamboyant tree and sent spray upon spray of scarlet and orange flowers dancing in the sun.

He went downstairs and nibbled at the breakfast dishes which had been left for him. Voices led him to the sitting room. Jill was going over the household accounts with Cook. She wore a green gingham dress with a broad white collar which showed off the lines of her throat and jaw each time she bent over the ledger. Guy found himself wanting to challenge her, to tell her she was wasting her talent and intelligence, her youth, probably her sexuality too. He bit his lip.

She sent Cook away. Guy went to her and kissed her on the cheek. In confusion he turned away and picked up a photograph silver-framed on the radiogram.

"What's this? Is this you?"

It was a portrait of Jill which must have been taken not all that long ago, probably since Harry married her. An open, un-shadowed face looked out at him, the wide mouth shyly parted, thick butterscotch hair curling around cheeks that were girlishly full.

"Have I changed that much?" she asked in all seriousness.

He looked at her. She was sitting, ankles crossed, in the middle of the room, on a stool supported by three brass, coiling serpents.

"Perhaps more than you think," he told her. "You had no secrets, back then. Now you have secrets. And some mystery. That's the difference."

The serpents gleamed in the shuttered gloom. She got up, with a little laugh. She said, "Oh, I wish I had! I wish you were right!"

She flew before him, on to the verandah, gathering up a pair of secateurs on the way. When he stepped out into the garden she came up to him with a wide-brimmed topi, snatched off the pegs

110

between the clay pots of ground orchids, anthuriums and maidenhair ferns that hung from the wooden eaves.

"You need this. We're creatures of the shade," she told him, dumping it on his head.

He could see what she meant. The hammering vitality of Nature in the tropics never ceased to offend his English instincts: the thick green knives of grass, the close-clustering bushes of crimson shoeflower and blue plumbago, drooping, alien flowers, cannas, crotans, poinsettias, huge-petalled and garishly tinted in stripes of cerise and magenta and sulphur-yellow – things growing and rotting and fertilising themselves, giving off a heavy odour sometimes sickly sweet like jasmine, in other places even sicklier with the inviting stench of corruption.

"This one's a moonflower magnolia," said Jill, reaching over to a bush with tightly furled blossoms. "Lovely chalice-shaped flowers. They only open at night."

Guy thought of her with his brother. For some reason a small shudder ran through him. He asked, "Does Harry take a lot of opium?"

"No. Almost never."

"Did he talk to you about what happened last night?"

"No." She was dead-heading an oleander.

"It's amazing, isn't it, what things lie hidden in families? Things you never knew were there until something happens like last night. Harry on opium. Me with too much to drink. Everything comes out, and you think you've cleared the air, but you haven't. I don't understand Harry at all...."

Jill did not reply. She went on cutting dead blossoms off the oleander bush. He gazed at her, so cool in the burning heat. Sweat gathered at the rim of his hat and trickled down his cheek.

"I've missed seeing you," he said.

"Oh, no. You've been terribly busy. Everyone tells me. And the Metropole. Aren't you settling in?"

"In a lonely sort of way."

She gestured with the secateurs. "You should get out more. Meet the natives."

"Oh, I do."

"Sylvia, for instance. She's wonderful fun: lovely, spirited. I've known her since she was in knickerbockers."

"If you're trying to tell me you're an old lady—"

"I'm not talking about myself." She turned and confronted him. Her eyes were wide and troubled. "Let's not talk about ourselves. Please, Guy. There's nothing I can do to help."

111

She started past him towards the house. He went with her, not knowing what to say except that something had to be said. But Jill spoke first, in a low voice.

"It's easy for you. You haven't been out here long enough to understand, or to think it matters. It's something about being out East, anything can happen, anything. This idea . . . a sort of *pressure* . . . of things getting out of hand, people losing their grip. The boy one day refusing to bring their tea. The colour of their skin changing. The dhobi-man walking out for good, leaving all their sheets dirty. . . ."

"You're frightened, aren't you? Of being out of control?"

Impatiently she shook her head. "It's not me, Guy. Try to understand what I'm telling you. It's the way of life out here, for all of us. Pleasant, easy, comfortable, yes; but it's balanced on a tightrope. One twist, one slip . . . you just wonder what's going to catch you."

She went from room to shadowy room, hands in the pockets of her gingham dress. He caught up with her on the verandah, where she stood quite still, the tips of her fingers on the parapet. A ray of sunlight between the rolled blinds melted her hair like butter. On the far side of the lawn a garden coolie watered a flowerbed. Nothing else moved; nothing else breathed.

"Sometimes it's so quiet I can hear my heart beating," she said in a voice that vibrated through him. "Have you ever listened to your heart? No, no, I'm sure you're much too busy. Sometimes all I can hear is my heart, pumping away. That blind, dull, monotonous, boring *thud*. God, I start asking myself why your great English poets ever used it as a metaphor for love and romance. It doesn't say much for love, does it? That the best they could come up with is a boring old pump."

She smelled of magnolia blossom, the kind that only opened its flowers at night. Sadness, anger, desire, ached through his body. He put his hand over hers on the parapet.

"You're wrong," he heard himself from a distance say. "You're wrong about the heart." He lifted her hand, and carried it, and held it over the strong beating in his chest.

"What—"

"Feel. Please. Just feel."

Nothing moved. Nothing breathed.

"No, Guy. No, it's not possible." She pulled her hand away, with something between a laugh and a sob, and gripped the parapet tight. "It's the heat," she murmured.

"Jill. . . ."

She moved back from him. The shaft of sunlight fell on her white collar. At the same instant there was a sudden sharp bang. Guy staggered back. Crows rose into the cawing sky.

Over the ridge, down through the rubber trees, came the black Morris 8. It puttered into the drive and drew up behind Guy's Wolseley. Michael Kandasala in his chauffeur's uniform got out and hailed them.

"New battery, Lady," he explained. "But very dodgy petrol."

Jill nodded. She looked at Guy, at the expression on his face.

"You must get back to Colombo," she said.

4 April 1942.   8.00 p.m. Colombo.

Most of one wall in the Operations Room of Sir Geoffrey Layton's head-quarters is taken up by an enormous map of the Indian Ocean. On it are plotted the relative positions of Sir James Somerville's Eastern Fleet, its faster division now at sea some fifty miles north-east of Addu Atoll, and Vice-Admiral Nagumo's Striking Force heading towards Ceylon from the south. The map markers demonstrate something of which Layton, gazing at the map, is all too painfully aware. The enemy is about three hundred miles closer to Ceylon than the British fleet.

Layton is under no illusions as to what this signifies. For the last seven days, ever since intelligence reports confirmed that an air attack on Ceylon was imminent, he has busied himself in clearing Colombo harbour of all ships which could be got to sea. Had he been entitled to give orders to James Somerville he would not have acquiesced in the return of the cruisers Dorsetshire *and* Cornwall. *As it is, they are due to be under way from Colombo in two hours' time.*

If Layton's intelligence reports are accurate, and the Japanese are approaching with the same firepower they brought to bear on Pearl Harbor and Port Darwin, there is no way Colombo's shore-based artillery can dent their attack. The only crumb of comfort is the precedent of Port Darwin, which suggests that Nagumo's bombers may restrict themselves to military installations and not do too much damage in civilian areas.

Air Vice-Marshal d'Albiac, Air Officer Commanding No. 22 Group in Ceylon, has provided Layton with a run-down on the fighter defences available. There are three squadrons of Hurricanes on the island. Two are in Colombo, one is in Trincomalee at China Bay. There are also two squadrons of naval Fulmars ashore, although these are unlikely to have the edge on the Japanese fighter planes.

The Hurricanes probably do have the edge. Not for the first time, the C-in-C congratulates himself on disobeying the Air Ministry by divert-ing to Ceylon two Hurricane squadrons bound for Java. In Java by now they would have been annihilated to little effect.

Layton turns away from the map to issue instructions to his staff. He needs a camp bed set up in the Operations Room, and a steady supply of black coffee. He is tempted to busy himself with subordinate details: to take telephone calls, to recall his commanders and once again go over the preparations that have been made. But the map draws him back. Its vast spaces of blue ocean and brown continent seem to revolve around the fulcrum of Ceylon like a belly-dancer round the diamond in her belly. To the east, the green pins of the enemy are gathering in strength, from Burma down to Java and Timor. To the west, a scattering of red pins in the emptiness marks the pitiful weakness of Allied forces.

In a few short months, the threat from Japan has materialised as more dangerous than the Chiefs of Staff could possibly have predicted at the end of 1941. Layton has been made aware, through unofficial channels, that if Ceylon falls, Churchill's government could well follow. The way would be open for the enemy to force Britain out of the war. They could invade India, now virtually defenceless, and link up with the German offensive through southern Russia towards the Caucasus. Or they could bypass India altogether and strike directly westwards at Britain's main supply route to the Middle East, up the coast of Africa.

It is this second option that would have the most immediately catastrophic effect. Madagascar is a few days' sailing for Admiral Nagumo. If he were to use it as a base, supplied from Ceylon, to sever the African supply route, it would in a stroke cut all reinforcements to Auchinleck's Desert Army of men, tanks, lorries, guns and ammunition.

The Desert War is in the balance. The British are desperately weak in the Middle East. Without reinforcements, and with the flow of oil from the Persian Gulf cut off, Britain's entire Middle Eastern and Mediterranean position would lie in ruins. Rommel would get to Cairo. The Mediterranean fleet base at Alexandria would fall. Germany would seize the Suez Canal and walk into the oilfields of Iraq and Persia, protected by Japanese carriers on their southern flank. Once Germany and Japan had closed the ring, the Soviet position in southern Russia would become untenable. The Axis would be in sight of achieving the main objective of the tripartite alliance – to attack its one remaining enemy, the United States, from east and west simultaneously.

It crosses Layton's mind, not for the first time, that it would have been more sensible to despatch the Eastern Fleet directly to east Africa, to secure Madagascar before the Japanese could get there, instead of maintaining the absurd pretence that Somerville's ships can somehow defend Ceylon. However it is too late now to send a signal to the Admiralty. Sir James is on his way. It is now unthinkable that the Royal Navy should turn tail and run without so much as attempting to engage the enemy.

With Dorsetshire and Cornwall not yet out of Colombo harbour, the vital thing now is to regain contact with the Japanese fleet. There has been no news since the early hours of this morning, when Catalina QL.A was presumably shot down after getting away its first sighting report. That leaves five Catalinas at Koggala Lagoon.

Admiral Sir Geoffrey Layton picks up one of the three telephones on the Operations Control desk. Within twenty minutes Flight-Lieutenant Jock Graham, armed with the sighting position transmitted by Squadron-Leader Birchall, is airborne in the 205 Squadron Catalina. His orders are to locate and shadow the approaching enemy.

Forward the Light Brigade. Onward the Six Hundred.

TWO

IT happened the day he had delivered his mistress to the Donald-sons' for dinner. Instead of going for a chin-wag with Uncle Albert – he had no intention of being made to sit on a bamboo stool in the kitchen while the old appu went on at him about his friends, his eating habits, his churchgoing – Michael wandered up Colpetty and across Galle Face Green to the Fort. Hitching a ride on the back of a tram, he crossed the bridge over the Harbour-Lake Canal.

All at once, like the hot smells of the Pettah borne on the breeze, he was conscious of a disturbance, a current of excitement in the air. Sinhalese faces were eddying around the Clock Tower, the small one at the edge of the open space where the Pettah started. A young Buddhist monk, shaven-headed and yellow-robed, had mounted the Clock Tower steps and was making a speech.

Michael had no particular place to go. He threaded his way through the honking traffic, and ended up at the very foot of the Clock Tower. He had never seen a Buddhist monk like this one. He was wearing broken spectacles held together by fuse-wire, and was punching the air with his black umbrella.

"Lanka is reeling under a hundred years of neglect!" he was shouting. His voice was hoarse, although he spoke the Sinhalese of an educated man. "It has been the British policy to make Lanka not support itself. We now depend for food on the rice they bring in ships from other countries! For centuries Lanka's central hills conserved rainfall. It rose in streams to irrigate the lowlands we kept under cultivation. What happens? The hills are planted with tea we don't drink and rubber we don't use! While British crops are watered, our canals and tanks run dry. Our low country is parched in the dry season and flooded in the monsoon. This is the price we pay for British rule!"

Fearful, Michael looked around. Some of the orator's audience had sensibly melted away. He should do the same, but something about this thin, passionate, billowing figure held him transfixed.

"In education it's the same. The British sow the wind and we reap the whirlwind. 'Education for all!' – that is what Mr E. Denham said to us – 'English! More English! Better English!' The consequence is that our sons scorn their father's trade and their father's tongue. They scorn to wear waistcloths and till the soil of their ancestors. They put on trousers and come to Colombo and waste their inheritance!" The monk rattled his umbrella on the steps with a sound like a collecting box.

"Great Britain has robbed Lanka of its lifeblood, its karma. Even in our small villages, which for two thousand years survived every famine, every drought, every invasion by the Dutch and the Portuguese, the little children now run into the street asking for school pens and sweeties. . . ."

Michael listened open-mouthed. Had he not been thinking such things in front of the mirror this very morning? His dark eyes fixed upon the speaker with a burning eagerness, he could never have seen the police charabanc which drew up on the other side of the market-place.

"What have the British done?" chanted the monk. "I will tell you what they have done. They broke the line of kings who ruled Lanka for two thousand four hundred years! They broke the rule of local chiefs and headsmen! They have killed the cow that laid the golden egg. They cut down our forests to plant tea, and they stole the profits for themselves!"

A large black-bearded man was distributing leaflets among the few who still listened. Michael had one thrust into his fist. The monk tried to wave the man away. He spoke more rapidly, in tempo with the running feet across the market-place.

"Even the colonialists are fighting one another now! Is that their idea of progress?" he shouted. "Progress is a blind alley. It has corrupted our people. The Christian missionaries have had it their way for hundreds of years. Now is the time to take things into our own hands!"

As the Buddhist raised his own hands, Michael saw that they were as smooth and unmarked by labour as a child's. The next moment he felt a violent shove in the small of his back.

He fell, sprawled across the steps. The police were in among the crowd. They were dragging people away to the van. Yells and curses rang in Michael's ears. Terrified, he dived forward across the steps, almost toppling the monk who still shouted above the din – "A new leader has arisen to free India! His name is Subhar Chandra Bose. The Mahatma himself. . . ."

Diving, twisting, Michael escaped the khaki ring of police and fled down an alleyway into the Pettah. He was still holding the leaflet. He crumpled it up and stuffed it in his trouser pocket.

It was then he heard the running steps behind him. With a moan of fear he took to his heels again. His pursuer was gaining on him. He looked over his shoulder. Swerving to avoid a trouser-press set up outside an Instant Laundry, he tripped, flung out an arm to save himself, and fell to the ground in a hail of tin saucepans.

A hand reached down and pulled him to his feet. It was the black-bearded man who had given him the leaflet.

"I thought you were the police," said Michael.

"Forgive me," the man replied. Tall and heavy-set, he spoke Sinhalese with a thick Moorish accent. "If I ran faster than you it was because I had the stronger motive. You see, comrade, if the police caught you, they would take down your name and address. If they caught up with me, they would send me to Bogambara Remand Gaol to join Philip Gunewardena and Dr Perera. Do these names mean something to you?"

"No."

"They are leaders of our great movement. They are martyrs in the Sama Samajist cause. Have you heard of the Lanka Sama Samaj?"

Michael found himself blushing, as if he had been obscenely propositioned. "Yes," he muttered, looking at his feet.

"Would you want to hear more? They have an office here, you know. Just round the corner. It's where I am going now." As Michael hesitated, he added softly, "Young man, if you believe in your country, you should at least know what we are fighting for."

Of the Sama Samaj, Michael had not so much heard as over-heard. Among people he knew, Ceylon's revolutionary national-ist party was spoken of in an undertone accompanied by much frowning and shaking of the head. Once or twice he had seen a little smile on the lips of J.P., his other uncle and the big gun of the Kandasala family, as if to concede that every nation had its hotheads, its firebrands... but when Michael eventually plucked up courage to ask him about the Sama Samaj, J.P. had stood on tiptoe in rage.

"Scoundrels! They want to accelerate the processes of history. As fuel, they exploit the discontents of the ignorant. What hap-pens? The whole caboodle explodes in their faces and we are all back to square one."

But even an old fuddy-duddy like J.P. had admitted that the

British number was up. Perhaps not in my lifetime, he'd told Michael last New Year, but you'll live to see Independence. Times change, he had explained, fanning himself with his bowler hat. We cannot afford to be left at history's postern-gate.

Emboldened by this thought, Michael followed the black-bearded man ("You may call me John") down a side-street and into a tailor's shop. Inside it was dark and smelt strongly of mothballs. Suits hung from the ceiling as thickly as bats in a cave. Instead of going up the stairs, John plunged into the back room which gave out on an alleyway.

Then he disappeared.

Michael stood at the door, staring up and down the alleyway. There was a muffled shout from behind him. He turned. A hand beckoned to him from the back of a cupboard full of suits. Pushing through them, he followed John up narrow back stairs. His fingers were slippery on the banister. He could smell printing ink. That would explain why the tailor used so many mothballs.

John knocked six times on a door at the top of the stairs. "Suryodaya Press" Michael read on the plate. There was a clattering of bolts. The door opened on a chain. A round, intelligent face, not much older than Michael's, peeped through the gap. Seeing John, it broke into a smile. The door opened; they were ushered in.

It was a long, narrow room, ventilated only by a desk-fan and one small window hardly big enough to escape through. At this end stood an awesome black machine, not unlike one of Master's mangles at the rubber factory, which Michael took to be the printing press. At the far end were two tables piled high with documents and leaflets.

All four walls were papered with posters, most of them in a bright school-pencil red. VICTORY TO THE PEOPLE they declared, in bold print laid over a field of toadstools, which turned out on closer examination to be a mass of clenched fists raised in protest. FREE LANKA others read simply, over a dramatic sketch of a man staggering under heavy black chains, forged to a huge black ball with a £ sign on it.

An older man came out from behind the mounds of paperwork. He had a long sharp nose on which perched thick-lensed glasses. His skull, as bald and yellow as an old billiard ball, glimmered with sweat.

"We were worried for you," he said, making it sound like an accusation.

"I've brought along a comrade. He was at the meeting," said

124

John. He pushed Michael forward. "The police arrested Vikrama this time, and no bad thing. I've told you before, this Young Men's Buddhist Association is a diversionist Trotskyite conspiracy. It must be suppressed."

The younger of the two Sama Samajists nodded. His hair more than made up for the older man's baldness: it stuck out round his ears and stood straight up in front like a toothbrush. "They are a danger," he explained to Michael, holding his gaze with an unnerving directness. "They distract the masses from acknowledging our legitimate demands. We say that the workers must rise up against the demon of British imperialism and take power into their own hands. What the YMBA wants to do is to return Lanka to the rule of Buddhist monks – and we all know what happened the last time. The Buddhists let the social fabric of Lanka crumble, so that when the Tamils invaded there was nothing to stop them."

This momentous event in his country's history had escaped Michael's memory but he nodded anyway. He could feel at his back the bulky presence of John, standing between him and the door.

"Don't believe the school-books!" broke in the older man as if reading his mind. "It was the Sinhalese, alone, who built up the great civilisations of Lanka. Nobody else. We threw the Tamils out, we Sinhalese! The British shipped the Tamils back here to be their slaves, yes. But one day soon we will throw the British out and the Tamils after them! We will lift up our heads again! Tell me," he added, putting his hands together with a gesture of pity. "Are you one of the unemployed?"

With a deep feeling of shame, Michael Kandasala told them about the Donaldsons and now the Tancreds. To his relief he was not immediately kicked down the stairs. The two Sama Samajists exchanged glances. They beckoned John to pull up a chair for him. The older man opened a desk drawer and produced a bottle of arrack and four glasses.

Michael had always scoffed at arrack as the sort of rough stuff Uncle Albert drank. But here of all places he could hardly admit he preferred gin, the drink of the Planter's Raj. With a polite shake of the head he took the distilled palm-toddy and swallowed it down.

The fierce liquor sang in his veins and fired his blood. Stretching out his legs, he listened to the revolutionaries. It was not long before the apparition in the mirror, which had bedevilled him all day, evaporated. Out of the heady fumes of arrack and revolution another image took shape – the dashing figure of a freedom fighter. It wore a crimson sari and a loose white shirt imprinted with the yellow Suriya flower, the symbol of peace, liberty and self-respect (as opposed to imperialism, war and slavery). The dark face was proud, its jaw determined, and this time there could be no mistaking – it was Michael's own.

Tears of happiness sprang to his eyes. He had discovered himself. He was at one with the oppressed people of his motherland, the poor enslaved masses whom the English warmongers had exploited through starvation, unemployment, immorality and disease. Thirstily he drank in tales of peasant smallholders, dispossessed by capitalist Sinhalese landlords and sent to work for a pittance on their coconut plantations. Basic material for the revolutionary struggle! The posters around him on the walls shook their fists and rattled their chains.

Eventually the older of the Sama Samajists stood up and leant across the desk, throwing half the room into shadow. "Michael, do you want to help us? Will you do as we ask?"

In the stillness, Michael could hear the whirring of the desk-fan. The noises of the Pettah seemed to have hushed; its toiling masses were waiting for his answer.

"I have a gun," he whispered.

"You have a gun? You?"

Michael swallowed. "Yes."

The two heads, the bald and the bushy, conferred together for a moment. Then the older man looked at him sternly. "We are in principle opposed to bloodshed," he declared. "Guns can never prevail against the will of the people. At the same time, if violence is used against us, we will respond with violence. Gun will answer gun. Do you understand?"

"Yes."

"Good. Then go back to being a car-man with your Kelani bosses. Act naturally, but keep your eyes and ears open. Take care not to draw attention to yourself by wearing a red sari or saying impulsive things. Behave as if nothing had happened; but keep your weapon to hand. Wait for us to tell you what to do." He took off his pebble glasses and smiled at Michael for the first time.

"We will be proud of you," he commanded.

We will be proud of you. As Michael Kandasala took a short cut through Slave Island back to Cinnamon Gardens, he repeated the Sama Samajist's words under his breath. Already in his mind's eye he could picture the scene: the lighted torches, the burning godowns along the harbour's edge, the ruthless dishing of any who stood in their way.

He, Michael, would be merciful. Armed with his gun (actually it was Uncle Albert's) he would see to it there was no looting or raping. But Millers Department Store would burn to the ground, he would organise that personally. So would Cargills, and the Elephant House, and Whiteaway Laidlaw. Then they would be forced to leave with their tails between their legs, the British. With no rubber or tea to trade, and nothing to buy in the shops, they would see that the game was up.

He hurried past the police barracks and turned down beside the Salvation Army headquarters. It was getting late. The Donaldsons would be passing round the coffee and liqueur chocolates. He looked for a rickshaw, but the only vehicle in sight was a big black hearse on its way back to the undertaker's yard. It put him in mind of the scene on his window-sill that morning when he had been trying on William's togs in front of the mirror: the ants struggling under the dead weight of the rhinoceros beetle. . . .

And in that second he understood, with a shiver of excitement and apprehension, that it had been meant as a sign for him. The dead beetle was the British Raj. He, Michael, must take his place among the ants in its funeral procession.

Was he resolved enough? Michael had asked himself this question every day since that meeting in the Pettah. Was he strong enough, when the hour struck, to do whatever the Sama Samajists demanded of him? Today, driving back down to the coast after the annual New Year binge in Nuwara Eliya, he forced himself to think about it harder than ever. Involuntarily he took one narrow hand off the wheel and raised to his lips the little silver crucifix he wore round his throat.

Master and Lady sat in the back. Young Master, Guy, was in the seat beside him. Michael had driven this road down from Nuwara Eliya tens of times: he knew every turn down through the tight green slopes of tea, through which the Tamil women waded slowly, with their baskets, plucking the green tips of the tea bushes. His passengers were talking about the war and about English politics, of which he didn't understand the head or the tail. At intervals they chucked cents out of the window to the small boys who hared down slopes too steep for tea, crying out at every hairpin bend, "Sir! Lady! I am making a small-coin collection!"

It was a tradition, this throwing money out to the children, a game that the British always played when they came away from Nuwara Eliya. Michael had never given it a second thought. But in his ears today rang the voices of the Sama Samajists in the printer's shop: *corrupt capitalist practices ... exploiting our children ... bribing the poor*.

The problem was working out how the struggle for a free Lanka was to be waged. Popular revolutionary movements had to spring from the corpse of imperialism, so Lenin had apparently said. But there was nothing corpse-like about imperialism in Nuwara Eliya. People talked about shortages: handing out long drinks of Lanka Orange on the lawn, carrying golf clubs, passing round the after-dinner coffee-cups, Michael couldn't see any shortages. Fewer men of Sylvia's set turned up to partner her at tennis, but there were still enough soldiers and sailors to go round. Mr Donaldson was a strange and complicated man, with his little jokes that nobody could understand, and his model railway up in the top verandah room – but he was no different from how he'd ever been.

As for Master, sitting behind him, he had such violent moods that he was impossible to understand. There were days when he would say nothing at all. He would fiddle with the great big crystal set he'd built, or shut himself away with books on Buddhism or Japanese dictionaries. There were other times – Michael didn't know which he dreaded more – when he would be cheerful and talkative, and summon him to answer questions about Sinhalese village life, or lecture him about Gandhi. On these occasions Master could almost sound like a Sama Samajist. Michael would seek any excuse to make his escape, thinking that there was some deep puzzle here that it might not be wise to know too much about.

Around him they were still talking about Winston Churchill and the war. Young Master Guy at least got them talking: he'd known times when this whole journey had been passed in silence. Young Master – now there was another mystery. Always restless, always distant, as if a part of him was missing. Michael imagined him as the kind of bachelor European to whose lonely bungalow a Sinhalese prostitute would come quietly at night, slipping in through the mosquito-netting and leaving before dawn with barely a footprint in the dust.

Three thousand feet down from Nuwara Eliya, at the foot of the Ramboda Pass, the air was already moister, the sun more sweltering. Under a piped run-off from one of the mountain

128

streams, two Tamil women tea-pluckers were bathing. Their wet saris clung to their full breasts and high rounded buttocks as they rinsed their long hair under the waterfall.

Michael slowed the car, then accelerated noisily over the bridge. Tamils, he despised them, always rutting, always breeding ... but, it was no good, he knew it was not the Tamil women he had thought of at the bridge at all – it was Sylvia Donaldson he had seen bathing in that waterfall, rinsing her bright blonde hair and letting the water cascade down her ivory back.

This was what shamed him. It made no difference telling himself, with many insults and slaps on the head, that saris were the most sensuous and tip-top garments ever invented, the glory of Ceylonese womanhood. The fact was that when he saw Sylvia Donaldson in her sun-dresses, or the white blouse of her new RNVR uniform, his lustful thoughts were terrific.

It was not that Sylvia gave him any encouragement. Just the opposite. From the way she ignored him it was obvious that she wanted to forget what they once shared together as children. In those days, she used to give him presents which she wrapped up herself and tied with string: an ivory-handled penknife, which he still carried in his trouser pocket, and of course the silver crucifix, which she had sent to him from England when his mother died.

He had a photograph (he'd looked at it this morning) of Sylvia and him dressed up in his best togs, Sylvia making faces at him behind his back. On the New Year's Eve before he was sent away to school, when he had been allowed to stay up until midnight to carry the champagne-glasses through from the kitchen, she had popped him a kiss under the mistletoe. He had smelt the milkiness of her skin and felt the down on her cheek, and the monster in his loins had bubbled and overflowed like the champagne.

He could still taste that kiss. It was more than just a kiss. It was the first secret between them, and the promise of more secrets to come. He didn't know then – how could he? – that if you weren't a white boy you weren't ever allowed such happiness. It didn't strike at him that in the eyes of these people he had grown up among he was worse than nothing. Nothing. Even a Vellala like him, the highest caste in Ceylon, in their eyes was lower than the meanest white man who crawled off the Boat.

It was Mrs Donaldson who had educated him to the real world, that weekend in Bentota where they had all gone to swim. He and Sylvia had found a secret sandy hollow among the rocks. First of all she'd wanted to arm-wrestle him. Then she got bored

129

with that. She dared him to take his swimming trunks off. She said she wanted to see if he was the same colour all over. He dared her back.

They listened. There was no one coming. Sylvia wore a one-piece swimming costume, bright blue, the colour of her eyes. With a casual shrug she let go the shoulder-straps and took it off, right down to the top of her legs. He dropped his swimming trunks and stood before her, naked. Hot with embarrassment he didn't know where to look. But she did. She began to reach out; then she stuffed her hand to her mouth, with a little giggle. "It's so *black!*" she'd whispered. And then, as she felt it, "Look what a monster it is!"

At which juncture her mother had come round the side of the rocks. And screamed.

That was the end of the first part of his life. He wasn't allowed into the main part of the house after that, not even to dust Mr Donaldson's model railway. And each year now, when they joined up with Master and Lady for the New Year holiday in Nuwara Eliya, Sylvia would say Hallo, Michael, and then pretend he wasn't there.

It didn't matter. He could wait. Sylvia didn't have anyone special, now. During her two days' leave she mostly played tennis or cut arum lilies for the dinner table, or else sat on the veranda and talked. She was full of chatter about the Naval Office: the movement of ships; the search for a safe harbour in case the Japs bombed Colombo; making percolated coffee to keep herself awake in the night watches; the frightful swizz of not being allowed to wear hats, unlike the Wren officers, which meant that you weren't allowed to be saluted. This morning Uncle Albert had told him that she'd talked and talked so much because she was heart-broken that Master Charles Bilbow had gone to sea –

But the silly old appu, what did he know a thing about, these days? He didn't have a brain in his head. Sylvia had not said a word, not a single word in his hearing about Bilbow, which showed how little she cared. And since the sailors he'd read about in comics always ended up dead, it was better she forgot all about him.

"Michael – you had better get petrol in Mawanella," Harry Tancred called from the back seat.

"Yes, Master."

"And you might check the oil. We're a bit overloaded."

"Yes, Master."

Wait for us to tell you what to do, they'd said.

130

They stopped at the garage in Mawanella, taking their turn for petrol behind two British army jeeps. Michael allowed himself to be bought a Lanka Lime by Lady. They were still some hours' drive from Kelani, but the hill-slopes of tea bushes had been left behind. Flat paddy-fields fringed with coconut palms now lay either side of the raised road. They went on, through sombre stretches of rubber plantation, and through villages where boiled paddy dried on coir mats in the sun and squatting women drove the hens away.

These were the people he had to educate. In these dirty children, playing under the castor-oil tree, flowed the life-blood of the revolution. Once the struggle had been taken to the masses it was all up for the capitalist big bugs and their henchmen who starved and oppressed them. Michael half-wished he could stop the car right here, in the middle of this village street. He would go down in the dust to that white-haired elder sitting motionless in the doorway of his thatched cadjan hut. Saluting him, he would offer to share his beggarly meal of rice-cakes off a plaintain leaf, and in return teach him how to break his fetters. They would come running after him of course, Master and Lady. He would throw the car-keys through the hut doorway and turn his back on them.

What was wrong with his family, that they had never made him return to his father's village, to seek out the wisdom of simple things? So much of his life he had resented never having a university education. Now he saw that he'd had a lucky escape. He could easily have become one of those *trouser-karens* the Buddhist monk had gone on about, who were so out of touch with village life that they wouldn't know what to plant in a *chena* if you gave them one. Flunkeys of imperialism, every one, salaaming their way to a job in the Commerce and Industries.

They too would be knocked from their perches by the revolution. Michael could think of more than one name to pass on to the LSSP when the day came. Meanwhile, he had not let the grass grow under his feet.

Behind him in Nuwara Eliya he had left his own seasonal greetings. He had done it last night, when they were all asleep in their beds. With a brush and a bucket of whitewash he had crept through the fence to the Hill Club. On the brick wall under the billiard-room window he had painted it in capital letters for all to see –

THE TIDE OF NATIONHOOD IS ON THE MARCH!

*

131

The opportunity Michael had been waiting for came a few days later. Lady told him to drive in to Colombo to return a canteen she had borrowed from the Donaldsons. Michael transported it in a large leather bag, which he had taken the precaution of stuffing with newspapers.

Uncle Albert's quarters were at the back of the Donaldsons' old Dutch bungalow. Michael crept down the side-drive and let himself in by the familiar door off the back veranda. The room was empty. Very carefully he took the canteen out of the bag and set it down without a sound on the cement floor. He waited a few seconds, wrinkling his nose at the smell of his Uncle's *beedi*, his horrible coarse cigar.

He knew where the old appu kept the gun. Quietly he opened the tin chest beside the teapoy and rummaged far down. The ancient smooth-bore pistol Albert had been given by the District Officer during the 1915 riots lay wrapped in oil-cloth under several pairs of cotton socks. Michael slipped it and the ammunition into the leather bag, closed the chest, and went outside.

Uncle was where he'd expected to find him – sitting outside on an upturned paraffin-tin, dressed in a banyan and a sarong.

Michael was ashamed for him. His quarters smelt of dried fish. Its two old leather humpties and the truckle-bed he recognised as Master and Lady's cast-offs. His uncle's teeth were betel-stained, and he was openly smoking ganja in his *beedi*; in fact, looking down, Michael could see the hempweed growing round the base of the small verandah. He sat down on the other paraffin-tin, the bag between his feet, hoping that the rust would not stain his newly pressed cotton trousers.

"Uncle, what is this? You are smoking too much ganja, and chewing too much betel and lime. I can smell it on your breath. You act as you were back in Kandaloya. Soon you will go back to sleeping east to west."

"I have always lain east to west. I am too old not to believe in demons. If you had any sense, you would believe in them too."

Michael was silent. He had been brought up a Christian, among Europeans, and yet the superstitions of centuries were too strong to be cut away by a few Bible lessons. At school he had jeered at other boys with their belief in devil-dancers and animal sacrifices, their terror of Rakshyos, spirits of evil who leapt out from the branches of graveyard trees and seized the unwary with madness – but he had also been secretly impressed. There was not much to choose, he concluded, between their spirits and demons and the angels and devils of the Bible – and there he had left it. Now, his rejection of the Europeans and their corrupt ways meant that, with no faith to hold to, menacing spectres had begun to stir in the corners of his night. Uncle had given them a poke.

"Uncle, you sit here looking into the past," he said defiantly. "You smoke ganja and think about the devil-priests, is that any way for an appu to carry on? What would your brother say? Do you suppose J.P. has time for *kappuralas* and all this mumbo-jumbo?"

"You do well to remind me." His uncle stood up and shuffled into his room. A minute later he was back with a satinwood box the size of a sewing case. He placed it in his nephew's lap, together with a letter addressed to J. P. Kandasala, BA (Lond.). "I want you to give this to J.P. from me," he said.

Michael opened the box, and drew in his breath with a hiss. On a bed of silky kapok lay a thick crescent of yellow tortoiseshell speckled with patches of brown. It was the family head-comb, the mark of high caste, signifying that its wearer had never had to bear a burden on his head. The most venerable object the Kandasalas possessed, it was conferred by long custom on the head of the family.

"I was the eldest of the three brothers," said Albert, sitting down again and pointing his cigar at Michael in the way Mr Donaldson used to. "But I am no longer its head. J.P. is now a very important individual in government service. The head-comb is his by right."

"Why don't you give it to him yourself?"

"The opportunity is not there. I am chucking it in next month. I am going back to live in Kandaloya."

Michael clutched hold of the box as though everything was slipping from his grasp. "What are you saying?" he cried. "Uncle, you are not even fifty-five yet! What is all this talk of retiring? And to a little village, without even a proper road so you used to say!"

The appu nodded.

"You have been here all your life," Michael persisted. "What is there to run away from?"

"I am not running *away*. I am running *towards*," said his uncle mysteriously. He dragged on his cigar and let his eyes drift with the smoke. Michael banged down the lid of the box and put it in the leather bag. The ganja made him cough; he got to his feet.

"Big changes are coming," he said in a bitter voice. "The British will be defeated. Imperialism is a dead duck. The

133

proletariat is awakening from its slumbers. This is no time to go and sit under a plantain tree in Kandaloya, Uncle, it is a foolish act."

Uncle Albert took out his pipe, and spat into the monsoon drain. "You know the saying," he remarked. "'When the cat puts its head into a pot he thinks all is darkness.' You, nephew, you put your head in a cloud and you think all is light."

Michael was not sure that he wanted to visit J.P. He had a suspicion that Uncle Albert in his devious way had given him the head-comb to take as a way of shaming him back into the bosom of his family.

But what family? His parents were both dead. Uncle Albert was about to bury himself in the middle of nowhere. His cousin Percy, J.P.'s son, had finished at university and was hoping to do as his father had done and take a postgraduate law degree in London. Percy would become a politician, and go the same way as all the other English-educated politicians in Ceylon. He would shout against the British in the State Council, and afterwards hobnob with them about Test Match scores over a cup of tea. Michael had no wish to see Percy.

But where to go for advice? The two boys at Kelani Lodge were Tamil, you didn't confide in Tamils (as they said, all the doctors were Tamil but all the coffins were full of Sinhalese). His one good friend, Victor Molligoda, had been arrested on a charge of pinching a bicycle bell. That left J.P. When Lady next had to go into Colombo Michael brought the satinwood box with him, and went looking for his uncle. He was directed to a hole in the ground opposite the Colombo Club, on Galle Face Green.

Forty or fifty workmen were busy on the site. Some were laying cables across the reinforced concrete walls and floor of a large underground chamber. Others operated mechanical shovels. His uncle, dressed like a British officer in white drill shorts and long white socks, with a khaki topi on the dome of his balding head, was engaged in a noisy row with a Senior Public Works Official. The cause of their argument lay on the ground nearby for all to see: a 120-foot pillar of chiselled granite, the famous Victory Column of Mr Lutyens.

"You say you have not the authorisation," he heard J.P.'s precise, high-pitched English. "I say I have neither the funds nor the manpower. If I did, I would re-erect the blasted thing anywhere you like. However, I am already at full stretch. Our

134

chaps are fully extended all over Colombo, digging wells, erecting first-aid posts, removing glass window-panes in the hospitals. . . . Very well! Very well! If the column is such a morale-booster, why not ask PWD to boost the column up somewhere themselves!"

The Senior Municipal Official threw his hands in the air, and stalked off across the grass. J.P. took off his rimless spectacles and wiped his perspiring face. Catching sight of his nephew, he looked more disapproving than ever.

"Michael? What are you doing here? This is a security area."

The box under his arm, Michael politely saluted him. Before he could be given an answer J.P. was off again, trotting down a ramp to consult the architect's drawings.

"This is top secret!" he called over his shoulder. "Our underground control room in case of attack from the air. Instant communications to every part of Colombo! If Hirohito comes over, we will be ready for him."

"Will you be down here, Uncle James?"

"Of course. It is my duty. The Deputy Controller has to stand at his post and issue instructions. He has to give a lead. Have you not been reading my Public Advice Notices?"

"Not in Kelani."

"No. Of course. You should be out of danger there." He studied the drawings, and began pacing out the concrete floor. Michael followed behind.

"My problem," continued J.P. as if talking to himself, "can be expounded in one single word; communications. Last week we had an air-raid warning, with sirens, and what happens? Everyone panics. In the Pettah there is a stampede . . . bullock carts overturned . . . people actually go and plonk themselves in the middle of the street and look up at the sky! Who reads my Notices? Who listens to the wireless? The fire-engines stayed put because the emergency lines to the Fire Brigade were busy with people ringing up to ask why the sirens were going. Why do they not read the Notices?"

"Is it possible that many of them do not read?" asked Michael, choosing his words carefully.

"They can hear. They can hear. I have sixty wardens and deputy wardens to call upon every household in Colombo. All they are requesting is a little co-operation. But people are the same everywhere, have you noticed? They expect government to do everything. Rasani! Excuse me."

J.P. ran across the concrete to speak to the foreman. Then he

135

hurried back up the ramp, fanning himself with his topi.

Michael began, "Your brother Albert—"

"This is another thing. Do you think I want to wear one of these dashed silly hats? We are all meant to be topped in steel helmets. There are no steel helmets. Nor any pumps. I will tell you why we are so delayed with this building. No pumps to pump out the water at bottom. I have had to authorise tons of dry cement poured down instead." He took out his pocket-watch with a distracted flourish. "I have to get back to HQ. Goodbye. Give my esteemed regards to the Donaldsons."

"You mean the Tancreds—"

"Yes. And come and see me one of these days, Michael. Make an appointment first if you please."

"Excuse me a moment. I have this to give you. It is from Uncle."

He passed over the satinwood box. J.P. opened it, and gazed at the head-comb. He stood still for a moment. His face registered irritation, amusement, and then a withdrawn look which Michael could not fathom.

"There is a letter," he prompted.

"Thank you, I will read it later." J.P. looked at his nephew with raised eyebrows. "Is my brother keeping his pecker up?"

"He smokes ganja. He says he is chucking his job and going back to Kandaloya."

"Yes." J.P. sighed, but made no further comment. He waved away the rickshaw waiting for him at the roadside. "Come. We will walk back together," he said.

Shoulder to shoulder, uncle and nephew walked the half-mile to the Fort, past fudge-sellers on the Green and children trying to fly kites in the dropping breezes from the sea. J.P. carried the satinwood box under his arm like a briefcase.

"The world is too much with us," he observed after a lengthy silence. "Getting and spending, we lay waste to our powers."

"Oh?"

"I refer to the Lakeland poet, Sir William Wordsworth. He hits the nail on its head, of course. We should all lead contemplating lives. Your great-grandfather never left his village." He sighed again. "Nevertheless. Times change, and we must change with them."

"Yes."

"Have you any idea of my responsibilities? As we speak, I am arranging a census of Colombo's entire population. I am preparing three ARP exercises, one of which fires off next week. I am giving

136

lectures on ARP. I am answering correspondence from people worried to send their nippers to school in Colombo. And all this time I am assailed – yes, *assailed* by people with foolish questions in the newspapers. How should they learn which side of a wall to take cover behind in an air raid? In their house, is a back room more blast-proof than a central room? Lying under a bed better than lying under a table? In a trench-shelter should they squat, or crouch on their hands and knees? Nit-pickers!"

"It may not matter very much," Michael volunteered.

"Precisely. Or should I say," J.P. corrected himself with lawyerly caution, "it may or may not matter. However, that is not my point. My point is that you and I are surrounded by detail, the minutiae of existence. There are times when we are unable to discern the wood for the trees."

"I know—"

"Which is why we must adapt. All of us. We must adapt. Look at the Veddhas. There were Veddhas in Ceylon long before our earliest ancestors came here. Today they are dying out. Why? Because they neglected to adapt themselves."

They crossed under the old lighthouse. Michael steered his uncle, still talking, through the traffic. "What about the British?" he asked.

"The British?"

"After this war. They have not adapted themselves. You told me that one day the British number will be up. What happens then?"

A sea breeze gusted up Queen Street. His uncle's topi left his head and floated into the gutter. Michael ran and retrieved it for him.

"It is an ill wind that blows nobody any good," replied J.P., smiling. The government offices were close by. In a nervous movement he pushed his spectacles up his nose.

"What will happen, do you think, Uncle? Will there be socialism? Will the workers take power?"

"Where have you been getting these ideas? Our people cannot manage a few estates: how can they manage the whole country? We will adapt, of course. But slowly. Remember that patience is the companion of wisdom." J.P. transferred the satinwood box to his other arm and shook his nephew warmly by the hand. "I must dash. Please express my thanks to Albert for the head-comb. Tell him I will write him a letter."

With that he hurried up the wide steps. At the top he paused for an instant to remove his hat, his neat figure dwarfed by the

Corinthian columns on either side. Then the tall doors engulfed him.

Michael Kandasala watched for a minute, his hands tucked under his arms, as the doors kept turning. Threshing stones, they ground important people in and out, until they became as small, in his imagination, as grains of rice. Uncle Albert and Uncle James: one the servant, one the master, just as the British had planned Ceylon to divide from the beginning. The same caste, and yet as different now, the two of them, as the Brahmin from the Untouchable. That was what the system had done. The demon of British imperialism.

He turned on his heel. His narrow shoulders hunched, he strode away, a solitary figure in the crowd. When would the men in the printers' shop make contact? What would they tell him to do? Whatever it was, he would be strong enough. He was prepared to fight and die in the cause of freedom – though of course it might not come to that.

WITH trembling fingers (it wasn't the flying that terrified her) Sylvia pulled on the thick gloves and buttoned the fur-lined helmet under her chin. Crouching in the long grass at the end of the runway she was invisible from the control tower. She recognised Model T at once by the self-important clatter of its engine. She waited until the silver wing-tips and racing propeller were visible above the grass-stalks, and ran forward in her sensible shoes.

David Gifford leant back from the front cockpit and pointed out the foot-holds. "Watch the machine-gun!" he yelled. "Goggles are on your seat!"

As soon as she was strapped in, he accelerated down the runway. The fuselage creaked and shuddered and bumped. In front, David pulled at a joystick. All at once the little biplane lifted in the air and began to bank over Ratmalana Airport, so steeply that Sylvia's stomach turned over. She closed her eyes, half-wishing she hadn't persuaded him into this.

It was the Colombo – Koggala patrol: down the coast-line to a narrow air-strip beside a lagoon used by flying boats, and then a bee-line back to Colombo over the low-forested hills of the Southern Province. This apparently was as far as the little 550-horsepower Wapiti could fly without taking on extra fuel – and if he took on extra fuel, as David was shouting to her now over the clattering of the engine, it would mean jettisoning the baggage in the back seat.

Sylvia managed a faint smile. On the ground, it would have been unthinkable for David Gifford to refer to her as a baggage. Up here, soaring and swooping in space (and she so *wished* David would stop showing off like this), he was a different person, laughing, joking, pointing out landmarks like the Beruwala lighthouse, handling the plane with a masterful arrogance which she had to admit was rather attractive once she got her breath back. Her hopes began to revive.

They had dwindled a little after the lunch last Friday at the Fountain Café. It had been *magnifique* to see him; she'd rather taken it for granted he had gone home to Blighty to learn how to be a Hurricane pilot and there he was waving at her from across the street. She'd nearly fallen off her bicycle.

"I say, you're looking a bit off-colour," he'd greeted her. "Not much of a life, just now, is it?"

Such a combination of tactlessness and sympathy lurked in this speech that Sylvia's lower lip began to quiver. She shook her head. Hastily David went on.

"How about letting me give you a spot of lunch? It would do wonders for my morale."

The more she apologised for being such a wet blanket, as they sat down to lunch in Union Place, the more fuss David made of her, pulling out her chair and offering to park her briefcase. It dawned on her that David had perhaps not viewed her before as a serious person, with deep feelings. She kept her eyes downcast as she studied the badly typed menu.

"I suppose you must be missing Charlie a lot," he said, after they had ordered their seer fish and roast potatoes.

She smiled bravely. "Tell me about you," she said. "I thought you'd gone away and left me too."

"So did I. But the CO had us all in the other day. Because of Johnny Jap in Malaya there isn't time to train us back Home. It's all going to happen out here. They're shipping the Hurricanes out in an aircraft-carrier and we have to put them together again, like model aeroplanes. Until then I'm still flying patrols in old Model T, that's what I call my Westland Wapiti."

"I'm awfully pleased you're staying."

"Are you?" He smiled, shyly. She noticed his hands resting on the orange check tablecloth, broad and sun-browned with pleasingly delicate fingers. She wondered if they had stroked Maria's face.

"I envy the freedom you must have," she said, after an awkward pause. "They're so stuffy at the Naval Office. It's as easy as pie being a cipherette; you're given pieces of paper with numbers on, and have to encode them by looking them up in a book and then put them through a decoding machine a bit like a typewriter. Totally menial, you know, but all the time you've got this senior naval officer peering over your shoulder to make sure you're doing it right, just like some horrid form-mistress at Cheltenham. And the rules, you wouldn't believe! Cipherettes work just as hard as most of the Wren officers, and underground too, because that's where the Cipher Office is, but people can only salute the Wrens, they can't salute us because we don't have hats. Only the people sent out from London have hats, can you believe?''

"Stuffy *and* stuffy."

"What? Oh well, yes. We're working in what used to be the dhobi rooms for Bauer's Flats. An old maid with gold braid – that's what we call them – was breathing down my neck yesterday and I said to Monica, 'Can you smell the starch in this room?' ''

Sylvia giggled despite her resolve, but David Gifford didn't seem to mind. In fact, when you got David talking, he quite seemed to enjoy a gossip and he noticed uncomfortably much about people, almost as much as she did herself. He had noticed how Ottoline Hoathly plucked at her hideous jade earrings whenever she talked about her husband the Archdeacon; and how Sylvia's father was always saying gravely, "It's the principle of the thing" (although David stayed tactfully silent when Sylvia told him how much it drove her mother to distraction); and how Guy Tancred tried to be terribly suave but was frightfully sweet and natural when you got to know him, and what a waste it was that Fiona and Audrey and Millicent had all fallen for Guy's sad eyes and rather stylish, world-weary air, and yet Guy didn't seem to care for any of them. . . .

"How about you?" asked Sylvia.

"What about me?"

"I bet you've got a secret *amour* up your sleeve!" She laughed brightly, and prodded her fish.

David shrugged his shoulders. In his worn-looking flying jacket he suddenly looked older; he looked about twice Charlie's age. "There's no time for that," he said. "It wouldn't be fair."

That was not the answer he was supposed to give. Sylvia said peevishly, "But you're staying. You said so!"

"Yes. For the time being. But you see, Sylvia, I'm not like Charlie. I don't have his glorious optimism. I don't have his feeling that everything's going to be all right."

"Why not? What do you mean?"

He gave her a lopsided grin. A lock of dark hair fell helplessly across his forehead, as if part of the internal disarray. "Here I am, sounding off like a Moaning Minnie, and I'm supposed to be cheering you up! All I mean is that I'm not going to get involved, that way, when I can't even see round the next corner. Let's talk about something else."

And so they did; although what it was she couldn't remember except that it was all rather flat and the table between them

141

seemed to have got bigger all of a sudden. Over the Cona coffee (he was already looking at his watch, he had a lecture in the Group briefing hut at 1500 hours), she plucked up her courage.

"David, if you really mean it about cheering me up, would you take me up in Model T?"

"Ah. I'd love to. But it's against all the regulations."

"Just for a spin."

"If the CO clapped eyes on us there'd be hell to pay."

He was weakening, she could sense it. She bowed her head, and slowly raised her blue eyes until they met his brown ones. "Nobody would see us," she whispered. "We can arrange it. Please, David. Don't grudge me a little bit of fun."

It worked. Sylvia knew it would. She smiled now to herself as she looked over the side at Galle, with the tiled roofs of its pretty Dutch houses looking no bigger than pink fingertips holding the sea back. In these cumbersome pullovers she'd been told to wear she was altogether a bit of a baggage. She had hoped that Charlie going away would put her off her food and help her lose weight, but it seemed to have the opposite effect, she felt hungrier and hungrier.

"Hold tight! We're going down!" shouted David.

Going down was hardly the word for it. They plummeted out of the sky into a grove of coconut palms. Sylvia screamed. The palm trees suddenly opened up to reveal a narrow strip of tarmacadam. At the end of the tarmacadam was the sea.

They landed. David seemed to be straining to brake the plane. Sylvia braced herself. The sea rushed towards them. Literally inches from death, as it seemed to her, David brought the Wapiti to a halt, and ambled it off the runway. He turned and grinned his lopsided grin at her. Shakily she took off her goggles.

When he helped her down she saw that it wasn't the sea at all but Koggala's immense palm-fringed lagoon, twice the size of Colombo harbour. To her disappointment there were no flying boats visible at all: just the jungle coming down in dark green and white tangled creepers to the water's edge. On the opposite shore a couple of Nissen huts were camouflaged in the undergrowth. Towards the sea, on a small hill, stood a white, peeling Buddhist temple, surrounded by temple trees. Far to the south, the road – railway bridge carried the occasional bullock cart to Matara over the narrow neck of water which joined the lagoon to the Indian Ocean.

It was a hot day, with scarcely a breeze to ruffle the clear water. In front of them lay a small beach of shelving sand attended by palms. Sylvia peeled off her sweaters. David, who had returned to the cockpit, came back with a large blanket and a canvas bag which was probably meant for navigational equipment but turned out to be bulging with bottles of orangeade, boiled eggs, corned beef, tomatoes and a bar of chocolate. To these Sylvia mischievously added the two king coconuts she had brought in a string bag.

"There's no barbed wire here like at Mount Lavinia," David said. "It's a restricted area, you see. So we've got it all to ourselves."

Sylvia felt quite weak for a moment. Palm trees, blue water, solitude, a fighter pilot (*almost* a fighter pilot). She would have to revise her ideas about romance. As soon as David had spread out the blanket she sat down on it, took off her shoes and wiggled her bare toes in the warm sand. "You know," she said, "this is the most adventure I've had in years."

"Trouble is, I can't be too late getting back," said David. He opened a bottle of Lanka Orange which spumed all over his hand.

"Don't let's think about Colombo. I bet we could think up a few minor problems for Model T to develop. Even on a short hop like this."

David laughed, and busied himself pouring out the pop. He said, "I shall tell Charlie that I carried you off to a secret rendezvous."

"I'm not married to him you know." She bit into a tomato. "Now I wish you'd tell me something about you. Maria de Vos thinks you're too good to be true. I said I was sure you weren't all that good really, deep down!"

"Did Maria say that?"

"In so many words." She let her mouth fall open and gazed at him, her face a picture of dismay. "Oh, David. I hope I'm not coming between you and Maria. I mean, inviting myself like this!"

"Sylvia! Stop being wicked." David grinned as he passed a picnic plate over to her. "Maria and I have a lot in common, that's all. We both feel... outsiders, in a way."

Sylvia felt a stab of pure jealousy, so sharp she almost choked on the corned beef. She looked at David, his English face with its long straight nose and sunburnt cheeks. "Maria, yes. She always will be, poor thing. But you? What makes you an outsider?"

"It's a long story."

They ate in silence for a while. Nothing stirred around them, not even the coconut fronds, drooping in the heat. Far out to sea Sylvia could see the catamaran sails of Malay fishermen, black commas on the blue horizon. She lay back on the blanket in a tumble of blonde hair, her hands behind her head, her breasts tight against her white blouse.

"We used to have a boy," she said. "His name was Michael. He's with the Tancreds now. His mother was my ayah, so we used to play together when we were little. Bows and arrows, that sort of thing. Every February we'd go down to a lagoon like this for a long weekend. A place called Bentota, there's a resthouse there. The whole household used to go down, and there would be terrible arguments because Daddy hated swimming and Mummy was always trying to get him to go in the water instead of sitting in a deckchair all day in a straw boater, reading official papers. Once, she tipped a bucket of water over him."

"Crikey. What did he do?"

"Oh, nothing. You know what Mummy's like. Everything's a drama with her. I suppose Daddy's used to it by now. He got up and moved the deckchair out into the sun, and carried on reading till his clothes were dry. Mummy felt so guilty, she let him eat two whole plates of Bentota oysters for dinner. I remember, he was sick the next day. But anyway...."

David had got up on one elbow and was looking at her.

"Anyway it was when I was – I don't know how old. I'd gone behind the rocks to change. I thought someone was peering at me, but there was no one there. I got undressed, and started to put my bathing costume on. And I looked up, and there was Michael, staring at me! I got such a fright. There I was, starkers! I must have shouted or something, because Mummy came rushing up, and after that I was told to stay away from the servants' quarters. I wasn't allowed to play with Michael any more. That's when I realised the Ceylonese were different from us; it wasn't just a matter of skin colour. It was funny, you know, like when you learn as a baby that the teddy you kiss to sleep on your pillow isn't really alive. It was a sort of growing up."

"Don't you think it might be you who was different? Not the other way round?"

She looked at him sideways, through a film of golden hair. "You mean, it's us who are the outsiders. Not the natives."

"Yes."

"*There!*" She screamed in triumph, and threw a tomato at him. "That's what you were *supposed* to say, noodle! You see, I'm an outsider too! We have *lots* in common!"

144

Halfway between laughter and dismay, David sat up. His white shirt was bloody with the squashed tomato.

"Sylvia! You beast!"

She hurled another tomato at him. "Who are you calling a beast!"

Boiled eggs and bits of bread sailed through the air, until Sylvia called Pax and got to her feet, breathless with laughter. She took off her blouse and her slacks and held them up with a wail of dismay.

"David! Look what you've done to me!"

"I'm just as bad. Look at me!" He pulled off his shirt. He was surprisingly hairy for such a civilised man, she noticed. The dark chest-hairs were sprinkled well below the wedge of sun-tan under his throat. A little trickle of them ran down from his belly button to the buckle of his trousers.

"Oh, come on," she exclaimed impatiently. "Let's go for a swim."

"We can't go for a swim. We've got nothing to wear."

"Don't be so boring. Nobody can see us. It's lovely to swim with nothing on." She ran down to the water's edge. Taking off her brassière and knickers, she flung them behind her with an air of abandon, and waded into the water.

It was colder than she expected. With much gasping and splashing she struck out from shore. When she turned on her back she saw David standing in his underpants at the edge of the water, his hands on his hips.

"Come on in!" she cried. "It's ripping! What are you waiting for?"

At that, he ran with giant strides into the lagoon and dived. Sylvia trod water and waited. But David surfaced some yards away from her, and lay on his back, and floated. He was so shy; painfully shy. In the distance between them she sensed the invisible presence of Charlie.

She swam quietly, for a few minutes, until she was close enough inshore to tread the sandy bottom. Then with a scream she disappeared. When she came up, her face looked anguished. She was holding on to her foot. David called out her name and struck out powerfully towards her.

"I'm here!" he shouted. Gently he picked her up. She threw her arms around his neck. He asked, "What is it? What happened?"

"I'm sorry. I'm sorry. It was my fault. I trod on something horribly soft and squelchy. I think it was alive. Ugh!" She shuddered.

"Come on, princess." With a sudden, awkward movement he bent his head and kissed her on the lips. "I'll take you to dry land."

He set her down on the blanket. She was shivering.

"Can I get you anything?"

"Yes please. My purple sweater." She nodded. "Over there."

When he came back, she was examining her foot. She pulled the sweater down to her hips and sat cross-legged on the blanket, in the sun. David perched on the extreme other edge of the blanket, clasping his hands round his knees, not speaking. Sylvia rolled over on her tummy. At eye level, a few inches away, a tiny pink crab scuttled sideways, at speed, and hid in a shell. She stole a look at David sitting there, so closed up within himself. But he had kissed her.

"I wish you would tell me about it," she said.

"About what?"

"You don't know how lucky you are. You can go and fight. You can *do* something. There's nothing we can do except try to help. And you won't let me."

"I can't. I can't let you."

"Yes, you can."

He wouldn't look at her. "Daddy told me once," she said, lying in a good cause, "he said, War is all about gathering rosebuds before they turn into Flanders poppies. What do you think he meant?"

"Sylvia. . . ."

"I think he meant there are times when you don't worry what's round the next corner. You take what's in front of you. You take what's offered."

She said this in a low voice, looking at the roots of the palm trees digging into the white sand. The day was fierce and still. She fancied she could hear the water wrinkling on the shore.

Then David was taking her up, he was lifting her into his arms. He kissed her on the lips, so roughly that it took her by surprise and she lifted her arm to resist him, before letting it fall across his shoulder. He must have felt her body soften, because he opened her mouth with his tongue and went on kissing her, in a hungry way Charlie had never kissed her, as if he was sucking out her marrow and her marrow was leaving her body with little shivers of pleasure and passing into his.

Sylvia's purple sweater was rucked up round her shoulders. She felt his hands exploring her body, in places they surely had never ventured on Maria's skin. She crossed her arms and lifted

146

the sweater over her head, shaking out her hair, and then pushed back against the hardness of his body, giving little moans of pleasure. Running her hands down his long muscular sides she traced with her fingers round the elastic of his underpants before sliding them down over his bottom, so unfairly neater and smaller than hers.

Who did what first she afterwards could not remember. What she did remember was sitting looking down at him between her breasts while his clasped hands pressed her bare back and he moved his, well, penis, up and down inside her, with such an expression of pain on his face, before he came, that it almost made her feel guilty for enjoying herself so much.

After it was over, she cleaned herself up with a paper napkin and got dressed. David sat naked on the blanket, regarding her. Behind him the sun speared off Model T's propeller blade.

He said, "Are you Florence Nightingale or do you love me?"

"Oh gosh. A bit of both."

"Come here."

She finished buttoning her blouse, and went over to him. With his delicate fingers he lifted a strand of hair out of the corner of her mouth and kissed her, gently this time.

"Are you still an outsider?" she asked with a tremulous smile.

"Not today. Not with you. Never again with you."

He gazed at her in such a strange, grave way that Sylvia dropped her eyes. In a moment he might tell her that he loved her more than anything in the world, and she wouldn't know how to respond. Why did he have to be so mysterious and intense, when sex was supposed to be jolly, sex was supposed to clear the air? She gave a little shrug of her shoulders and said with a grin, "Do you think we should get airborne again?"

While David got his clothes on, and went to warm up the engines of Model T, Sylvia finished stuffing the picnic things – the empty bottles, the chocolate wrapping – into the canvas bag. Pulling the heavy blanket towards her to fold it, she saw it obliterate the impress of their two bodies in the sand. She paused for a second, with a little frown, then gathered everything into her arms and ran to the plane, leaving behind the two coconut husks.

5 April 1942.   12.15 a.m. Indian Ocean.

In the destroyer Isokaze, in the vanguard of Vice-Admiral Nagumo's Striking Force, sailors hear a solitary aircraft overhead. A message is radioed to Akagi. Nagumo sends up six Zero fighters under the command of the fighter escort group leader on board Akagi, Lieutenant-Commander Shigeru Itaya. Within minutes, Flight-Lieutenant Graham's 205 Squadron Catalina has been shot down with the loss of all her crew.

Nagumo is well satisfied. His Zeros have once again shown themselves to be proficient at night take-offs and landings. The enemy Catalina may have transmitted the position of his Striking Force, but almost certainly had no more time than the other flying boat to find out its composition and strength. If the element of surprise has been lost, the element of unpredictability remains in his favour.

Only one matter still has to be seen to before Nagumo can turn in for the sleep he badly needs. Yesterday, as the Striking Force turned north towards Ceylon, his fellow-Admiral, Jisaburo Ozawa, sailed into the Bay of Bengal with a carrier raiding force consisting of Ryujo, five heavy cruisers, one light cruiser and a number of destroyers. A signal has to be despatched to Ozawa to make sure he is in a position to co-ordinate his first raids on British coastal shipping in the Bay with Nagumo's dawn attack on Ceylon.

If Naval General Staff intelligence is accurate, Ozawa will be able to take his pick of British merchant shipping all the way from Madras to the Ganges Delta. He should have no trouble either taking a heavy toll of the shipping cleared out of Colombo and Trincomalee and sent north to India to escape the Ceylon attack. The Indian economy is known to the General Staff to be dependent on its coastal trade. If Ozawa can disrupt this traffic, and possibly launch his intended raids on the Indian mainland at Cocanada and Vizagapatam, it will be a crippling blow. Carried on for any length of time, it would mean that the British forces opposing Lieutenant-General Shojiro Iida's Fifteenth Army in Burma would be forced to bring all of their supplies overland.

A crippling blow ... not only in military terms but psychologically as well. Nagumo is aware of the open discontent with British rule in India. Gandhi has been making speeches; so has Nehru. Already, in Malaya, some of the 60,000 Indian troops defeated by the Imperial Army have begun to throw in their lot with the Greater East Asia Co-Prosperity Sphere. India is like a rotten tree, leaning towards the axe. ... The opportunities opening up before Nagumo are almost too painfully bright to contemplate.

After Pearl Harbor, Nagumo was invited to the Imperial Palace for an audience with his Emperor. This, the most illustrious moment of his life, was blighted when, against all the prior advice of his Chief of Staff, he unaccountably lapsed into inelegant phraseology, and addressed himself (which was even worse) to the Emperor in person instead of to the household officials beside him through whom all intercourse with the Emperor was channelled. Only a second audience with his Imperial Majesty will mitigate the shame of this blunder, which remains indelible. If, after crushing the British Eastern Fleet, Nagumo were to sail on and join forces with Ozawa in the Bay of Biscay and bring India to its knees, that audience would be granted, he has no doubt of it.

The Admiral gives orders that he should be woken one hour before the Striking Force reaches flying-off position. Then he retires to his cabin. The Yamato spirit, the spirit of old Japan, burns within him; but he feels the baleful spectre of Yamamoto at his shoulder.

He will wait upon the outcome of this mission before deciding his next move.

On the map in Guy Tancred's office, Bruce MacAlister's rubber estate at Kitulgala was marked with a black pin. He was refusing to slaughter-tap his rubber trees – one of the very few planters to hold out against the directive issued by Guy in Dunlop Orient's name.

It meant a long and tiresome journey up into the hill country. Guy had put it off for two reasons. The first was that in a face-to-face interview he would be obliged to issue the ultimatum which courtesy forbade him to put in writing; that if a planter persisted in his refusal, Dunlop Orient would reserve the right to dismiss him from his estate – in effect destroying his career.

The second was that Bruce MacAlister was Jill's uncle – and a father to her in all but name, so Harry had said.

Gradually, after much hard talking and hard feeling, the other black pins – even Harry's – came off the map. At the end of January, when only MacAlister's remained, Guy picked up the telephone and rang Kelani Lodge. In a formal voice he explained the situation to Jill. It was not his fault . . . he was obeying instructions from Dunlop and the Rubber Controller . . . the fall of upland Malaya had put enormous pressure on Ceylon rubber supplies. His sister-in-law evidently had seen this coming. She sounded neither surprised nor particularly upset. It would be best if she came with him to Kitulgala, she advised. Michael would drive the two of them up together to see her uncle.

That night, when the rickshaw girl came up to his narrow room at the Metropole, Guy gave her a lady's watch and a pair of rayon stockings and sent her back to York Street.

He took a taxi out to Kelani the following morning. He wore the pale cream suit – possibly to demonstrate to Jill that the East had not at all succeeded in changing him; possibly to convince himself. When the taxi came round the steep bend in front of the Lodge he half-expected to see her standing on the verandah, shading her eyes in the sun. Instead, there was the Morris with its boot open, and the sound of her voice organising the blankets and the picnic basket.

151

He paid off the taxi. He stood with his briefcase on the gravel drive, his eye caught by a flash of sun from a tall aerial he hadn't seen before, on the roof. Jill came round the side of the car. She was wearing a bush-jacket and slacks, and – the first he'd seen of them – a pair of sun-glasses. When she took them off, he saw she had been crying.

"Something I have to ask you," she said, stopping some few feet away from him. "Would you mind doing some driving later on?"

"Not at all. Why?"

"Harry's taken Michael off somewhere. I was hoping I wouldn't have to drive the whole way there and back." Before he could say anything she hurried on. "I hope it's all right if I don't offer you coffee? I'd like to get started. Kitulgala's quite a long way."

Jill's driving was stylish, impulsive, cavalier. Guy wanted to say how women's driving always reflected their natures, and tickle her curiosity, but he thought better of it. In profile her face looked blurred, as if tears had washed away the strong lines of her jaw and cheekbones. He scratched his ear.

"How is everything?" he enquired.

"Fine. The factory's working at full capacity; Harry's pleased. The Hoathlys – you know – came up for Saturday lunch. We played tennis. I've done a fair bit of painting. The garden's really coming into its own. Did you see it?"

"Up as far as the drive I saw it." He paused. "When I said How is everything, I really meant How are you."

"Thank you, I get by. Talk to me about Colombo, Guy. Open a window in my life; bring some colour in. How are you and Sylvia?"

He was affronted. "Really, I hardly see her. She's still pining for Charles Bilbow. We went last week to see Tyrone Power in *Blood and Sand* at the New Olympia."

"Rather a smelly little cinema, isn't it?"

"Is it? I suppose it is. Sylvia came equipped with newspaper to spread on the seats. She said the Indian troops brought cane-bugs in."

"Was she bitten?"

"No."

"Good."

"Jill—"

"How about Kitty Clarke? She's always good for a bit of colour. Usually an unlikely shade of cerise or magenta."

152

"Do you talk about me in these terms behind my back?"

"I haven't colour-coded you yet. I was thinking of amber."

Guy decided to move on from this topic. "I had dinner at the Clarkes', as a matter of fact. Shortly after the New Year. Your friends the Hoathlys were there. Eric Hoathly doesn't have much social conversation, does he?"

"This is a country of strong, silent men."

"Kitty told me he's a brilliant preacher. Perhaps he's more talkative in a surplice and cape."

"Let me guess. You had roast beef in batter, and suet pudding with golden syrup."

"Nearly. It was chicken à la king."

"Dear Kitty. Does she still have her tank of tropical fish? All those blind mouths opening and shutting, like I imagine dinner at the Colombo Club. It used to put me off my suet. What else is going on?"

"The war mostly, I suppose. Colombo's rapidly turning into a refugee centre. At the Colombo Club they're grumbling that nobody dresses for dinner. According to my boss the Galloping Major, Ceylon is now officially a Bastion, if not yet the Last Bastion. Apparently Field-Marshal Wavell honoured the island with a flying visit last week. And you know, you need a permit for everything – government buildings, the harbour warehouses. You even need a permit for the officers' beach at Mount Lavinia."

"I bet Sylvia has one."

He ignored this. "I went to drinks at the Ingram Bywaters', to speak for a moment of social climbing. They don't only have boys, they have major-domos. One of them brought round corned beef canapés, which is presumably one of Mrs I.B.'s contributions to the war effort. Percy Buller was there—"

"With the invisible Mrs Buller?"

"No. His excuse this time was that they've just had a break-in. His wife got into a panic, thinking Singapore was going to fall and what were they going to do with the house and the furniture. She packed all the silver, because she's planning to leave in the first evacuation. Then she unpacked it to make sure it had been packed properly and nothing had been stolen. The same night they had a burglary and it all went."

This time he got a smile out of Jill. "She made him write to the *Ceylon Times* last year," she said, "about men she saw, 'big, hulking Ceylonese' bathing in the river with nothing more than a pocket handkerchief around their middles, and how it was a disgrace to public morality. Poor old Percy. Him and that little dachshund. At least it's preferable to that horrid, snappy little Pekinese of Mrs I.B.'s."

"Popo. It collapsed of the heat during the drinks party and had to be carried away – probably to the punkah-wallah, Tony Apple said."

"It was lucky to escape internment, if you ask me. Harry calls them flying foxes, that Colombo crowd. He says they all hang together in their plump furs on the same fruit trees and screech at one another. I think that's a bit unfair. Mrs Ingram Bywater is doing a lot for the refugees, which is more than I am, stuck out here."

He hadn't seen his brother since the New Year. "Why," he asked, "doesn't Harry ever seem to enjoy himself?"

She turned her face slightly, and then looked back at the road. "What would you know about it?"

"Except when he's alone. Climbing up Mount Pedro, or tinkering with his transmitter in the garden shed."

She said defiantly, "I don't see what's wrong with that. Look at George Donaldson and his model railway. It takes up the whole of the top verandah. Anyway, Harry doesn't have much time for your social pleasures. Donald, his *Sina Dorai*, is in hospital with a bad bout of malaria. It's left Harry having to do all his work as well."

Guy fell silent. If Jill wasn't prepared to talk about Harry he couldn't force her to. He looked around. They had left the railway behind them at Avisawella and were driving towards the foothills of the Central Province. The Kitulgala road went on to Hatton, up one of the steepest passes in Ceylon.

Jill picked up the pieces. "I had a call from Liz Donaldson yesterday. I don't think she's having much fun either. She says George spends most of his spare time looking through newspapers for bullish news about Singapore and then reading it out and driving everyone silly. We're either poised for a major breakthrough or else heavily outnumbered and fighting back inch by inch. She says she can't take much more of it. They had *their* car battery removed last week, and everyone is convinced there's somebody going round stealing these things to power a transmitter to send secret information to the Japs. As if that wasn't enough, she's still waiting to hear where her son's been posted. And she's got Sylvia moaning that just when Charlie Bilbow's gone, her Burgher friend Maria de Vos has been tactless enough to start going on dates with some airman. . . ."

"David Gifford."

"Yes."

"The one at Sylvia's party, that time I'd at last got you to talk about yourself." He went on bitterly before she could answer. "Was that such a crime? Am I never to be forgiven for it?"

With a squeal of brakes, Jill skidded the car to a halt at the side of the road. For a moment she sat still, her hands on the wheel. White dust hung in the air.

"You drive," she said.

Guy got out, stumbling on the loose dirt verge, and went round to the driver's side. This was an area of spice gardens; he smelled cinnamon, and something sharper, the smell of burning. He pushed back the seat in silence and drove away.

"Let me tell you about Bruce MacAlister," Jill said in an even voice beside him. "Then I'll have talked to you about me. My grandparents were Scottish, like everybody else's. They had two sons, Bruce and my father who was two years younger, and they both emigrated in 1905. Bruce came here. My dad went to Australia. It was a kind of rivalry, I think, to see who would do better. And Dad was doing rather well for himself in Melbourne. He set up a photographic studio which specialised in Society portraits – if you can believe there was Society in Melbourne forty years ago. Then he decided to go off and fight for the British in that place you mentioned called Gallipoli, and he didn't come back."

"I'm sorry."

"Don't be. I was only five at the time. Mum tried to keep the studio going, and packed me off to convent school plus a few other ropy institutions. When Uncle Bruce twisted her arm to let me come out to Ceylon I was pleased as Punch. He never had any children, you see. He married late: an Australian farmer's daughter, Diane, he met at a Boat Dance at the Bristol Hotel – they used to save up to come to Ceylon and marry Brits, you know – and she died in childbirth three years later. Conditions were none too grand up here then, you can imagine."

"So you stayed with him?"

"For six months. Getting things straight. I'd had enough after that, you'll realise why. And Bruce could see that Kitulgala was no place for a young girl. So I came down to Colombo, and he put me through nursing training at the Fraser Home. For which I owe him a lot."

"And then you met Harry and lived happily ever after." He glanced at her. She was twisting the elephant-hair bracelets on her wrist. "Isn't that right?"

155

"Yes it is. I was telling you about Bruce. He was very kind to me. I trust and respect him more than anyone I know – respect his judgement, I mean. He can be hard. He's had a very hard life. It isn't easy getting rubber trees to produce at nearly 2500 feet. He's the kind of man . . . how to explain . . . he believes hot baths brought about the fall of the Roman Empire and we're going the same way. An old Empire type, I suppose. But not the sort of planter you find hanging around Colombo." She glanced at Guy's cream suit. "I don't know what you're going to make of him."

"You mean, you don't know what he's going to make of me."

She laughed shortly, and leant over the seat to get lemonade from the back. She had a deliciously neat figure, he noticed again. Compact but feminine; not chubby, like lots of the Cinnamon Gardens girls. To appraise her in these terms, he knew, was a form of retaliation for her disinterest in him. It served her right.

He drank the lemonade she gave him, and drove on. The subtropical landscape of the low country was thinning out. The ground became hillier, and the rice-paddies less frequent. Beyond Yatitantota the road was blocked for some sort of war exercise, and they had to make a diversion of twenty miles. The picnic basket in the boot, Jill informed him, was full of groceries for Bruce MacAlister, not their lunch, as he'd hoped. They stopped at the rest-house in Kitulgala and ate curried chicken and rice.

The Kitulgala rubber estate was still some miles away, far enough up the Hatton road to take them, to his amazement, right into the hills. As they embarked upon the Ginigathena Pass, literally among the tea plantations, a dirt road took them sharply down to the right, and over a rocky spur of hills. Ahead lay a broad valley, its floor darkly carpeted with rubber trees. As if from the air, they could see the estate in its entirety, basking in a dream of greenness under a blinding sun.

MacAlister's bungalow was directly below them, at the head of the valley. Its galvanised-iron roof stood out amid sheltering Casuarinas, flame trees, tulip trees and silk-cotton trees with their deeper crimson blossoms. In isolated dignity it commanded the valley, much as Guy imagined its owner did.

"I used to call it the Lost Valley," said Jill, leaning out of the window. "In my romantic youth."

"Did he plant it himself?"

"Yes. Dunlop Orient bought the ownership from him during the Slump."

156

He drove on. The road – hardly more than a track in places – twisted downwards through the trees, within sound of an invisible murmuring waterfall which three months ago must have been a thundering torrent. It came out at a square brick-and-timber building, bigger but scarcely more pretentious than a settler's log cabin. The ground sloped front and back, and the servants' quarters had been built off to one side, across a flat square of grass on which Guy thought he caught a glimpse of cricket nets.

He pulled up at the porch. Jill jumped out of the car and ran up the steps. A young man, red-cheeked and broad-shouldered, came out to greet her. His amiable face was screwed into a look of acute embarrassment.

"This is Bobby Loomis, Bruce's *Sina Dorai*." Jill introduced them. "Bruce was expecting us for lunch. He's had to go back to work."

"A drainage problem, sir," said Loomis uncomfortably. "We had a storm last night and we've got some flooding down the far end of the estate, where the rubber's interplanted with cacao. Mr MacAlister should be back in an hour or so. . . ."

Guy looked at his watch. Then at Jill. She was frowning.

"It's not his fault, you know," she said. "We were the ones who got delayed. I'll phone Harry. We'll have to stay the night."

The two of them sat on the verandah, mostly in silence, while the house boys came and went with rattling tea-cups and the SD made what little conversation he could. He talked of anything but rubber. He talked about the Planters' Club in Kitulgala and the weekly rugger game on Saturday afternoons; and had they heard the report of Carole Lombard's death in a plane crash, what a jolly awful thing to happen; and how he wished he'd seen Joe Louis defend his world heavyweight title against Buddy Baer at Madison Square Garden.

All the time Guy could hear the invisible waterfall, and the high bark of wanderoo monkeys in the forested slopes around them. Jill was restless. She got up and prowled around the bungalow; he could hear her banging drawers and moving things. A triangle of shadow began to enlarge across the plantation.

There was a light crunching of hoofs on the gravelled drive. A Boy ran out and held the reins of a piebald mare. Its mud-spattered rider dismounted and came up the steps. Jill ran forward and embraced him.

Guy looked nervously at this uncle of hers. He stood roughly his height, a couple of inches over six feet, but his thinness made him seem taller. He had a bony head, its narrowness accentuated by his close-cropped hair, and a high, weathered complexion. Only in the clear dark eyes was there anything of Jill in his face.

Guy stepped forward to introduce himself. MacAlister greeted him with a perfunctory handshake and a slap on the back. Loomis got the smile.

"Thanks, Bobby," the planter said gruffly. "Could you give the *kangani* a hand? He's still at the factory, trying to sort out the mess." To Guy he added, "Give me a tick while I change out of my things. Veeraswami will bring you a whisky."

Guy paced the verandah. It was patently ridiculous that he should have to waste all this time on one obstinate old planter, who proceeded to behave in such a high-handed manner. He glanced at Jill. She was grinning.

"I'll leave you two while you talk business," she said.

Just then her uncle reappeared, in slippers and a bulky plaid dressing-gown and what looked like a pair of long johns underneath. "You're staying the night," he said crisply. "Veeraswami is making up the beds. Don't disappear, Jill. Stay and see fair play. Tell me how Harry is doing. Is his *Sina Dorai* still peelie-wally?"

"Yes. Malaria, I'm afraid. He's in the nursing home in Hatton. We've traced it to the drainage at his bungalow. Harry reminded him to pour sump-oil on the standing water, but the mosquitoes had bred by then."

"Poor Donald. Should have remembered, though. It's one of the first rules of life in the East, Mr Tancred," he went on, addressing Guy as if he were a child. "Don't let your drains back up." He sipped his whisky and studied the younger man. "That is a very smart suit. Did you buy it in Colombo?"

"London."

"I bought a tussore suit like that to go dancing with my wife. The snag was, it went yellow after a year out here. You learn better after a while. I don't know how long you've been in Ceylon, Mr Tancred?"

"I came out in late November."

"November? *Late* November you say. I came out to Ceylon thirty-seven years ago this summer. All the money I had was borrowed. I took over a plantation that had gone to seed; I cleared it; and I started from scratch. It was seven years before I could build this bungalow. Another ten years before I could repay my loans. That's seventeen years of my life, Mr Tancred, before I could consider buying a new suit to go courting my wife."

"Yes."

"I was the first planter in the history of Ceylon to operate a high-yield *Hevea* plantation at a height of 2500 feet. Nobody thought it could be done. Dunlops didn't think it could be done. Too much rainfall! Not enough sun! I proved them all wrong, and when I had to sell, let me tell you, Dunlop Orient came cap in hand."

Guy nodded. "It must have been a wrench, having to sell, after you'd built this place up from nothing."

"Don't humour me, Mr Tancred. I had to sell because of blasted government interference, the same blasted interference that's brought you here today. I was getting twelve shillings a pound for my rubber in 1911. In 1931, after the government allowed a free-for-all in rubber exports from Ceylon and Malaya, I was getting fourpence a pound. Three years later, once the big companies had moved in and bought out all the entrepreneurs like me, they brought back export restrictions and pushed the price right up again. Now – don't interrupt me – I believe in commerce, Mr Tancred. Commerce is what made Britain great. Not politicians; not the Army. It was the merchants who got things done. And I don't mean the get-rich-quick types who want to take out of a country and put nothing back. I mean the producers. People like me, who build something up and cherish it. We're a dying breed, Mr Tancred. The more meddling there is from Head Office, the less it's worth our while, God damn you all."

MacAlister's glass was steady as he raised it to his lips. Guy suspected he'd prepared his fine speech. He leant forward, his hands between his knees. "You say you're not an opportunist, Mr MacAlister. You're a team player. You believe in staying and seeing something through. How do you reconcile that with being the only rubber planter left in the Dunlop Orient group – probably the only one left in the whole of Ceylon – not to slaughter-tap your rubber trees? Have you realised the advantage that would give you in the first few years after the war?"

"You dare to sit there and accuse me of sharp practice!"

"No. Not sharp practice. Short-sightedness. Have you any idea of the prices you'd be able to command? Don't think other planters haven't got the interests of their rubber trees at heart. They've made the sacrifice."

"Tancred, this is not a normal plantation," explained MacAlister with a display of self-restraint. "If you had any experience of planting, you would know that. At this height, rubber trees are very quickly exhausted if you slaughter-tap them. There's a higher risk of root disease. New trees take longer to become lactiferous, even if you succeed in grafting them on to old stock. After three years of increased production you'd have nothing, nil production, for at least as long again. As your files will have told you, I retire in four years. I want to leave a going concern, not a wilderness."

"You'll leave a graveyard if the Japs arrive." Guy was beginning to get angry.

"What do you mean?"

"Have you heard of scorched-earth? That's what the Japs have been doing to plantations in Kelantan and Perak. Probably Selangor too, by now. It's not just simply pressure on Ceylon rubber supplies. It's what could happen if the Japs get to Ceylon. You talk about government interference. I'd say we were at the last ditch. Are you prepared to see thirty-seven years of work here put to the torch?"

"Is that what you were told to say by Rawling?" MacAlister enunciated the name with disgust.

"It's common knowledge in Colombo. I don't have your experience of plantations, Mr MacAlister. But I do know what's going on in the world outside."

It was getting dark. He couldn't see the expression on the planter's face. MacAlister clapped his hands – mockingly, Guy thought for an instant, but it was for Veeraswami to come and light the Aladdin lamp on the verandah table. In its suddenly brilliant flame their faces looked white and strained.

Jill got to her feet. Without looking at either of them she said, "I think, if you don't mind, I'll go and see Cook about dinner."

"It's curry," said MacAlister. He raised an eyebrow at Guy. "I hope you can cope with hot curry."

"Yes."

"Good. If you'll excuse me, I'm going to take a bath before dinner. If you want to use the thunderbox, Jill will show you where it is."

Guy was left alone on the verandah. He stared at the Aladdin lamp. "Made in Britain" was inscribed round its base. Its glare dimmed in the horde of flying insects which had swarmed out of nowhere and hurled themselves in wave after wave at its fragile glass. *Was* all this what Rawling had told him to say? Well, no: not in so many words. But if one stood back and looked at the strategy behind it – it was Rawling's without doubt. The furious

160

drive on production quotas, the tactics of last resort – it was Major Rawling mobilising for war.

A muffled bang beside him made him start out of the chair. Under the insect invasion, the Aladdin lamp had exploded in a puff of smoke. Rescuing him from the darkness Veeraswami put his head round the verandah door.

"Dinner is served, Master," he said.

Inside, the bungalow had a spartan air. Its rooms were large and comfortless. Cumbersome pieces of teak furniture stood around the walls in forlorn muster. In the bookcase, propped up by old ginger-jars, stood some dog-eared detective stories, McIan's *Highlanders at Home*, a volume entitled *The Rattle of the Stumps* and a complete set of Wisden.

The only colour came from four or five oil paintings, which Guy presumed to be Jill's. One, in the dining room, had an almost luminous intensity. It made him think of the Douanier Rousseau. It showed a bay encircled by low rocky cliffs and lit by the reddish glow of the dying sun – except that the bay was dark green and writhing with jungle foliage and the twisted branches of tall trees as far as the eye could see.

He had drunk enough whisky to cope with the hot meat curry, served with rice pancakes, curry puffs, a fish sambal and plenty of vegetables chopped in coconut. Jill ate sparingly and said little. MacAlister, dressed now in a dark suit, had got his second wind.

"Ten years ago you wouldn't have had a meal like this," he said with a dour satisfaction. "No electric light, of course. No refrigerators. Just blocks of ice in zinc-lined boxes packed with sawdust. Sewage went into a hole in the ground. Your brother will remember those days."

"He used to write home about the rats in his bungalow."

"Rats, and worse. I've had leopard around once or twice. And when you're a young apprentice you don't get a bungalow like this. It's a four-room cabin built of rough brick, with a corrugated-iron roof. You're there by yourself, miles from the nearest out-station, in the middle of nowhere. Nobody to talk to. You're too junior to be allowed to join the local planters' club. You fall back on your inner resources, and if those aren't strong enough, heaven help you. Even rats can be company then."

Guy shuddered at something he wanted to forget. MacAlister smiled grimly. "You probably haven't seen a rat, have you, Tancred? There can't be many on the loose at Head Office. It's a pity a few more people from London can't come out and see what life's really like here, before instructing us what to do."

161

"The pity, Mr MacAlister, is that I can't invite you to London right now to see what life is really like back where everything is so civilised and easy." Guy was controlling himself with difficulty. "I worked as an ARP warden, sir, during the Blitz. Many of us at Dunlop's did. I saw plenty of rats, oh yes. Hackney rats. Mayfair rats. City of London rats. And it's true that they sometimes enjoyed human company. Except that the humans were dead and the rats were feeding on them. You sit out here, six thousand miles away, and read in your newspaper and hear on the radio about how Britain Can Take It and everybody's Smiling Through and life goes on with a few sacrifices here and there. You don't hear – because they don't tell you, it's bad for morale – about the dead, and the ones pinned under tons of masonry, and the others with bits sliced off them by shrapnel or flying glass. Women and children too, and thousands of them in London alone, you just ask the hospitals, they'll tell you. I should think a few of them wouldn't say no to a lonely jungle cabin if it meant they could keep all their limbs and the bombers weren't coming over night after night. . . ." The memories had seized him and he sat there quite oblivious, his breath coming in shallow gasps. After a moment he excused himself, and went out to the lavatory.

When he came back, they were in the verandah room. MacAlister pointed to a chair. "I've told Jill she must bring you with her for a weekend up here if you'd like it," he said gruffly. "There's mahseer in the rivers, which means the fishing's first-class. Best game fish in Asia, the mahseer."

"Oh, yes?"

"And it's coming up for the butterfly run," said Jill, leaning back with her hands behind her head. "Bruce will tell you," she added, glancing at her uncle. "Do you remember the week I arrived, it was the week of the annual butterfly migration? I couldn't believe my eyes, I thought I was in Paradise. Millions of them, in a continuous stream, that drifted overhead all afternoon down the valley. Yellow and black, pinks, a lovely periwinkle blue: I'd never seen such colours. And you said they were all on their way to Adam's Peak to die."

"That's the coolies' story," returned MacAlister. "Hence their name, Samanaliya, from the Hindu name for Adam's Peak, Samanakande, Hill of Siva. It's never been disproved. But then, nor has it been disproved that Ceylon is the historical Paradise. It is what the Mohammedans believe. It's perpetual spring, near enough. And there's Adam's footprint on the Peak for all the pilgrims to see." He nodded upwards at another of Jill's paintings, above the mantelpiece, in which Ceylon's most famous peak reared its perfect pyramidal shape above a cloud-mass cloven by its dawn shadow.

"Buddha's footprint according to the Sinhalese," said Jill. Her face looked troubled. "Harry always used to quote Sir John Mandeville," she continued. "'From Seyllan to Paradise is forty miles, the sound of the fountains of Paradise is heard there.'"

They fell silent, as if listening. Bullfrogs croaked. An owl hooted from the trees. Guy felt calmer. He thought of the invisible waterfall he'd heard from the verandah. Paradise was always just out of reach, whether it was the kind that was guarded by an angel with a flaming sword or the kind that sat just a few feet away from him, her heart-shaped face lifted up thoughtfully to the painting on the wall.

It was getting late. By tacit agreement they talked about things that did not vex them but brought them closer: Bruce MacAlister about growing up in Aberdeen where his father worked as a foreman in the comb works of Messrs Stewart & Co., who each year converted eleven hundred tons of horns, hoofs, indiarubber and tortoiseshell into eleven million combs, spoons, cups and paper-knives; Jill about her one memory of her father in Melbourne, walking up Heidelberg Road towards their home near Darling Gardens pushing a wheelbarrow in which squatted a large Grecian bust – presumably to use as a studio prop, since it went on collecting dust for years after his death, until her mother one day slapped its marble cheek in a fit of exasperation and knocked it off its stand.

Guy, perhaps because it was late and a long way from anywhere, found himself recalling an expedition he'd made fifteen years ago into the Tancred past. From his mother's house in Kensington he had got up before the rest were stirring. With his bright new birthday sovereign in his pocket he'd bicycled to Paddington Station where he'd bought a railway ticket to Tiverton and back. Unloading his bicycle the other end, he had ridden the seven miles to the River Rubble and then along the valley to Rubble House, where his grandfather had lived and his father, Reginald, had been born.

The lovely Queen Anne house was locked and shuttered. Its American owners had gone away; there was no sign of the housekeeper. He found a scullery window unlocked, and wriggled through. It felt grand and sad to be there, like visiting a family vault in which the coffins all were empty. He wandered through rooms of dust-sheeted furniture, and opened windows on to the same view down the narrow lawn that generations of his ancestors must have looked out upon. In the drawing room he stared at the Tancred crest worked into the stone fireplace, and then at the smoke-darkened portrait above of Sir Henry Tankard, Bt, 1670–1726, who rebuilt Rubble House and whose dissolute, snobbish son (to judge from his own portrait) changed Tankard to Tancred because it sounded more impressive.

Then he heard the back door open, the footsteps in the kitchen. In a panic – he was all of fourteen – he thought about lying low and escaping through the scullery door when the housekeeper's back was turned. He gazed up at Sir Henry Tankard; he saw an expression of deepest shame on the cracked features; he knew that here of all places a Tancred could not turn and run. He went down and hung his head to the housekeeper. . . .

Guy hesitated at this point in the story, a little puzzled now by what had seemed then perfectly in the nature of things.

"Don't be theatrical," said Jill.

"I was just thinking. You see, she burst into tears. She was an old woman, she'd known my grandfather and 'Master Reginald'. She made me sit down all by myself at the big kitchen table and served me with crumpets and cherry cake. A Tancred was master of the house again. And yet I couldn't wait to swallow my tea and belt back up the road to Tiverton. At that age I felt I didn't belong in that wonderful mansion with its portraits of my family and the view down the river valley. I belonged in a little terrace house in Kensington with a backyard and a few photograph albums and the traffic going past the door. I was frightened, I suppose. I'd opened up this grand and glorious past and it was too big for me. I wanted to be my own size again."

He stopped. Bruce MacAlister, still bolt upright in his chair, had started to nod off.

Jill said, very softly, "I think we should get the Empire to bed, don't you?"

Breakfast, MacAlister had warned them, would be early and light – *chota hazri* he called it, using the Indian term. Guy was woken at dawn and came out to find Jill and her uncle already on the verandah, drinking pineapple juice. Below them a cock crowed out of the whiteness. They were floating in a sea of mist which obliterated the valley.

MacAlister stood up when he arrived. Clearly impatient to get to his beloved rubber trees, he stamped his riding boots on the coir matting. His mare whinnied.

"I assume you don't want to see over the plantation, Tancred, so I'll say goodbye." He extended his hand. "I will do as you ask and slaughter-tap the estate. I'm in the middle of a replanting programme, it will mean abandoning it, but I can made a sacrifice as well as the next man. You know my views. I should like Head Office to have them."

As Guy made some reply, MacAlister bent and kissed Jill farewell. He mounted and rode away, very thin and erect, until the mist swallowed him up.

Guy and Jill sat in silence on the verandah. A flock of jabbering parakeets flew overhead, making for their feeding grounds. The boy brought out bacon and eggs for them on a covered plate.

After a minute, Jill said, "You know, I started painting here. Bruce had paints and canvases sent up from Colombo. I got to be pretty good at landscapes. Not so good at the human figure."

"I suppose not."

He felt her touch on his arm. "Don't let it upset you, what Bruce said last night. He's not the kind of man to give in without a fight. He's bitter about Major Rawling, because Dunlop Orient put him straight in as *Periya Dorai* of one of the best-run estates in the low country and let him learn the business from the top; then they made him an Agent. And Bruce . . . you can see he's got a bee in his bonnet about governments. He's always said that Ceylon shows what a lie the old maxim is that Trade follows the Flag. The Portuguese came here because they were searching for curry spices to flavour their salted meat in the winter months. The Dutch were single-minded about cinnamon and couldn't have cared less about the Ceylonese. And now the British: Bruce says we make all this fuss about administration and village welfare, but if the rubber and tea estates were wiped out by disease we'd be out within a year."

"Was Rawling really put in at the top?" The more Guy found out about the Major, the more it fascinated him. He added in a solemn voice, "You mustn't suppose it bothered me, what your uncle was saying. I was actually thinking I might have been too hard on him. You have to be careful how you handle the old Empire types."

Jill smiled to herself. "Do you have a lunch appointment in Colombo?" she enquired.

He shook his head.

"I was thinking, if you didn't have to get back in a hurry, we could do a detour. There's something I want you to see."

She wouldn't tell him what it was. As they returned through Kitulgala and Yatiyantota she seemed nervous, preoccupied. Before the road swung west towards Avisawella along the Kelani valley, she took a left turn and began driving back in the direction of the hills.

After a few minutes, she said with a tremor in her voice, "I can't remember how far this is. Perhaps we'd better turn back."

"I've got lots of time," he lied to her. "Besides, there's plenty to look at."

And indeed there was an unusual amount of industry in the paddy-fields. January was the end of the Maha season, and the ripe paddy was being harvested. In some fields, the women, in cotton waist-cloths and flowered headscarves, were working the furrows in rows of six or eight, scything the paddy and leaving it in sheaves to dry. In others, under the gaze of white paddy birds wheeling like seagulls, men tied the dried paddy in bundles. These they took back in bullock carts to the village threshing grounds where they lay stacked, waiting for the water buffaloes to come and trample out the rice from the stalks in the cool of the evening. Like the view from Rubble House, he was looking at something which could not have changed for hundreds of years.

"The Sinhalese could double their rice crop with modern farming methods," said Jill. "These people could be self-sufficient in rice if they didn't rely on astrology and the devil-priests. Instead we end up with rice rationing; it's absurd."

"Harry would probably say it was the Buddhist way of doing things. You don't meddle with it."

His arrow hit its mark. Jill's hands tightened on the steering wheel. "Don't talk to me about Buddhism!" she cried with a passion. "All that reverence for life, what does it amount to? A mother picking lice out of her daughter's hair and putting them down safely so they can reinfest the child. A Buddhist bus driver putting his passengers in the ditch rather than run over a rat-snake in the road. Do you know why Colombo has a Pasteur Clinic? It's because Buddhists are forbidden to kill rabid pariah dogs. If you'd tended all the rabies cases I have, you'd see a different side to Buddhism."

"Isn't it also the Christian doctrine: thou shalt not kill?"

"I don't see much sign of it in the Christian world at the moment, do you?" She changed the subject. "Was it true, what you

166

said to Bruce about the Japanese putting Malay rubber estates to the torch?"

He hesitated. "Yes. Some of them. So the intelligence reports say. Others they just leave, and I suppose they'll return to jungle."

"So it was a half-truth."

"Look," he said. "You've got to realise. If the East Indies go, Ceylon is the only major rubber producer left to the Allies. India itself only produces one-seventh as much rubber. It's crucial to get maximum production. From everybody."

Jill was silent for a minute; on her face, the inward, mysterious smile. "Well," she remarked finally. "You got what you came for."

They passed a rubber plantation, and then another which was running to seed. The metalled road had narrowed: several times they had to go down on the verge to pass laden bullock carts. They came to a village and Jill stopped the car. There were beads of sweat on her face.

"What time do you make it?" she asked, looking at her own watch.

"Coming up to a quarter past eleven."

"OK." She seemed to reach a decision. She let her hands fall from the wheel. "Let's go for a walk, shall we?"

Guy knew better than to keep on at her with questions. He got out of the car. The heat reflected off the hard earth; he flinched, and shaded his eyes. An acrid scent, perhaps of burning *chena*, mingled with the sour, muddy smell from nearby paddy-fields. Around them were the usual whitewashed cadjan huts, some with a tiny verandah and a kitchen at the back, their roofs thatched with plaited coconut leaves. Each stood in a little clump of trees. He remembered what old Albert had said to him one day at the Donaldsons' – "If a man has six coconut trees, a jak, a cow and a part-share in a rice-field, he needs nothing else in life."

Jill had put on her dark glasses again. She took a paper bag out of the glove-box and held it tightly in her hand. To his surprise, the village verandahs were almost deserted. Even the high barking of the pariah dogs didn't alert the usual curious adults and pestering children. They must all be in the rice-fields, it occurred to him. The pi-dogs, with their narrow eyes and ginger coats stretched over bony ribcages, he shied away from, remembering the Pasteur Institute.

He followed Jill down the village street. An old man, plantain-shaded, beckoned from a doorway, offering king coconuts; Jill smiled and shook her head. He could hear children now, and see the school, a one-room cement building with a galvanised-iron roof and a fenced playground set back from the roadway.

The children, dressed in ragged, spotless white, poured across the playground when they saw Jill and hung, panting and laughing, over the stout cadjan fence.

"Ayubowan!" she called to them in Sinhalese.

"Good morning, Lady!" they chorused in reply.

Opening the bag, Jill took out a handful of boiled sweets and began to distribute them, placing one in each upturned palm as gravely as a priest. They thanked her, each in turn, and craned their necks to make sure nobody got extra. Then they darted back to their barefoot games.

Guy observed this scene with mystification. They were handsome children, to be sure, with their white teeth and shining faces. One in particular, paler-skinned than the others, with brown hair and a serious expression on his face, who took Jill's sweet shyly and lowered his eyes. But was this why she had brought him so far?

"Is this what you wanted me to see?" he called to her.

She paid no attention, but leant on the fence and watched the children playing. Some kicked a football about; the brown-haired boy had picked up a laundry bat and was defending stumps black-chalked on the cream-painted wall.

Not until he came up and took her arm did she snap out of her reverie. "It's not far now," was all she said to him.

They drove on through the village, and up a gentle, forested slope on another curving red-dirt road. The road narrowed as they went upwards, and became a track. Long grass brushed at their heels and scoured the chassis. At a place where there was room to turn – she knew where to find it – she stopped the car and switched off the ignition.

"Do you have any matches?" she asked him.

"Yes. What for?"

"Horse leeches. Just in case."

"You mean we're walking through the jungle?"

She laughed at his dismay. "Up the track, what's left of it. Anyway, you know what the coolies say: Only he who fears snakes sees them!"

"Am I to be told where we're going?"

"You'll know when you get there."

From the boot she took a sun-hat, and tied it with ribbon under her chin. Guy went bareheaded. When they set off, he realised with a shock that what he had taken to be primal jungle was the ruins of an abandoned rubber plantation. Instead of rows of arrow-straight trees, there was a tangle of vegetation. Many of the rubber trees had fallen. Others leant at crazy angles under the weight of lianas, vines and rattans that climbed up them towards the sun. From somewhere underneath there rose a smell like rotting compost. It appalled and fascinated him, this spectacle of Nature attempting to suppress the man-made aberration of itself, like a panther biting at the bullet in its flank.

"What happened?" he asked. "What went wrong?"

"Too much water," Jill replied, a little out of breath. "Chronic root disease. There was nothing anyone could do."

They had walked for ten minutes when the slope reared steeply. The secondary jungle fell away. They were climbing through coarse, waist-high grass that might once have been a lawn. The track, by now no more than a faint trail, came to a dead end. Concrete steps led upwards. Guy could see ahead of them, in the lee of the high ridge, the remains of a small bungalow.

He scrambled up the last few steps, pulling Jill by the hand. This was the kind of place MacAlister had described: the four-room cabin of an apprentice planter, as lonely as hell, a place to go mad in. Now that human life had left it, another kind of life had gradually taken charge. Insects had moved in. Creepers and grasses had pushed through the wooden floor and sprawled up the walls of sun-dried brick.

Gingerly he trod the boards of the narrow verandah. There was a stink in his nostrils of dead matter and animal dung. He kicked open a cobwebbed door: its hinges broke from the rotting frame and it crashed down, sending scuttling things into the dark corners. Peering in, he saw the margarine-coloured walls, the worm-eaten skeletons of chairs around a rusted grate. Someone had tried to make a home out of this godforsaken shack. Next door lay a pile of dry bones, probably left by hunters seeking shelter. From the ceiling hung the metal hook for a mosquito net: the only sign that this had once been a bedroom.

He backed out. Jill was sitting on the verandah in a battered rattan chair, the one piece of furniture that still survived. She looked up at him.

"This was Harry's bungalow," he said.

She nodded.

"My God."

He gazed out over the verandah rail. The ruined plantation stretched in every direction as far as the eye could see.

169

Somewhere there would have been a factory down there, line-rooms, a planter's comfortable dwelling. None of them was visible. Harry would have had to walk a mile or more to hear the sound of another human voice. From this desolate retreat his brother had written those letters, full of humour and adventure, that had so fired Guy's imagination. Letters composed by the flickering light of a gas-lamp, reaching out across a gulf of solitude to a world of friends and family who would not have understood the language of despair.

"This is why you brought me," he said, not looking at her. "You want me to understand the man you married."

She got up and stood behind him, her light cotton jacket brushing his sleeve. "He stayed up here for four whole years as a *Dorai*. The plantation had begun to die around him. Then the manager had a nervous breakdown, and Dunlop Orient decided to cut its losses. Harry was lucky; they would have made him redundant. But he'd contracted some kind of bug – they thought it might be malaria – and by the time he came out of the Fraser Home, there was a vacancy in the Estates Office for a Junior. Then the Assistant's job at Kelani came up, and the Visiting Agent recommended him."

"I wouldn't have lasted six months," Guy reflected aloud.

"Harry was so lonely he trained a gecko to take its meals with him. It was five years into our marriage before he could bring himself to take me here. He said there were too many devil-spirits in the bungalow: he wouldn't tell me what they were. Ghosts of the person he used to be? I don't know. I think he was afraid of them: the only thing I've known him ever be frightened of. He didn't stay long, even then. Not even to look at China Bay."

"China Bay?"

"That was the name he gave it." She looked at him for a moment. "Come. I'll show you. I want you to see everything."

He followed her up a short path behind the cabin that led to the top of the ridge. They walked through a clump of bushy camphor trees, and came out to a patch of grass with a simple wooden bench.

The sight that opened up before him took his breath away. They were standing on the brink of a semi-circle of steep cliffs that curved in twin promontories for a mile or more on either side of them. One hundred and fifty feet below, thick jungle crowded to the base of the cliffs, filling the round valley and surging out the far end in an emerald flood which lapped the sides of a high mountain range in the distance. In its wildness and beauty the

170

scene reminded him of the canvases of the first American romantic painters, who invested landscapes with their vision of the second Eden as they travelled westwards into the unknown.

Awed, he sat down beside her on the bench. He murmured, "It's your picture in the dining room!"

"Yes." Jill took off her sun-hat and put it on the seat between them. "When the monsoon wind gets up it ruffles the tops of the trees and makes them ripple like green water in a bay. It's the westernmost part of the Peak Wilderness Sanctuary: you're looking straight at Adam's Peak when the cloud is off the mountains. Harry made this bench. He used to come up here a lot. He said it gave him reasons for existence. It kept him from losing his grip."

Guy stared at the ruthlessness of jungle below him. China Bay was one great clotted battleground of ironwoods, satinwoods, banyans, fig trees, all fighting upwards against the teeming undergrowth of climbing plants which latched on to them and dragged them down. "Poor Harry," he said at last. "Caught between his devils and the deep green sea."

Jill was silent. He looked at her. Light breaths of wind were brushing her hair against her cheek.

"You would be a reason for anyone's existence," he said with a huskiness in his throat.

"Oh. Harry had others." She looked at her hands, touched the moonstone ring on her finger.

"What do you mean?"

"In the school playground, did you notice that boy? The one with the brown hair?"

"Yes."

"That's Harry's son. Your nephew. By a Sinhalese village girl."

He stared at her. She was looking at her hands. He repeated stupidly, "Harry's son? By a concubine?"

"It happens a lot in the out-stations."

"Sandy Duncannon—"

"Yes. For one. Harry pays her money. Enough for them both, I suppose. He never told me there was a child. When he knew I'd found out he was very angry, he said it was none of my business. He'd had this . . . this girl visit him for eighteen months up here, and he'd paid her off, and that was that." Jill looked up. "You mustn't tell him we went to the village," she said sharply. "He doesn't know I see the boy. . . ."

"Of course I won't."

171

She bent her head again. "His name is Peter. He's very bright. He comes top of the class in English and History."

"Is it because of him that you haven't wanted to have any children?"

"No. It's Harry who doesn't want children. Not me."

"Oh, Jill."

She brushed a stray hair out of her eyes. "I know what Harry means about China Bay. He called it that because it's like the real China Bay, south of Trincomalee harbour where he used to go on leave, sea-fishing for amberjack. It's an aerodrome now. The RAF use it. When we went there – it was before we were married – it was incredibly peaceful. Coconut palms. The sun on the water. Everything I used to dream about the tropics in my convent school. We took a boat out, went swimming, caught a seven-pound kingfish, at least Harry claimed it was seven pounds. He sang songs – *On the road to Mandalay, Where the flyin'-fishes play, And the dawn comes up like thunder outer China 'crost the Bay! . . .*"

Her voice trailed off. Guy reached out and took her hand. Instantly she snatched it from him. "I don't want your pity, you know! If I wanted children, I would have children. If not with Harry, then with someone else! Anyway I have plenty of time, and – things might change." Tossing her head, Jill got up and strode round the bench, her hands in her pockets. "It's not the end of the world," she exclaimed.

Guy was lost in admiration for her mettlesomeness. Lydia would have accepted her fate, or else hired lawyers and sued for divorce. Jill was resolute. He saw her that last time at Kelani Lodge, standing on the verandah in a shaft of sunlight, berating the poets for getting it wrong about the heart. And then again in the garden, warning how the East made people lose control. She had kept hers. She had said nothing.

"Why now?" he asked her. "Why are you telling me this?"

"Why not?"

"Tell me. Please."

Jill sat down, straddling the bench, and put her sun-hat on. Tilting her chin to tie the ribbon, she grinned at him. "Did I tell you what Bruce thought of you? I told him you were arrogant, obstinate – a typical Tancred, I told him. But he liked you. In fact he respected you. He said you had great strength of character and a nice smile."

"Your uncle said that?"

"Well," she admitted. "I added the bit about the smile."

The wind had dropped. The sun burnt his face. He gazed at

her through motionless air. "I want to tell you this," he said. "I love you."

"Oh, Guy." Jill smiled and brushed the back of her hand tiredly across her eyes as if she wanted to sleep. "I think we should go back now," she said.

"Wait."

This time she did not withdraw her hand from his.

"I may be arrogant," he said. "Probably obstinate too. And I expect my mother spoiled me as a child and I pulled the wings off butterflies for all I know. But I am not deceitful or insincere. I know who you are. If I could have stopped myself loving you. . . ."

He could not see her clearly. The sun burnt him through. Jill moved close to him and put her arms round his neck. She was trembling. He could feel the tears on her cheek.

He pulled her round to face him and kissed her on the mouth. To his half-appalled delight she did not pull away from him. She pushed her whole body closer, pressing her soft mouth on his in a kiss which seemed to penetrate to the roots of his being and to lick every part of him with little tongues of fire. He swallowed the flame of her. He pressed her body closer still, to melt it into his. He wanted nothing else ever to exist, except this kiss which united them.

After an unknown while she broke free. Blindly she stumbled forward. For an instant he thought she was going to throw herself over the cliff; he leapt after her in terror. She turned to face him. Her eyes were bright with tears, but she was smiling. She straightened her sun-hat; she pushed under it a stray ringlet of dark-gold hair.

"Don't worry," she said with an effort at lightness. "I'm not going to lose my footing, Guy. Even for you."

The clouds were massing over Adam's Peak. A few drops of rain reached them on the wind. Bending their heads they hurried down to the car, not pausing to glance back at Harry's bungalow. Jill gave him the keys. Guy drove down the track and through the village to the Kelani road.

"We've missed the storm," said Jill. She snapped her compact shut. "It'll spend itself in the mountains and that will be that."

"Do you want anything to eat?"

"It's too late to stop anywhere. Anyway, I'm not hungry."

"Nor am I." He hesitated. "Will Harry be at home?"

"I don't know. He may be in Hatton, arranging Donald Fraser's transfer to Colombo General. But I'm afraid you'll have missed the last train. You'll have to stay over."

Guy felt the car wheel go slippery. His palms were sweating. He said, "I should like to spend the night with you."

She flushed.

"If not in Kelani, then come to Colombo."

"Where? The Metropole? Besides, I'm sure you've found a local girl to spend the night with when the need arises, haven't you? Most bachelors do."

"I'm leaving the Metropole. I'm going to rent a small flat in that block opposite the Galle Face Hotel."

"You haven't answered my question."

She was mocking him. He said indignantly, "Of course I haven't been seeing native women. What do you take me for?"

"Then I think you should. You have to relax sometimes, you know."

"I don't think that's very amusing."

"Oh, don't be pompous, Guy. Have you got something against the Sinhalese women? I asked Harry what *his* girl had been like in bed. Shall I tell you what he said?"

"If you want."

"He said that she was incredibly pliant. *Pliant*, that was the word he used. And that she had a lot of hair, much more than he was expecting. Do I shock you?"

"I'm not completely ignorant of these things."

"Ah. Now we're getting there. What was she like, Guy? Did she moan a lot and call out your name? Did she get your name *right*?"

He felt himself reddening. "Listen, I'm sorry," he said. "I say I want to spend the night with you, and you think all I'm interested in is sex. Well, you're wrong. It shows what a low opinion you must have of me. Or what a low opinion you have of love, I don't know."

She sighed, and fell silent. They had passed Avisawella and were driving high above the wide, muddy Kelani-ganga. Below them in the last of the afternoon sun a mud-white elephant lay on its side in the river squirting water over itself with its trunk, while a mahout scrubbed its caked hide with a brick. After a minute, Jill said in a small voice, "I don't have a low opinion of you, Guy. I know that's not all you want from me, and I wouldn't care if it was. I suppose it's a form of jealousy in me, if you can believe that. The idea of freely making love. You see Harry . . .

he's made certain vows to himself. I shan't tell you what they are. He's not becoming a Buddhist priest, or any of the wilder rumours that people in Colombo put round at the drop of a hat. It's just that he's embarked on a kind of one-man crusade for peace—"

"Harry has!"

"Yes. Based on the Buddhist example of Ceylon. It's meant him immersing himself in the Buddhist experience, its codes of self-discipline. . . . Please keep all this to yourself. It's why no one has seen him recently. In fact I should prefer they didn't."

"Why?"

"You'll see."

"Does Harry know what he's doing to you? Does he apologise for the life he's making you lead?"

She shrugged. "Harry needs me."

Guy thought about their embrace at China Bay. "Then you need me," he said.

He drove up the familiar dirt road to Kelani Lodge. Already he felt the pain of leaving her. The terrible thought occurred to him that he would literally kill his brother for Jill if she asked him to. He could hardly tolerate the thought of sleeping under the same roof as her but in another bed, and then departing for Colombo in the morning.

They left Rasani and Kelamuttu to unload the car. The green verandah blinds had been drawn against the late-afternoon sun, submerging the rooms in an aqueous light through which they trod slowly as if under water. Stirrings of guilt began to trouble him – and Jill too, from the way her eyes anxiously searched up stairs and through open doorways.

"He must be working out in the office," she said.

The office was a large garden shed, made of corrugated iron, close to the tennis court. The garden coolie sat with his back against it, eating an early dinner of boiled rice and vegetable curry off a plantain leaf. When he saw them he scooped the leaf up, tapped on the wall and hurried off towards the servants' quarters.

The shed door opened. Harry came out, scowling. Guy froze. He had shaved every hair off his head.

"Where have you been?" he demanded. "Jill, you know what day it is. The ceremony starts in an hour!"

Jill bit her lip.

"Never mind," he said gruffly. "Guy, you'd better come in."

Guy followed him into the shed, suppressing a terrible urge to

175

giggle. His brother's bald skull shone like an ostrich egg. He still looked like an eminent fakir, with his prominent forehead and deepset eyes, but now a fakir who had been struck by lightning. Guy looked back to see Jill's expression. To his dismay she had vanished.

The garden shed was deceptively spacious. It smelt of cheroot smoke. To Guy's left, beside the almirah, was a truckle-bed with a thin mattress and two coarse-fibre blankets. On the desk against the far wall, lit by a gas-lamp, lay a small pile of phrase-books and dictionaries, most of them Japanese so far as he could make out, and a scattering of notes. A Buddhist treatise lay open on top of them.

Taking up much of the right-hand wall of the shed stood an enormous home-made radio transmitter, about four feet high and two feet wide. It stood on a low steel table which had its legs in tins of paraffin to keep the ants away.

"It's powered by this bank of car batteries," explained his brother, pointing them out. "I could have wired it to the electricity supply, but that's damned unreliable these days. I'd appreciate it if you kept all this under your hat," he added, glancing at him. "I'm sure I can trust you, Guy. I don't want some confounded bureaucrat in Colombo coming up here with a lot of forms to sign. If you bear with me a minute, while I change, I'll tell you about it on the way."

Harry took off his shirt and draped it over the back of a chair. Out of the almirah he took a long white cotton garment, like a night-gown or a Moroccan djellaba, and pulled it over his head.

"On the way to where?" asked Guy, mesmerised.

"I'd like you to come with me to the temple ceremony at Kelaniya. I think you deserve to know what's going on."

"Does it have to be tonight?"

"Yes. Today is a Poya day, the full moon. It's the most important night in the Buddhist month. And I think you'll be impressed by the Kelaniya ceremony. The Kelani dagoba is one of the most sacred in Ceylon, and one of the least corrupted by Hindu idolatry. It is where Gautama Buddha himself, according to the legend, feasted with the Naga King on one of his three flying visits to Ceylon, the one when he left the imprint of his foot on Adam's Peak."

"I thought it was Field Marshal Wavell who paid flying visits to Ceylon."

His brother stared at him. "There is room for levity in Buddhism," he said, "but perhaps after tonight, Guy, you'll feel less inclined to it. Shall we go? I hope Michael has put petrol in the car."

The journey took them down beside the Kelani-ganga on the Colombo road. Michael, the chauffeur, evidently took Poya Day seriously. He had dressed in a clean white buttoned jacket. Guy saw no reason why Harry could not have done the same instead of robing himself like a Brahman. He thought of Jill, left alone at the Lodge, and his anger turned in on himself. He could have been with her now. Only his contemptible, Sunday School mis-givings about adultery had stopped him turning down this ludicrous invitation to a Buddhist temple ceremony. At this very moment he could have been holding her, touching her, leading her to a room where the mosquito net would cascade whitely around them—

"You must be sitting there wondering what the attraction of Buddhism is for me," observed his brother. "Perhaps you will recall my mentioning to you the stories of Leonard Woolf. Like most European men of real intelligence who lived in Ceylon for any length of time, Woolf came to the view that if he had any religion it would be Buddhism. He sees it as I do, as more of a philosophy, a civilised code of conduct, without all the theologi-cal mumbo-jumbo of Christianity. The point is, it's up to the individual Buddhist to find salvation for himself. He doesn't need the paraphernalia of gods and priests and churches. There are no magic carpets in Buddhism: that's what I respect about it. You'll see a chief priest tonight, a *bhikkhu*, but he is simply the master of ceremonies. He isn't running the show, like Eric Hoath-ly does at St Peter's."

"Ordinary people need leadership, surely?" retorted Guy. "Look at you. Do you think your rubber estate would carry on producing, if it were left up to the individual natives? Didn't you marry Jill when she was in the Pasteur Institute? You must have seen the other face of Buddhism then: the laziness, moral laziness I mean, the callous disinterest—"

"So Jill's been talking to you?" Harry seemed to find this amus-ing. "Well, she's quite right. I'm not saying Buddhism is perfect. There are two sides to self-absorption, and the bad side is the callousness, and the begging-bowl priests who expect everybody to subsidise their idleness. I don't deny any of that: but it's an Indian, Hindu corruption of Buddhism, not the real thing. What's different about Buddhism is that it practises peace. There's nothing peaceable about Christianity. It believes in progress, in the lessons of history: that's why it's such a blood-thirsty faith. In the last war – Max Fremantle watched them – our

177

bishops blessed the tanks as they went into battle. You can be damn sure the German bishops were doing the same on the other side. You'd never find a *bhikkhu* commending glory-fodder to the greater glory of God. Wars on this planet have been started by Christians or Mohammedans, or by barbarians with no faith except in the sword. You won't find a war that Buddhists have started.''

Guy looked at him in disbelief. "Look, we're in the middle of fighting Japan! The Japs are a Buddhist people!"

"They were once. And it's my belief that they will be again. Nippon's religion, if you can call it that, is State Shinto. The Nipponese government took over Cult Shinto, an offshoot of Buddhism, and have turned it into a kind of flag-worship, such as the Nazis have. That's what encourages them to fight. Emperor Hirohito is the living equivalent of Lord Buddha for the average Jap soldier. And that is where my transmitter comes in."

Guy noticed Michael in front listening intently. He wondered if Harry had dragged his driver in on this lunacy. "What you're getting at," he suggested, "is some sort of propaganda exercise."

"No exercise. This is in earnest. The Japs are an all-powerful fighting force. They've proved it in China and Malaya. They won't be stopped by a few toy aircraft and outdated battleships. If they are to be stopped, it is by a direct appeal to their deepest beliefs of all – beliefs that go deeper than Shintoism, even deeper than Hirohito. I mean Buddhism, and its central commandment, Thou shalt not kill."

Harry leant forward in the seat. He fixed his blue gaze on his younger brother and spoke with the same earnest intensity he had brought to his explanations of rubber planting. "Ceylon is the key," he said. "This is the purest of all Buddhist nations. Ceylon can set the example of peace better than anywhere in the world. If the Japs reach this far, we have to remind them of the pacifism which lies at the root of their ancestral religion. We've got to. We've got to do it. If it avoids a single unnecessary drop of blood being spilled, it's got to be done."

He sat back, clasping his fingers together tightly as though to stop his hands shaking. "You may be thinking this is a pointless, futile gesture," he added more calmly. "You're clever; you've made your mark. But answer me one thing. Is it any more illogical, any more pointless and stupid, than this senseless slaughter? Hundreds of thousands of young men killed in the West. Probably millions killed in Russia. Tens of thousands of men already dead among the rubber trees in Malaya. This is the madness. We have to put a stop to it. And not by picking up weapons and joining in the fight.''

''What you're saying is, Forget about civil defence and the RAF. If the enemy arrives, tell them that war is wrong, and wait for them to go home.''

''No nation knows better than the Japanese that surrender is the way to mastery,'' replied his brother. ''It is the essence of their martial arts.''

The car slowed, and joined a procession of other vehicles on their way to the dagoba. Darkness had fallen. Crowds of Sinhalese, most of them in family groups, passed them on either side, carrying flowers, fruit and lighted torches. Guy looked out of the window at them. He was conscious of the feeling of estrangement which his brother always managed to induce in him, since that very first day in Ceylon, at the rubber factory, with his talk of submitting to nature in order to be able to control it. Harry had surrendered to Ceylon, and it had mastered him. A line from ''Mandalay'' came to him – not one that Jill had recited. *If you've 'eard the East a-callin', you won't never 'eed naught else.* Harry had heard the call, and had gone over, and the sitars were sounding for him on the other side.

Michael parked the car against a low red-brick courtyard wall. Harry got out, followed by Guy who for once was inconspicuous in his pale suit. Through the window Michael handed his master a tray of lotus flowers which had lain on the front seat.

They joined the many hundreds of worshippers flocking into the temple courtyard with their gifts to the Buddha. Swaying women wore jasmine and gardenia flowers in their hair. Guy looked with longing at the offerings of fruit. He hadn't eaten since their early breakfast; his stomach was complaining.

They fell in with the ritual procession around the courtyard. In the middle rose the Buddhist shrine, or dagoba, its mountainous, teated dome, like a young woman's breast, wavering palely in the light of the torches. Around it grew the white-blossomed trees of Ceylon: the low, spreading temple trees, an ironwood tree, and four champacs adding their sickly-sweet scent to the incense of the worshippers. Further away stood an ungainly bo tree, its branches hung with coloured lanterns in commemoration of its sacred ancestor under which the Lord Buddha gained enlightenment 2500 years before.

Harry muttered in his ear. ''This is a side of Ceylon you won't have seen in Colombo. Buddhism is the karma-force of the Sinhalese, but most Westerners haven't the faintest idea what it

179

means to them. And the few I know who have become Buddhists are the fashionable, begging-bowl types who think it's all to do with sitting around and contemplating their navel."

They completed the circuits of the courtyard. Harry stepped forward, a pink-skulled giant among the small, dark Sinhalese. He placed his offering of lotus blossoms on the low altar, and rejoined Guy. They waited in silence, as the congregation swelled and seethed in the courtyard until there was scarcely room for those in procession to tread in single file round the perimeter wall.

At last the chief *bhikkhu* emerged from the interior of the shrine. In his horn-rimmed spectacles he looked to Guy like a successful businessman who had put on orange robes for an evening Rotary address. His sermon on the Brahma Viharas would have passed him by, he suspected, even if he'd understood the language.

Guy by now was starving. The smoke of torches, the incense mingling with burning coconut oil and the heat from the packed bodies around him compounded his discomfort. As from a long way away he heard the monks chanting the sacred Pali verses, and noticed Michael the chauffeur abasing himself over his hands joined in prayer. He was still wearing his crucifix; Guy wondered if he was witnessing a conversion. The Pirith ended, and Harry beside him was chanting the Tisarana, the three Jewels –

> *Buddham saranam gacchami*
> *Dhamman saranam gacchami*
> *Sangham saranam gacchami. . . .*

and the ceremony was completed.

"You can come back and sleep at the Lodge," Harry told him as they made their way back to the car. 'Or I can drive you in to Colombo. It's only five miles from here.'

Guy hesitated. Jill was probably in bed by now. He would have to be in the Dunlop Orient office by mid-morning at the latest, for a meeting with Rawling. The Metropole moreover, for all its scruffiness, cooked the best fish dinners in town.

"I should get to Colombo," he said.

5 April 1942.   5.45 a.m. Indian Ocean.

Thirty minutes to dawn. The search planes are already airborne, scouting ahead of the great fleet. At centre of it the five aircraft-carriers Hiryu, Soryu, Zuikaku, Shokaku *and* Akagi *are steaming slowly ahead in V-formation,* Akagi *out in front. The seas are calm. There is no sign of the enemy.*

The silence is broken by the clanging of bells. Flight-deck lights snap on, dimmed for safety. There is a rumbling sound: the enormous hatches are being winched back to reveal the ghostly light from below of giant elevators bringing the first wave of attack aircraft up to the flight deck. As the forward elevators deliver the fighters, and the midship and stern elevators deliver the dive-bombers and level bombers, maintenance crews of seamen in khaki overalls run forward to manhandle the planes into their line-up positions and secure them against rolling.

In Akagi, *as in the other four carriers, loudspeakers issue the staccato command, three times repeated, "Aviators assemble!" The pilots are ready and waiting. Rapidly they make their way to the Operations Room under the bridge, where the controllers of the air attack have gathered to brief them.*

Several of Akagi's *senior officers surround the Fleet Navigator, Commander Gishiro Migura, at the map board. The Commanding Officer, Captain Taijiro Aoki, is present, as is Commander Shogo Masuda, the Air Officer. Not far away, Lieutenant-Commander Ono,* Akagi's *intelligence officer, is studying the latest signals sent by the Japanese submarines as they range well in advance of the Striking Force.*

As soon as Vice-Admiral Chuichi Nagumo arrives in the Operations Room, Masuda addresses the pilots. There is not much he can tell them that they don't know already. His airmen have been trained exhaustively. They have studied the bombing and attack plans until they are familiar with every detail. Masuda exhorts them to stay calm, to put their strength in their abdomen, to keep their excitement and nervousness under control. He warns them that for the first time in the war they can

181

expect to meet immediate enemy counter-attacks. *The British have been given prior warning; they will be in a state of readiness.*

It remains for Lieutenant-Commander Mitsuo Fuchida to say a few words, and then pass over to his two deputies, Itaya and Murata, to confirm the attack plans for the Zero fighters and the dive-bombers respectively. The briefing is over. The pilots leave the Operations Room and double out to the flight deck. Their ground crews have completed the task of wheeling the heavy bombs and torpedoes out of the Ammunition Room and loading them on the bombers. The mechanics have given each aircraft engine a final test.

A bugle call shrills over the loudspeakers. At the flight control station Commander Masuda issues his orders.

"All hands to launching stations!"

The watertight doors of every bulkhead in the Akagi are closed, as a precaution. The deck-lights dim; the pilots can see only a few feet ahead. At a signal from Masuda, Captain Aoki proceeds to bring the giant carrier round head full into the wind. Simultaneously he increases its speed to match a wind velocity of fourteen metres per second.

"Start engines!"

All the aircraft engines of the first attack wave roar into life at once, shooting livid white flames from their exhaust pipes and sending tremors from the vibrating deck through the bodies of every man on board, from the deck crew to Nagumo on the bridge. Immediately beneath the C-in-C, Lieutenant Saburo Shindo, leader of the first wing of fighters to take off, flicks on the blue and red wing-lights of his Zero to indicate that he is ready. Within sixty seconds every other pilot has done the same.

A deck orderly reports to Commander Masuda. "All planes ready!"

Masuda gives a last look round. Then he signals the bridge, "Planes ready for take-off."

Akagi is now in position. The order comes, this time, from Vice-Admiral Nagumo himself.

"Commence launching!"

Floodlights suddenly bathe the carrier's flight deck in a brilliant, unnatural dawn. Lieutenant Shindo revs up his engine. He waits for the deck control officer, who monitors the pitching of the ship, to give him the go-ahead by swinging a green signal lamp in a luminous arc over his head; then he gathers speed along the upward-sloping flight deck towards the blue light at the far end; and with a farewell wave through his open canopy he takes off into the darkness.

From the deck crew there is wild clapping and cries of "Banzai!" and waving of caps in the air; but already the rest of Shindo's wing are lining up, waiting for the green signal lamp and roaring off, dipping momentarily after leaving the flight deck, then turning to climb. In just a few minutes a neat pattern of blue and red wing-lights indicates that the Zeros have sorted themselves into formation. Looking back, the crew of Akagi can see the thin streaks of light following each other into the sky as Hiryu, Soryu, and Zuikaku send up aircraft to join theirs.

As the early paleness of dawn begins to uncover the horizon, the first attack wave of Nagumo's Striking Force, consisting of thirty-six fighters, thirty-six dive-bombers and fifty-three high-level bombers, is airborne and on its way to the target. On board Akagi, where a moment ago there was a hubbub of planes, the deck-lights dim over a scene of eerie stillness and silence. Into this stillness the voice of the Commander-in-Chief breaks over the loudspeakers.

"We go on to victory!" rasps Nagumo. "May the unparalleled Yamato spirit prevail!"

All the seamen on deck take off their caps when they hear Nagumo's voice. They lift their own voices in the Imperial Anthem —

"May our Sovereign's reign last
A thousand generations and eight thousand generations
Until the gravel of the river
Becomes rock
And these rocks are covered with moss."

The sound is snatched by the wind. There is nothing they have left to do but wait.

"THE sun was risen upon the earth when Lot entered into Zoar.

"Then the Lord rained upon Sodom and upon Gomorrah brimstone and fire from the Lord out of heaven;

"And he overthrew those cities, and all the plain, and all the inhabitants of the cities, and that which grew upon the ground.

"But his wife looked back from behind him, and she became a pillar of salt."

According to the Church of Ceylon prayer book in Sylvia's gloved hand, it was the first Sunday in Lent. Through the east windows of St Peter's Garrison Church ("imbecile Gothic" said the local guidebook) the sun threw gold lozenges on a congregation grown bigger and more pious since the recent Japanese victories in Malaya. After the prayers, Eric Hoathly turned towards the congregation to intone the Collect for the Day. His face above the ridiculous little pointed beard wore a solemn, gloomy expression which made Sylvia wonder for a moment if he knew her secret. Then she remembered that of course it was how the Archdeacon always looked in church: an expression he put on with his Sunday vestments out of respect for God, the spiritual equivalent of her mother's bright smile when the Ingram Bywaters came to dinner.

"O Lord," said Eric Hoathly, "Who for our sake didst fast forty days and forty nights, give us grace to use such abstinence; that, our flesh being subdued to the Spirit, we may ever obey Thy godly motions in righteousness and true holiness, to Thy honour and glory, Who livest and reignest with the Father and the Holy Ghost, one God, world without end. Amen."

Sylvia returned a low, fervent "Amen"; not that it was going to help. Appeals for abstinence had come too late. Her flesh could no longer be subdued by the spirit. She was pregnant. That much she knew for certain.

She had told no one. Not even Mummy yet, although in the intervals when her mother wasn't worrying about Piggy in north Africa, Sylvia had intercepted a speculative glance or two. Her

184

first instinct had been to rush to her mother in tears, and be comforted and told what to do. Then she realised that in the excitement of David and the Naval Office and the war she couldn't be certain when she had first missed her period. The dreadful truth dawned on her that she couldn't be a hundred per cent certain whose baby it was – Charlie Bilbow's or David Gifford's.

She could not go to Mummy and admit she didn't know who the father was. This was something she was going to have to sort out for herself. After the first blind panic, her natural optimism began to filter back. Perhaps the beastly thing would go away of its own accord. She took hot baths. She played tennis. She pedalled furiously to and from the Naval Office, often taking long detours around the Lake. She made the hard trek out to see Miss Utteridge's Buddha. With some of the other cipherettes she went to afternoon dances with the troops in smelly, stuffy halls where she nearly died of the heat.

Nothing worked. Her embryo would not abort. It clung to her with a stubbornness which Sylvia began to think rather endearing, a symbol of her self-reliance. But that didn't alter the fact that something was going to have to be done, and quickly. She had come to church to pray to God for guidance. It didn't help that everyone else was offering up prayers to abstinence, fasting (she was so *hungry* all the time) and being generally ashes-and-sackcloth.

> *Forty days and forty nights*
> *Thou wa-ast fasting in the wild:*
> *Forty days and forty nights*
> *Tempted, and yet undefiled.*

Sylvia was swept along in the thunderous moan of voices in a minor key, above which Ottoline Hoathly's soprano descant could be heard in short, shrill bursts like a locomotive whistle –

> *Shall not we Thy sorrow share,*
> *And fro-om selfish joys abstain,*
> *Fasting with unceasing prayer,*
> *Glad with Thee to suffer pain?*

There was the trouble with the Anglican Church, in Sylvia's view. It was so ... *censorious*, that was the word. Protestants never left it to God to pass judgement; they always wanted to do it themselves. They absolved all their own sins in church so that they'd be free to reproach people like her, when actually she just hadn't *thought*, that was all.

Admittedly, it was Lent. But then it was always Lent in St Peter's; the Archdeacon was always scolding his congregation for one thing or another. Maria de Vos had taken her once to a Catholic service at St Mary's Bambalapitya, and that was actually rather fun, with Father de Souza's rich robes, and the incense, and the thrice-struck bell. Even the temple-worshippers in Kataragama had the temple-curtain in front of which the priest danced and moved the lamp-light over the painted likeness of Naga the Snake God: the curtain covering the doorway to the inner sanctum in which the raja cobra was rumoured to lie. And the Buddhists had mantras and white temple-flowers. ...

Sylvia had laid a rather crumpled temple-flower (it had been in her handbag) at the feet of the giant Sasseruwa Buddha, after the others had gone back down the hill. That had been on Monday, the fateful Monday. The Expedition had been planned for the end of the month, but it had had to be brought forward a couple of weeks. What with petrol rationing, and the curfew, and troops everywhere on the roads demanding passes or setting up Diversion signs, they might otherwise have had to call it off altogether.

The Expedition was Miss Utteridge's idea, it went without saying. Her constant complaint (to anyone who would listen) was how the European colonisers of Ceylon refused to accept that the island had once had a civilisation as great as theirs. Leaving her bungalow in Anuradhapura, where she had lived with her books and servants ever since her husband was killed in the Relief of Ladysmith during the Second Boer War, Miss Utteridge would periodically descend on Colombo, full of crusading enthusiasm, to organise an expedition into the Interior. From her suite of rooms at the Galle Face Hotel she would sally forth in her sun-hat and gym-shoes, a familiar figure in Cinnamon Gardens, to beard the memsahibs over tea.

Sylvia had managed to steer clear of her godmother for most of her adolescence. When she went to school at Cheltenham Ladies' College, Miss Utteridge had given her an annotated guidebook to what she called the Vic and Bert. During her time in London Sylvia had not once darkened the doors of that museum.

It was Maria de Vos, oddly enough, who had brought the two of them together. She had dragged Sylvia, somewhat against her will, to a meeting of the Ceylon Historical Society. Hardly knowing her formidable godmother except through the articles she penned to the *Ceylon Observer*, usually in a state of dudgeon, about some new failure to protect the island's ancient monuments, Sylvia was unprepared for the thin, sprightly, cheerful figure in slacks who mounted the rostrum. The subject of her talk had sounded dire – some sort of protest about siting the proposed Anuradhapura New Town right on top of some ruins. By the time Miss Utteridge had finished describing the Toluwila ruins, the only remains in Ceylon of the form of highway used by the ancient dynasties two thousand years ago, and the most suggestive evidence anywhere of their daily social life, Sylvia was bristling with indignation at the heavy-handed bureaucrats (probably her father had something to do with it) who could callously bury such treasure under brick and concrete.

Maria had persuaded Sylvia to open Robert Knox's *Historical Relation of Ceylon*, telling her it was the best book about the island and not just because it was written during the rule of her own Dutch ancestors. Discovering this, Miss Utteridge had summoned her god-daughter to the Galle Face Hotel. Before she knew what was happening, Sylvia had found herself drafted in as one of the old buzzard's campaigners, and a subscriber to the Antiquities' Protection and Archaeological Research Society of which Miss Utteridge was a founder-member. In no time she was persuaded to grill her father on the political background of what became known as the Great Toluwila Ruins Debate. Daddy provided what assistance he could, grumbling the while that Miss Utteridge was a classic example of an antique who needed no protection whatsoever.

The road, hardly more than a track through the jungle, to the forty-foot-high standing Buddha at Sasseruwa, had only just been opened up. In wet weather not even a jeep could traverse it from Aukana. On this February morning, the Expedition party press-ganged by Miss Utteridge gazed anxiously at the sky. To their silent dismay there wasn't a cloud in it.

"Are we finally all here?" enquired Miss Utteridge. She counted them off with her umbrella.

"Sebastian *did* say...." Kitty Clarke looked helplessly back down Lotus Road.

"I am afraid we jolly well can't hang about," Miss Utteridge returned decisively. "They've put on a Special, you know. It's no bally good unless we keep to the timetable."

The fact that in the middle of wartime a special tour train

should be put on for them was testimony to Miss Utteridge's powers of persuasion. Obediently her little party traipsed into the station. Sylvia stole a glance at Maria de Vos who had not yet spoken to her. The Burgher girl had put on her showiest outfit: a ruched summer dress in pretty pastel colours and bright red shoes. Sylvia wondered if it was an act of defiance. Did Maria know that David was seeing her? Had David told her? She didn't even know if the two of them had met since her party: David was so enigmatic if you got him on to things he didn't want to talk about. . . .

A week ago Sylvia would have brooded on these possibilities. Her being *enceinte* put all such petty jealousies into perspective – so she had decided before coming out today. Even so, when she felt Maria's eyes on her, she found an excuse to look away.

As they crossed the Fort station platform an obsequious inspector pushed a path for them through a babble of Tamils besieging the ticket office for rail tickets to the ferry for India. Sylvia knew most of the group. Her mother had announced she was coming at the last minute, slightly to her dismay. As well as Maria and Kitty, Mrs Ingram Bywater had come along, and so had the Hoathlys.

"I fail to understand those natives back there," remarked Mrs Ingram Bywater as soon as they were all seated in the single carriage (coupled to an ancient locomotive with a bulbous funnel which must have pre-dated Miss Utteridge's Boer War days). "If the Nipponese, as we're told to call them, take Ceylon, they will surely take India. I should have thought it better to face one's fate in the relative comfort of one's own home surroundings."

"They might have heard what the Nipponese Army do to minorities like the Chinese," suggested Elizabeth Donaldson. "There haven't been many Chinese among the refugees arriving from Hong Kong and Singapore. Or Tamils, for that matter."

Her words did not lighten their sombre mood. They had all at one time or another been down to the jetty to watch the refugee boats come in from Singapore. Sylvia had witnessed the shock on the faces of women who had left husbands, servants and possessions to the mercy of the Japanese. With wretched smiles they came down the gangplank, often with nothing more than what they stood up in. At the Refugee Centre there were clothes in plenty, and toys for their children. It didn't seem to do much for their morale.

Still, there was no point in making a to-do about it. Already the delicious smell of fresh coffee was filtering from the buffet at the end of the carriage. Leaving the city behind, the train chugged strenuously past paddy-fields and terraces and estates of coconut palms, their branches bending with fruit. In the distance sparkled the flag-bedecked pagoda of a Hindoo temple, swarming with goddesses painted light blue and pink. Away from Colombo, Sylvia began to feel the burden of her guilt lifting. She had brought the new Daphne du Maurier novel to read. Best of all, Maria had organised a late-breakfast snack of chicken sandwiches. She passed them round with the coffee.

Spirits rose, even Kitty Clarke's: "I do declare this blackout's a blessing in disguise. I'm sleeping so much better than I did before, what with the traffic slowing down! I just wish poor Sebby could get home earlier and didn't have to walk in the dark!"

Mrs Ingram Bywater, who had never yet invited Kitty to any of her coffee mornings, could not resist a malicious rejoinder. "Apparently the people hit worst by the blackout are divorce lawyers," she said in a clear voice to Ottoline Hoathly. "Identification of adultery is said to be impossible in the pitch dark."

"I'm sure I wouldn't know about that," said Mrs Hoathly hastily. "But you don't know what's going on, do you, these dark nights? All these stories you hear, about spies and enemy agents. How does anybody know, I mean, when you can't see more than two feet in front of you?"

She glanced at her husband for confirmation. The Archdeacon kept his counsel behind a blue haze of pipe-smoke. Miss Utteridge took up the cudgels.

"Don't believe all you hear," she declared. "We had these rumours in the First War. There was a German boat, *Emden*, in Ceylon waters in 1914. People reported frightful stories of how it had been provisioned by German merchants in Ceylon, and was passing back information to the Kaiser. It turned out that *Emden* couldn't have cared one bally bit about Ceylon. The stories were put about by British businessmen who thought the Germans were pinching their trade."

"Oh, so you don't think it's true?" asked Kitty Clarke.

"I shall tell you what I think," said Miss Utteridge, after a pause. "I don't think it matters a frightful lot what happens in the war as far as Ceylon is concerned. Win or lose, things are going to be different from now on."

This delphic remark momentarily silenced the carriage. "In what way, Miss Utteridge?" Sylvia ventured to ask.

The old lady pursed her lips. "We've lost too much ground,"

she said. "The effect on the Ceylonese is going to be the same as the effect of the Great War on the British lower classes – they're going to get their Independence. That's what I think. I come from a family of soldiers and I married into a family of soldiers and I've got an instinct about these things."

Nobody was impolite enough to contradict her, although Sylvia could see from Mrs Ingram Bywater's expression that she thought Miss Utteridge should stick to archaeology. Even Archdeacon Hoathly, who prided himself on his liberal views, had his arms folded across his chest and was gazing out of the window at carts, loaded with household belongings, heading into the countryside. His wife had picked up Joyce Cary's *Aissa Saved*.

"I asked my father what would happen when the British left Ceylon to the Ceylonese," remarked Maria, taking her seat again.

"What did he say, dear?"

"He didn't say anything, Mrs Hoathly. He had some pencils on his desk. He picked one up and just pushed it slowly into the fan until the blades caught it."

"Goodness me!"

"But I know what he thinks. He thinks there's going to be a free-for-all when the British leave. He says that everybody talks about Ceylon as the Pearl of the East, whereas if you look at it, it's more in the shape of a ham in a butcher's shop, waiting for the moment when it's carved up."

"Oh, Maria, aren't you being a bit melodramatic?" protested Sylvia.

Maria did not answer. Sylvia sighed. They were passing through Gampola. It was where the British had grown the first rubber trees in the East, transported in 1876 as seeds smuggled illicitly from the Amazon Valley. She glanced around the carriage, trying to imagine what it was like to be Maria, to feel herself the odd one out (though by rights it was Maria who belonged here). Eric Hoathly, puffing at his pipe, now studied a back number of the *Church Times*. His wife was deep in *Aissa Saved*. Her mother and Mrs Ingram Bywater were talking quietly. Kitty Clarke sat back with her eyes closed, a half-knitted scarf in her lap.

Here they were before her eyes; it was impossible to imagine that tomorrow they would all be gone. They had invested one hundred and fifty years of their time and money and labour in this small island and for better or worse transformed it utterly – how could they possibly just turn round and walk away? Sylvia had a sudden vision of the carriage they were sitting in emptied

190

of everybody except her, and then filling up with Sinhalese, one or two at first, very polite, then five, ten, a hundred, pushing and shoving until there was nowhere for her to sit or even stand except forced half out of the window and the train was picking up speed all the time. . . .

Maria got up, and walked down the aisle to where Miss Utteridge was sitting, opposite Sylvia. The old lady had pinched a pair of eye-glasses on to her nose and was studying a large-scale map. Sylvia could not help noticing that on this map her god-mother had herself green-inked in a new road and extended a number of others with a regal stroke of the pen.

Miss Utteridge smiled up at Maria and patted the seat beside her. "Here's Aukana where the other giant Buddha is," she explained, pointing to a green asterisk. "Sasseruwa is here, seven miles to the west. The road cuts through the bush from Aukana and stops at the foot of a hill. The Buddha is carved out of the cliff-face at the top of the hill. It's very like the Aukana image, only softer, more impressionistic. We think it must have been carved about the same time, fourth century AD, by a pupil of the Aukana master." She glanced at Maria. "Are you all right, my dear?"

In a low voice Maria said, "Miss Utteridge, will you leave? When Independence comes?"

"Gracious me, no. My home is here. Just as yours is." Noticing her expression, Miss Utteridge added, "Mind you, I expect you'll have married a nice man and gone abroad."

Maria sighed.

"I know you think optimism comes easy from an old lady like me," continued Miss Utteridge, her hand, patting Maria on the wrist, as splotched and yellow as an English autumn leaf. "But don't tell me a pretty girl like you hasn't got her eye on a young man somewhere?"

Sylvia buried her nose in *Frenchman's Creek*.

"Yes," said Maria. "But he's an airman. He's training to fly Hurricane fighter planes."

Miss Utteridge was silent.

"What I wanted to ask you," Maria said with difficulty. "If something happens . . . is there anything left inside? Does the feeling of love go on? Is that what keeps you going?"

"Love." Miss Utteridge folded up the map, smoothing the creases into place. "I was married to Reginald for nine years," she said slowly. "It is now nearly forty-two years since he died, in the Relief. Not a single day goes by without my thinking of him, and sometimes writing him a note in my diary. Yes, love does go on,

191

if you don't brood about it and turn it to self-pity. But you, young lady, should enjoy what you have," she added with firmness. "Make hay while the sun still shines, my dear."

The engine let out a long hoot. Ottoline Hoathly dropped her book, which Sylvia retrieved from between the high wooden seats. The landscape now was broken up by terraced ridges and brutal escarpments of gneiss. There were plumbago mines here, and squares of betel vineyards carefully fenced against marauders. At Kurunegala, in the shadow of Elephant Rock, they stopped for ten minutes to take on coal and let members of the party answer what Kitty Clarke liked to apostrophise as the call of Nature. A detachment of Indian troops watched them curiously from the opposite platform.

They trundled on northwards. More coffee was brewed for elevenses. Mrs Ingram Bywater brought out a Jubilee tin of shortbread baked by her cook. Eric Hoathly and Miss Utteridge pursued an argument about the value of missionaries, Miss Utteridge insisting that the cruelties of the Spaniards in Mexico or the Portuguese in Ceylon were due to them being Christian missionaries first and traders afterwards.

Sylvia heard this in snatches, as the train ride was making her unaccountably sleepy. Once, she opened her eyes to find herself in a steep valley alongside a fast-flowing river where small children were riding the rapids in inner tubes. The next moment, the landscape was a carpet of green jungle and Miss Utteridge and Archdeacon Hoathly had moved on to an argument about the Buddha's tooth.

Shortly after midday they clattered over points and rocked to a standstill in the siding of Aukana Halt. The jeeps Miss Utteridge had ordered from Anuradhapura were already waiting beyond the whitewashed railway building, their drivers standing stiffly beside them holding big blue parasols. When Miss Utteridge waved her umbrella they came running across to unload the hampers containing the expedition's picnic lunch. It was the first sight the party had had of their lunch hampers, and they followed them out of the train and into the jeeps with animation.

Sylvia found herself in the back of a jeep with the Hoathlys, together with someone she didn't know, a grey schoolmistressy woman with bony ankles and a flushed gin face who suffered in painful silence against Ottoline Hoathly's sharp sides. Miss Utteridge as promised took the convoy past the Aukana Buddha, for comparison. Sylvia caught a glimpse of a sand-coloured figure cloaked in rippling stone and raising a gigantic hand in threat or blessing, before they went on down a white dirt road into the jungle.

It took them fifty minutes to cover the seven miles of track. It was gouged out of thick jungle, which crowded forward again on either side. Wanderoo monkeys thrashed the branches overhead. A large pig trampled away through the undergrowth. They passed an overgrown *chena* and a clearing of cadjan huts set among jak and cotton trees, its inhabitants so dumbfounded by the convoy of vehicles that even the little children stood stock still without so much as raising their cupped hands to beg.

The road ended abruptly in what looked like the forecourt of a ruined monastery at the base of an enormous rock. There were no dagobas or wiharas here: simply a collection of hermits' huts built of ashlar and sheltered by bo trees. Behind them rose a stairway of wide stone steps, cracked and upheaved by giant lianas. They led to a platform on which stood a small modern hut like a sentry-box. Steps carved in the rock continued up from the platform and disappeared from view in a clump of eucalyptus trees.

Whatever Miss Utteridge might have preferred, there was no question of the Expedition proceeding until an important rite had been observed. Blankets were spread on the grass. The hampers were produced, and their contents devotionally brought forth. Knives, forks and spoons were distributed. Lemon barley water was poured into glasses. Boiled eggs were shelled. Loaves of bread were sliced and buttered. Tomatoes were handed round. Sausages were stabbed with toothpicks. Kraft cheese slices were unwrapped, bananas unpeeled and two tins of Peek Frean savoury assorted biscuits opened and devoured; the whole ceremony – conducted in prayerful silence except for brief petitions and responses and occasional exclamations of thanksgiving – taking place under the vaulted canopy of blue parasols held up by the ministering drivers.

The picnic might have gone on long into the afternoon, and the point of the expedition been sacrificed to contented digestions, had not Ottoline Hoathly decided to go exploring. It may have been that she was looking for shade in which to finish *Aissa Saved*; or that she needed privacy to relieve herself of the lemon barley water – whatever the reason, a piercing scream issued from one of the empty hermits' dwellings, followed at speed by the Archdeacon's wife, her face the colour of her beige blouse. Eric Hoathly ran towards her. She clutched his arm.

"In there!" she cried, pointing to the hut. "A *snake*!"

193

Kitty Clarke and Maria comforted her. Two of the drivers approached the stone doorway, parasols at the ready. As they did so, a grass-green serpent slid its length unhurriedly over the stone threshold and disappeared in a cleft in the rock.

"It's only a rat-snake," called Miss Utteridge. "No need for kittens! Come on now, or we'll miss the Buddha!"

With a flourish of her umbrella she started up the ancient steps. Kitty Clarke trod gingerly behind her in her patent leather shoes, followed by Sylvia's mother and the schoolmistress. Ottoline Hoathly, aided by her husband, set off next. Sylvia took up the rear. She had tissues in her bag. If the worst providentially happened, she would slip away to the side without anybody noticing.

As she began to climb the two hundred and eighty steps, taking deep breaths, Maria came up beside her. For a while they walked in silence, neither wishing to be the first to speak.

"It's just the right time of year for this sort of thing," said Maria eventually.

"Yes."

"I'm so glad for Utters. I'd hate it to have been the sort of weather we've been getting in Colombo, so stuffy and rotten, it makes you feel like jumping out of a window."

"Dire, isn't it?"

"I suppose you manage to get out of town a bit, do you? I ring you sometimes at the Naval Office and you're never there," she added piteously.

"Well. A bit. Not much. I'm working so hard now," said Sylvia, "what with one thing and another."

"Do you see anything of David?"

"David?"

"David Gifford."

"Oh. Yes, a bit. He's flying a lot, you know. They've got the Hurricanes now."

"I know."

They walked on. Maria had her head bent. Her glossy black hair, which Sylvia envied, hid her face. Sylvia could not see her expression. She could hear Miss Utteridge ahead, pointing out hermit caves in the rock-face, their doorways as brightly ornamented as a Hindoo temple.

"It was so mad of me," said Maria suddenly. "You're my friend, you should have made me see. Whatever made me think I had a chance with him? I've got none of your social graces: the sort of thing you and your friends went to school in England to learn. I've never *been* to England, except in books. I've never been to the opera, or a grand London ball. I can't gossip on and on about Ascot, and Henley boating, and the Cheltenham Gold Plate—"

"Cheltenham Gold Cup," said Sylvia. "What I mean is," she went on hurriedly, "those aren't the important things. I mean . . . you know. . . ." She struggled to find an example. "Love?"

"Oh yes. Love." Maria brushed the hair off her face. Sylvia wanted to look at her, but dared not. "I believe in love. I believe in a lot of things. I believe in God and in stones with a hole in them and a ring round the moon bringing rain. But most, I wanted to believe in David. Do you know what he said when I went home after your party?"

"What?"

"He said, *I shan't ever forget tonight, you know.* He said that. I thought it meant . . . but I was so mad, it was obvious what it meant, it meant Thanks and goodbye, Maria, goodbye, I shan't be seeing you again."

Sylvia said nothing. The baby inside her, which might be David's baby, seemed to be no trouble (although she was perspiring a lot, her face felt clammy with it). Luckily a breeze cooled them as they climbed past trees that grew at perilous angles from clefts in the rock. Maria hadn't gone the whole way with him, that was all she'd wanted to be sure of.

Maria quickened her pace. She said in a muffled voice, motioning ahead, "At the party after *Cinderella* – do you know what Mrs I.B. said to me? She asked me if I would like to put in for the position of Ayah to the children of some titled friend of hers. *Ayah*! She called it 'governess', but I knew what she meant perfectly. I'm a Burgher, I'm chi-chi, it's as simple as that."

"Very nearly there!" cried Miss Utteridge, as Sylvia muttered words of sympathy (though frankly she thought Maria was laying it on a bit thick). The steps were shallower now, the trees more thickly clustered. Without warning they broke out into a grassy arena. The Sasseruwa Buddha stood before them, carved out of the sheer rock-face, a scattering of temple-flowers at its feet.

In this deserted spot, the Buddha's presence was overwhelming. Overhung by a tall velvet tamarind, it towered above them in an attitude of sublime stillness. Its purplish-black granite was set off by sand-coloured splashes in the niche behind, so that it might appear to the superstitious to be lit by the rock itself. One hand held the folds of its robe to its shoulder. The other lifted an open palm towards them in a symbolic gesture of *abhaya* – "fear not".

Its stillness entered into all of them. They stood for a minute without moving or speaking: Miss Utteridge grasping her umbrella, Kitty Clarke with one hand on her sun-hat, the Archdeacon and his wife arm in arm. Sylvia, a little apart from the others, gazed at the face of the Buddha. Unlike its fellow at Aukana it wore an expression of benevolent contemplation. The heavy eyelids were closed, the mouth unsmiling but peaceful. That this granite colossus could be instinct with yielding spiritual grace was a mystery which defied analysis or description.

Miss Utteridge broke the silence. "There is a legend about the Sasseruwa Buddha," she said. "The legend is that in the reign of King Dhatusena there was a competition between a master and his most brilliant pupil to see which of them would be the first to carve a giant statue of Buddha. A bell would be rung when the first was completed, after however many years it took. The Aukana Master, a supreme technician, chose to carve the transcendent majesty of Buddha through perfect balance, poise and absolute clarity of form. The Sasseruwa Pupil chose to convey his spiritual benevolence, compassion and grace, which meant discarding all he had learnt to do by the rule-book and relying on inspiration and prayer to guide his hand. The bell rang for the Aukana Master, and this Buddha was forgotten for many centuries."

"I must say one finds the idea of a *race* a trifle vulgar," said Ottoline Hoathly eventually. "I doubt whether one would find a similar disrespect shown by people who were carving images of Christ in our great cathedrals."

"There were no statues of Christ," replied Miss Utteridge patiently. "This Buddha was sculpted while the Angles were fighting the Saxons. I believe a gentleman called Attila the Hun was running things in Europe. . . ."

She was interrupted by the arrival of the schoolmistressy person, plainly out of condition, who advanced wheezing to confront the colossus.

"It's very fine, Miss Utteridge," she exclaimed plaintively when she got her breath back. "But why did they have to build it so far from the main road?"

Time was getting on. Shadows were already beginning to creep across the grass. Their train was waiting. After thanking Miss Utteridge for the Buddha and the excellent picnic, they each began to make their way back down the hill. Only Sylvia stayed behind.

196

She was alone with the Buddha. The immensity of her confrontation sent a tingle down her spine. Deep-shadowed, the Buddha's inward-looking face seemed to be contemplating an image of her, Sylvia Donaldson, in the vastnesses of its mind.

What did it make of her? Was it passing judgement on her incapacity to love? That was something else about Maria: she seemed to be able to give her heart away as easily and gracefully as a kiss. To Sylvia's mind, love should never come that easy. She suspected it was something frightfully difficult and strenuous, like ballet lessons. And yet, without it, she felt as she gazed at the Buddha's awesome equanimity a strange giddiness, a lightness of being, as if it was love that anchored you to the earth and gave harmony to things, so that you felt you could co-exist with the rocks and trees, like the Buddha, and feel they were a part of you and you a part of them.

David Gifford was like that – *weighty*. It scared her sometimes. On his one night off last week they had gone to the Silver Faun nightclub (known to *tout le monde* as the Septic Prawn) and danced to "Whispering Grass", and then sat at a table by themselves in the smoky half-darkness. David had fumbled around inside his uniform.

"I've got something I wanted to give you."

He brought out an object wrapped in tissue paper. He unfolded it, clumsy with a boyish awkwardness. Inside, there lay a gold charm in the shape of a cross, except that in place of the top bit there was a loop, with a gold chain to fasten round her neck. Gently he took her wrist and placed it in the palm of her hand.

"It's called an ankh," he told her, blushing under his sunburn. "It's the ancient Egyptian symbol of eternal life. I've got one too. I had one of those Ceylonese jewellers on the road from Mount Lavinia make them for me."

Sylvia picked it up and held it in her fingers. Eternal life. It was as light as a feather. She shivered. "David, it's lovely," she whispered.

"It's pretty, isn't it?" David had not taken his eyes off her. "I say, Sylvia, you will wear it for me? Won't you?"

"I think I've got one or two things it will go with," she'd said. And flowered into a brilliant smile.

It had been that night, checking the white tape on his car bumpers before driving her home, that he'd suddenly asked her if there was anything she really believed in. He had meant it seriously; she was taken aback. It was not a question she'd ever been asked before.

"Gosh. I don't know. I'd have to think about that one." She'd got into the car with a rustle of her dress. "What about you? Oh, in eternal life I suppose you'll say!"

"That was the ancient Egyptians." He had shut her door and gone round to the driver's seat, smiling grimly.

"In what, then?" she persisted.

"I don't know." He was leaning over the wheel, peering and peering into the blackout as he drove. "I don't know," he repeated.

"You must believe in something."

"Why?"

"Because everybody does." She considered this further, in the clarity of the three pink gins she'd drunk in the Septic Prawn. "Don't you have a *need* to believe in something?" she asked, describing a vague shape in the air with her hands which might have been God or the world or a ball of twine.

David was silent. She felt a vague unease. Colpetty in the partial blackout looked shrouded in mystery, like a huge banked-down fire that only showed the intensity of its burning in little chinks and crevices through the mantle that covered it.

"Well?" she asked.

"Are all your needs and wishes granted, Sylvia?" David gave a laugh. "How lucky you are. A true Cinderella!"

She was shocked by the bitterness in his voice. David may have sensed this, because he took his hand off the wheel for a moment and squeezed her fingers.

"I was frightened last night, Sylvia," he said quietly. "I woke up in the middle of the night, in a strange room, in a strange country, and there was nothing to hold on to. Do you know what I mean? There was no God out there. There were no voices, from home or Cranwell or anywhere, telling me to hold my head up, fight for King and Country, any of that guff. There was just silence. And emptiness. Like there is in a plane when you're flying and the engine cuts out and you know it's just you and this lump of metal all alone in space." He squeezed her fingers. "That's why you mean so much to me, you know? You're my anchor. You're my runway lights on a dark night, shining up at me and bringing me down safe, Sylvia. So – believe in something for me. Will you?"

"I believe in us," she had said. Trying hard to be brave. He had dropped her off at the top of her drive and they had kissed under the rain tree, its leaves in clenched purses waiting for the sun to open them.

"Sylvia! *Sylvia!*"

It was her mother, somewhere down below. With clumsy fingers Sylvia opened her handbag and took out the waxy temple-flower she had picked during lunch. Stepping carefully between the scattered stones, she laid it with the other offerings between the Sasseruwa Buddha's stone feet. The spreading shadow had given the giant figure an air not of repose so much as of boredom, as if it no longer found Sylvia as interesting as she found herself. She turned and ran down the hill, her sandals barely brushing the stone steps, and almost collided with Miss Utteridge at the bottom. The old lady smiled at her with a trace of irony in the wrinkles of her face.

"Well, Sylvia," she said. "I think that was a great success, don't you?"

Everybody seemed to think so. Their venture into the interior behind them, the Expedition embarked on the homeward journey in a talkative mood. Kitty Clarke, rubbing Pond's Cream into her face to counteract the effect of so much direct sunlight, speculated that the Buddhists of old set up their religious images in such ungetatable places to prevent ordinary passers-by from taking them for granted. Archdeacon Hoathly pronounced it more likely that the ancient heathen sculptors were guided by where they could carve a suitable slab of rock. (Christians, he explained, knew better than to tamper with the natural landscape which was evidence enough of the glory of God.)

Maria de Vos and Mrs Donaldson were chatting about William: how he had now gone out to the Western Desert – was it Tobruk? – with the Northumberland Fusiliers, and how they'd had a letter from him saying how warm it was, it reminded him of Ceylon, and he'd had no repetition of that dreadful influenza attack which had them so worried. Her mother only ever became animated nowadays, it seemed to Sylvia, when she could talk to someone about her darling Piggy. The fact that she had another child, actually at home, who might have a few problems of her own, seemed never to occur to her.

With a jittering of china cups and saucers, the tea-trolley came down the aisle. As well as the shortbread, there were deliciously crunchy rock cakes baked by Ottoline Hoathly in the run of her weekly consignment to the Victory Shop. Miss Utteridge's Special rattled southwards, straining every piston to make Colombo before the blackout, and not stopping at all until they reached Kurunegala. Refuelled, they were just moving out of the station when Mrs Ingram Bywater climbed to her feet and pulled the communication cord.

There was a squeal of breaks and a smashing of tea-cups in the galley. The train jerked to a halt. Her arm outstretched and quivering, Mrs Ingram Bywater pointed at the scruffy, grinning newspaper-boy running alongside the train. He was holding up an evening newspaper, whose shocking headline could all too easily be deciphered as they pressed their faces to the window. SINGAPORE SURRENDERS it read.

With some difficulty (the Sinhalese train driver was an impudent beggar, of a type they had all too frequently encountered in the last few months) the train was kept waiting until the Archdeacon had purchased ten copies of *The Times of Ceylon*. For the rest of the journey the Expedition was forgotten. The war (from now on spoken of as the War) had spilled into their own backyard.

Sylvia read the news report over her mother's shoulder. British forces had fought magnificently to the end. Morale never faltered. The resolute demeanour of the troops surrendering their arms would have been a shock to any Japanese general expecting to find a cowed and vanquished enemy. The instrument of surrender, signed yesterday at 7 p.m. local time by Yamashita for the Japanese and Lieutenant-General Percival for the British, in the Ford motor plant at Bukit Timah, was a humanitarian act. Our boys could and would have gone on fighting: but Singapore was full of refugees and running low on water supplies, and Percival wished to spare the city the ordeal of a full-scale assault. It would be unrealistic to deny that the loss of Singapore was a grave setback: but its effect would be to stiffen the upper lips of British forces in the East and spur them to fight on with ever greater determination towards final victory.

That was it. There really wasn't very much for anyone to say. Ottoline Hoathly burst into tears. Her husband patted her awkwardly on the arm.

"You can see why he's called 'Rabbit' Percival," Mrs Ingram Bywater said in a loud voice. "The chap just didn't have the stuffing to stand his ground."

It was all very well to say such things, Sylvia thought at the time, but what if the Japanese were simply too good for any of them? Mrs. I.B. could dismiss them as little yellow monkeys – indeed she was doing just that – but were they not living, all of them, in a world the monkeys were rapidly taking over? Apparently most of our troops in Malaya had been Indian people, but

200

The Times of Ceylon, right in front of her, said that Sumatra was being invaded and Java attacked as well. What if the Orientals had trained a new breed of warrior who were better, man for man, than the British Army itself?

Sitting there in her seat, watching Maria help one of the boys clear up the splinters of smashed coffee-cups, Sylvia had listened to the ancient locomotive pounding back to Colombo. The clatter of its wheels had sounded in her ears like the rattle of machine-gun fire. She had had visions of David Gifford in his Hurricane fighting off hordes of Japanese fighters; of Charlie Bilbow in HMS *Dorsetshire* going down in a blaze of guns. For the first time she had felt a stirring of fear, as if the seed inside her had woken in alarm and kicked its unformed legs in her belly.

Someone was tapping her on the shoulder. Sylvia looked round with a start. It was her neighbour, a nice old colonial type. He was pointing downwards. Her bag had fallen to the floor. Stifling a yawn (it was *very* hot in St Peter's, with the sun coming through those diamond windows) she picked it up and put it on her lap. It still smelt of the temple-flower.

She had missed most of the sermon: not that Eric Hoathly would notice. "Let me turn now to the hymn we are about to sing," he was saying, shuffling his notes in the pulpit. " 'The tumult and the shouting dies; The' – uh – 'Captains and the Kings depart.' "

(Ill-at-ease, thought Sylvia, with his chosen text, perhaps because such an array of Ceylon's captains and kings were present in his congregation, beginning with Governor Prescott sitting very straight-backed in the front pew, flanked by Lady Lusted and the legendary Admiral Layton who only last week, she'd heard her father say, had called one of the Cabinet ministers a wobbly old jelly.)

"Kipling's famous 'Recessional' reminds us lest we – indeed – forget, that in this dark time of strife between nations, when we are anxious, not merely for ourselves, but for our friends and loved ones across the seas, reminds us, I say, that there is one who is a greater General, a General to whom we shall all, in due course, have to account. Kipling's hymn, written in 1897, echoes the famous sentiments of Queen Victoria expressed at about that time – 'An Empire without religion is like a house built on sand.' In Lent we do well to remember that strength of arms is as

201

nothing without a proper humility and faith in God. When we use humility and faith like a light to guide our dealings in this world, then we are indeed a house builded upon a rock, able to withstand all assaults of our enemies. . . ."

(What so complicated things was that Charlie had asked her to marry him. He was now quite unexpectedly back in Ceylon. With Singapore fallen there was nowhere else for *Dorsetshire* to go. She was being dry-docked in Trincomalee, and from what Charlie had heard, Ceylon could become an important naval base. She'd said No, of course. She couldn't imagine why Charlie should want to get married in the middle of a War. Unless it was something to do with his brother Edward getting married in London – an occasion she remembered being told about because they had held the reception in his father's house in Glebe Place just up from the Chelsea Embankment, and Lady Lusted had given Edward an incredibly valuable Crown Derby dinner service. Not that that made any difference.)

"We will be asking that, after the kings have departed and the clamour of battle has died away, 'Still stands Thine ancient sacrifice, An humble and a contrite heart.' Humility, let me say to you, is the supreme virtue, because it meekly accepts all that this world can confront us with – blows and blessings, triumphs and disasters – in the knowledge that God and. . . ." The Archdeacon paused momentarily at this juncture because Admiral Layton had got up and left with a clatter of boots by the vestry door. ". . . that God and the goodness of God will prevail. I want us all to go out into the Fort today in that humble frame of mind which Christ taught us when he said, 'Blessed are the meek, for they shall inherit the earth.' Let us go out, I say, as children before God, renewed in His Holy Spirit. In the name of the Father. . . ."

(The more she thought about it – not about Glebe Place, especially, but about her pregnancy – the more convinced she was that it was Charlie's baby she was carrying. It was quite early after her period but frankly she was a bit vague about these dates and Mummy probably wouldn't be much help. Besides which she wanted to present Mummy with a husband-to-be she'd feel safe with.)

God of our fathers, known of old,
Lord of our far-flung battle-line,
Beneath whose awful Hand we hold
Dominion over palm and pine. . . .

(Besides which, too, David for all his terrific tenderness and his Laurence Olivier qualities was so *dark* – dark where Charlie was blond, deep where Charlie was open – you could never be quite sure of his reaction if the baby turned out not. . . . whereas dear Charlie and his relations wouldn't notice the difference. And, quite honestly, when all was said and done it was the future of her baby she had to consider, and at least with Charlie one knew.)

> *The tumult and the shouting dies;*
> *The Captains and the Kings depart. . . .*

As the lusty chorus of Colombo's upholders of the faith, defenders of the free, sank to a dramatic hush for the last verse of Kipling's hymn, Sylvia, with a grateful glance heavenwards, reached her decision. Now she could tell Mummy about it . . . although on second thoughts she might wait just a little longer, there was no point in rushing things. Feeling that a burden had dropped from her, Sylvia with a gloved finger found her place in the hymn book, and adopted a suitably solemn expression as she sang the last chorus in her clear soprano –

> *Lord God of Hosts, be with us yet,*
> *Lest we forget – lest we forget!*

SIR OLIVER PRESCOTT had learnt to live with his physical appearance. His head was somewhat pine-cone-shaped, a peculiarity he shared with William IV. In recent years, as Mollie had never ceased to remind him, he had begun to verge upon the portly. True, he had lost a fair amount of weight since Mollie died. But one detail of his physiology never failed to embarrass him. At emotional moments he flowed, not from the eyes, but from the nose.

Standing here on the wooden jetty, watching a launch from one of the last (perhaps the very last) refugee ships from Singapore speed across the harbour, he could feel the mucus begin to prickle in his nasal passages. This wasn't the only refugee boat he had turned up to greet, but the truth was that the early arrivals hadn't affected him in the same way. It must be knowing so much more now about the utter disaster these poor devils had escaped that brought the lump to his throat.

Coolies secured the ropes. Feeble waves from the launch were answered by cheers from the crowd behind the harbourmaster's barriers on the quayside as the first arrivals were helped on to the jetty. The Ceylon Police Band, rather heavy on the tubas, struck up "There'll Always Be an England". The Governor wiped his nose. The whole scene put him in mind of one of those mid-Victorian genre paintings. Really, if he was as handy with oils as Mollie had been with watercolours, he would have painted it under some such legend as "Safely Home": the brass instruments of the band flashing in the bright sun, the gaily dressed crowd on the quayside waving their sun-hats and the answering waves from the refugees hobbling towards the gangplank, and across the water the vessel itself, its name invisible under streaks of oil, parts of its rigging shot away, a jagged hole in the poop, and a lifeboat swinging dangerously from a single davit....

And where was all their luggage? In January it had been gleaming steamer trunks. Now it was bags and wicker baskets and a few bulging and broken suitcases, flapping like the stained and crumpled clothes of the figures carrying them. And what were they doing wearing headscarves? On closer inspection they weren't headscarves at all, but bandages – the one he'd thought had red flowers on, that was a bandage too, poor old dear. He blew his nose, so sharply that he got a ringing in his ears.

The refugees were shepherded into lines on the covered jetty. Sir Oliver, swagger-stick under his arm (everybody had a swagger-stick nowadays), joined the harbour officials in their white uniforms and gold braid, at the Harbour end of the jetty, near the foot of the gangplank. The genre painting had vanished, to be replaced in his thoughts by other, more contemporary images: the Singapore godowns burning with a thick black smoke; the Naval Base abandoned to looters; Allied troops, riotous with booze and misery, rampaging through the city they'd never had the chance to defend; generals, an admiral, an air marshal paddling sampans to find a junk to take them across the Malacca Strait – Sumatra, Java, anywhere to get away from the Japanese.

These had been the stories out of Singapore for a fortnight now. They filled him with shame and the sense of unreality which comes when the nightmares which plague sleep are relived in the callous light of day.

Exactly four years ago, as a guest of Shenton Thomas, Sir Oliver had attended the official opening of the Singapore Naval Base. One vast, humming war machine, it was a sight as formidable in its way as the Tower of London must have been to Wat Tyler's peasants. Underground workshops and armament depots capable of surviving a direct hit from a 2000 lb bomb, acres of machine shops, repair shops and power plants, a graving dock, a floating dock, cranes the height of a fourteen-storey building, fuel-tanks, barracks, cantonments, messes, all under the protection of menacing batteries of heavy artillery, minefields, airfields. . . . No wonder Shenton was bursting with pride and complacency from the soles of his boots to the tip of his white cockaded topi. The Gibraltar of the East, impervious from the sea and invulnerable from the land, a fortress. . . .

From which, seventy days after the confounded Japs landed at Kota Bahru ("Well, I suppose you'll shove the little men off!" Shenton Thomas had laughed to Rabbit Percival), a pitiful Dunkirk of motor-launches had set out to flee from those same little men. Whereupon they were blown out of the water by Admiral Ozawa or, more probably, beached on one of the many desert islands in the Strait, where at this moment their passengers would be facing imminent death from malaria and starvation.

These images had been with Sir Oliver Prescott in his waking and sleeping hours. They had been confirmed and embellished by every new batch of refugees, adding their tesserae to a black mosaic of apocalypse. Their stories, needless to say, had been cheerful anecdotes of individual acts of fortitude and ingenuity, of gallant good humour in the face of death. It was what was unwittingly revealed when each piece was fitted into place – the blind, dogged, obstinate imbecility of Malaya Command, the blithering muddle of Sir Shenton himself – that made the Governor want to weep when he looked at these brave souls on board. Wiping his nose he stepped forward, swagger-stick under his arm, to welcome the new arrivals and shake them by the hand.

They happened to be stretcher-cases, unfortunately. He had to step back to avoid getting in the way of nurses who rushed them into waiting ambulances. The last stretcher-case put out a bandaged arm. Sir Oliver lifted the end of it and moved it up and down.

"Welcome to Ceylon," he said. Cameras clicked.

"To where?" asked the head on the pillow. Man or woman, he couldn't be sure.

"To Ceylon."

"Oh," said the head. "Oh. We must have missed. . . ."

The voice trailed away. The stretcher moved on. A merry-looking Englishwoman in a blue dress, one leg blown off, followed on crutches. She put out her hand.

"Nice to meet you, Your Excellency," she said cheerfully. "I'm Jane Purfleet, Mrs. Can't tell you what it's like to be back on the old terra firma. I don't suppose you've come across a sister of mine. Betty Warrender. Have you? She was heading your way." With that she swayed, and would have collapsed if the Governor had not supported her. "So sorry," she murmured faintly. "Sea legs, you know."

The band started up again. Another launch was coming in. To Sir Oliver's astonishment, the huddle of refugees in it were singing. Stirred by the music to memories of happier days, of Sunday lunchtimes at Raffles and the Sea View Hotel, they sang raggedly at first, gradually gaining strength, until by the chorus the whole boat-load of starving, tottering refugees had joined in a defiant refrain –

> *There'll always be an England*
> *And England shall be free,*
> *If England means as much to you*
> *As England means to me.*

Everybody cheered and waved. White handkerchiefs fluttered. Children sat on their father's shoulders and waved little Union Jacks. Mothers leant over the barriers (Customs formalities could not be waived unless for the Japanese) to embrace relatives and friends – British, Dutch, Malays, Indians, Americans, Chinese – who had somehow survived their peril on the sea.

The Governor was wielding his handkerchief for the fourth or fifth time, when the singing on the launch faltered and died away. He looked round. A Ceylon Planters' Rifles platoon was marching smartly along the quayside in front of the Customs House. The refugees from Singapore stared at them with blank faces. What were they pointing out to each other? It must be the CPRC's Lee-Enfield 303s.

Like the host at one of his cocktail parties the Governor continued to stand there smiling and shaking hands as the line staggered past him into Customs. He knew what they were thinking. Out of the frying pan into the fire. If 67,000 troops and some of the biggest guns in the world hadn't stopped the Japanese in Malaya, what were a few units of old-timers with First World War pea-shooters expected to do against them in Ceylon?

Thank God that wasn't his problem any more. That was Layton's can of worms. And since Vice-Admiral Geoffrey Layton, RN, Commander-in-Chief, Ceylon, as of a fortnight ago, clearly enjoyed playing Mr High and Mighty, Sir Oliver was not going to stand in his path.

There were similarities, he reflected malevolently behind his fixed smile, between Geoffrey Layton and Chaplin's great dictator. They were both small men. They both strutted. They both had a tendency to gesticulate and to bang everything in sight with fists or sticks whenever they were crossed. When Churchill had given Layton his plenipotentiary powers in Ceylon – one of the lessons learnt from Singapore where nobody was in overall command – Sir Oliver had immediately tendered his resignation. Cranborne, the new Colonial Secretary, had refused to accept it. In a long cable, signed 'Bobbety', larded with flattering phrases, he had contrived to suggest that the entire War Cabinet would be deeply offended if in "this hour of peril" such a loyal and conscientious public servant as Sir Oliver were to resign before he could be properly rewarded with the laurels that crown so distinguished a career.

Sir Oliver understood perfectly what this meant. It was a clear threat to the G in front of his CMG, as well as to his full pension rights. Graciously he consented to withdraw his resignation and suffer the dreadful Layton as patiently as he was able.

Nevertheless there were times like the following morning, visiting the Ladies' Golf Club, when the motto of his Order of St Michael and St George, *Auspicium Melius Aevi*, aroused in the Governor the thoughts that lie too deep for tears. How sadly fitting it was that he should be decorated for his lifetime's service with the Token of a Better Age. As he sat in the Club Committee Room, listening to the opening address and hearing in the background the bulldozers plough up the familiar fairways and fill in the bunkers to make a site for another army camp, Sir Oliver felt his life slipping through his fingers like ash through a grate.

They were all there, rustling on the rattan chairs in their Hirdaramani's silks and cottons: representatives from the Services, the Rotary Club, the Women's International Club, the European Association, the Wives' Fellowships and the Ceylon Planters' Association. They had come to hear him talk about Singapore and discuss the requirements of the refugees. Mrs Ingram Bywater presided over the tea and biscuits (coffee was now in short supply), and Lady Lusted had rounded up a gaggle of refugees to deliver each a short soliloquy on The Most Thrilling Moment of My Escape from Singapore.

Token of a Better Age. Was it a fault in him, some strain of pessimism or nervous exhaustion, that made him take it for granted the Better Age lay in the past, not in the future? It was to the past that he found himself returning when he told them about Singapore – the shopping for presents in Chinatown, coffee at Robinsons, the crush in Raffles Hotel at Sunday lunch (was Robinsons or even Raffles still standing? He did not dare ask) – for the painful reason that he could not go into detail about the fall of the city: it was too profoundly humiliating.

How could he expect them to take him seriously? How could he expect them to believe that the main reason Singapore fell was because all its guns pointed out to sea? Or that Malay Command had abandoned the Naval Base and its equipment even before Percival's troops had withdrawn across the Causeway; had refused to respond to the Japanese pre-assault bombardment because Percival didn't think it was serious – and then the searchlights to direct our counter-barrage were never switched on because apparently the signal ordering it never arrived!

He put the best face on it he could. "I can tell you no more than

Winston Churchill told the House of Commons," he said. "We lost Malaya, in a ten-week campaign, to an enemy we outnumbered three to one. Our own troops fought bravely and well; it was only an overwhelming superiority in air and sea power which gave the Japs an edge. I know some of you have friends and relatives left behind in Singapore. From what my people tell me, the Japs aren't treating them too badly. It was General Percival's final request that the Nipponese army would protect the women and children and the British civilians, and Yamashita promised that he would guarantee it. As to how things are going in Java, your guess is as good as mine. Frankly I fear that Batavia will go the same way as Singapore."

A buzz of indignation swarmed through the Committee Room. Sir Oliver swallowed. Deirdre Lusted's expression said plainly that if she had been in Wavell's or Percival's place she'd have chased every last little yellow man out of South-East Asia. And, by God, she probably would have, too. He cleared his throat and soldiered on, raising his voice against the noise outside.

"I can promise you this, though. We've already got more and better fighter aircraft in Ceylon than were available in the whole of Malaya. And keep this under your hats – ha! – but I have it on good authority that an aircraft-carrier or two are on their way to Colombo as we speak. We've learnt our lessons from Singapore. It's taught us a trick or two. If the Japs come this way, they're going to come off a very bad second best!"

There was a polite drizzle of applause. A tall woman in a blue spotted dress raised her hand. The Governor squinted at her uncertainly.

"What are your evacuation plans?" she asked.

He recognised her now. "You need have no worries on that score, Mrs Buller," he declared. "Everything will go smoothly into operation."

"Isn't that what they said in Singapore?"

It was time to move the discussion on to the pressing problem of refugees and their need for board and lodging. As they talked – was he the only one to notice? – coolies kept coming in and carting away the furniture! With brazen nonchalance they removed the chairs, one by one, until all the empty seats had gone. They lifted the sideboard (there went any hope of a drink) and took it outside.

What the blazes was going on? They were taking the bookcase now – and the curtains – and the Ladies' Golf Club team

209

photographs off the wall. Nobody was paying the slightest attention, that he could see. When at last with respectful bows the Sinhalese came for him – in the event for the little table beside him with its carafe of filtered water – Sir Oliver felt he really had to make an issue of it.

"What's going on in here?" was what he actually burst out with.

The representatives of the Ladies' Committee smiled at him as if he was making one of his jokes.

"Surely you know, Sir Oliver," said Mrs Ingram Bywater after an embarrassed pause. "Admiral Layton gave us the news last week. He has requisitioned us. Tomorrow, the building is reclassified as officers' quarters. Isn't that right?"

The Governor hesitated for no more than the second it took him to digest this information. "So it is," he said, controlling himself with difficulty. "Quite right. So it is."

He was in no mood to carry on after that. As soon as he decently could, he left the Committee Room, negotiating a passage through rolled carpets, piled furniture, stacked pictures, old golf-bags and glass cases of stuffed and moulting birds. He was extremely angry. Layton had gone too far. He was damned if he was going to be made a fool of in this way. Layton, confound the man, had no prerogative to take these decisions without first consulting him.

Banging his hat down over his ears, Sir Oliver stormed out to his waiting car, a pi-dog sniffing at his heels. That was what war did. It sprang upon one out of nowhere, rude mechanicals with swagger-sticks whose only experience of human contact was shouting at troops on a barracks square. For him to have in effect stepped aside for Layton had required the kind of tact and self-lessness that only came with years of service. Layton seemed determined to repay it by humiliating him. First he'd pinched one of his best men, Sebastian Clarke, to work as one of his aides under the ridiculous title of Second Flag Officer, Shore Command. Then he had commandeered the whole of Victoria Park as an army camp. (The man obviously had a chip on his shoulder about golf, he'd put *cows* out to graze on the Nuwara Eliya golf links.)

And now this. It was too much. His hands twisted and flexed his swagger-stick across his knee as if it were Layton himself he was twisting in his hands, stocky, balding, arrogant Layton with his flat, red face and stubborn, obstinate jaw which would break the bones in any hand that punched it – not that the Governor would mind having a go. Was this what it had come to – seeing one territory after another that he'd spent his life looking after falling to the Japanese, and ending up on a little island off India being bossed and bullied and browbeaten by Layton, of all odious specimens? He ground his teeth. The man was odious, odious. Him and his miserable little black and tan bitch terrier which had twice bitten his white trousers. He had no tact. He revelled in being a "naval type", abrupt, forceful, given to using the kind of salty language that might be acceptable on the lower deck but had already been the subject of complaints by his Ceylonese ministers. . . .

Under normal circumstances, Layton and he would have divided up the military and civil government of the island between them. It was Shenton Thomas who had queered Sir Oliver's pitch. Shenton had put up such a poor show at the end in Singapore – neglecting to sign minutes in Council so that he could countermand decisions, arguing with Duff Cooper, Wavell and virtually the entire Malaya Command, refusing absolutely to accept the fact that defeat was staring him in the face – that every time Sir Oliver moved to intervene with Layton, the spectre of wretched Shenton loomed up before him and robbed him of the initiative.

It was going to be like that today. He knew it as soon as he made his entrance into the War Council room on the first floor of Queen's House and saw them sitting there: Sebastian Clarke, Layton, Air Vice-Marshal d'Albiac, the First Secretary and Sebastian's old boss George Donaldson. They rose when he came in. With a curt smile he nodded at them and took his seat at the head of the table.

"Well, gentlemen. What's on the menu today?"

Simon House, hovering beside the false fireplace, hurried over and put a single typewritten sheet in his hand. Layton started talking at once, without giving him time to look down the agenda.

"With your permission, Sir Oliver, I have ordered the demolition of the Racecourse grandstands, along with the houses of the Chief Justice and Colonel Kotelawala which are in the flight-path."

"What? What are you saying? The Racecourse?"

"You will find it at the head of this morning's agenda, Sir Oliver. I must have a new runway for our Hurricane squadrons that will take Hirohito's pilots by surprise. I regard it as a matter of supreme urgency. I have asked the PWO to get hold of every elephant in Colombo for the job."

The agenda convulsed in the Governor's hand. He laid it down on the leather-edged blotter in front of him and smoothed it out with quivering fingers. Control. He must control himself.

"This is a desecration," he declared, very deliberately. "It is an act of vandalism, there is no other word for it. I myself opened the new grandstand in January. It was subscribed for by the whole of Colombo. Yet you are proposing, if my ears do not deceive me, to demolish it, demolish the whole complex, together with the residences of two of Ceylon's most distinguished public servants – for a *runway*."

"Yes," said Vice-Admiral Sir Geoffrey Layton.

There was silence. From far beneath rose the faint clattering anguish of the boiler.

"Sir, we have considered alternative sites," said Air Vice-Marshal d'Albiac. "Nowhere else offers the twin advantages of shelter and the element of surprise in an air raid."

Another silence. Sir Oliver looked at Sebastian. He sat playing with his pencil. George Donaldson, beside him, lifted his shoulders in an almost imperceptible shrug.

"I cannot accede to this," Sir Oliver said, speaking rapidly. "Even you, Layton, must appreciate the damage it will do to morale. The whole recreation of the people of Ceylon consists in going to the races. The Colombo Racecourse is to the Ceylonese what the West End is to Londoners; you might as well build a runway between Piccadilly Circus and Leicester Square. Our job should be to reassure the people here if we want their co-operation. This will destroy all confidence in us. Take my word, the effect on morale would be catastrophic. We must build the runway elsewhere. This is a matter on which I cannot give way."

"*Bad for morale.*" Layton spat the words out with such intense disgust that Sir Oliver started. "That is a phrase I had hoped never to hear again for the duration of the War. We surrendered Singapore because of decisions not taken because they would be *bad for morale*. We consistently refused to create defensive positions in Malaya because the sight of them would have been *bad for morale*. We delayed evacuation because it would be *bad for morale*. We pushed thousands of troops and weapons into the city as it was about to surrender because to divert them elsewhere would have been *bad for morale*. We refused to destroy stocked warehouses and factories on Singapore Island because Percival thought it would be bad for bloody morale. When the bloody Japs were on the outskirts of the city we went on telling the citizens the situation was in hand because it would have been bad for

212

your bloody morale to tell them different. *Don't talk to me, sir, about morale!*"

He stopped. Nobody moved. Sir Oliver turned his face to the window. Outside in Gordon Gardens a butcher bird gave a piercing cry and swooped to impale a bundle of fur in its claws upon a strand of barbed wire.

"I spoke, perhaps, with more heat than was necessary. I am sorry," said Layton.

The Governor did not reply.

"You will understand, Sir Oliver, that I had to withdraw my command from Malaya. I do not intend to withdraw it from Ceylon."

Sir Oliver looked at him, his face expressionless. "I understand perfectly," he replied. "You will do what you will. May I suggest that we move on to item number two?"

Sebastian Clarke stopped playing with his pencil. He cleared his throat and looked at Layton for permission to proceed. Layton nodded.

"The Scorched Earth Committee has held three meetings so far, in the Chief Secretary's office," Clarke began. "We have agreed that the naval, military and Royal Air Force authorities will be responsible for the destruction of their own installations, establishments, vehicles, equipment and stores, together with all important strategic bridges. Civilian demolition and denial-to-the-enemy schemes are now being worked out, but we have agreed the main points. . . ."

Sir Oliver stared straight ahead at the print on the wall, above Layton's head, of Queen Victoria at Osborne receiving a deposed Kandyan princess. The princess lay prostrate in a ring of ninepin courtiers; the Queen graciously put forth her hand, one ringed finger extended downwards like the Sistine Chapel Jehovah offering life to His creation. What the Lord giveth, the Lord also taketh away. . . .

"Harbour installations will be destroyed, including warehouses, coal stocks and lighters, the lighters preferably being fired and sunk in the harbour entrance and in the berths. All West Coast petrol stations will be rendered inoperable. We're working on a scheme to pollute petrol stocks with rubber latex. . . ."

Was it really necessary to destroy the island in order to save it from the Japanese? Through half-closed eyes the Governor envisaged the city of Colombo burning with bright flames, his telephone dead, the lights flickering and going out, the stench of

213

smouldering rubber, the smash of glass as whisky-bottles were uncrated and thrown against the wall. Was this how it would end, after all the flag-waving, the brave words, the Tank Weeks and carnivals to drum up war funds?

Six weeks ago – it seemed no time at all – he had been borne at the head of a tank division into the Government Press Grounds to open the second Printers' Pie Carnival. Escorted by Kandyan dancers and nautch girls, and followed in procession by ARP trucks, ambulances, and a fire-engine, his brightly decorated tank had rumbled over a mock minefield into the Press Grounds and crashed slowly into a huge cardboard pie.

When the cheering and clapping had died down he had stood erect in the turret and delivered a short address on the virtues of the tank as a fighting machine; how it had won the war on land for us in 1918; how the Germans had relied on it to beat the French Army to a frazzle two years ago and had very nearly done the same to our gallant ally the Russians; and now the Allies were turning the tables by using tank divisions, with splendid support by the RAF, to beat the enemy back from Moscow and hurl them headlong out of Libya too. "By tanks-giving today we can help our brave fighting men to give us cause for thanksgiving tomorrow!"

The money rolled in, to the tune of "Rule Britannia" on a scratchy gramophone. It went on rolling in. It passed the million-rupee mark, then the two-million mark for the RAF alone; enough for eighteen fighter planes. Large cheques from businessmen, smaller donations from tradesmen and clerks, roadsweepers, fruit-sellers, one day's pay from the overseers and labourers of nearly every estate on the island, to fund a war that meant nothing to them yet but would do soon enough if Sebastian Clarke's plans came into operation. . . .

"The Committee recommends that there should be three stages in regard to the destruction of property," Sebastian was saying. "The first we have called the 'Alert', the second the 'Close-up' and the third 'Action'. This of course is the 'Alert' stage, and preparations are proceeding smoothly. Preparing stores for explosives, drilling holes in the harbour sills and constructing tunnels in coal stacks are all being carried out under the guise of Air Raid Precaution exercises—"

"ARP?" interrupted Layton. "What about the underground command post? Perhaps Sir Oliver will bring us up to date."

"I beg your pardon?"

"Item three, Sir Oliver. The underground civil defence HQ. It was due to be finished at the end of February."

"Yes." The Governor looked at George Donaldson for succour. "Isn't it that fellow Kandasala in charge?"

George Donaldson shuffled through his sheaf of papers and produced a handwritten memo. Layton groaned.

"According to the chief ARP overseer, Mr J.P. Kandasala, there have been delays . . . where are we . . . problems with the extensive and very complicated wires . . . problems with the high water table on Galle Face Green . . . movement of the concrete base, let me see . . . the roof to go on, and he says everything should be bang on in a fortnight." He looked up with an amused expression.

"A fortnight?"

"Yes, sir."

Layton clenched his fist and pounded the table. Coffee-cups rattled. The secretary taking the minutes put her nib through the paper.

"What the bloody hell's going on!" shouted the Admiral. "Gentlemen, we are at war! I arrived expecting to find myself in a country mobilised for battle. What I found was no fewer than three different strikes in the port, which resulted in forty-eight vessels lying helpless in the outer anchorage. Civil defence appallingly inadequate. Fire-fighting arrangements ditto. No radar warning systems. A total defence force of three battalions, a Town Guard of three hundred businessmen and two anti-aircraft batteries that spend their time square-bashing because they don't have equipment!" He glared at George Donaldson. "I'm not making any accusations. I know it's been a job to get London interested. But civil defence is not a London matter. It's up to us! If Oliver Goonetilleke needs more resources to get the underground command post finished, he must be told to ask for them. With your permission, Sir Oliver, I should like Mr Goonetilleke to be present at our next meeting."

The Governor nodded to George Donaldson, but did not answer. Indeed he had only distantly heard the C-in-C's tirade. It wasn't as though Oliver Goonetilleke hadn't done a damn good job. There were ARP wardens in every other street, spotters on every high building in Colombo. What was it Deirdre Lusted had been complaining about before the Golf Club meeting? The ARP spotter on the roof of the Galle Face Hotel. She had been in the bathroom and opened the curtains and there he was, with his binoculars, staring straight at her window! The blackout was bad enough, it was an open invitation to thieves; was she to have no privacy either?

215

The Governor had promised to look into it. On reflection, an unfortunate choice of phrase. He imagined Deirdre Lusted rising from her bath: soapsuds careering down her pendulous breasts and plopping from huge, purplish nipples, soapsuds on her flaccid belly, soapsuds on her sagging, dimpled buttocks. Was there something wrong with him, that he hankered after women so much younger than himself – *poppets* if he was honest – with their budding young figures and firm-all-over skin?

Even when Mollie was alive . . . but there was nothing harmful in it, it was an aesthetic appreciation of form and shapeliness. He saw himself standing on a high roof, searching the sky for enemy aircraft, swinging his binoculars until they came to rest on the bathroom window of Miss Hartington, his social secretary. Miss Hartington was a model of efficiency, neatly printing in his appointments diary every name but her own; but tonight, naughty girl, she had defied the blackout and taken a bath with the lights on. What's more, she had failed to draw down the blind, all innocent of ARP spotters with binoculars on high roofs, and there she stood in the bath, in a shower of chestnut tresses, bending to soap her thighs. He had imagined the discreet fullness of her exquisitely pointed breasts, but he would never have guessed at the existence of those three little brown moles on her hip which drew your eyes, like the Belt of Orion, towards the shiny, dark, curling triangle between her legs—

"Sir Oliver!"

He dropped the binoculars.

"Sir Oliver, I should be grateful for your views on how these Defence Regulations can best be publicised."

"Ah." The Governor showed his teeth in a smile. "I think this is a case of *inter arma, silent leges*, is it not?" When Layton's only response was a gloomy frown, he allowed a note of condescension into his voice. "He saw enough wars, Cicero, to know that in time of war the laws are silent. The regulations can be put into effect immediately; I'll have a word with the Attorney-General."

He sat back and savoured his small victory. Layton of course was not musical enough to know that in orchestras it is always the second horns who carry the melody. He had already taken off on another tack, banging away about importing rice from Egypt and America now that supplies from Burma were almost exhausted; drawing up a list of indigenous foods which could help provision the newly completed top-secret naval base at Addu Atoll for Admiral Somerville's Eastern Fleet (Sir Oliver still remembered it as the China Fleet from the days when it was based under Somerville in Hong Kong). . . . Most of it was, in the Governor's opinion, a waste of time.

Why not admit it? Destroying the Racecourse was an abominable waste of time. The Japs had shown what they could do in Malaya and on the Burma Road. If they wanted to take Ceylon, they would. No power on earth could stop them. ARP was vital. Food production was vital. The rest was whistling in the wind. The only aspect of the War which had given him any encouragement at all, recently, were Rawling's brilliant schemes for guerrilla warfare. . . .

Major Rawling had not been idle these past few weeks. His scheme to round up Sama Samajist dissidents by following their messengers back from the printing shops had met with remarkable success. He was now engaged in vetting patriotic young Ceylonese men who could be trained for sabotage and fifth-column work in the jungle. It was his view that the Japanese, when they came, would hold Ceylon with only a token garrison, a garrison which could be successfully harried and sabotaged by a highly trained, highly motivated guerrilla force. To this end he had employed volunteers from the Ceylon Defence Force, working under conditions of utmost secrecy to reopen and clean a long underground tunnel (which the Governor hadn't known existed) from the seventeenth-century Dutch fort at Kalpitiya towards the sea.

Rawling had also been experimenting with a new long-wave transmitter. This had rather less auspicious consequences. Shortly before Christmas he had sent out a sergeant in the Ceylon Engineers with the transmitter to Port Blair in the Andaman Islands. His instructions were to sail from there to the northern tip of Sumatra and make his way down the island towards the Malacca Strait, transmitting every twenty-four hours on a pre-arranged frequency. The transmission grew fainter each day as the sergeant made his way down the east coast of Sumatra until, by the time it was necessary to recall Sergeant de Mel before he ran into trouble, contact was lost altogether.

Two weeks ago, long after Rawling had given up hope of the man, his transmitter crackled into life, its signal strong and clear. *Konnichiwa. Seiron do ittara ii desu ka*? ("Good afternoon. How do I get to Ceylon?") There followed some untranslatable phrases and a high crackle of laughter. Evidently Sergeant de Mel had fallen into the hands of the Japanese. Worse, the Japs had tinkered with the transmitter to give it a longer range than it had previously possessed.

Rawling appeared to regard this incident as an insult directed personally at him. His conviction that there were Japanese spies in Ceylon took on a new animus. Restrained by the Governor from physically forcing his way into Buddhist temples with a search warrant, the Major had members of the Young Men's Buddhist Association followed and aerial photographs taken of their sanctuaries, which he then scrutinised with a magnifying glass for evidence of radio transmitter antennae.

It was the conversations he had with the Major about psychological warfare which most enthralled Sir Oliver. Rawling had read an article in *Nature* about infestations of soldier ants, and a certain kind of chemical spray which had been developed to neutralise them by making them lose all sense of direction (the Governor had not remembered the precise details in the excitement of the moment). Rawling had spotted instantly that the principle behind this spray could be utilised against the rigorously structured and disciplined Japanese Army.

He asked the Governor for funds to set up a printing operation to flood Japanese-occupied territories with forged currency. Sir Oliver had authorised them. He saw now, with a momentary unease, that this constituted item five on the War Council agenda.

There came another scream from the butcher bird. Round the table every face was turned in his direction. He gave a small cough behind his hand.

"I think we can all agree with Major Rawling," he said. "We can't sit back and wait for trouble. We have to take the war to the Japanese."

"How?" asked Layton.

"I beg your pardon?"

"How does Rawling intend to distribute the forged currency? The Japanese have command of the air over their occupied territories, I need hardly remind you."

"Ah, I've thought of that one. British-trained Chinese and Malay agents would smuggle them into enemy territory. Rawling has hand-picked a team of operatives to train for this mission."

The C-in-C's face registered scepticism.

"The consequences could be devastating," persisted Sir Oliver. "There would be widespread unrest. Rioting. The Japs could have a civil war on their hands in no time. Malaya, Java...." He gestured with his hands in a vague illustration of countries collapsing like a row of dominoes.

"I am not blind to the possibilities," Layton replied. "I question, however, whether we should be placing bets on outside chances when the defence of the Empire is at stake. I seem to remember that Major Rawling's last proposal was to equip a corpse with a radio and drop it on a dud parachute into Japanese-held territory, in the expectation that the Japs would use his radio to try to deceive our Intelligence. What was the outcome of that?"

The Governor flushed. It was typical of bully-boys like Layton to look no further ahead than the indent for the next piece of military hardware. "There has been a delay due, I am told, to the problem of obtaining or stealing a corpse in a suitably fresh condition to be flown to Sumatra," he said stiffly. "This does not invalidate the tactical merits of the forged-currency scheme. I think we should recognise that Rawling has had a pretty good success rate."

Layton shot out a hairy wrist and looked at his watch. "Well, he's got the money," he conceded ungraciously. "If he wants to spend it setting up a printing press, let's hope his notes don't have 'Made in Ceylon' across the watermark. I have just one further announcement to make, gentlemen. You will all have heard the news that Bandung has fallen. Our troops, and the Dutch, have been forced to retreat from Rangoon towards the coast." He put on his spectacles. "D'Albiac, you will testify that I was given stick by the Air Ministry in London for diverting two squadrons of Hurricanes here from Java. My decision has been borne out by the message I received as I was leaving to come here today."

With a regrettably theatrical flourish, Vice-Admiral Layton unbuttoned his breast pocket and took out a cable. He unfolded it, and read from the decoded message underneath. "At 0425 hours this morning, the Foreign Office received a communication sent eighteen hours earlier by Mr Yencken, our man in Madrid. It read: 'I learn from a reliable source that the Japanese Embassy is saying next objective will be not Australia but Ceylon.'"

In the silence that followed, Sir Oliver felt his bowels begin to churn. What would he do if he ended up in the bag like Shenton Thomas? Would he cope any better when the chips were down?

The dreadful thing was that he saw himself all too vividly in Shenton's shoes. Cowering under the dining table or behind the refrigerator in the Government House pantry, like poor Shenton, as the bombs fell all around. Not discovering until too late that blowing up the Causeway also blew up Singapore's mains water supply and having to rush home from War Council to fit taps to all the stand-pipes. Having to deal with frightened servants, telling them to stay put under the billiard-table. Being forced out

219

of Government House, dodging the craters in the drive; and finally having to walk under guard through the streets – so he'd heard – into Japanese captivity.

Frankly, it was not pain or torture or imprisonment that Sir Oliver was suddenly afraid of. It was the humiliation: the indignity of having his office and all that it represented exposed as futile in front of the Ceylonese. He had always argued (usually to Mollie's free-thinking friends from London, whom she'd invited to stay when she wanted to annoy him) that the justification for British rule in the East, above and beyond the spreading of social benefits, was the maintenance of order. If order collapsed, if the British proconsuls failed to protect the local population from external attack, then they forfeited the right to govern.

He saw himself being led in handcuffs, hatless through the streets of Colombo . . . his route to prison lined by Moors, Tamils, Sinhalese, their expressionless faces luridly lit by the flames from Sebastian's torched warehouses . . . his plumed hat kicked along the street in front of him by a monocled Japanese officer. Before his eyes the feathers turned into a chicken and scuttled into the crowd which exploded on every side into cackles of derisive laughter—

Layton was rapping on the table with his spectacles. "Gentlemen, we are in a sticky corner. General Wavell made it clear to me, as a friend, when I took up this post that my job was to make a defensive stand, whatever the cost. . . ."

What were they all anyway, reflected the Governor, but dragonflies, flashing and skittering over unfathomable waters? They landed on the dark, sullen river of the East and let themselves be carried along for a while, resplendent on the tide – he, Layton, all of them – and vanished; but the river flowed on.

Golden lads and girls all must, As chimney-sweepers come to dust. . . .

He had been to some of those forts in Uva province built by the British over a hundred years ago, in the last war the Ceylonese had been made to fight. Forts at Paranagama, Dehiwinna, Badalkumbura, Palatupana, Kalugodella: hilltop strongholds with their parapets of stone and earthwork and bastions at each corner – and now? A few melancholy, ruined walls half-submerged in jungle or patana grass.

In one they showed him a skull with a piece of gun barrel lodged in the bone. He asked if they knew who it was had died in this horrible way. The guide had grinned at him through broken teeth.

220

"English, Master!" he'd said with satisfaction.

The Governor looked round the table. In the silence that followed Layton's speech he could hear the tumultuous murmur, never stilled, of the Ceylon that lay beyond the high windows.

"Gentlemen, I think we should call it a day," he said.

5 April 1942.   7.15 a.m. Addu Atoll.

The morning skies are still overcast this Easter Sunday morning. Eight-tenths storm clouds have been reported over most of the west coast of Ceylon by the two Hurricanes from 30 Squadron which took off on a routine patrol at first light from Ratmalana. Six Fleet Air Arm Fulmars – slow, awkward, two-seater fighters given some limited value as recon-naissance aircraft by the introduction of lightweight, high-frequency wireless telegraphy sets – followed them into the air and are patrolling down the west coast, round towards the east and back again. Six other Fleet Air Arm antiques, "Stringbag" Swordfish from 788 Squadron at China Bay, have taken off for the 160-mile overland flight to Colombo, each carrying a small torpedo in case they sight the enemy fleet.

There has been no news of the whereabouts of Nagumo's Striking Force since the abruptly silenced report at midnight from Flight-Lieutenant Graham's 205 Squadron Catalina. A third reconnaissance aircraft, Flight-Lieutenant Bradshaw's 240 Squadron Catalina, has taken off and flown in the direction of Graham's sighting report, expecting to meet with the same fate. There are now just three flying boats left under the netting on Koggala Lagoon.

At 7 a.m. Bradshaw's crew, flying low over the waves to escape detection by enemy radar, spot a large number of aircraft directly above them, flying north. They have been briefed to expect British carrier-borne planes in these coastal waters, so they do not break radio silence to report them. They fly on south, towards the Japanese fleet.

Admiral Sir James Somerville, at the head of his Fast Division in the battleship Warspite, *is not much more than a hundred miles ENE of Addu Atoll. Events are overtaking him. The sighting report from Graham's Catalina has shown the Japanese carrier force making full steam for Ceylon. Almost as worrying are reports coming in from the Bay of Bengal. In the last hour, two merchant ships off the east coast of India,* Malda *and* Sinkuang, *have reported being attacked – one by aircraft, the other apparently by a battleship! It confirms his worst fears.*

223

A two-pronged attack by the Japs in the Indian Ocean is bad enough. That his Eastern Fleet should be out of position to deal with either is almost too much to bear.

The last-ditch strategy Somerville has agreed with the First Sea Lord at the Admiralty is at all costs to keep the Eastern Fleet "in being". There are to be "no adventures", in Churchill's words when the two men met before Somerville left England. If Somerville's fleet remains "in being", so the argument goes, the Japanese will not necessarily be able to cut Britain's sea routes to the Middle East up the east coast of Africa, even if they do capture Ceylon – and they would then have to divert valuable naval forces from the Pacific to defend Ceylon against Royal Navy attacks.

On one thing, however, Somerville is absolutely clear. He is not prepared to slink back into the funk hole of Addu Atoll. He has not come all the way out East from the Mediterranean, and put his ships through weeks of training, in order to sail his men up and down and back again like the Grand Old Duke of York. He has a reputation as a fighting admiral; he does not intend to gain one as the Vanishing Admiral. His plan is to be in a position 250 miles south of Ceylon by the time the sun is up.

By his estimation this will place the Eastern Fleet within reconnaissance range of the Japanese ships. His old Albacores and Swordfish are no match for the Japanese by day, but Somerville can see no reason why he should not close in at nightfall and launch them to deliver torpedo attacks on the enemy by moonlight. His aircrews are experienced in using their radar for search and attack, as well as in using flares, if need be, for target illumination. It is a known fact – so he believes – that the Japanese dislike night action. This way he should be able to give them one or two hard knocks while keeping out of their way during daylight hours. Always supposing (as he does) that the Japanese fighters have approximately the same 200-mile range as his Albacores.

All that remains is to rearrange his rendezvous with Dorsetshire and Cornwall, currently heading towards Addu Atoll. Sir James Somerville is no historian but he knows all about the carnage Admiral Togo inflicted in 1905 on the ill-prepared Baltic Fleet.

On the bridge of Warspite, steaming at nineteen knots towards an enemy whose range and depth of striking power he cannot possibly judge, Somerville now sends a signal to his two heavy cruisers to join him on latitude 0°58' N and longitude 77°36' E – a change of course southwards which (according to a sighting report of the enemy transmitted by Bradshaw's Catalina at 0715 hours but not received by Somerville until the forenoon) will bring Dorsetshire and Cornwall within reconnaissance range of Nagumo's fleet.

It was an improbable scene which greeted Guy Tancred that March morning, shortly after dawn, when he lifted the blackout blind on his living-room window overlooking Galle Face Green. Of all people old Ingram Bywater, carrying a golf umbrella, was leading a procession of Sinhalese coolies across the grass.

They appeared, at least, to be coolies. Clad in banyans and sarongs they hauled heavy drays like gun-carriages. But as they gathered obediently near the fenced-off site of the new Civil Defence Headquarters, Guy could have sworn he recognised among them familiar faces from the Colombo Club: a cook, four waiters, the porter and the doorman, still incongruously wearing his turban.

Dismantled to make way for the underground HQ, Lutyens's Victory Column still lay in six sections on the ground, as it had lain since Guy moved to his flat from the Metropole. I.B.'s men now set about slipping ropes under three of the granite shafts. With much heaving and straining and raised voices they were manhandled on to the gun-carriages, which were then solemnly trundled off the Green, back across the road and round to an out-building at the rear of the Colombo Club.

Guy went away to shave and get dressed. When he returned and opened the window some time later, I.B. was directing the second loading. As the last of the Victory Column disappeared from view, the old man stood to attention on the grass. Stiffly he raised his umbrella in salute.

The sun was up. Below Guy's quarters in Galle Face Court the daily trek of Europeans and Ceylonese commuters from Colpetty and Bambalapitiya up to the Fort was under way. Guy made no move to join them. He watched from the window. Resting his forehead against the glass, he tried to work out what had gone wrong.

Nothing at Dunlop Orient's; he could be sure of that. There were no black pins left on the rubber-estate map in Guy's office. Everything was running like clockwork. Rubber production had shot up to something approaching maximum workable output: the turnover each Thursday now at the Chamber of Commerce was in the region of 4500 lb *a week* of smoked sheet and crêpe rubber. Bought *en bloc* by the Ministry of Supply in London, at a fixed price of 11*d* a pound, it was convoyed in cargo ships to Tilbury. At least half of it (a fact not generally explained to Ceylon planters) then doubled back East, to the Soviet Union.

In the eyes of the world, Guy had made a success of his assignment. He had come out to Ceylon as an investment adviser, a person who could deal with figures. He had proved he could deal at least as well with men, and run a sizeable department into the bargain. All this would have added greatly to the self-esteem of the young London businessman in the tussore suit who had disembarked from SS *Burdwan* nearly five months ago. It did nothing for Guy Tancred now, as he looked down at the bicycles and rickshaws and hooting cars. He felt restless, jaundiced, unfulfilled.

He had been ill, he told himself: illness had this effect on the system. Lying in the Fraser Home clinic with a fever – at first diagnosed as malarial until it was discovered to be nothing worse than a bad attack of tick typhus – he had stared up at the dark green shutters on the windows and wondered what it was that barred him from the simple pleasures that run-of-the-mill types enjoyed.

He saw them everywhere in Ceylon. They worked up a healthy sweat playing tennis and rugger. They drank a lot and became boisterous, or maudlin, but they always presented themselves in good order at the office in the morning, as they had been brought up to do. They had a fling or two with the sort of fast girl their mothers would disapprove of, and then married the little home-maker who wept at christenings and debated with her chums about the frightful price of a good dinner service nowadays. They expected to get from life what they put into it, neither more nor less.

Guy had never seriously had to think about such people before he arrived in Colombo. In the clinic, isolated, vulnerable, he forgot his sociable London life, happy and at ease with his like-minded friends. It seemed to him in his weaker moments, when the fever took hold, that he carried some germ of apartness which alienated him from these happy-go-lucky characters. When his temperature subsided, and he could think clearly again, he realised that the fault was not in him but in everybody else. They had no spirituality, he decided. This was the dimension they lacked. They might have shrewd heads, warm hearts, healthy bodies; but when it came to intimations of immortality, they were about on a par with wood-mites in an organ loft.

This conclusion afforded him little relief. It was not enough to know himself to be different; he had to share it with someone. In these five months he had met only one person he could share it with. Jill. Jill knew him, in a deep, instinctive way that nobody, not even Lydia, had known him. He loved her for it.

And she was avoiding him.

It was this that turned Guy's success at work into a hollow mockery. What was it worth, if there was nobody he loved and admired who was prepared to acknowledge it? Rawling he respected almost as a father, and Rawling had been complimentary. But the Major was nowadays so preoccupied with Japanese spies, Buddhist monks with radio transmitters, Sama Samajist fifth-columnists, all his grandiose deception schemes, that he had little time for the mundane business of rubber production. On Guy's very first day back at work Rawling had come bowling into his horse-box to ask his assistance in finding a fresh corpse, apparently a vital ingredient in some intelligence operation against the Japanese in Malaya. After an hour spent ringing round his contacts with this request, Guy had begun to wonder if he was not imagining it in delirium from his hospital bed.

Jill had come to see him in the Fraser Home. Just once. He was papery with fever and she had been cool and professional like the nurse she was trained to be. He couldn't remember what she said to him, but she had peeled a *Suwandel* plantain, the small, reddish banana that was his favourite of all the fruits of Ceylon, and with her fingers broken off a bit at a time and put it on his tongue. The plantain tasted tender and sweet: the first solid food he'd been able to stomach since the infection.

Since he had come out of hospital, not a word. He knew that she was back in Colombo during the week working at the Pasteur Clinic, and that she slept most nights at the Donaldsons' in Cinnamon Gardens; but she was never to be found at either place when he came calling. Harry was unreachable at Kelani. Elizabeth Donaldson was evasive. He'd have suspected a conspiracy if he'd been able to think of any conceivable motive for one. The East did strange things to people; Jill had said so herself. Perhaps that was it.

He turned away from the open window, and threw an angry, almost contemptuous glance around the room. His new lodgings made him think of Bruce MacAlister's bungalow: the same shabby-forlorn neatness of unloved furniture; dark rings left by whisky-glasses on the drink-tables; through the bedroom door the crumpled sheets on one side only of the double bed; a smell of furniture polish and airlessness. On the desk lay an unfinished letter to Lydia.

The letter was mostly about his brother. He couldn't tell her about Jill; to talk about Harry seemed the next best thing.

". . . It's the same when he goes on about Gandhi and passive resistance. There's something about him which quells disagreement. All my best arguments come to me hours later. On Gandhi, for instance, this satyagraha business is just the other side of the coin to appeasement. Look at Lord Halifax. As Baron Irwin, Viceroy of India, he had all those meetings with Gandhi and got totally taken in by him. Back home as Neville Chamberlain's Foreign Secretary he tries to apply the same satyagraha principles to Mr Hitler, who promptly proceeds to invade Czechoslovakia. That's something I should have pointed out to Harry. But could I think of it at the time?"

In London, in a mood like this, Guy would have escaped for a day or two to the countryside; perhaps to Exmoor or the Brendons, to walk for long distances in the fresh air. Here it was too sultry for that. The worst of the hot weather was supposed to arrive in May, but already the wind from the north-east was torrid, as if from some terrible furnace hundreds of miles away which was slowly firing up to full blast. As an economy measure the Governor had decreed that shorts and open-necked shirts could be worn to work. Even so, with the fans going in his office, desk-work gave him prickly heat on his elbows and forearms. He was as trapped there as he was here. . . .

On impulse, he went to the phone and rang Edward to tell him he would not be coming in that morning. A familiar voice answered.

"Yes?" it said abruptly.

"Major Rawling—"

"Who is this I'm speaking to?"

"Guy Tancred here."

"Ah, Tancred. I've had a bit of a leg-up, actually. They've made me a Lieutenant-Colonel."

"Good heavens."

"The papers aren't through yet, so keep it under your hat for now. Are you free at lunch, Tancred? I thought you and I might have a spot of lunch at the Club. Can you manage it?"

Guy hesitated for a second. Rawling never made any social

gesture that did not have an ulterior purpose. His curiosity was aroused.

"I'll meet you there," he said.

After he'd spoken to Edward, he looked at his watch. He had five hours before lunch. Alone in his flat, he came to a decision. If it took the ingenuity and persistence of Rawling himself, he would track down Jill Tancred. It could not be put off any longer. He needed her more urgently than he'd ever needed anyone.

He phoned the Pasteur Clinic. Jill was not there. He dialled the Donaldsons' number, then put the phone down. He was not going to give advance warning. To call at the Donaldsons' unexpectedly was the best idea.

At first he thought he'd come to the wrong address. The house looked right; so did the number on the gate. But the beautifully tended green lawn, so treasured by Mrs Donaldson, had disappeared overnight. In its place was a ploughed field. Two barefoot garden coolies straddled the turned earth, planting seeds by hand.

Guy walked up the drive, the gravel already warm under the soles of his shoes. Ushered in by a flustered houseboy he found Elizabeth Donaldson in the cool of the verandah room, where Sylvia had had her twenty-first. She was bent over a leather-bound photograph album; he saw the threads of silver in her tightly curled brown hair.

"I'm awfully sorry to come bursting in like this," he said awkwardly.

Elizabeth Donaldson looked up, her eyes oddly bright. For a moment she seemed not to recognise him. Then she smiled and patted the sofa beside her. "Come and sit down," she said. "Look at this album. See – that's silverfish. You know, I don't think God intended us to have memories, in the tropics. The ink's faded on all my letters. The photographs all fade and mildew. And if they don't, the silverfish eat them."

Guy nodded, listening for footsteps, voices. Holding his hat between his knees, he said politely, "It must have been a tremendous wrench to sacrifice your garden. What do they want people to grow? Yams, pulses, cereals, that sort of thing?"

"Yes. Look. Look at this one. William had just got his Harrow uniform, that's less than six years ago but it's bleached out, you can hardly see his face! And yet if you look back at those old studio photographs they're so clear – that's me at Wimbledon High School in 1911. Did they use a different method then?"

"I don't know."

229

"He's twenty-one today, you know. I was just looking through some old photographs. George pulled lots of strings and we got a birthday cable sent out to him in Tobruk. I think we're still holding Tobruk."

"Yes."

"The awful thing is, George says, Rommel seems to know in advance every move we make. Still, I mustn't bore you." Mrs Donaldson closed the album and held it on her knee, not wanting to let go. "It's a strange thing, about memory, isn't it?" she went on. "Even when you've made something you think is going to last. Do you remember that dreadful drought two years ago? No, you wouldn't, you weren't here. Everything went. All the climbers, the cannas, a beautiful jacaranda which I'd grown from a seedling. And can you believe, I can't picture in my mind what my garden used to look like, back then?"

"Jill thinks you're the best gardener in Colombo."

A houseboy brought in the tea on a tray. Guy wondered what had happened to old Albert. Mrs Donaldson poured.

"Milk? Sugar?"

"No thank you."

"If it's Jill you came to see," said Mrs Donaldson, carefully passing him a cup, "I'm afraid she's gone in to the Clinic."

"Oh yes. Really?" He cast around for something to say. "She's working very hard at the moment, Jill."

"She's lucky. She's got a skill. She can use it. I trained, you know. After London University, I trained as an English teacher."

"Did you, Mrs Donaldson?" He swallowed down his tea and looked at the cloisonné ware on the drinks-tables.

"But the men all came back from the War. They took the jobs that were going." She clutched the photo-album, repository of fading memories. "I had a good degree. Eventually I obtained a minor musical post at Haberdashers' Aske's. I suppose it might have come to something if I hadn't married George."

"Do you think so?" He set the cup down on the tray.

"But then, ah! George held out the promise of exotic parts." The blue eyes in the lined face appraised Guy with a sardonic look. It suddenly occurred to him to wonder how much Jill had told her.

"I suppose that's true." Guy stood up. "Mrs Donaldson, I won't take up any more of your time. Thank you for the tea. I didn't deserve it after turning up so unexpectedly." He held out his hand. "I hope you hear soon from Tobruk."

Sylvia's mother twitched a smile. "Try the Pasteur Clinic," she said.

Since all civilian parking had now been prohibited around the Echelon Barracks and the Police Quarters, Guy eventually had to drive across the Canal and leave his car at the Railway Station. He made his way through the crowds that now seemed to besiege Colombo Fort Station day and night, and walked back over the bridge. Above the street noises he could hear the crisp shouts of NCOs drilling troops on the Barracks parade-ground.

The Pasteur Clinic was a low, white building set back from Lotus Road, not far from the Quarantine Department. Like every other public building in Colombo its glass windows had been removed as an air-raid precaution and either shuttered up or replaced with panels of cellophane. In the reception area somebody had posted up an Evacuation Notice, the first Guy had seen.

In view of the unsettled state existing, and the problems relating to food supply, etc., he read, *all those persons not normally resident in Ceylon and not engaged in essential war work – including the wives and children of military personnel – must arrange to leave as soon as passages are available for them. With regard to residents in Ceylon, non-Ceylonese women with young children who are not employed on war or important Social Welfare work are advised to leave as soon as they can conveniently do so.*

The Notice, signed Layton, C-in-C Ceylon, had been posted up outside the Emergency Operating Theatre, no doubt to remind emergency cases that if they survived this ordeal another awaited them. Jill Tancred, as a nurse, would qualify to stay behind. She would have stayed in any event, Guy knew.

This time he did not leave his name at the desk. Avoiding the receptionist's eye he hurried up the stairs and down a long corridor, following signs to the Rabies Wards. A nurse, a Burgher by the look of her, came towards him pushing a metal trolley. She directed him to the Sister's office.

The Sister was filling out forms. A pair of grey eyes looked up at Guy severely over half-moon glasses.

"I'm afraid Mrs Tancred isn't here," she said. "Did you wish to leave a message for her?"

"May I wait?"

"In the normal way I should say yes. Unfortunately we're very, very busy. We're taking overspill from Colombo General,

231

not only rabies but malaria transfers from the garrison at Trincomalee. If it's urgent, I think you may find Mrs Tancred at the Refugee Centre. She told me she had letters to deliver, so try there. Her shift here doesn't start until lunchtime."

The Refugee Centre, in St Peter's Church Hall, disoriented him for a moment. It wasn't just the cool and dark after the brilliant sunlight outside. The smells of cooking and disinfectant, the scattered junk-shop piles of books, toys, suitcases, dresses and old slippers, brought back painful images of the London Guy had left behind – the church halls and school-rooms to which he had guided the shocked, shaking victims of the night's bombing raid, clutching to their night-clothes the few dusty oddments of their life that they'd rescued from the wreckage.

But this was Ceylon. Everything here was much more cheerful and optimistic. People laughed and chattered like old friends. Trestle tables had been set out with all kinds of clothes contributed by the good citizens of Colombo. The latest batch of refugees – not all Europeans by any means, he could see a sprinkling of brown and yellow faces – were picking up garments and examining them critically before disappearing behind discreetly positioned canvas screens to try them on.

Little girls sat on the floor, dressing old dolls out of bits of material. Small boys ran around with model aeroplanes and made dive-bombing noises. At the back of the room a row of food-safes stood with their legs in bowls of paraffin to keep away the ants. Ottoline Hoathly, who had sold her jade earrings to swell the Refugee Fund, presided over a prodigious, pot-bellied tea-kettle which rattled and puffed on top of a little electric ring.

"Hallo, Guy!" she called out when she saw him. "You look as if you could do with a cuppa!" Before he could reply, a mug of hot tea was pressed on him. "Jill says you've moved into Galle Face Court."

"Yes. Do you know where she is?"

"It must make you wonder how you ever managed before. So much nicer than those dreadful chummeries young men still seem to enjoy. Socks everywhere and the smell of old curries on unwashed plates. Kitty, do you remember?"

Kitty Clarke, dressed as if for a church fête, had arrived with a large tin of powdered milk. She shook her head, spooning out the powder into a line of mugs. "Sebastian never went into a chummery. He had his own suite of furnished rooms in a large house in Horton Crescent. A very distinguished family, so he always used to say. Do you know," she added with a nervous laugh, "Sebby wants me to join the evacuation?"

"Surely not, dear!" Ottoline Hoathly looked horrified.

"He's serious. I told him I was engaged with essential war work, but he's serious. He says the whole place could go up in smoke. I told him there are fifteen hundred miles of ocean between Singapore and us and there'll be plenty of time to think of that when the time comes—"

Impatiently Guy scanned the Hall. There was no sign of Jill. He caught sight of a very pretty raven-haired girl talking to a group of Dutch refugees – that girlfriend of David Gifford's, Maria de Vos. He went over and greeted her, rather more curtly than he'd intended.

"I didn't know you spoke Dutch," he said. "Is that where you're from?"

Maria de Vos pushed her hair back with a diffident gesture. "I'm taking a correspondence course," she explained. "These poor people from the East Indies, there's no one to understand what they want—"

"Have you seen Jill – Mrs Tancred – anywhere?"

"Oh. No. But I haven't been here very long. She may have gone down to the harbour with some of the other nurses. I think there's a boat coming in. Is there anything—?"

"No. Thanks," said Guy.

At the docks, he showed his pass to the military policeman by the Yacht Club entrance. The sun blazed down; his shirt was clammy with perspiration. It was possible Jill had been sent down to cope with the landing of stretcher-cases. The only stretcher-cases Guy could see were called *Royal Sovereign*, *Ramillies*, *Resolution* and *Revenge*: the four First World War battleships currently lined up at the north-eastern jetties for refuelling, like a row of old ladies on intravenous drip.

He ran into Tony Apple, and could hardly recognise him. The puffiness had left his face. His eyes, a month ago dulled and bloodshot, were alert with the old humour. Two financial blows had allegedly bankrupted him. The loss of his investments in the Malay States was closely followed by Layton's demolition of the Racecourse, which had forced him to repay his debts to every bookie in Colombo.

It was Governor Prescott who had come to his rescue. A word in the right ear, and Tony Apple found himself employed as an Assistant Quartermaster, Naval Stores. The horrifying idea of earning his living (most senior jobs in Ceylon, he had once told

Guy, required industry rather than intelligence and were therefore the sort of thing Scotchmen did best), he discovered to be not so horrifying after all. He sold his horses. He stopped drinking. He had become, from all accounts, a model of diligence and punctilious book-keeping.

Some of his interests had not changed. "I take it you've found other fish to fry," he said to Guy with an inquisitive air.

Guy realised he was talking about the rickshaw girl from the Metropole. "Something of the sort," he said, avoiding his eye.

"Well, don't concern yourself about her, old boy. Since the Navy came to town the tarts have had their hands full, in a manner of speaking. Yours was officer material of course," Tony Apple added smoothly, noticing the expression on Guy's face. "The ratings go to Mrs Mary on St Andrew's Road. She's known, I believe, as the Training Ship."

Guy grinned. "I heard about her from Rawling. He sent one of his agents to check that she wasn't passing on naval secrets."

"Was she?"

"He doesn't know. The man never reported back."

"Then Rawling should go himself. Mrs Mary would be a match for him. She's the size of Tiny Anstruther, and Tiny's so fat he's had to have special permission to wear his bayonet at the front of his belt instead of the back."

Laughing, they walked along the quayside towards the RN Store Depot on Kochikadde. Guy was tempted to envy the older man. Women for Tony Apple were a simple matter of having a good time. He had no trouble finding women who went along with this for a small consideration. Not for him the aches and pangs of love: he loved himself too well to suffer for other people. What emotional storms did you have to weather to reach such passionless calm?

"I'd forgotten how deaf Sandy Duncannon is," Tony Apple was saying. "I read out to him, in the Club yesterday, the news about Ronnie Smythe breaking his collar-bone falling off Miss Dorothy Pagett's Golden Hackle in the Cheltenham Gold Cup. "Who fell off Dorothy Pagett?" bawls old Sandy, and the old buffers all crowd in, thinking I'm telling a dirty story!"

"It's those years of quinine, in case he caught something from one of his native ladies." Guy thought of Harry's life as a *Sina Dorai* up in the wilderness of China Bay, and the laughter left his face. A current of sympathy for Jill flowed through him, and with it – sympathy releasing intuition – a certainty that he knew where he would find her.

The Colombo General Hospital was in Regent Street, not far from the Donaldsons', where he had started that morning. The main reception was a hubbub of ringing telephones and scurrying orderlies; Guy could not imagine a greater chaos if the Japanese invaded. The outpatients area was awash with refugees sitting in chairs or on cushions on the floor – most of them evidently in the clothes they had worn all voyage. Several Sikhs in uniform wandered about with puzzled expressions, holding small pink cards. A bald-headed Sinhalese gentleman in a frayed white hospital robe had come down from one of the wards to talk to his wife, who sat, surrounded by bags of food, on a stool in the middle of the concourse. A small boy had emptied a box of British soldiers on the floor – tin machine-gunners, commandos with hand grenades – and spat fire at the hurrying nurses.

He enquired at the main desk. "I believe you have a malaria patient here. His name is Donald Fraser."

"Oh, yes." The woman at the desk glanced up at him. "Second floor, Ward 15."

Clutching the bag of fruit he had bought as an offering, Guy climbed the stairs. If Jill wasn't there, bringing Donald's letters, it would be no bad thing to have paid a courtesy call on Harry's sick *Sina Dorai*. His own ten days in the clinic had taught him how oppressive it was to be ill in a foreign country. Even worse for a boy like Donald, not long off the boat from Glasgow and eager to make his mark.

Ward 15 was full, but he could see no sign of the ginger-haired young Scotsman. By the swing doors at the far end stood a bed with screens round it. Guy pulled open a screen and looked inside. The bed was empty.

"Are you looking for Donald?" asked a voice behind him.

He turned. Jill was standing there. She wore a dark blue, belted cotton dress, buttoned up to the neck. Her face was stony.

"He's dead," she said. "Donald's dead."

He stammered. "Oh? What? Is he?"

"There were complications. A pulmonary infection. It's not uncommon when the malaria takes hold."

"Surely not nowadays!"

"Oh yes. It happens. People do die out here, you see."

"I'm sorry." He held the bag of useless fruit.

"Yes. Harry will have to look for another *Sina Dorai*." She turned up her sleeve and looked at her watch. "I must get to the Clinic."

"Jill. . . ."

"Yes?"

She wouldn't look at him. She fiddled with the elephant-hair bracelet on her wrist. He could see the sign in bold red letters on the wall above her: 'WARNING – If Incendiary Bombs Are Dropped, Fires May Ensue.'

He said, "I was going to ask if you would have dinner with me tonight."

"Until this happened? Well it was kind of you—"

"I mean, I am asking."

Still she looked away. "It's very kind of you, Guy. I'm far too busy, I'm afraid, and it's not just Donald. Things are in such confusion, you know, everything's so confused, vaccines held up in the warehouses, red tape, nothing delegated to the regional hospitals, everybody hanging back, making difficulties—"

"I want you to have dinner with me."

"No."

Stepping forward he grabbed her, he pulled her behind the screens. Jill put up her clenched hands. He pinned her arms in an embrace and kissed her.

"No!"

Her bracelet snapped and rolled on the floor. She struggled against him silently. The top button of her buttoned-up dress undid. He kissed her throat. Pinning her glorious suppleness in his arms he muttered furiously, "Come to dinner. Promise, and I'll let you go."

There was a breathing-space. He heard footsteps approaching down the ward.

"OK, I promise." Her voice shook with an equal fury. "Just don't expect me to eat your stinking food."

He released her. Jill sank down on the dead man's bed. Strands of butterscotch hair uncurled over her brow; she pushed them back with trembling fingers. Guy bent and retrieved her bracelet.

"Eight o'clock at the Galle Face Hotel," he told her.

Jill stood up. She slapped his face, so hard that if she'd been wearing rings it would have cut his cheek open. She brushed past him and went out through the swing-doors.

Guy stood there for a moment, shaking. He couldn't think straight. He couldn't think at all. A nursing sister in navy blue, with a white bonnet over her grey curls, put her head round the screens.

"Are you a relative?" she asked.

*

236

Guy got to the Colombo Club at one o'clock. Rawling was waiting for him. Despite his promotion he'd had the unusual modesty to dress in mufti. He greeted Guy warmly, almost effusively, and took him inside.

In the few weeks since Guy had been here, the Colombo Club had changed – so much that for a moment he wondered if it was another of Rawling's deception schemes. It had lost its robustly British nature entirely. It seemed to have gone native and taken on the atmosphere of an Indian temple. The chandelier-lights were turned down to save electricity: a shadowy dimness enveloped the classical lines of the entablature and obscured the frieze with its emblems of Britannia, its shields, helmets, crowns, laurel garlands and crossed trumpets. An insidious incense of balsam perfumed the air. It came from joss-sticks glowing on the mantelpieces and in saucers on the tables.

"It's those damned fish rotting," said Rawling. "Let's go straight through and have some grub."

The scent of incense followed them as far as the small dining room, at which point it was overwhelmed by the decent English smell of boiled cabbage. Three or four planters sat at the long table, including one of Harrison & Crosfield's people whom Guy knew slightly. To his relief, no Dunlop Orient planters were to be seen.

"I ought to tell you, Tancred," said Rawling over the mulligatawny soup, "I've written a very positive report of your work to London."

"That's extremely good of you." Guy was taken aback. He dabbed his mouth with his napkin. "It's a matter now of keeping the lid down, I'm afraid. First the Excess Profits Tax and now this Compulsory Purchase Scheme. I'm getting one or two of our better producers threatening to throw their hand in altogether. It's not the hardship: they accept that. It's the news of all this synthetic rubber flooding on to the market."

Rawling nodded. "You must leave them in no doubt that the Allied governments won't suddenly deregulate rubber after the War. There will be compensation, and close restriction on synthetics. They'll get their profits back." He lowered his voice. "Frankly, Tancred, we've got more pressing problems. The Japs are looking in our direction; I can't tell you more than that. At a moment like this we need all the talented chaps we can get. I'm desperately short of good men. Now that things at the office are running smoothly, what do you say to coming over to my side for a spell?"

Before Guy could think of an answer, Rawling held up a pudgy hand in warning. Ingram Bywater and Percy Buller had come into the dining room. They sat down next to them breathing heavily. Percy Buller flapped a hand in front of his nose.

"That confounded voodoo pong," he grumbled. "Next thing, we'll be summoned to lunch by blasted temple bells. Doesn't surprise me that Layton hasn't shown his face; he probably thinks we all wear sarongs. What's on the menu?" he added morosely, raising bloodshot eyes to the boy. "Fish curry?"

"Roast meat, Master. And boiled cabbage, Master."

"All right."

"Layton might have had the decency to reply to our invitation," snarled Ingram Bywater. Like Buller, he seemed to Guy to have aged visibly in the few months he had known him. "The last man to be offered honorary life membership of the Club was the Prince of Wales, and he had the decency to thank us for it."

The mulligatawny soup had steamed up Rawling's pebble glasses. He took them off and polished them. "He's a modern sort of chap, Layton," he remarked. "A first-rate soldier, of course."

Nobody had a reply to this remark. Guy broke the silence. "I notice you rescued the Victory Column, sir," he said, addressing I.B.

"What?" The Treasurer of the Colombo Club started, as if caught out in a guilty secret. "Oh yes. Well something had to be done, Tancred. A bit of a scandal having it lying there. Damn bad for morale, too. Especially after Singapore. Imagine the Nips arriving and finding our war memorial in pieces on the ground!"

Percy Buller clattered his spoon in the soup-bowl. "I beg your pardon, I.B. The Nips arriving, d'you say? I'd like to see 'em try. We've got the Eastern Fleet in harbour and fighter planes all over the sky. The troops aren't top-hole, I'll agree. But they aren't decimated by VD, as I gather they were in Singapore. That's what let the Nips in. VD and foreign troops."

Ingram Bywater lifted his upper lip. "If you're so sure of this Percy, what were you doing in Cargills last week, buying one of those weighted truncheons?"

"How d'you know that?"

"My wife saw you."

"Did she?"

"She saw you, Percy."

"Well I don't mind telling you, it's not for use against the Japanese. It's in case of civil unrest. Social disorder. If the locals

238

start running amok, like they did in 1915, it might be necessary to crack a few heads. . . ."

The two men were still baiting each other when Rawling excused himself and took Guy out for coffee in the smoking room. "I don't like the look of Buller," he remarked when they were by themselves. "His wife went off to Tanganyika in the first evacuation. His investment capital from selling his shipping business went down the drain with the Straits dollar. He's signing chits for everything. In my line of country you've got to watch a man like that."

Guy was puzzled. "Vulnerable to blackmail? Percy Buller?"

Rawling put a match to his pipe and sucked it alight. "Nobody's above temptation, Tancred. One of the first things you learn. Religion will drive a man to desperate measures. So will politics. But a rich man who loses his money is the one to watch."

Guy looked at him. Rawling's eyes were very clear, very calm. He wondered, not for the first time, what he was getting himself into. "I suppose I shall need permission from Dunlop Orient," he said doubtfully.

Rawling shook his head. "I'll take full responsibility. The less anyone knows, the better. Lesson number two: no paperwork and less telephone calls. It's a risky business, Tancred. There are spies. Everywhere spies, even in a peaceful-looking billet like Ceylon. The only way to beat the other chap's intelligence network is to have a better one of your own."

"What sort of risks will I be running?"

Rawling paused. "Nothing very hazardous *at the moment*," he confessed. "It's more a question of scouting out the shoreline where the Japs might try to stage an invasion of Ceylon. I'll give you the gen when we're back in the office. I've got some naval boffins who can pitch in to help. I'll tell you this much. It was discovered in Britain early in the War that the most critical time for an invasion force is when they are in the actual landing craft, coming in through the surf. From the enemy point of view, the shorter the run-in the better. We also know, from Malaya, that the spearhead of any Japanese infantry attack will not be via motorised transport, which will come by heavier craft to a secured beachhead, but via the ordinary bicycle. The bicycle, you will realise, can get them at speed through coconut and rubber plantations. What I will want you to do, Tancred, is to find out which beach, on the West Coast, the Japs would choose for an invasion attempt, taking all these variables into consideration."

"All right," said Guy.

They talked about other things. Sir Stafford Cripps had flown into New Delhi to stiffen India's backbone ("He will offer them self-rule if they beat off the Japanese," predicted Rawling with a cynical grimace, "and then Churchill will back down"). A lieutenant-general had taken over from a major-general as army commander in Ceylon. And, more evidence that things were hotting up, Admiral Sir James Somerville had arrived by air in Colombo to take command of the Eastern Fleet.

Meanwhile, if Rawling was to be believed, there were elements among the local Ceylonese population who remained unimpressed by all this gold braid. The Sama Samajists continued to undermine the war effort. They distributed hysterical propaganda sheets among the troops. They had burnt down another warehouse, outside Colombo (an incident kept out of the newspapers). They had even attempted – if not the Sama Samajists, who else? – to derail a train at Beruwela and put the main Colombo – Galle railway line out of action.

"Are you familiar with the banyan tree?" asked Rawling. "There's a splendid specimen in Trincomalee, in the gardens of Admiralty House. Birds take its seed and drop them in the branches of other trees. Instead of dying, the seed germinates in the branch. It drops its roots down to the ground, and flings up branches which also develop roots and become trees, d'you see, until the banyan seed has completely taken over, suffocated, killed the host tree. That's how I view nationalist movements like the Sama Samaj. They infiltrate other movements, take them over and eventually destroy them. Unless, of course, you cut them down first."

Guy nodded. He could no longer keep his mind on this talk of spies and invasions. Was it really he who had manhandled Jill, like some drunken layabout? His cheek burnt more at the memory than from her slap. He had behaved worse than any of the rugger types he'd been sneering at. She would never speak to him again. Never. It was finished between them.

As they got up to leave, he asked Rawling, "Have you ever been to China Bay?"

"Of course. Next to Ratmalana, it's our main airbase."

"No. Before the aerodrome."

He could feel the pale eyes behind the thick-lensed glasses searching his face.

"Yes. As a matter of fact," said Rawling. "I used to keep a boat there. At the Sea Anglers' Club, years ago. Beautiful place.

First-rate fishing at China Bay. Off-limits now, of course."

They went out into the afternoon heat. The Lieutenant-Colonel had somehow acquired an impressive new car, Guy noticed, a 4-litre Sunbeam Talbot, like the Governor's. A driver too, who, as soon as he saw them, took a small container out of the glove-box, ran round to open the rear door, and sprinkled something white on the back seats.

"Insect powder," said Rawling. "It's a constant battle, don't you find?"

With blackout curtains over its windows the Galle Face Hotel looked forbidding, aloof, like a Scottish seaside hotel after the end of the season. Barbed wire and sandbag emplacements, creeping up the shoreline from Mount Lavinia, had cut off all access to the sea except for a gap below the terrace. It was a very small gap, which a fat Japanese – if such a creature existed – would find difficult to negotiate with or without his invasion bicycle.

Guy ran up the steps into the big marble entrance hall. A small knot of uniformed men from Army HQ, and a larger group of Eastern Fleet naval officers, lounged around with an air of being conscious that they now far outnumbered the old colonial hands for whom Colombo's Galle Face Hotel had been as famous an imperial caravanserai as Shepheards in Cairo, Raffles in Singapore or the George V in Rangoon. Boys hurried backwards and forwards with Revelation suitcases. The switchboard operator at the wide reception desk had been replaced by a servicewoman in a neatly pressed uniform, who pushed her mouthpiece aside to repair her vivid scarlet lipstick.

It was five minutes to eight. There was no sign of Jill. Guy strolled in a casual way through to the pillared verandah, his hands in his pockets. On the hotel board a handwritten notice announced that *Bryony and Basil, after a thrilling escape from Jap air raids in Batavia, will be starring with Felice's Blue Star Band on Saturday night in the first-floor Lounge – don't miss them!* A large head-and-shoulders photograph of a dusky Latin American beauty, teeth parted in a brilliant smile, had been pinned up beside it. Not Bryony, Guy discovered when he read the sprawl beneath, but *Dinah! She's dinah-mite! The new hot rhythm sensation!* Someone had inked in a blue moustache on her upper lip.

Guy surveyed the notices for five minutes or more. He then sat down in one of the teak and rattan chairs and flicked through a

241

copy of *Vanity Fair*, his eyes darting to the hotel entrance whenever an angry screech announced another turn of the swing-doors. At ten minutes past the hour he got up, walked into the restaurant, and sat down at his table. The head waiter, brother of the Italian restaurant manager, nodded his head sorrowfully.

"I know which way you feel about it, Mr Tancred," he said. "We feel the same way."

"Oh?"

"This restaurant never closed. Not even in the First World War One it closed. Now Emperor Hirohito has won. After seventy-two years, he has managed the closure of the Popular Restaurant and Grill Room."

"Already?"

"Next week it closes. They are going to *partition* it into dormitories for the military officers. What you want to eat?"

"Nothing." Guy looked at his watch. "Not yet. Just a whisky and water. Make it a double."

"I know which way you feel," said the head waiter. And took the menu away.

"Guy!"

He looked up. Sylvia Donaldson was tripping towards him across the room waving and smiling. Charles Bilbow, wearing his Acting Sub-Lieutenant's rig as grandly as an Admiral of the Fleet, followed her with a shade more reluctance.

"Heavens, what a surprise! Are you waiting for anybody? Can we join you?" Without a moment's pause Sylvia sat down opposite him – and immediately shot up again, her pretty face screwed up in mock agony. "Charlie showed me round *Dorsetshire* this afternoon," she said with a giggle. "I scraped my poor bottom sliding down one of those – what do you call them? Companion ladders? Oh do pull up a chair, Charlie," she added. "Guy will throw us out as soon as he's had enough of us. Won't you, Guy!"

Charles Bilbow shook Guy's hand with a mixture of friendliness and deference. He accepted a chair swiftly found for him by the Boy who brought Guy's whisky. "It's true: we had a sort of an open day and I showed Sylvia all over the ship," he said, looking at her proudly. "Captain Agar took quite a shine to you, didn't he, old girl?"

Sylvia glowed. "His first words were 'You must be Charlie's darling'," she confided to Guy with a little laugh. She lowered her blonde head, fiddled with a sapphire ring on her finger.

"What's it like?" Guy asked Bilbow.

"*Dorsetshire*? Oh, it's ripping fun. In a sort of way. It gets pretty baking below decks in this weather; it tends to put some of the fellows I mess with on a short fuse, I can tell you. But I don't mind. I don't mind the heat. And Captain Agar's the best there is. He won a VC in the Kronstadt Raid, you know. A lot of the chaps say he's the best captain in the fleet. Somerville wouldn't ever say so of course. They say he's never forgiven *Dorsetshire* for closing with *Bismarck* and sinking it before Somerville could get there in *Renown*."

"*Renown*. Isn't she one of those museum-pieces in the harbour?"

Charles Bilbow shook his head wryly. "No. *Renown* was refitted three years ago. She's much too good for the Eastern Fleet. You know why they're known as the Weeping Ladies, those battleships? Their ballast is so bad, they can't hold their water. They lose so much, dribbling down the sides, that the crews can't even do their laundry. The heat below is even worse than ours; it's unbearable."

"It can't be as bad as our dances with the troops at the Institute," interrupted Sylvia. "Can you imagine it, Guy? Tuesday and Thursday afternoons from four to seven? All the cipherettes not on duty are bussed along to the BSSI. It's absolute murder in that heat; we're sweating like *cochons*. Ugh!" She shuddered. "I'm ravenous just thinking about it. Aren't you, Charlie?"

Charles Bilbow took the point and signalled for a waiter. Guy let his glance stray towards the restaurant entrance. Sylvia leant towards him, blue eyes sparkling with inquisitiveness.

"Do tell!"

"Tell you what?"

"Who you're waiting for, of course! I *know* you, Mr Guy Tancred. I can see into your inmost secrets!" She leant forward, her happy gaze barely skimming the surface of him. "Do you want us to go?" she breathed.

Guy smiled and changed the subject. "I saw your mother today," he said. "She was looking at old photographs. There was one of you in nothing but a pair of frilly knickers. I think you must have been a bit younger!"

Sylvia pouted prettily. "I should jolly well hope so. I don't know what's up with Mummy at the moment, she's always sitting around with old albums and diaries. When you ask her about it all she says is she's taking stock! As for the garden, it's just *ruined*."

They ordered the meal of the day, which was fish and chips.

243

Guy had another drink. He listened sombrely while Sylvia told him about her loved one's exploits in HMS *Dorsetshire*: how Charles had sailed north to Burma to harass the Japanese; how he escorted the last convoy of evacuees, troops and civilians, out of the burning city of Rangoon and Charlie had acquitted himself so well that Captain Agar, VC, was making him his Acting Secretary next week while his Secretary was on a week's leave up-country. All this while, Charles was content to look bashful and say nothing, occasionally pulling his arm gently away from Sylvia's hold so that he could put another piece of fish in his mouth.

Watching them exchange loving glances, Guy burnt with a fierce self-hatred. He had robbed himself of every advantage the gods had bestowed on him. They had given him the capacity to love, and he had channelled it into an infatuation with his brother's wife. They had given him a war, so that he might go and find glory on the field of battle, and he had ended up as a functionary organising sales of crêpe rubber. Meanwhile here were youngsters like Charles Bilbow and David Gifford, with half his own experience and *savoir-faire*, living life to the full, with a joyful intensity as if every moment might be their last. He said, staring morosely into his drink, "I gather from your mother that that exotic friend of yours, Maria, has fallen head over heels in love. It must be something in the air."

"David Gifford, d'you mean?" Bilbow laughed. "She'll get over it. Mind you, she's a real corker that Maria de Vos. If she wasn't half-native, I wouldn't mind—"

"Charles!" Sylvia had coloured up. "Don't be beastly. Maria can't help it if she has a tiny touch of the tar-brush. How can you talk like that?"

Charles Bilbow grinned. "It's all very well, Sylvia. What about that houseboy you told me about. Michael Kandasala."

"That's quite different!" Sylvia slapped his wrist. "I told you, I used to play in the garden with him when I was a little girl. Everybody does that sort of thing when they're little. It's not my fault if the poor boy still looks at me like a moon-calf whenever I see him." She appealed to Guy. "Well, is it?"

Bilbow pursued her. "All right, so you didn't know any better. But David's new here. It's not that different. He doesn't know the ropes. Do you remember the day after he'd got here from Bombay . . . we were sitting here and David was coming to join us?" He looked at Guy. "Has Sylvia told you this story?"

Guy shook his head. He felt for his watch under his shirt cuff.

"We were sitting right here in the hotel and David came

rushing in. I promise you he was choking. I thought he was going to pass out. He said: 'Out there! The sea! It's full of blood!' We ran and looked out of the window, and the sea had turned that vermilion colour you get when it's filled with infusoria. We told him, you know, there was a simple scientific explanation. But the next day we were walking along and David suddenly stops and says 'There's blood on the pavement! Look at the blood on the pavement!'"

"Betel spittle," said Sylvia, wiping away tears of laughter. "Poor David. But Charlie, you're no better. Remember that time in Bentota you heard the banshee owl and thought it was evil spirits!"

"Whose evil spirits?" asked Jill.

The laughter stopped. Guy got to his feet. Jill wore a low-cut, dark green evening dress which showed off her brown, freckled shoulders and the curve of her throat. She had put her hair up. It gleamed like coiled brass serpents in the light. Ignoring Guy, she looked down at Sylvia with a half-smile.

"My goodness, Sylvia, is that an engagement ring?" she asked.

Guy stared at the sapphire, the colour of Sylvia's widening eyes.

"Can I tell them, Charlie? Mrs Tancred, Charlie asked me to marry him this morning. And I said Yes!"

"That's wonderful." Jill bent down and gave the younger woman a kiss. "May we celebrate it? Perhaps Guy will stand us a bottle of champagne, if the hotel has any left. Guy?"

She looked at him. He could read the mockery in her eyes. There was no half-smile for him. Her mouth was set. Off-limits.

"I was expecting you at eight," he said.

"I lost a button off my dress. I had to change." Glancing at his empty whisky-glass she added, "You seem to have found plenty to entertain you."

The champagne he bought cost an arm and a leg. Jill drank most of it. The two youngsters were ill at ease. They talked about the clamminess in the air (not helped, they agreed, by the blackout blinds on the restaurant windows). Sylvia had a story about Ceylonese boys in the front row at the New Olympia. She'd been with Charlie to see Tyrone Power in *Blood and Sand*, and these boys, they had *booed* the National Anthem; at the end, when everyone else had stood up, they sat there and *booed*.

"You'd think they don't owe us anything, not even a decent respect," exclaimed Charles Bilbow, frowning.

245

"I was bicycling to work at the Naval Office yesterday and this Sinhalese man – really, a man, not a boy, at least twenty years old – he ran behind and whistled at me," continued Sylvia.

"Wolf-whistles," Bilbow elaborated, colouring up.

"Wolf-whistles. Yes. All down the street. I saw a policeman and stopped and reported him, but he'd run away by then. And this policeman – d'you think he could have cared? Not a bit of it. He took my name and address and said, 'I'm sorry, Missy. It's these ne'er-do-wells.' Ne'er-do-wells! I mean, really!"

Charles Bilbow had been studying Jill's face. "Would you mind awfully if we pushed off and had our coffee on the terrace?" he asked.

"Charlie—"

"Come on, old girl." He stood up abruptly.

"Charlie, half a sec." Sylvia beamed at them, a little tipsy from the champagne. "*Do* come on to the Septic Prawn with us," she pleaded. "*Everybody's* going to be there. The music's jolly square but there's a terrific night-club comic who does impressions—"

"Sylvia!"

"All right, all right. Who does impressions of George Formby and Gilbert Harding. And Tommy Handley. Do you promise?"

"I prefer Guy's impressions," said Jill sweetly. She tipped the last of the champagne into her glass. "He does a very good one of Ronald Colman, don't you, Guy. Or is it Errol Flynn?"

"Oh, Guy! Do show us—"

"Come on, Sylvia." Firmly the Sub-Lieutenant linked arms with his fiancée and marched her away from the table.

"I didn't know Guy did impressions. . . ." They could hear Sylvia's bubbly voice spilling into Bilbow's ear. "Have you ever seen . . . ?" and the rest was lost in the roar of a Fleet Air Arm Fulmar overhead as Charles Bilbow opened the door on to the covered terrace.

Guy stared at his glass. He had nothing to lose. Whisky and champagne on an empty stomach had convinced him of that. Not looking at Jill he said, "Which impression would you like? The one of the reformed sinner, on his knees and begging for forgiveness?"

"Suit yourself." Jill's eyes were on the terrace door. "Did you hear that stuff about wolf-whistles. They're only about twenty and already they sound like Colonel and Mrs Blimp. Don't the English ever learn? Do you think it's something in their genes?"

Guy raised his head. Jill had her elbows on the table, her chin cupped in her hands. There was a faint odour of jasmine; he caught his breath. She had taken trouble over how she looked tonight. Why? Was it to provoke him further? To taunt him with her remoteness.

"It's easy for you to say," he fired up. "You think you're different, but you're just like everyone else out here. You say your life is boring; actually you wouldn't have it any other way. You like it like that."

"Do I?"

"No risks. Aren't I right, Jill? A no-risk policy, in case things get out of control. Keep out. No admittance. Trespassers will be prosecuted. I said that to you – remember? And you said, it wasn't you, it was the East, it was the way people have to be out here. You said it was up to me to be different. Well, I've tried. God knows, I've tried to break down the fences. I tried this morning – all right, I'm sorry, it wasn't the time or place. But you've been avoiding me."

"Have I? Yes. I suppose I have."

"Why? What have I done?"

Jill looked at him. He stared straight back at her. Her glance went past him, to the blind windows.

"It's only poachers I keep out," she said.

"What do you mean?"

"People who break down my defences and then retreat. People who invade my feelings and then run off. Your memory is selective, Guy. We spent a day together not long ago, don't you remember? I took you to the school and to the bungalow. China Bay. I showed you everything that was precious to me. We made love—"

"We kissed!"

"Yes. Perhaps that's all it meant to you. And when we got back to Kelani Lodge you went off with your brother. Two old pals. And that's the last I saw of you."

He was silent. "Harry was there," he said at last.

"Harry was there. And I expect you thought to yourself – oh, Jill will be asleep. . . ."

She signalled to a hovering boy and ordered cheese, biscuits and coffee to get the man away from the table. Guy watched her. In place of the elephant hair bracelets she wore a thin gold band on her wrist, curved in the shape of a heart and clasped where the two halves met. A love-token Harry had given her, most probably. Worn to put him in his place.

"Well, Jill wasn't asleep," she continued, so quietly he had to lean towards her. "Jill was lying in her bed, under the mosquito

247

net, waiting to hear the sound of footsteps. Harry to his bedroom, you to the spare bedroom next to mine. And then in the morning, at first light, oh. . . ." she leant back and clasped her hands behind her neck, laughing softly and shaking her head, like a boy. "And then just the one pair of footsteps. A bit like yours only more measured, deliberate, familiar. Very familiar. And I thought – is it brotherly love that's kept him away? Or the prospect of a good dinner at the Metropole? I made a joke of it, you see. I think one should. Don't you?"

"Oh dear God. I didn't ask to go to the blasted temple ceremony. At least you could have let me see you to explain."

She looked at him, her eyes sad. "Explanations always come too late," she said.

A boy had opened the terrace doors to let a draught of air into the long room. Above the brisk officerly voices and the bursts of braying laughter, they could hear the ocean brushing on the beach, like the soft brush of fingers at a closed door. The food came: dry biscuits, a sliver of butter, regulation cubes of imported cheddar. They ate in silence for a minute, watchfully.

"I hate condensed milk," said Jill, emptying the miniature jug into her coffee. She wrinkled her nose. "Ugh, it's so sweet."

"Come back to the flat," said Guy. "I've got some real coffee."

"No. Thank you."

"I don't know why I didn't think of it." He signalled to the head waiter for the bill. "Rawling gave it to me. It's real Kenya coffee, it tastes like nectar. Really."

"I'm sure it does, Guy. But I have to get back to the Donaldsons'. I don't wish to be late."

"You won't be." He signed the bill with a flourish, ignoring the head waiter's sorrowful gaze. "I promise."

"Don't be juvenile. Please, Guy."

The sharpness in her voice made him start. She was looking at him with real anger. He grinned, and saw in her clear eyes a flicker of unease, or fear.

"This is my night off from temple ceremonies," he told her, the smile all over his face.

Her answer was to get up to go. He pushed his chair back and stood behind her.

"At least you will walk with me on the terrace," he said in a low voice.

Without replying, Jill went ahead of him to the screened terrace door. He watched the ease of her walk, her head high, her back straight; the dark green dress shifting with the lissom movement

248

of her hips. At the door she addressed him quietly. "Let's not talk any more. Let's just get some air."

It was very dark. The ships at sea had extinguished their lights. Colombo was blacked out. Razor-thin streaks of yellow light escaped from the Galle Face Hotel shutters, like flak rising towards a night bomber. In spite of the darkness an eerie phosphorescence was in the air. It painted the wave-tops as they crashed gently on the sand. It back-lit the huge explosions of cloud which drifted through the black sky. It flecked the leaves of the bushes around him. It glimmered in the trees. Only themselves it left entirely in blackness. He could not see Jill at all, until they brushed together, and then they kept close for safety's sake.

"I wonder how Charles and Sylvia ever found their way," he said, forgetting.

"Oh, don't worry." Her laugh came out of the darkness. "Sylvia knew her way already. Sylvia had her wedding planned weeks ago. The only thing that worried her was that they might get married in the dry season and there wouldn't be any white gardenias to go in her bouquet."

They walked on to the grass, dark spectres in the glimmering. There were no other passers in the night.

"They should have married straight away," said Jill, half to herself. "There's so little time for anything any longer."

"We make time for the things we really want to do," he replied with a feeling of self-pity.

"Do we?"

He put his arm round her waist. Jill stiffened and pulled away from him. "Let's go back, we've come far enough," she said, her voice brisk.

"Which way?"

"I don't know."

"Up here. There's a path."

This time it was she who touched him for reassurance. "Go slowly," she said.

The path, between the black shapes of bushes, must have curved round in a circle because it came out on to the grass again. In front of Guy's face appeared a bush that opened round, white, sweet-smelling blossoms to him, ghostly in the phosphorescence. He stopped still.

"It's a moonflower magnolia. You must have seen them before, for goodness' sake," whispered Jill.

"In your garden. But the flowers are open, see? Aren't they glorious?"

He turned round. Jill had vanished. The darkness had swallowed her up. He called her name.

"Jill!"

No answer came. He turned back. The flowers of the magnolia were like cupped hands. The way she had cupped her chin in her hands, her face like a heart, gold-edged like the bracelet on her wrist. He stood without moving, in the fragrance of the magnolia. Tears filled his eyes.

Then, imperceptibly, he became aware that Jill was standing there. She had returned to find him, or perhaps she had always been there, just an arm's length away.

Small waves glittered and sank. Moonflowers hung in the darkness.

He pulled Jill into his arms. She strained from him like a kite straining from a high leash but her face, her soft, lovely face was already raised to his, her mouth accepting the kisses he pressed on it.

They pulled each other down. He fumbled with her dress. *Oh, Jill*. He recited it over and over again like a Buddhist prayer, fumbling with her dress. *Oh, Jill*. Impatiently she thrust his hand away. Raising herself off the grass she wriggled her dress up, and tore loose the thin strip of satin which joined her camiknickers between her legs. Now at last she was visible to him. Her thighs glimmered with the whiteness of the moonflowers, the sailing clouds, the long dancing wave-crests that rose and fell.

Guy buried himself in her fragrance. He pressed himself into her with a keen anguish of delight, so keen that he drew sobbing breaths like a man recovering from a long pain. Jill made no sound. She lifted her stockinged legs and crossed them over the small of his back. Her eyes were closed; she moved her head from side to side as if to do everything to avoid the look in his eyes – of lust, of triumph, whatever she might see in them. Her hair uncoiled around her in ecstasies of curls and ringlets. While he was still approaching his climax he felt a constriction within her and, in the end, a long low animal moan that seemed to issue from all over her body.

He had climaxed inside her, without thinking. Jill opened her eyes and stared up at him. There was no expression on her face. Without saying a word – there was nothing to say – he moved back from her. He rolled over to lie beside her on the hard earth. His brother's wife.

"Guy?"

"Yes."

He quaked, waiting for what would come.

"I think we should go," was all she said.

He helped her to her feet. Jill picked her bag up off the ground. They went down through the barricades to the beach, and walked along it for a few yards, slipping on the sand, until they were out of the hotel grounds and could climb up the concrete steps on to the Galle Face.

Jill cleared her throat. "I can't go to the Donaldsons' like this," she said. "I'll have to come back to your place and straighten myself out. Do you mind?"

"Mind? Oh no. No."

Grateful for the darkness, Guy led the way. They skirted the site of the Civil Defence HQ and crossed the road to Galle Face Court. To his relief, the lobby was empty. In silence they walked up the stairs (the lift as usual was out of order). Guy opened the door of his flat and went straight through to draw down the blackout blinds.

"Don't do that."

He looked round. He heard the door close, the noise of her kicking off her shoes. Her silhouette came soundlessly up beside him, jasmine-scented, and opened wide the window.

A gibbous moon had broken cloud cover. In its half-light her skin had a lustrous transparency, like the wash on artist's paper. He saw the contours of her cheeks and throat, and the curve of her breasts under the silky dress.

"It's a nice flat," he began. "I was lucky to get it, considering. Rawling got it for me, in fact. He's not a bad chap, you know. He's been sending reports to London praising the work I'm doing. I have a modicum of respect for him."

Jill was standing so close that he could feel her body move inside her dress as she drew in breaths of the cool air.

"Shall I make some of that coffee?" he asked.

"No."

"I'll leave it, then."

She was wriggling inside her dress. "I think some of that grass got down my back," she complained. "I have to tell you, Guy—"

"Yes—"

"I think the missionary position is ungallant when you're doing it on the ground. It's not as if there's been any rain for days."

He was too stunned to answer. Jill turned her back on him.

"Undo my dress, please," she said.

251

The zip was easy. The dress fell to the floor. She stepped out of it, and stood in her white undergarment. It was made of some silken material: it shimmered when she wriggled.

"Bloody grass," she muttered. She pushed the straps off her shoulders and peeled down until she was standing in nothing more than a brassière and a pair of brief elastic trunks with suspenders to her stockings. The trunks left bare the tops of her thighs. Guy could see the white moons of her rounded bottom and, when she bent to unstrap her suspenders, the dark hair in between. His mouth dry, he took her arms and raised her towards him.

Her head fell back on his shoulder. For a minute or more she stood still, panting with shallow breaths, while his hands undressed her further, undressed her and stroked her breasts. It was her turn to murmur his name – *Oh, Guy* – and when she began to move her hips against his – *Oh, Guy* – and he could bear it no longer, he picked her up in his arms and carried her in the half-light through to his bed.

This time they had freedom. They had comfort. They were no longer embarrassed or afraid. Jill smiled up at him from the pillow, narrowing her eyes in the darkness.

"Light a candle for me, lover," she murmured.

He had it there, burning for her, and she would not let it go but fell upon it, caressed it, played with it, moved it around inside her; and when it burnt low she revived it with her tongue and her lips until it flared again. She was insatiable; she wanted more and more; and when he lay back exhausted, in a bath of sweat, she lay sprawled half across him, murmuring in his ear, running her fingers up and down his body.

He fell asleep, and dreamt he was a water buffalo, contentedly scratching its tick-bitten hide against the bark of a tamarind tree, its day's work done.

When he woke up, it was to the light streaming in through the window, and the song of a magpie robin clear above the early-morning street noises. Jill was already awake. She lay naked under the mosquito net, in a rumple of white sheet. In the morning light he saw how beautifully pale were her breasts against the sunbathed brown of the rest of her. He put out his hand and stroked her hair back from her forehead. It was slightly damp still. She smiled at him, and brushed his cheek with her hand.

"God, I feel better," she said.

"I love you," he told her. "I love you more than anybody has ever loved you, or ever will love you, or ever can love you."

252

"Darling Guy." She brushed his cheek.

"Will you stay? I want you to stay with me."

"You mean, draw the blackout blinds and pretend it's night again?" She smiled, and yawned, and smiled again. "What fun. Actually I think I might finally let you seduce me with some of your Kenya coffee."

"Of course." But he had no inclination to get out of bed. He wanted to look at her, to drink her in as at a fountain. *From Seyllan to Paradise is forty miles*, she had quoted from Mandeville, *the sound of the fountains of Paradise is heard there.*

But water was not, somehow, Jill's element.

He murmured, "If incendiary bombs are dropped, fires may ensue."

"What's that?"

"A notice. You were standing underneath it at Colombo General."

"Was I?" She gurgled with laughter. "I think there's a little man somewhere who spends all his time trudging round Colombo sticking up warning signs. Have you seen that other one on fire precautions? 'If your clothes catch fire, clap your hand over your mouth, lie down, and roll,' signed The Inspector General of Police. Why your hand over your mouth? Is it to stop yourself screaming and waking up the neighbours?"

"It's to stop you breathing in smoke."

"Oh I don't think so. I think it's protocol, like burping at table. Well-mannered people cover their mouths when their clothes are burning. Do you see?"

Hand on her mouth, Jill rolled over in bed, on top of Guy, and yelped when he tickled her.

"Do you know you've got freckles on your shoulders too?" he asked.

"I can't help it."

"I think they're delicious."

"I've got one on my bottom, as well."

"Where?"

"Here. See? And in front. . . ." She rolled over and showed him a little scattering of brown spots on her belly, just above the honey-dark curls that clustered into her groin. "It's the sun. Harry used to say they were the eyelets on my chastity belt."

Guy drew his hand back. Jill's Australian unaffectedness never ceased to disconcert him. She must have sensed his reaction because she pulled the sheet up and raised herself on one elbow. Her eyes travelled past him to the window.

253

"You've probably worked out that Harry and I gave up making love a long time ago," she said.

"You said he'd taken vows. Buddhist vows."

"More or less. Harry... you know. He believes in codes. I suppose it must have been his public-school code first. Not the blind duty, King and Country bit, he's much too intelligent. I'd never have loved him if he'd been a sort of Percy Buller like the others; what would Bruce have said?"

"What, then?"

"You should know." She hesitated. "Paying his dues. Not cheating. Helping the weak. Never hitting a fellow when he's down. No, I'm not mocking. It's a more tough-minded code than we got at convent school. But Harry thinks codes of behaviour are what keep the world from splitting in two. He lives by them. Conduct, discipline... all the things he sees the war destroying. And now that he's decided the Buddhist code is best, he's determined to live by it and persuade the rest of us to live by it too. Including the Japanese. He could," she added bitterly, "teach Gandhi a few lessons."

"You could always divorce him, you know."

"Divorce Harry?" She threw him a sidelong glance. "It's not like that."

"But you must!" Impatiently he got up and strode about the room, unheedful of his nakedness. His mind was made up. "You must," he repeated. "You can't go on being unhappy, I won't let you! How could anybody not love you and cherish you? Oh Jill, I should, given half a chance!"

She was very still, her chin still propped in her hand, turned away from him. "Harry loves me," she said.

Guy's hands went down to cover his crotch. He got back into the bed beside her and pulled up the sheet.

"I know it's mad," she went on. "Harry spends all his time when he's not down on the estate in his wretched garden shed, with his radio thing. Michael Kandasala's the only person he allows in there. I hardly see him from one week to the next. But you see," she sighed. "I know how bloody important this is to him. I have to support him through this. It will all be different after the War. We'll go back to being the way we were. That's what I have to hope."

"*After the War.*" Guy's voice was harsh with sarcasm. "Everything's supposed to be back to normal *after the War.* Reunited happy families. The British back in Singapore and Hong Kong, taking their tiffin in the office as if nothing had happened, except for some queer little Japanese types coming in and wiping the dust off their desk-tops. That's what they all think in Colombo, you know. None of them realises that we're in a fight to the death. People like Rawling and myself engaged in highly sensitive intelligence work, and all Harry can do is sit around and play games."

"Are you?"

"Am I what?"

"Doing top-secret intelligence work with the Galloping Major?"

Guy nodded, and frowned. "It's not something I can talk about. Even to you. But yes. It's to do with potential Japanese invasion beachheads."

"Guy! What a dark horse you are!" With a small grin, Jill stroked his hair. "And have you found any?"

He hesitated. He could hardly tell her he had only just been conscripted. "Let's just say there are contenders," he declared with an air of containing himself. "What I'm telling you is absolutely confidential, Jill."

"You haven't told me anything yet. How long have you been doing this? Ever since you came to Ceylon?"

"For a while."

He would not be drawn. He had made his play for her and it had had the desired effect. No longer was he the contemptible rubber agent, fiddling with figures while the East burned. He was a warrior. He wore an invisible uniform. David Gifford and Charlie Bilbow had nothing on him now. When Jill, running her fingers through the scattering of hairs on his chest, begged him to tell her what other hush-hush missions he had carried out, he looked down at her and smiled.

"How about that coffee?" he suggested.

The week which followed seemed to Guy the happiest of his whole life. He hardly set foot inside the Dunlop Orient office in Chatham Street. Instead, armed with a large-scale map and three official-looking passes provided by Rawling, he jaunted up and down the west coast of the island, from Udappuwa in the north to Matara in the south, looking for the beach which the Japanese might have targeted for an invasion landing.

Rawling's naval boffins had explained what to look for: the degree of shelter from the prevailing dry-season winds; the rate of shelving most suited to landing craft; the nature of the terrain

255

beyond the beach which would present the first wave of Japanese with the fewest problems. Most of the west-coast beaches would have set the Japs up as sitting targets; but with the camera he'd been given Guy dutifully shot rolls of film, occasionally managing to include a Malay fisherman and his catamaran in the picture to introduce a touch of artistry into his work. The late-March days were uniformly hot and cloudless, and Guy often found it necessary to test the water himself, boldly striding out into the rippling water and swimming a few lazy yards while he turned over in his mind the suitability of the place for a Japanese attack.

To be making this military contribution to the war effort impressed him greatly. It impressed Rawling too, to judge by the urgency with which he seized on Guy's findings each evening in the various rendezvous he arranged – an upstairs room in the Pettah, a corner table at the Pagoda Tea Rooms, once in a hideously damp underground tunnel, smelling of guana and rotting seaweed, where, in the light of paraffin lamps, Guy saw cardboard boxes full of tinned spam and Bombay duck stacked to the dripping roof.

The news was bad, except from Russia. The Japanese were heading their way. As Guy squatted in a dinghy off Dondra Head, plotting the slope of the sea-bed with the aid of a lead line and sheets of waterproofed graph paper, he tried to imagine the crump of shells, the slicing bullets, cries and barked orders, smoke rising above shattered palm trees, blood clouding the translucent water and attracting curious fish.

He tried to imagine it and failed. The war was even harder for him to summon up now than it had been in his vision of it at Kelani Lodge, sweeping through Harry's rubber estate. As he leant over the side of the gently rocking boat and gazed down at the flickering pebbles, all that came to him was the marvel that this geographically was the last landfall in Asia before the South Pole; and the reflection, sentimental but pleasing, that human love was the only thing in existence which was unalterable across such a vast distance – in form, in consistency, in temperature, in energy, in strength.

Only something as impervious as Jill's love for him and his for her, he decided, could have withstood Colombo's gossiping tongues. George Donaldson had let slip to Ingram Bywater in the Club that Jill was hardly using their spare room at nights. Mrs I.B. had forced Elizabeth to admit it. Rumours ignited and spread like brushfire through Cinnamon Gardens: everyone had her own version of the story.

Guy was shielded from the effects of this; he had been on the move constantly since that night at the Galle Face, and, anyway, he was the man. Jill was unprotected. She had to run the gauntlet of horrified looks and whispered asides every time she left the Pasteur Clinic. As a result, she worked longer hours than ever, and reached Guy's flat at night looking pale and exhausted.

"Guess what! Kitty Clarke thinks I've put a spell on you!" she announced one evening. The Boy had cooked them fish mouli with carrots for dinner: Jill had left half of it on her plate.

He caressed her arm, its down of tiny hairs pale against the tan. "Well, it's true."

"According to Elizabeth, opinion is about equally divided. Either I'm a painted harlot or Harry's Buddhist practices have driven me into your arms."

He laughed. "Who cares? Who cares what any of them think?"

Jill was silent for a moment. With the end of her spoon she traced circles on the tablecloth. "Don't underestimate what we're doing," she said. Her voice was strained. "You will be going back to England after the war. You hate it here. Oh I know you do, Guy. You think Colombo is a dreadful little backwater, full of dead fish – and perhaps it is. I see you going off and being terribly successful somewhere, and probably buying back Rubble House and making a new generation of Tancreds there—"

"Oh, nonsense—"

"And I hope you do. I think you should. But Ceylon is my home. I belong here. I shall be staying, as they say, to face the music. After the way I've behaved, I don't expect angelic choirs."

"You can't stay. You can't stay. Not when Harry finds out."

Jill looked at him oddly and said nothing. He put his hand over hers on the table.

"I swear to you, Jill," he said with a huskiness in his throat. "I'm not leaving Ceylon without you."

She said nothing. The Boy knocked and came in with the pudding in a glass dish. He set it down on the table between them.

"Sir, I have made special-recipe banana custard," he said.

"How lovely!" Jill took her spoon and tucked into the yellow glutinous custard. "One thing to be said for the War, it's meant we can all eat nursery food again. I know what I was going to ask you. Have you found your invasion beach yet? Well have you?"

"It's at Beruwala," he answered her sulkily. "If you're interested. The beach by the lighthouse. It's the only one that fits. Rawling thinks so too."

257

"Why are they so sure the Japs won't land on the east coast?"
She gave a nervously bright laugh. "China Bay, I suppose."

"They'll want to move fast on Colombo." He leant forward.
"You heard what I said. I'm not going to leave without you."

"I heard what you said. I don't want to talk about it now."

"Why?"

"Because . . . oh, *because,*" she answered impatiently.
"Because you were right. The War's here. We're in the middle of
it. We could all be killed tomorrow. Let's leave after-the-War until
it's over."

That night, the last they had before Easter, she came to him in
her smart nurse's uniform, naked under it, gladness in her eyes.
She was no longer voracious. She responded to him with an
awesome tenderness and unselfishness as if it was Guy who now
needed all the transfusion of love she could give. She told him
how strong he was; how good-looking; how sexy he was to have
inside her; how good he was; how good he made her feel – *so
good, oh Guy, oh so good* – drawing him down and holding him fast,
as though to keep him there for ever. . . .

In the morning, as she left, she told him the truth. That Harry
knew about the affair. That she had told his brother Harry everything. "There was no other way," she said, in a phrase Guy could
not get out of his mind, "no other way I could go on."

258

5 April 1942.   7.20 a.m. Indian Ocean.

At 25,000 feet, near the service ceiling of the Kate high-level bombers, the cloud is still pillared above them. However, it is not storm-cloud, presaging the kind of conditions which, disgracefully, had prevented the Genzan Air Corps attacking Singapore on the first night of the War. Looking out from his cockpit, Commander Mitsuo Fuchida, leader of the air strike, can clearly see the glowing red, yellow and green lights of his bombers in formation behind him.

Fuchida it is who led the attack on Pearl Harbor. Ever since, he has had to bear the burden of hero-worship from the young pilots under his command. Pearl Harbor was four months and more than 50,000 miles ago, since when the Carrier Striking Force has ranged the oceans destroying targets hardly worthy of its mighty power. In Fuchida's view it is high time to return to the Pacific to strike at the American aircraft-carriers, the only enemy capable of putting up a fight.

Today's attack will take them a distance of 450 miles. Three years ago, over China, that would have been their maximum range. They have all learnt much more now about these aircraft – how to adjust the power settings and get the fuel mixture right, how to take advantage of wind conditions – so endurance will be no problem today. Also, the Kates are carrying 800-kilogram bombs instead of torpedoes. It allows them more fuel.

There is nothing Fuchida can teach these youngsters now. He watched them in Akagi before dawn, their faces intent, putting on their clean mawashi or loincloths, and their thousand-stitch body-belts, each stitch (contributed by friends and neighbours back home) representing a prayer for good luck and for the chance to fight with honourable courage for the divine Emperor. He saw the serious expressions with which they wrote their short letters home and placed them in their lockers along with a carefully wrapped snippet of hair or a nail-clipping in case they do not come back. He made sure they took with them into the cockpit the delicacies which boost their morale – the vacuum bottle of coffee syrup and the bean-paste-coated rice cakes called ohagi.

They all know what they have to do. Following whatever height Fuchida's distinctive red and yellow striped aircraft makes its bombing run over the harbour, the first attack formation will unfold in a fan. Most of his fifty-three high-level bombers, protected by the Zeros, are going to attack harbour installations, oil-tanks and railway workshops. The thirty-six Val dive-bombers will level out at a height of 4300 feet and then dive on the British Eastern Fleet in the harbour, releasing bomb-loads totalling over 13,000 kilograms between them. Itaya's Zeros will be ready to deal with any enemy fighters that come up to meet them. The remainder of the Kates meanwhile will veer off over the airfield and destroy the hangars.

It is 0725. Breaks in the cloud are beginning to appear. Commander Fuchida looks down through his goggles. He can see the blue-shadowed sea, and, directly ahead, a long white line of breaking surf.

They have reached the south-western shoreline of Ceylon. Fuchida eases the stick forward, and starts to go down.

THE gun, still wrapped in oil-cloth, lay on the seat beside him. As he drove out of the cover of the rubber trees, Michael Kandasala brought the Morris 8 to a stop. Muttering to himself, he picked up the gun and put it in the glove-compartment. There might be roadblocks ahead. There was no point in asking for trouble.

He was tired. It had been a long night. The forest around him was silent, with the silence that always lay on the land in the hour before dawn. Ahead of him, the sky seemed to be getting paler although it wasn't easy to be sure, it might just be the effect of squinting through the windscreen at a road he could hardly make out. His lights were so feeble with this silly blackout tape on them.

Something ran across right in front of him. He braked violently, and heard the thud of metal against bone. Trembling, he got out of the car. The animal – it was a baby deer – lay peacefully at the side of the road, its flank rising and falling as if in sleep. In the moonlight, he saw the dark blood trickling out of its open mouth. He placed his hand on its wet fur. As he did so it gave a shudder, and died. With clumps of grass he wiped the blood off his hands and returned to the car.

It was a bad omen. That was why his hands were slippery on the wheel. What would the *bhikkhu* have said? *Beware of harming any creature.* But it was not his fault. It had been an accident. Was he being punished for something he had done? Was he being reminded, as if it was not already on his conscience, that to do this with his gun was not the end but only the beginning? Evil thoughts, impatience, self-interest, forgetfulness – these things also could kill, also must be thrown away.

He came at length to the T-junction, and turned south down the road towards Hanwella. On his left the land fell away towards the Kelani-ganga. There were other, quicker ways of getting down to it, but Master's instructions had been precise.

"Take the early-morning ferry," Master had said. "Go out to the middle of the river. Throw the gun into the water; throw it as far

261

as you can. If you make this ceremony, the Buddha will know that you are resolved to follow the Path.' So saying, Master had shown him his moonstone ring, which he had been given by a monk at the high temple in Kandy. "The moonstone represents the first step on the path to understanding," he had explained, "because the moonstone is always the threshold of the steps leading up to sacred Buddhist temples." Michael, his eyes still full of tears, had shaken his head in acquiescence.

It had been the Lord Buddha himself who had directed him to confess to Master about the Sama Samaj. In accordance with the Dharma he had sat in his room with his eyes shut and concentrated on his breathing. He placed himself in front of the big rusty mirror, where he had practised to be a white man in William Donaldson's cast-off clothes, where he had practised being a nationalist revolutionary dressed in a white sarong with old Albert's pistol tied with string to a belt round his waist. But this time he confronted no image of himself, neither as an imperialist nor as a revolutionary. Squatting in front of the mirror he strove to clear his mind of all thoughts, all worries, and, in meditating upon nothing at all, to find the peace of mind and serenity which Master had.

The first few times he had been unable to rid himself of angry thoughts. All the humiliations he had suffered in his short life came crowding through his mind, like Rakshyos, or like the ghosts in the school play who came to King Richard III of England in his tent.

Not until yesterday, squatting there with his eyes shut, had he found a way to concentrate on his breathing. It was to experience each breath as evidence that he was alive, healthy and alive, and in relation to this wonderful fact of being alive, all his worries, fears, hatreds, humiliations, were as leaves on the guava tree which withered and blew away.

Comprehending this, his mind had become clear and joyful. He *knew*, without having consciously to think, that the right way had to come from within himself. Violence was exterior. Violence destroyed the Way before it could be travelled.

Mr Tancred, with his great bald head and penetrating eyes, filled him with apprehension as well as with respect. It was obvious to him that Master was some kind of holy man. If not actually a *bhikkhu*, he was filled with the spirit of enlightenment, of *samadhi*. It was in this spirit that he had taken on a humble person such as himself, Michael Kandasala, to help him with the transmissions.

Every evening, after his work on the rubber estate had finished, Master would call him into the radio shed and take him through the drill. It was hard slog. The language especially was difficult, even after Master had spelt out on paper how he had to pronounce it, syllable by syllable. It had taken Michael an hour just to get his tongue round *"ohayo gozaimasu"* – *"o-highyoh gaw-zymahss* – "good morning" in Japanese.

Tonight, thinking about his confession, he had muddled the words. Master had been patient; all the same he tapped his fingers on the desk. It was then that Michael had burst into tears and made a clean breast of everything. He told him about the Lanka Sama Samaj, and about the slogan painted on the Hill Club wall. And about the gun he kept in his mattress.

When he had finished he went down on his knees in front of Master. He expected to be instantly sent packing – or worse, locked in the dhobi-room while Master telephoned the police. Instead, there had been a long silence. Then he had been made to sit on the edge of the truckle-bed, while Master proceeded to tell him about the Mahatma Gandhi and the Salt March from Ahmedabad to the Indian Ocean.

It was a story Michael knew well. But the way Master told it made him understand its meaning. It was evidently not an act of rebellion; it was a parable of what rebellion could do. Harmless in itself, it was at the same time more powerful than any deed of violence.

It was the kind of action of which Gautama the Buddha would have approved. As Buddha himself said in the Suttas, "Just as the mighty ocean has but one savour, the savour of salt, even so has the Dharma but one savour, the savour of release." And if it could work for Gandhi, in the vast continent of India, it could work against the British in Ceylon.

Once this war was stopped. As it had to be.

Headlights bore down on the Morris 8. Michael swung into the side of the road. An army truck full of troops clattered past; it was too dark to tell if they were Indian or British. His lip curled in amusement; it was all so futile. So much money wasted on this War, as Master said. So many men and machines of destruction. So many politicians, generals, important people, all buzzing round this small island like flies around a bowl of mango chutney. *And all barking up the wrong tree!*

Master and the *bhikkhus* were right. There had been too much killing. It had to be stopped. The longer it went on, the easier it became to think there was no choice except kill or be killed. That of course was how the Sama Samajists saw it: kill or be killed. No wonder they resented the Buddhists, and gave him all that eyewash. As he drove on, Michael thanked Buddha that he had found the Way before it was too late, before he had done something for which his Karma, in time to come, would take its revenge.

The first light of dawn unmasked the landscape as he turned down towards the ferry. On the edge of a dry paddy he saw two crows perched on the branch of an ironwood tree. Three months ago he could not have dismissed from his mind the villagers' superstition which said crows seen at first light are omens of disaster. Now, he tooted the horn and giggled as they took flight.

This was what Buddha had done. The Lord Buddha had shown him how to recover all that was good in his past without having to take the bad things as well, the demon-priests, the ignorant superstitions. Buddha had showed him how to enjoy again what he had enjoyed in childhood. As he drove, he could taste on his tongue the crumbling sweetness of rice cooked in coconut milk, which Mother had made for him as a special treat when he was ill. That and talla-ball sweets, and hoppers cooked and eaten with wild honey. . . .

The sky in the east glowed with a pink light. It caught the surface of the wide, slow river which was now stretched out before him, giving it a pale, pink milky whiteness that rippled into shadow. As he got out of the car (there was only a bullock cart ahead) the jungle behind him at that instant stirred itself awake. It rustled in anticipation of sunlight. The screech of a peacock was answered in the cooing of spotted doves and the tap-tap of an invisible nightjar.

The ferry, when it emerged out of the darkness shrouding the opposite bank, proved to be hardly more than an outsize raft, powered by an engine not much bigger than an outboard motor. Gingerly, Michael drove the Morris on to the timber deck and secured it with ropes. Two grimy vans, one loaded with coconuts, the other with crates of chickens, followed him on board. He saw with relief that their drivers paid not the least attention to what must have been the unusual sight of a young Sinhalese in sole charge of a very expensive car.

With no more fears, he followed the instructions Master had given him. Halfway across he got out of the car, holding his uncle's old gun still wrapped in its oil-cloth. Shielded by the open car-door he leant over the rail. Then he hesitated. He was here to perform a ceremony, to show respect for Buddha. He moved away from the cars, back across the ferry deck, to give himself a run-up. He trotted to the rail, and with an over-arm toss he bowled the gun as far as he could into the pearling water of the Kelani-ganga.

The splash disturbed a spring of teal. They rose in the air and stalled for a second, flapping their wings, before flying back over the trees. Most of the Christian Englishmen he knew would have shot them: he, a Buddhist, had just thrown his gun away. As far as he knew the ancient firearm had never been used – not by the old appu, certainly not by anyone else. It was white men who killed for pleasure, and from killing animals went on to kill each other.

Last month he had overheard Master at dinner (this was before Lady became a fixture in Colombo), telling a story about the passenger pigeon. The passenger pigeon had existed since before the beginning of history. Up to 1850 it was the commonest bird in North America. A bishop in Canada drove them away with holy water because they had eaten all the local crops. Passenger pigeons flew in such great swarms, so Master said, that they sometimes obscured the sun.

Then, for the next fifty years, they were hunted without mercy. Nesting colonies were destroyed. Men shot them. Snared them. Captured them in nets. Migrating flocks were slaughtered wholesale. In September 1914, according to Master, the last passenger pigeon in the world died in an American zoo in Ohio. That month, Michael heard him say, was the start of the Great War.

Now Michael stood at the ferry rail watching a reddish sun peep over the grey horizon. By throwing the gun away he had not lost a link with his family: he had made himself more worthy of being one of them. He thought of Uncle Albert, waking at dawn by long habit in his whitewashed room in Kandaloya and slowly remembering that there were no longer any household tasks to occupy the long, empty day. J.P. – he was another early riser. He would be adjusting his dark tie under his stiff collar, and planning his schedule with the precision of an egg-timer (while grumbling that all the big shots as normal would be wanting their eggs done differently).

Meanwhile the sun was high enough to make the dew sparkle on the grass and on the leaves of the trees as the ferry came nosing into the south bank of the Kelani-ganga. To the convert, the dew and the glittering spiders' webs in the grass were more priceless than any jewellery shop in Main Street. He sniffed the heady morning air and listened to the suck of water among the swaying reeds. There was a better life to lead than the city life of a *trouser-karen* he told himself, and he, Michael Kandasala, had been granted the way to find it.

The journey back to Kelani through Hanwella took him on to the main Colombo road. He did not hang around. Master had put him on constant standby in the radio shed. Already at this hour – it was only seven o'clock – there was an excessive amount of traffic. Townspeople were still leaving Colombo in bits and bobs although the panic about air raids, started by J.P.'s ARP tests, seemed to have calmed down. Most of it was army activity: troops in lorries, military big bugs in jeeps, engineers at the side of the road putting up tall telephone-poles.

He stopped at the petrol depot in Hanwella. The roadblock, a flimsy thing of empty oil-barrels and a lowered pole, was a little bit further on. To the English officer who questioned him, Michael explained that Mr Tancred of Kelani Lodge had sent him out early to get the tank filled. The officer examined the date-stamp on his petrol coupons, and waved him on without another look.

Michael whistled as he drove home. Whistling was something he never did: but today was different. A pain had fallen from his heart. A week ago he would have been smarting with rage at the foreign troops on the road, the litter of petrol-cans, the bullying food-posters, the roadblock with its pink faces in charge, the English officer with his curling moustache turned up like a sneer. Today, because his mind was on higher things, he accepted these sights with unconcern, as if he was calmly viewing the antics of an enemy who was powerless to do him mischief.

Besides, waiting at the roadblock, he had seen something he had never expected to see as long as he lived. Behind the sentry-block he had seen four white soldiers – *privates*, as it was the British joke to call them – clearing the jungle. Stripped to the waist, sweating heavily, they were attacking the undergrowth with pitchforks and scythes. Here was a labourer's task, a *Sin-halese* labourer's task, being done by white Masters! He had sat, open-mouthed, until the officer had shouted at him to drive forward.

One of the soldiers, long-haired, his skin still pink and white, had stood upright, rested the pitchfork handle against his leg and wearily wiped his arm across his forehead. Michael saw this. It was a gesture you would have seen a hundred times a day, all over Ceylon, for the last thousand years – but always before it had been a brown arm, wiping the sweat off a brown forehead.

266

It seemed to Michael that in this glimpsed scene, a mile outside Hanwella, on this Sunday morning in April, a thousand years of history had come to an end in Ceylon. A barrier had been torn down. A high hill had been levelled with the plain. In the vision that entranced him, motoring along the road with the air blowing in through the open windows, he saw East and West joining hands across the great divide, brown skins and white skins working together in the sweat of their brows, as the Lord Buddha in his wisdom had surely intended. Things were going to be different, now. The signs were there. He was beginning to see them.

The sky responded with a roll of drums. Michael looked up and saw the planes, and saluted them as they flew past, out of the rising sun.

THREE

It was a humid Easter weekend in Colombo. On Saturday night, for the fourth night in a row, the April sea breezes failed to come inland and lift the suffocating heat that had clamped down over the city. People slept with their windows open, restlessly, under a single sheet, waiting for the monsoon to break and release them. Kitty Clarke's son, Edward, woke in the early hours of that Easter Sunday morning and began to scream. The moonlight had caught the wrinkles in his sheet and turned them into long black snakes that teemed and slithered as he thrashed his legs to be rid of them.

"It's a nightmare, sweetie-pie, only a nightmare. Nothing to cry about," Kitty comforted him as she held the sobbing boy against her rayon shift. But Edward knew that the snakes had just disguised themselves as long thin shadows; they would be back, crawling over his legs again, when she went out and closed the door.

In a smaller flat, further south towards Bambalapitya, David Gifford lay awake under the same fitful moon. His hands behind his head, he stared up at the ceiling. Shivering clusters of shadow were cast on it, from the barely trembling leaves of the tree outside his window. He made clouds out of them through which his Hawker Hurricane IIB flew upwards, circling, looking for height from which to dive on to the tail of enemy Zeros. Tonight he was merciless. As soon as he was in their slipstream he opened up with all eight .303 machine-guns, and in his frustration went on pumping in bullets until the Jap exploded in a ball of flame.

He had woken up an hour ago, with a raging thirst. Too much drink, that was his problem. Not last night, but earlier in the week. It caught up with you after a while. He never used to drink anything more than the occasional whisky: but recently he'd been starting with a few Nuwara Eliya beers in the mess and then dragging some of the boys off to the night-club where they would

271

dance and have a good time and he'd stand with his back to the bar. Not moving except to raise his glass to his lips, he would stand and gaze at the shadowy faces in the smoke.

He had been seeing something of Maria de Vos in the last ten days; although in his imagination it wasn't Maria in bed beside him. It was a pink and brown, rounded figure, small and very pretty, with delicious little residues of puppy fat on her upper arms and her hips. She lay peacefully with her cheek on his pillow, one arm curved around the nimbus of her blonde hair; on her face the mischievous sleepy half-smile with which she had sought out the hollow his body made in the soft mattress. If he lay perfectly still, and held his breath, he fancied he could hear her breathing.

He counted clouds, he counted enemy aircraft, but his thoughts kept shooting him down. With a groan he turned on his side. It was his own fault. And really it was Maria who had the grace, the intelligence, the fine-tuning. He could talk to Maria about anything: about plays, music, ballet, all the things he took for granted back home but which she had only ever seen and heard in the second-rate versions which had toured to Colombo. Her cultural range astonished him, though it shouldn't have. Her father, Rex de Vos, was a top lawyer in the Chief Justice's office. She evidently came from a distinguished Burgher family, with any number of aunts, uncles and cousins who were scientists, librarians, archivists, legendary figures on the racetrack – she had delightful anecdotes about all of them.

And yet Maria herself was so modest, so unassertive. Only in her dancing did she assert herself. He had been to see her in Mademoiselle Orliga's studio: she had pirouetted and pranced like one of those Hindoo goddesses with a dozen legs and arms. Such an innocent, enchanting creature, with her 'Hollywood-style' American handbag, and those big dark anxious eyes which seemed always to be looking for reassurance, even after reassurance was given. . . .

David pushed the mosquito netting aside, and drained his glass of water. There was no sense in him sleeping, even if he'd been able to. He had his alarm clock set for 3 a.m. to be on standby at the Racecourse aerodrome at 0400 hours. Somerville's fleet had left Colombo harbour, all except for Charlie's ship and another cruiser which had come back to escort a troop convoy, so he'd heard. It must mean that the Japs weren't yet closing in.

He put the glass back and looked at the luminous hands of his watch. It was almost three. He sat on the edge of the bed for a moment. Then he got up and pulled his clothes on. His back and shoulders were clammy. His head was aching.

As he got to the door he thought he heard something, and turned back. Nothing moved. The bed was empty. There was no blonde head on the pillow. In the moonlight, though, he'd caught a glint of gold. It was the Egyptian ankh on his bedside table, the match of the ankh he had given Sylvia at the Septic Prawn. On an impulse he returned and put it round his neck on its gold chain, tucking it under his vest so that his fellow-pilots wouldn't know. He went out, buttoning up his jacket, and closed the door quietly on his daydreams.

Guy Tancred had slept, but not well. He was growing a military-style moustache and it prickled, as though mosquitoes were constantly settling on his upper lip.

Groggy, he lay back and watched a grey dawn seep round the edge of the blackout blinds. He listened to the faint susurrus of the breakers on the Galle Face shore. The oppressive heaviness of thunder hung in the air. He dozed off again, and was woken by the bells of Christ Church ringing for the early-morning service. He pulled aside the mosquito net and went into the bathroom to shave.

Jill had scoffed at his moustache. She seemed to find a lot of what he did funny at the moment. This Easter weekend she'd said she was spending with Harry in Kelani. Guy had acquiesced – which was probably a mistake. It wasn't so much a question of playing fast and loose with his affections: Jill knew better than to do that. But there were important things he had to discuss with her. The unexpected Dunlop Orient cable for one.

It was a whole day since he'd seen her; two since she'd told him about Harry knowing... *"no other way could I go on"*. He'd spent a sleepless night failing to reconcile himself to that. Over and over again he'd tried to imagine the scene with them in Kelani when she'd spilled their secret out. Sometimes she and Harry were in the garden, sometimes on the verandah, sometimes at dinner over coffee, sometimes in bed together (this was the hardest to imagine). Harry's reaction was always identical. A look of shock would cross his face, followed by momentary anger that his little brother could behave in this way, before his face hardened into a Buddha-like expression of compassionate forgiveness.

When Guy was unable to stand it any longer he'd stormed into

273

the Pasteur Clinic, on the pretext of having an urgent family message for Jill. She was not to be found in the rabies wards; Guy had no desire to beard the formidable Sister again. Restlessly he prowled the antiseptic corridors, nodding to Singapore refugees straying from their sick-beds in borrowed slippers and dressing-gowns. The third nurse he stopped was able to tell him Jill was on theatre duty: he kicked his heels outside the emergency operating theatre, scowling at Layton's evacuation notice, until the double doors swung open and a sheeted figure was wheeled out, one of the nurses holding up a drip as she hurried alongside.

Guy edged in, brushing past a doctor who looked too exhausted to ask him what the devil he was doing. Jill was in the anteroom, running water into a washbasin. When she turned round he saw that her hands and the front of her white tunic were spattered with blood.

"You shouldn't have come here," she said.

"You shouldn't have left like that. Without explaining."

He went up to her. She raised her bloodstained hands as though to ward him off.

"Look at this. This is what I have to worry about. Not enough gloves to go round. We're running short of everything: drugs, sterilisers, trained nursing staff. And you should see the state of some of the refugees. It makes you wonder why anyone should want to bring children into a world like this."

"You sound like Harry."

"Is that a crime?"

"Jill. I want to know. What did you mean, there's no other way?"

She turned away. She plunged her hands into the basin of water.

"It's true."

"What is?"

"Think about it, Guy. Try and see my side."

She was scrubbing her hands furiously. He saw the gold of her wedding-ring in the cherry-red water. He blurted out, "Did you tell him you love me? That you're coming to live with me? Did you tell him how good we are together?"

She stopped, and bent her head over the basin so that he could not see her face. After a moment she said in a low voice, "I told him how much I needed you. He understood."

He was silent. She lifted up her face. He kissed it, holding her tight, like a boy with his first date. She broke away from him with

274

a little laugh. "That moustache! You're getting more like Major Rawling every week!"

And then the doors had opened, another patient was wheeled in. Guy had squeezed her hand, and left.

Now, he put down the razor and rubbed his face vigorously with the towel. He could be patient. Where need was, love naturally followed. "She doesn't know me as well as she thinks," he said to the mirror, and strode back to the bedroom to dress.

Lydia's letter was on the bedside cabinet. Putting it to his nose Guy sniffed the faint, sophisticated scent which had somehow survived the journey from England. There was something quite erotic about Lydia's lily-like decorousness, it occurred to him, at least in contrast to the sexual directness he had met from Jill. With its gossip about Langham Place, "Bobby Helpmann" and the Fulham Forum, the letter was totally superficial of course, as was everything Lydia said and did. But at least it had the virtue of being predictable. You knew where you were, in Lydia's world, which meant in practice you could be one step ahead. Out here . . . but out here too it was just a matter of time.

The telephone rang. He went into the sitting room and picked it up. Rawling, through a hail of static.

"Tancred? It's on. Meet me at the office. Give me—"

Without warning the static accelerated into a bray of heavy turbine engines directly overhead. Rawling's voice faded. Guy sped to the rattling window and pulled up the blind. He could see them – ten – twelve – strung out in line astern. They looked like Blenheims except for the red discs circled with white on their fuselage. Fighter-bombers. Japanese fighter-bombers.

He flung on his clothes. He ran down the empty stairs and out into Colpetty in a chaos of horns and sirens. He saw the explosions above the harbour, brighter than the sudden sun. He saw gouts of fire and smoke.

The Imperial Japanese Navy had reached Ceylon.

Eric Hoathly had taken especial care over his Easter sermon. This was an opportunity to say things that needed to be said. He had had complaints from parishioners about the behaviour of sailors on shore leave in Colombo. There had been carousing. Worse than carousing. Prostitutes had returned to the environs of Church Street, he had seen them himself. Ottoline, who took an emancipated view of missionary work, had been down among them and talked to them about the dignity of womanhood. It had

had no effect. That was the tragedy of war. It not only claimed men's bodies but corroded their souls. Morality, propriety, the social graces – all corrupted, all progressively destroyed.

He proposed to remind his congregation that although Easter derived from the Teutonic pagan festival of *Eostre* (as we find in the Venerable Bede) a thousand years of Christian usage had supervened. The words of St Clement, writing to the Corinthians, would make an apposite resurrection text: *Let none of you say that this flesh is not judged and does not rise again . . . for as you were called in the flesh, you shall also come in the flesh.* That should make them prick up their ears and take notice.

While the Archdeacon perused his notes, during the First Lesson which was read by Sir Oliver Prescott, George Donaldson glanced around St Peter's. It was a very creditable muster to say the least. Most of the nabobs had turned out, and a decent number of rankers too. A few of them had to stand at the back, which he hadn't seen before. Even Sylvia had been coming to church of her own accord recently, although this morning she was on duty in the Naval Office. The Ingram Bywaters were here. So were a fair number of their other neighbours, in a demonstration of pluck the local population could have done worse than to copy. Yesterday Sinhalese had joined Tamils falling over themselves to get out of Colombo. People had been hanging on to the sides of trains out of Fort Station, like the natives did in India.

George Donaldson thought of his Hornby train set. In its uncluttered harmony it was a model of how society should order itself. But what if those little wooden people on the platform were all suddenly to find their voice and demand to be taken somewhere? He imagined cramming them into the trucks and carriages, balancing them on the roofs – and of course they'd fall on the floor in their silly way and he'd have the irritation of having to pick them up and scrub them clean, one by one, while all his train schedules went awry. . . .

Distant thunder rolled. He could not restrain an involuntary shudder. That was where, in the end, the East defeated them all, defeated the best systems of the most brilliant administrators. Its populations were unmanageably large and unstable. The imposition of order was always superficial, establishing a surface calm, like weighted nets upon the sea.

" 'Christ is risen from the dead, and become the first-fruits of them that slept,' " read the Governor in a sonorous voice from

I Corinthians. " 'For since by man came death: by man came also the resurrection of the dead. For as in Adam all die: even so in Christ shall all be made alive.' "

The Church of Ceylon was another net, cast to still the sea as much as to capture little fishes. Psalms and the Creed would follow; then Archdeacon Hoathly would lift up his eyes to God and request Him to defend them from all assaults of their enemies, that they, confidently trusting in God's inclination to the British cause, might not fear the power of any little yellow adversaries. George Donaldson thought of his brother in London. Thirty years ago this month, aged twelve and fourteen respectively, the future colonial administrator and the future merchant banker had been taken by Mamma and Papa to the Savoy Theatre to see Reginald Owen as St George in *Where the Rainbow Ends.* George Donaldson remembered even now the embarrassment with which he had tried to hide his tears at the end when St George took off his shabby cloak and revealed the shining armour in which he would defeat the Dragon King.

That production at the Savoy had sown the seed of his ambition to be a proconsul of Empire, fighting aggression and the forces of tyranny. These last few months – ever since, he supposed, William had gone off to the war – he had been grappling with the knowledge that his ambition would never be realised. The age of the proconsul was over. Sir Oliver Prescott was proof enough of that. The best one could expect was to be like Kipling's centurion, standing on the walls of Rome and watching, on one side, barbarism, on the other, decay.

The Governor closed the heavy Bible with a thud and nodded familiarly at the altar before returning to his pew in front of the Donaldsons. The organist played the first few bars of a hymn, and the congregation rose. In the pause before the hymn, another sound took over. It began like the buzz of a mosquito and soared to a wail, a high, keening wail which sang through St Peter's Church like the scream of a falling angel.

A subdued commotion. A scraping of chairs. The Governor half-turned and raised an eyebrow at his Acting Chief Secretary.

"I don't think it's a practice, sir," said George Donaldson.

"Don't you?"

"No, sir. It's a Red Alert."

"I'd better get back, then."

Sir Oliver picked up his hat and his prayer book and strode

down the aisle. He did not appear to notice Eric Hoathly, who ran up into the pulpit and thumped his hymn-book on the lectern to get their attention.

"The crypt!" shouted the Archdeacon, above the blare of the air-raid sirens. "Follow me!"

Somebody opened the main doors. Sir Oliver heard the thunder of bombers overhead. His lower lip jutting, his face grim with disappointment, he marched out into the sunlight and back towards Queen's House, accompanied by a Sinhalese servant who unfurled an umbrella and carefully held it over His Excellency's head to shelter him from any falling bombs. Panic-stricken figures ran past him in all directions. Explosions in the harbour behind him shook the pavement and sent up puffs of dust from the street.

Sir Oliver did not look back. He did not look up. All he could think was that, once again, he hadn't been put in the picture. Layton and the others must have conspired to keep this from him. Either that, or they simply hadn't bothered to tell him the Japs were coming. They were fighting the blasted War without him.

On the Racecourse airfield, the men of No. 258 Squadron were sitting down to a breakfast of bacon and eggs and orange juice. They were a mixed bunch. At Ratmalana, where they'd been re-formed virtually from scratch, they were known as the Kedgeree Kids. David Gifford was one of only two English pilots – the others were from Canada, Australia, New Zealand, South Africa, Rhodesia and the Argentine – but they all ate the same breakfast with the same hearty appetite, having had nothing more than black coffee for the three and a half hours they had been on alert for a Japanese raid.

The tension had eased. Even the cooks and the waiters in the mess hut could feel it, and passed out the plates to the usual jokes about hot food to fend off the Nip in the air. If the Japanese had been going to attack, they would have done it by moonlight and enjoyed the element of surprise. That was the view of the boffins in Fighter Operations, and who were the Kedgeree Kids to disagree?

Shortly before dawn there had been a brief, violent squall of rain. Now the clouds were beginning to clear. David Gifford finished his last cup of coffee and stared at the sky. Its woolly grey reminded him of Wiltshire skies. What would have happened if

England had enjoyed Ceylon's climate – would it have been conquered by waves of invaders who wanted to be able to sit out every evening on a warm verandah with their drinks, and be able to play eighteen holes of golf in the sun without having to run for shelter to the clubhouse halfway through? And if the golfers and tennis players and tea merchants were thrown out of their tropical islands in the sun? Imagine all these Englishmen, like Sylvia's father, trained through generations to govern far-flung natives, being asked to limit their horizons to governing London or Liverpool or Stoke-on-Trent – wouldn't they end up treating the poor ratepayers like natives too?

To the north, between the clouds at about 8000 feet, a flash of silver caught his eye. If one of the Hurricane Squadrons from Ratmalana was airborne it would mean the alert was over – though surely they'd have been told at the Racecourse by now. It must be one of the Fulmars returning from a dawn patrol. But there were only about six Fleet Air Arm Fulmars – weren't there? – and he could see ten or twenty flashes of silver . . . maybe a hundred . . . the whole sky to the north over the harbour . . . and then more planes to the south, over Ratmalana, coming low over the airfield, and he heard the CO barking down the phone to Fighter Operations – "Of course we can see the bloody enemy!" – and he was grabbing his leather helmet as the alarm blared out and racing, racing to his Hurricane, clambering into the cockpit and checking the fuel and the switches while the mechanic unplugged the trolley battery and sprinted away.

There was no time to think about what a communications cock-up there must have been. The main thing was to get up there. Plugging in his oxygen-mask, he set the throttle forward and started her up. Usually on a humid day like this he would wait until the engine was running smoothly, but there was no time, the twelve cylinders were all firing, the propeller was turning OK. David Gifford let the plane gather speed, and tucked up the wheels as he lifted its nose above Victoria Park.

Height. It was height they needed. Height and speed and power. Straight after take-off any fighter plane, even a Hurricane, was as vulnerable as a young blackbird taking its first flight out of the nest. Once he was up through the clouds. . . . Diving out of the sun his Mark IIB Hurricane was surely a match for any plane in the world, even the Japanese Zero fighter, about which the Air Ministry had told them nothing, nothing at all, despite the fact that they'd been operational over China and Malaya and escorted the attack planes at Pearl Harbor. . . .

He nursed the Hurricane up into the sunlight, moving the throttle to keep her steady. Squadron-Leader Fletcher, the CO, was on his port side, leading the formation in a Vic-pattern towards the sea. He must have seen what David had seen: a tight formation of Japanese bombers escorted by Zero fighters, still several thousand feet above them to the north, heading inland to attack the harbour. 258 Squadron would have to turn in from the sea for a head-on attack.

Height. More height. So far they were lucky: no Zeros on their tail. They couldn't have been expecting an airfield on the Racecourse. It was the poor beggars at Ratmalana who would be copping it, shaken by bomb-blasts as they got airborne, always supposing any of them had managed to take off.

Through his perspex hood David Gifford saw two Japanese bombers dive down at a steep angle and disappear into a lump of cloud above the harbour. He kept the Hurricane steady in formation and waited. The CO would probably go for 20,000 feet, he thought, so they could take a crack at the Jap fighters on equal terms. But he was wrong. With a "Tally-ho!" that crackled in David's earphones, Fletcher led the formation on a turning dive into the thick cloud, heading straight for the bombers low over the harbour, machine-gunning as they finished their bombing runs.

In the cloud David lost them. It was every man for himself now. Flak was rising from the AA batteries. Coming out into clear visibility he had a sudden view of smoke and flames rising from ships in harbour, before he pulled out of the dive and began firing all eight .303 machine-guns from dead astern at the bomber in his sights.

Closing to nearly point-blank range David saw its rear turret shatter, and then its forward turret. The bomber bucked and swerved towards the open sea. He didn't see it go down. There was one – no, two – enemy fighters on his tail. He banked steeply, seeing the lines of tracers curving past his wing-tip, and marvelled to himself at the speed and manoeuvrability of these Jap planes. Just as he'd inched enough height to turn and fire a long machine-gun burst at one of his two attackers, another four or five Zeros came at him from out of the clouds.

He turned on his back and dived vertically down through cumulus, doing aileron turns, until the cloud cleared and he was pulling out frantically over the tops of palm trees somewhere inland from the city. He couldn't shake them off. He smelt burning, he could feel the heat at his back. The Hurricane's engine was in trouble. Oil spattered his hood and filled his cockpit. Frantically he ducked in and out of the palm trees, playing hide and seek in the close green hollows of paddy-fields.

Still the Zeros came at him firing cannon shells from both wings. He felt a panic that started in his abdomen and worked its way up towards his throat. This wasn't fair. They were four to his one. They'd had their fun with him. Frantically, he climbed into the watery sun – but the plane wasn't responding – the controls were soft – he'd stall if he didn't pull out right now – and the Jap was coming at him from behind, shredding his fuselage with the bullets that kept cracking around him – *Out of control* –

J. P. Kandasala's devotion to duty very nearly killed him. It being Easter Sunday, he had risen at cock-crow to make a tour of the Pettah churches, knowing bally well that their priests and *bhikkhus* et cetera wouldn't have the faintest idea what to do in an air raid, or where to locate the nearest water-hydrant in the event of fire.

After eating his breakfast (his wife had pushed off to stay with friends in Kandy) he hailed a rickshaw. He visited St James's, St Anthony's, St Lucia's, St Mary's, St Anna's, eight Hindu kovils, three mosques and a Buddhist temple. At about 7.45 a.m. he left the Old Dutch Church, just as its largely Burgher congregation was arriving, dressed up to the nines, for morning service, and walked down Wolfendahl Street towards the covered market.

For a dreadful second, when the sirens went, J. P. Kandasala thought he had ordered an ARP practice and it had slipped his mind. What to do? Then he looked up, and saw the bombers come in over the sea, and heard the unfamiliar bark of the anti-aircraft guns, and knew that his hour had come.

He got out his whistle and blew it shrilly. Then he began running down Wolfendahl Street, an incongruous figure in his regulation helmet and grey worsted Sunday suit, waving his arms and shouting to people to take cover. Not until he got down to the market-place did it sink in that there was nobody on the streets. They had all melted away. He was alone.

At that moment an explosion knocked him sideways. He scrabbled in the dust for his spectacles and his tin hat. A bomb had fallen, he didn't know where. It occurred to him that he himself was not invulnerable to the enemy attack. There was a shelter underneath the old Town Hall. His best black shoes crunching on broken glass, J. P. Kandasala ran across the square, through the covered market and down the stone steps.

From the point of view of a scientific observer he would have preferred to wait out the raid in one of the hundreds of specially constructed slit trenches and cabook-walled squares he had planned and supervised. The Town Hall cellar made one of the safest natural shelters in Colombo. Even so, to his chagrin, he found fewer than twenty people in it, including the local ARP warden who had forgotten to put on his helmet, his uniform or the white brassard stamped ARP on his left arm.

"What's your tally?" he asked the man curtly. "How many dead and wounded? Have you got enough dressings?"

Wilting under this rapid fire, the warden made a sweeping gesture with his arm at the little band in the cellar. J. P. Kandasala looked round. An elderly white gentleman with a handlebar moustache, dressed like J.P. in a grey suit, sat in a corner by the ventilation grilles, muttering to himself. A prosperous Sinhalese couple, with three small girls in frilly pink party-dresses, were anxiously discussing the special biriyani lunch they always prepared at Easter and whether Cousin Mary would know where the saffron was kept. A group of Tamils, perhaps porters from the market, crowded round an upturned petrol-drum playing cards and rolling cigarettes. Two families of Burghers, obviously caught on their way to Wolfendahl Old Church, sat silently, clutching their knees, looking with anxious expressions at the ceiling. A couple of bespectacled young locals – probably attorneys-at-law like half the educated population of Colombo – hawked round tickets for an end-of-season cricket match against the police to celebrate Sinhalese New Year. They were explaining to anyone who would listen how the Japanese could be pushed back across the Pacific.

"But you yourself are injured, sir!" exclaimed the ARP warden, gazing at him in dismay; and J. P. Kandasala realised that in the heat of the moment he had indeed sustained a nasty scratch above his left temple, from which a trickle of blood had run down his cheek. Since there were no safety plasters in the First Aid Box he good-naturedly took off his helmet and allowed the warden to wind a bandage round his head, giving him the appearance of an unnaturally small Sikh with half his turban missing. The cut was actually much less painful than the nick he'd given himself shaving that morning, when his thoughts had turned to the not-yet-quite-finished underground Civil Defence HQ . . . and, ye gods and little fishes, what about that? Was it OK? It would only take a single thousand-pound bomb through the plank-and-tarpaulin roofing to blow it all to kingdom come!

Made quite ill by the thought of this, J. P. Kandasala opened the shelter door and looked up the steps. His ears were still buzzing from the explosion (the headgear they'd at long last been sent was absolutely bally hopeless against blast, and the supplementary pads of cottonwool were still being made up) but it did seem quieter now, up top. Eyeing the warden severely, J. P. Kandasala told him to start assembling search parties. Then he ascended the steps.

He was immediately enveloped in a powerful smell of fish. The air battle was still in progress. He could see puffs of smoke from the ack-ack batteries and a pillar of black smoke from something burning in the harbour. As he gazed at the sky, a plane with RAF roundels came spiralling lazily out of the sky trailing a ribbon of white, and crashed somewhere out of sight and out of hearing. Dauntless, J.P. followed his nostrils and arrived at the fish market in St John's Road.

The scene would stay with the Deputy ARP Controller for many nights to come. The fish market had taken a direct hit from a Japanese bomb. Fish were scattered for a hundred yards in every direction: seir fish, whiting, mackerel, sole, baby sharks, some headless or cut in two, some still moving convulsively in the road. A lobster claw had somehow attached itself to the metal strut of a lamp-post. A dog sniffed at a crab which had lost most of its shell and one eye-stalk and was still trying to inch its way down the pavement.

Against a lamp-post slumped a fish-market porter, his white apron stained with blood. He must have been cutting up fish when the bomb fell. J. P. Kandasala stopped and asked him what had happened.

The porter made no reply. He stared at the Deputy Controller through eyes that did not focus. From under his apron a narrow puddle of dark blood and bile seeped slowly towards the gutter. Horrified, J. P. Kandasala extended his hand. As he did so, the porter took hold of his apron and lifted it between his fingers and thumbs. He opened his mouth to say something, then slid slowly sideways. J. P. Kandasala saw the hole where his stomach had been. He bent his head and was sick into the red-running gutter.

Wiping his mouth, he lifted the porter back against the lamp-post. The man's face had gone grey. The Deputy ARP Controller looked around him in dismay. He had established thirty first-aid posts in Colombo, yet there was no sign of an ambulance or a stretcher-party. He was alone, in a deserted street, with a dying man, several hundred fish and half the stray dogs and cats in the city.

If he was at his Control Centre he could do something. The Control Centre had direct lines to the first-aid services as well as to the police and fire-brigade HQs. It also had fully operational direct lines to the Naval PDO control room and the RAF fighter operations room which would give him a chance to find out what the bally hell was going on. But how could he get there? It would take half an hour to walk. This man was dying.

"Damn and blast!" said J. P. Kandasala, aloud.

A fighter plane, trailing black smoke, flew overhead, so low that he could see the red sun of Nippon on its fuselage. Small flakes of ash began to drift down from the fires in the harbour. He repeated to himself the inspiring words of Civil Defence Commissioner Goonetilleke: "We will not allow our beautiful city to be burnt; we will not panic and run away; we will rescue the wounded and fallen."

At that moment he saw an old lady in gym shoes, pedalling slowly towards him down the street on a mud-stained bicycle. He ran towards her.

"Madam, you are risking life and limb," he said, panting.

"I am paying for this War, and I intend to see it," replied Miss Utteridge. Nevertheless she dismounted from her bicycle.

"I must beg you. I am" – J. P. Kandasala tugged at his arm-band to show her – "I am Mr J. P. Kandasala, I am Deputy ARP Controller. There is a man dying here. I must please borrow your bicycle to go to the Control Centre and call for help. I must beg you to take shelter. There is one immediately posterior to you in the Town Hall."

Miss Utteridge reacted with surprising speed. In a matter of seconds she was at the porter's side. She studied his glazed pupils, and felt his pulse. Taking a small mirror from one of her bewildering number of pockets, she held it to the man's lolling mouth.

"Poor chap's a goner," she remarked, getting to her feet. "Nothing God or science can do for him, I'm afraid. Have you got something to write on?"

J. P. Kandasala produced a visiting card from his wallet. Miss Utteridge wrote on the back of it.

"Take the bike," she said. "Here's my address in Colombo. Let me have it back by midday Tuesday, there's a good chap. I've got a luncheon engagement."

"Please, madam." J.P. put his hands together in supplication. "Please take cover. You will be killed!"

One hand on her straw hat, Miss Utteridge looked at the sky. "The enemy appears to have retired for the time being," she asserted. "No more Easter eggs, I fancy. Besides, Mr Kandasala, I think I am correct in saying that the timber strutting in your air-raid trenches is made of jak wood?"

"Yes."

"Jak is particularly susceptible to termites. I should prefer to die on the surface than to be buried alive. May I refer you to the excellent advice distributed in leaflet form by the Ceylon Churches? 'In the event of an air raid, remain calm and resigned. If your soul is at peace with God, you will have nothing to fear.'"

The Deputy Controller rode off, wobbling between the dead fish, his bicycle chain making a noise like the grinding of teeth. Miss Utteridge squinted down towards the Town Hall. It looked all right to her. No obvious signs of bomb damage. Quite honestly, she was more worried about the Old Post Office. Its eighteenth-century colonnades weren't built to withstand high-explosive bombs. Frowning a little at the temerity of the Japanese (they'd bombed Singapore, but what was there in Singapore worth preserving?) she stuck her hands in her pockets and footed it towards Prince Street.

The ancient 25-pounders on Galle Face Green were having their moment of glory. Firing indiscriminately into the heavens they narrowly missed a crippled Hurricane, which crash-landed further up the promenade. Guy Tancred gave up any hope of reaching the Dunlop Orient office while this was going on. He took shelter in the Colombo Club.

Nobody was about. The Head Porter's cubby-hole was deserted. Guy leant over the counter, picked up the Porter's telephone and dialled Kelani Lodge. The static flared at him like a forest fire. At the far side of it he could faintly hear ringing and then a voice. Jill's. He shouted down the line, "Are you there! Thank God! Can you hear me? Are you all right?"

She said something interrogative, it might have been to ask what was going on, but the forest fire was raging now. He shouted, "I'm all right! Stay where you are!" and put the phone down.

It was quiet in here; dangerously so. He could hear his breath coming in short gasps. The muffled tumult in the sky sounded like the coiled paper horns that children blew in each other's faces at Christmas. He realised that all his fear, all his anxiety, had been for Jill in this attack.

He loved her. He forgave her. All he found hard to forgive was Harry's damned idiotic, unmasculine, self-sacrificial behaviour. He'd have preferred his brother to come down to Colombo and knock his teeth in; then they'd both know where they stood. It must be the War that made people behave like raving lunatics. The War and the heat. And being out East.

An explosion on Galle Face Green set the Porter's keys rattling on their hooks behind him. Guy gazed around. Nothing had been done about the rotting fish in Beira Lake; the exotic smell of incense was stronger than ever. Coloured triangles of bunting, of the sort used to decorate Hindoo pagodas, led past an easel-mounted blackboard on which was chalked in neat yellow letters GENTLEMEN GO THIS WAY TO THE AERIAL BOMBARD-MENT SHELTER.

The flags directed Guy downstairs into the wine cellar. The Cook had thoughtfully provided a cold collation of sausages and hard-boiled eggs, and handed him a plate. There was no tea or coffee. A white-coated Boy with profuse apologies offered Guy a cup of white wine from the bottles which surrounded them. Several elderly Club residents had gathered in the candle-lit gloom (electricity had not descended to the basement of the Colombo Club). One of them, recognising Guy from his last visit, shuffled over in a state of high excitement.

"It's Ingram Bywater," he breathed, putting a whiskery mouth close to Guy's ear so that the servants wouldn't hear. "He said he was going outside to have a dekko at something. We haven't seen hide nor hair of him since."

Guy remembered the scene from his window not many days ago. He turned towards the Boys, then checked himself. This wasn't their War. Putting down his breakfast he hurried up the steps and through the kitchen quarters to a door which opened on to the back lawn. A young casuarina lay across the path, its trunk neatly sliced in two by the machine-gun bullets of a strafing Japanese fighter. Above his head three planes were having a dog-fight. Guy leapt over the tree and sprinted to the rusty corrugated-iron shed down by the servants' quarters.

In the gloom, Sir Edward Lutyens's dusty granite Victory Column lay in sections on the ground, like the fallen tombstones of a race of Titans. Ingram Bywater, dressed in white flannels, lay slumped across one of them, his hand still clutching the tarpaulin he had been drawing over the Column to protect it from shrapnel. His face was covered in blood from a deep gash on the side of his head.

Guy thought at first he was dead. Gently he turned the old man over and propped him against the shaft. I.B.'s eyes opened. He stared at Guy fiercely. Guy folded his handkerchief and began to dab at the blood.

"Are you a member?" demanded I.B.

"Guy Tancred, sir. We must get you to a hospital. You've had a nasty crack on the head. Must have been shrapnel."

"Shrapnel? What shrapnel?" The old man irritably waved his hand at the war memorial. "Cover it up, will you, Tancred?"

"As soon as I've got you out of here, sir."

Guy ran back to the Club and summoned a couple of servants. The raid seemed to be over; he couldn't wait around. Not until he was on his way to Dunlop Orient again did a curious fact strike him. The shed had been in semi-darkness. If there had been shrapnel holes in the walls or roof he would have seen the light they let in. Could the Colombo Club Treasurer have been attacked? Was this Japanese raid the signal for some kind of native uprising?

He dismissed the thought. The streets were too quiet and still. He felt at home in them. The acrid smell of smoke, mingled with the brick-dust still hanging in the air, brought to his mind the streets of London after a Luftwaffe raid. Britain could take it. Could Colombo? He could not repress a feeling of grim satisfaction that at last all that Cinnamon Gardens set, the Bullers, the Lusteds, Tony Apple and Ingram Bywater, would know what it had been like in the Blitz. They would learn how it felt when the War came to your street, and came back and back and back, knocking down the doors, tapping at the windows. Oh, it would teach them a lesson! The one Rawling had been trying to get them to understand (and been cold-shouldered for his pains), that in war there was no place for amateurs. In war there were only winners and losers, and if you weren't ruthlessly professional, you didn't stand a chance of winning.

A wail of ambulance sirens followed him up the wide Dunlop Orient stairs. Rawling, in uniform, was sitting in his horse-box at the far end of the empty office. The blinds were drawn down. Piled on his desk, thousands of yellow Straits dollars fluttered in the draught from the electric fan. When he saw Guy he opened a drawer in his desk and shovelled them in. Guy stood to attention and saluted.

"Come and sit down, Tancred," said Rawling. He took off his little round spectacles and polished them with a handkerchief, allowing a silence to develop. Then in his deceptively mild voice he said, "It's only a matter of time."

"What? The Japanese?"

"Invasion, yes. Their organisation inside Ceylon is incomparably too sophisticated for any other explanation."

"I thought you'd got most of the sleepers."

"So did I. I was wrong. I've failed. We're surrounded by traitors, Tancred. I mean it. Europeans too. That's why we were taken by surprise today."

Guy was confused. Rawling took a cigarette out of a box on his desk and lit it. It was the first time Guy had seen him smoking.

"D'you know, there was no radar warning of the attack?" The Major seemed to be controlling his voice with difficulty. "The radar posts were on the alert all night. They were linked over commandeered telephone lines to Fighter Operations HQ. The Japs arived over Galle at 0720 hours this morning. They flew up the coast and reached Ratmalana at 0755 hours. In those thirty-five minutes, although the planes would have been visible to the naked eye, not a single radar message was sent to Fighter Operations. Until those damn planes arrived over Ratmalana, nobody at HQ even knew of their existence."

Rawling sat back and raised his hands in a gesture that was almost Italian in its despair. Guy stared at him. "Could it have been sheer incompetence?" he ventured. "Watches being changed, people dozing off . . . that sort of thing?"

"Incompetence? It was sabotage! Nobody is that incompetent. I have my own theory about this, Tancred. Either the telephone lines or the radar itself were jammed, sabotaged, by high-frequency radio transmissions from a nearby source. Do you see it now? That's the reason I should have been looking for a clandestine radio transmitter – not for propaganda but for sabotage! And if it's been done once it can be done again."

Was it anger or frustration which impelled Guy to speak? As he told himself later, it was a clear sense of his military responsibility. "My brother has a radio transmitter," he said in a casual voice. "He keeps it in a shed in his garden."

The silence could only have lasted a few seconds. To Guy it seemed to stretch out to eternity.

"Your brother Harry? Harry Tancred?" asked Rawling in the same mild tone.

"Yes. Of course I don't—"

"Of course nothing. Why didn't you tell me this before?"

"Sir, I really don't think—"

"It isn't a case of what you think, Tancred." Rawling's face had gone a puce colour. To Guy, appalled and guilty, he seemed to have swollen to twice his normal size. Only his voice remained deceptively calm. "This is a security failure of the worst kind. We must act at once. War is no respecter of fraternal bonds, Tancred. I expected better from you." He looked at a travelling clock on his desk. "I am due at a council of war in Queen's House in a quarter of an hour. I should be obliged if you would come with me."

There were people in the streets again. Oddly, none of them appeared to be Ceylonese, except for one staggering past with a pile of clean sheets and laundry in his arms – a dhobi-man, obviously, who'd had no time to steal off with anything else. A straggle of Europeans who had taken refuge in the crypt of St Peter's during the raid were making their way home on foot, since no drivers or rickshaws were to be seen. They scattered to make way for a convoy of jeeps which roared up Queen Street and turned right, in the direction of the Pettah.

"Malay States police," remarked Rawling, nodding at the stockily built men in mufti who sat squashed tightly in the back. "Rescued from Singapore. They've been convalescing at Mount Lavinia. Just the kind of reinforcements we need to stop looters at a time like this."

Guy made no response. He had worked out why Rawling wanted him along. Rawling had evidently decided that if he was left to himself he might telephone his brother and alert him. He was determined to keep Guy in his sight.

The realisation mortified him. He had lost Rawling's trust. But had he ever really had his trust? Had anyone? He thought back to the most revealing, and surprising, conversation the prospective Colonel had ever had with him. It was during the search for a Japanese landing beach. Guy had reported back late at night to Rawling and found him still at his desk in Dunlop Orient, eating a snack sent round from the Elephant House. The talk had got round to the Japanese, and the need to match cunning with cunning.

"Think of rats," Rawling had said suddenly. "Had rats in Leicester when I was a boy. I don't know how much you know about rats, Tancred. Know your enemy is what I've always said.

Mus decumanus was the beggar we had. It's bigger than *Mus rattus*, fiercer and faster on its feet. I found out where their rat-holes were, and I crawled under the boiler and behind the milk-safe and I watched them. Too cunning to take ordinary rat poison, of course, so I trained up a young terrier, kept him in the outhouse. One weekend, I was alone in the house, I cleared out the cellar and flooded it in a foot of water. Then I went round in gumboots and unplugged all the rat holes I'd sealed up." Guy could hear his chuckle now. "I can remember the beating I got to this day. But, by God, my little brown friends never came back."

They turned in at Queen's House, past the sentries who saluted when they saw Rawling. Guy, a step behind, looked apprehensively at the broad, round-shouldered back in the unclassifiable dark green uniform. He could imagine what it would be like to join the ranks of Rawling's little brown friends. Thank God he'd not admitted to telling Jill they knew which beach the Japs would land on.

Sir Oliver Prescott had made two concessions to the air raid. One was a steel helmet. It had evidently been made for Indian use, like the Queen's House lavatory seats, for it perched uncomfortably upon the crown of his head and held out no hope of protection against anything heavier than a falling coconut.

The other concession was to move out of the War Council room, at the front of Queen's House, into the back dining room, where he now sat with George Donaldson, fiddling with a small box that contained two cottonwool plugs. If the Japanese came back, he had been told, he was to stuff them in his ears to protect his eardrums against blast.

If the Japanese came back. Geoffrey Layton seemed to think they would. The Jap admiral, Nagumo, had been cheated of his main target which was plainly Somerville's Eastern Fleet. If Nagumo hadn't yet discovered Addu Atoll, he would presumably work on the assumption that Somerville was circling around somewhere out there in mid-ocean, waiting for the opportunity to return to the shelter of Colombo to refuel. It would therefore make tactical sense for Nagumo to send his bombers back to finish the job of knocking out the oil refineries and harbour workshops. From the figures Air Marshal d'Albiac had given them so far, the Japs wouldn't face much of a challenge in the air any longer.

Layton, John d'Albiac and the rest of the top brass had

decamped to their various HQs, much to the Governor's relief. He had accepted that they'd been as much in the dark about the air raid as he had (d'Albiac was almost in tears about the failure of his radar bods). This had improved Sir Oliver's temper no end; it had almost disposed him for once to tolerate the C-in-C. Frankly, as they'd all sat here in their steel hats, maps unfolded on his calamander table, talking about a "Kota Bharu-style attack" on China Bay, he'd begun to see that these military chappies who'd been striking poses all over the shop had no more idea what Nagumo's strategy was, and what they were going to do about it, than he himself. It gave him, for the first time, a genuine fellow-feeling for poor old Shenton Thomas in Singapore, faced with the bumbling strategists of Malaya Command.

Layton ran true to form, of course, issuing orders right and left as though he had some secret personal access to the Nipponese master-plan. The Governor, fiddling with his ear-plugs, was tempted to put them in and protect his ear-drums. Instead, adopting an expression of deep thought, he got up and with his hands behind his back walked to the window. There he had the intense pleasure of watching Layton's black and tan bitch, who had escaped in the general confusion, being rogered by a pi-dog with a pizzle the size of a swagger-stick.

Sitting now alone with George Donaldson he allowed himself a smile. There was nothing else to laugh about. The civil defence shortfalls remained appalling, with only three fire-engines and six trailer pumps for the whole island – hardly enough to cope with one large building, so God knows how they were getting on down at the harbour or what would happen if the Japs returned for another raid with incendiary bombs. No gas-masks yet. The Colombo hospitals still dreadfully vulnerable, with none of their medical facilities evacuated to the suburbs. He himself presiding grandly over a half-deserted city, whose local populace, with animals' instinct, had sensed the earthquake before it happened. . . . He was no longer the actor-manager, ensuring that the show went on. At this moment he felt more like a stagehand, waiting, in the wings of Asia, for the curtain to fall.

Meanwhile, and most urgently, he had the task of fabricating a communiqué to be released to the local press. George was very helpful over stuff like this. Years of offering advice to government ministers had taught him just how much of the truth it was sensible to reveal.

The first consideration was to restore calm in the civilian population. The second was to make it clear that Ceylon's brave

291

fighter pilots had given the Japs their first bloody nose since Pearl Harbor. It wasn't yet clear how many Hurricanes had been shot down, but according to d'Albiac at least five Japanese Zeros had been seen to crash over land, and double that number would have ditched in the sea on the way back to the carriers. The word from Colombo General Hospital was that apart from a few dozen people killed in the harbour area (mostly black east African troops unloading food ships) and a direct hit on the Angoda mental hospital, civilian casualties from this first attack were relatively few.

Sir Oliver put on his reading spectacles and checked through what they had composed. Under the heading "Colombo Provides Best War News of Week" (a safe enough assumption), the eventual press communiqué read as follows –

Colombo was attacked by a large force of Japanese aircraft at 8.00 this morning. Dive-bombing and low-flying machine-gun attacks were made on the Harbour and Ratmalana areas. Material damage done was comparatively slight. A small number of civilians were killed or wounded.

The enemy were successfully intercepted by our fighters and heavy losses inflicted. Twenty-five enemy aircraft were shot down for certain by our fighters whilst five more were probably shot down and twenty-five more damaged.

The courage and calmness shown by the population of Colombo had to be seen to be believed, and made me proud to be your Governor. Owing to the gallant manner in which you behaved and acted, casualties were far below what might otherwise have been incurred, and would have been negligible except for an attack on one of our medical establishments. It is significant indeed that such an institution should have been singled out by our barbarous enemy, especially on the Christian festival of Easter Sunday.

I should like to take this opportunity of expressing my deepest sympathy with the relatives of those who lost their lives, but they may feel proud in the fact that those lives have not been wasted but given in the defence of Ceylon. You have now had your first air raid, and I trust you are relieved to find that the experience is not as bad as you may have anticipated.

I can only thank you for your co-operation, and say that I look forward with confidence, after today, to whatever further air attacks we have to face together.

"Do you think we leave the impression that you are *looking forward* to more air attacks?" asked George Donaldson anxiously. Unlike the Governor he had his wife to think about, and his daughter in the Naval Office.

Sir Oliver took off his helmet and held it, for a moment, against his heart while he mopped the perspiration off his skull. "The watchword is 'solidarity'," he said firmly. "I believe it helps their morale to know that their captain stays on the bridge. I'm not going to let them down, George. We sink or swim together."

George Donaldson might have been forgiven for thinking that most of the captain's crew and passengers had already leapt overboard, to judge from the unnatural quietness in Colombo's streets.

But Sir Oliver had been struck by a different aspect of his metaphor. He had suddenly remembered Singapore's Chief Censor. This individual, who had been responsible for suppressing every reference to the military superiority of the Japanese from the time they landed in Kota Bharu to the moment they invaded Singapore, had last been spotted in the sea on 19 March, struggling to get away. Here, exemplarily, was a man who had fallen a victim to his own propaganda, so successfully had he stopped information getting through.

Thoughtfully, Sir Oliver took out his fountain pen and added another paragraph to the communiqué –

We must not be complacent. It is entirely due to the manner in which we prepared ourselves to meet this danger from the skies that we came through so magnificently. So long as we do not relax, so long as we continue to work together with willingness and uncompromising resolve, we shall be able to face the future with our heads held high.

"What do you think, George?" he asked, passing it over.

George Donaldson studied the Governor's coda.

"I think it puts it in a nutshell, sir," he replied.

Simon House put his head round the door. "Colonel Rawling is here, Sir Oliver. And Mr Guy Tancred of Dunlop Orient."

The Governor nodded. "Simon, will you get the girls to type this up?" Getting to his feet he signalled his ADC to show the two men in. As he now did out of habit whenever Rawling was announced, he went to the window to close the curtains. For once there was no shipping waiting to clear the bar. The ocean was a dull blue-green emptiness, except for a thin pillar of smoke on the distant horizon. He wondered if *Cornwall* and *Dorsetshire*, which had not left Colombo harbour until 10 p.m. on Saturday night, had made good their escape.

"What d'you say, Rawling?" he asked as he turned to greet him. "Are the Japs coming back?"

"Yes, sir."

"You seem very sure."

"I am. This morning they effectively blocked all warning of their arrival. This means that they must have an organisation on the island of an extent and a sophistication I never anticipated. They would not have set such a network up in order to monitor a few raids."

The positive tone in which this assertion was made disconcerted the Governor. He glanced at George Donaldson for reassurance. "Air Marshal d'Albiac seemed to think it was the radar chaps nodding off," he began uncertainly. "Wasn't that it, George? Either that, or the radar went on the blink—"

"Precisely so." Rawling had advanced into the middle of the room, his dark green uniform and swagger-stick giving him a faintly theatrical authority. "A powerful transmitter could have been responsible for that. The same powerful transmitter which might now be informing the Japanese of the whereabouts of our Eastern Fleet. Sir, I do not wish to exaggerate, but we are facing an emergency of crisis proportions. Earlier today I discovered the existence of one clandestine radio transmitter on the island. It belongs to a well-known planter in the Kelani valley. I refer to the brother of my colleague here, Mr Harold Tancred."

"Harry!" George Donaldson, sitting at the rosewood table, laughed aloud. "Rawling, you surely aren't suggesting that Harry Tancred is helping the Japanese?"

Rawling hesitated. Sir Oliver looked at the young man he had brought with him, Harry Tancred's brother. He had turned very red. This was surely all quite unnecessary. "Have you any evidence?" he demanded.

"Direct evidence? No."

"Well then," said the Governor heartily. "I think *festina lente* should be our watchword, don't you? I can't believe that one of our most reliable English planters—" He broke off, and then went on more slowly. "Of course I gather he's become some sort of Buddhist – George, you were telling me – but then so did Henry Janvrin and one or two others. I don't think you can hold a man's religion against him. Perhaps Mr Tancred here will go up to Kelani and see the thing's put out of action, eh?"

There was a silence. They all looked at Rawling who stood frowning by the table, his mouth set in an obstinate line. Eventually George Donaldson spoke to him.

"You said, direct evidence. Would you care to amplify that?"

Rawling nodded. "I'm afraid it may be more serious, sir, than at first appeared," he said, addressing the Governor. "Tancred here tells me his brother employs as his assistant in the radio shed a young Sinhalese by the name of Michael Kandasala – his head Boy, I believe. Now as you will know from my report on potential Japanese invasion beaches, prepared by Tancred here, they will almost certainly attempt a landing at Beruwala, thirty-five miles south of Colombo. You will also know that in the old Customs Station at Beruwala we recently discovered a cache of arms, almost certainly belonging to the Sama Samaj nationalists. Our files show that Mr Kandasala has had contact with the Lanka Sama Samaj."

Sir Oliver felt suddenly old. He had knocked around long enough to think he knew the sort of chaps planters were: steady, unimaginative, loyal, incapable of treason. But the world was becoming the kind of place where you couldn't be sure about people any more. Just when long experience in government had begun to convince him that everybody was much the same underneath, a war came along and they all turned out to be as unpredictable as foreigners.

"Well, I don't know," he said. "George, what do you think?"

George Donaldson had gone grey. He stood up slowly, his head bent forward, his hand clutching the chair-back.

"This boy Kandasala," he began unsteadily. "We – that is to say Elizabeth and I – he used to be on our staff. The last time we used him. . . . Guy, you tell them."

"At the New Year, yes, sir. In Nuwara Eliya," Guy nodded. "He came over to you and helped old Albert serve meals and drinks."

"Yes." George Donaldson paused, and went on with difficulty. "We had Sylvia up – my daughter – from the Naval Office. Sir Oliver, I am most deeply sorry. I have to tell you that this little wretch may have got wind of Addu Atoll."

The Governor's anxieties fell away. Given a crisis all his own he was cool, decisive. "Rawling, get hold of Brown at Military Police. Take however many of his men you need and get to Kelani. I want you to go in person. You might decide to keep the transmitter going to broadcast false information. I leave that to you. But let's waste no more time."

"Yes, sir. The one other matter was to bring you up to date with the movements of our fictitious 33rd British Infantry Division sent over by General Wavell's deception unit GS1 (d). I thought you would like to know that we have, so to speak, moved them south to the plain inland of Beruwala. I hope the Japs will have intercepted our radio messages—"

"Yes. Yes. Good, Rawling. Tell me about it later," interrupted

Sir Oliver, enjoying the rare pleasure of being impatient with him. Noticing young Guy Tancred's harrowed expression, he softened. "Tancred, you'd better go along in the jeep to Kelani."

"Yes."

"Life is full of hard decisions, Tancred. I appreciate you have just made one of the hardest."

With that, the Governor passed the two men over to Simon to see out. George Donaldson had already left the room, disconcertingly. But Sir Oliver wanted this time alone. Something had begun to make music in his head: fugitive images, the thread of an idea. He sat down at his dining table and pulled paper and pen towards him.

No Roman wreaths, no thunderous cries,
Met these frail gladiators of the skies

It was a long time since he'd felt like a sonnet.

There had been no time to think about David. As soon as the raid was over, Maria de Vos had pulled a sheet off the bed and left the house, locking the door (her father was in Kandy). Finding her bicycle gone, she half-walked, half-ran towards the harbour, guided by the thick black smoke. To have sat outside the Racecourse compound in a huddle of RAF wives and girlfriends, waiting for news, would have driven her mad. It was better to go somewhere that she could do some good.

Later she was to place the moment she entered her dream world – more properly a world of nightmare – at the instant she walked over the shattered level crossing and went down towards the harbour warehouses. In this dream she kept meeting familiar people doing unfamiliar things. In this terrible dream, events happened around her in slow motion and she was helpless to alter them or even to cry out in fear.

Nobody stopped her. The military police were nowhere to be seen. Dock coolies and harbour officials, their white shirts grimed with dust, ran aimlessly up and down like ants in an anthill laid open to the sun. A European was shouting orders; his voice sounded like Tony Apple, but his face was blackened and his clothes hung in tatters, there was no way to be sure.

Dock labourers rushed past her paying no attention to a man slumped against a bollard crying out to them. Blood ran down his arm from a deep shrapnel wound. Stumbling over the ropes that led nowhere on the quayside, Maria ran to help him. She tore a strip from the sheet and bound it round the gash, closing it as tightly as she could. Then she was off again, past the cliffs of water-drums and ships' supplies, the stacked munitions, slipping in the pulped remains of fruit and vegetables and bloodier debris of the raid, her sheet getting smaller as she bandaged casualties the stretcher-parties hadn't got round to.

She saw sights she would never forget. She saw the long grey cigar-shape of a submarine, miraculously intact, sitting beside its heavily listing depot ship. She saw a merchant ship burning under the sea. She saw men in boats in the harbour, manoeuvring amid the smoke and fires, hauling bodies out of the oil-slicked water. Worst of all, worse even than the stench of burning rubber that hung over the harbour so thickly it made her gag, was the man trapped under timber in a blazing godown, screaming at the firemen who were driven back and back from him by the ravenous flames.

Maria's sheet was finished. The last of the dead and injured had been taken to ambulances. Her throat dry, her eyes stinging, she set off on the long walk back to the Racecourse. David Gifford would surely be there to greet her. She had lived through too much suffering in the last hour to bear the existence of any more.

People came to her out of the smoke. Did she imagine Kitty Clarke, dressed in her churchgoing best, looking for Sebastian on the quayside? Tears had furrowed through the powder on her cheeks; her hand fastened on Maria's wrist like bird's feet.

"Have you seen him?" she demanded.

"Your husband? No. Is he all right?"

"It's all over, my dear. It's finished."

"Oh, Mrs Clarke, I don't think so."

But it wasn't the Japanese Kitty was talking about, it was Sebastian. Inflamed by his mission to prepare the destruction of Colombo to deny it to the enemy, on Saturday night he had taken steps to pull down his marriage as well. Telling Kitty he had been unfaithful to her, he had gone on to list the names of six women, none of whom she'd heard of, until she had buried her head under the pillow to shut out the sound of his voice.

Alone of all the people Kitty could have made them to, Maria had no interest in hearing these anguished revelations. She resented every second Kitty Clarke delayed her, every sentence of consolation drawn from her reserves of compassion. In her mind's eye she was already at the Racecourse gates, scanning the field for a lanky figure in a flying jacket, a lock of dark hair falling carelessly over his face. Two days ago she had made him crab curry, and they had played Monopoly together on London streets she had never seen. . . .

And then Kitty was gone, bearing her sorrows into the smoke, and Maria was alone in the sweating streets. Much more alone than she had ever been, in the Pettah, she realised (not with surprise but with the calm matter-of-factness which accompanied dreams). The streets were quite empty. The bazaars were all deserted. Their owners had fled so fast at the sound of the first bombs that they hadn't paused to shut up shop. She could see in one a pile of rupees still standing on the counter; in another, a single shoe on a cobbler's last. A bolt of vivid blue cotton for saris had unrolled into the gutter. Flies gathered round a sweet-stall, its jaggery candies slowly melting in the heat, under a poster that warned in large type THE PENALTY FOR LOOTING IS DEATH. A pink umbrella lay abandoned in the middle of the street, one spoke snapped as if in a crush of people who had disappeared. The exodus had been so sudden, so complete, that she fancied she could hear the echo of it vibrating in the air. But when she stood still, all the sounds she could hear were the ghostly patter of stray dogs, padding down Main Street.

The Ceylonese had gone, and left Colombo to the British. They had left the Europeans to fight their foreign war and get it over with. Maria did not see how they could be blamed for this. It was not their quarrel. It was not even their city. White men had built Colombo. White men conducted their own business in it, with little reference to the Ceylonese. If white men now wanted to fight over it, in the name of defending the Empire, it was not cowardice but common sense to keep out of the way. Besides, the British in the East, disregarding caste and race, always judged the Ceylonese by the simple standard of how efficiently they could be hired to help in the business of government and trade. They had never asked the Ceylonese to risk their lives for them.

As Maria crossed over the Main Street bridge into the Fort she saw two Tamils walking ahead of her. Both were naked except for white dhotis. The shorter of the men had actually taken off his loin-cloth and wrapped it round his head. As Maria came closer she saw that it was soaked with blood.

Hearing her footsteps they turned, grinning vacantly. The uninjured Tamil had a huge round unwrinkled forehead bulging above eyes which flickered everywhere, never resting for a moment. His companion looked older, though it was hard to be

298

sure. With his lips he kept framing silent sentences then breaking off with a cackle of laughter.

Maria de Vos kept the distance of the street between them. They had stopped, and she stopped too, not knowing what to say.

"Do you want a hospital?" she asked them.

"*Aaspatiri*," the tall man replied, nodding.

"It is in Regent Street." She pointed. "South. One mile from here. South."

"*Aaspatiri*," the man repeated. Smiling, he caught his companion, swaying from loss of blood, and swept him up into his arms like a baby. "*Aaspatiri Angoda*."

Maria understood. They had escaped from the Mental Hospital. It must have taken a direct hit. How many other lunatics, injured or dying, were wandering the streets of Colombo? Carefully, so as not to frighten the two men, she stepped across the road. They would never get to Colombo General. Somewhere there had to be a First Aid Post. If only there had been an ARP warden in the street to tell her where. She heard an ambulance siren, getting louder. An ambulance would take them, even if she had to stand in its path.

But the man with the huge head and the wandering eyes was already walking away, holding his dying friend in his arms as lightly as a bundle of red flowers. He was walking in the direction of the sea.

'*Nillu!*" she cried after them in Tamil. "Stop! Wait!"

If the big man heard her he gave no indication of it. One direction was as good as another. And who was to say that Colombo General would have been able to take them in?

Maria went on her way. Her feet were beginning to ache. There would be glass all over Mademoiselle Orliga's parquet floor: no Orchid Dance today. At the shuttered Fountain Café in Union Place a solitary soldier sat on the grass drinking passionfruit juice out of a bottle. Jeeps began to go past, and a few private cars driving north to see the damage. There was nothing in the sky. All the Hurricanes must have got back long ago. All the ones that were going to get back.

She passed the Donaldsons' house, but did not stop. It was not far now. She could see the tall buildings of the University and Royal College. There was everything to hope for. She had given up the fortune-tellers, after a crystal-gazer had seen her in an old Dutch-period style wedding dress with a simply cut bodice, a high neckline and lace-edged collar. The detail so clear: but a mist where the groom should have stood. If only David's 250 Squadron had gone to join 261 at China Bay!

The gate in the airfield fence was shut, but the armed MPs recognised her and let her through. She seemed to see David winking at her and smiling his teasing smile. *What about that Dutch courage?* she heard him say. None of the planes she could see had the distinctive gold cross David had painted on his fuselage. But she was in too much of a hurry to look properly, and there were the mess tents and the Ops hut, and an airman coming out now, a white flying scarf knotted loosely over his khaki shirt. He looked curiously at Maria as she ran across the grass.

"Excuse me," she said. "Excuse me bothering you, but have you seen David Gifford?"

The airman studied her face. "Are you a relative of his?" he asked. An American accent.

"I'm . . . no. I'm a close friend. Maria de Vos."

"Well, Maria." The airman gripped the ends of his knotted scarf. "David's plane hasn't come back yet. I'm sorry, that's all we know. He hasn't come back."

She woke up out of the dream in that instant. She saw it had all been real, the nightmare had been real.

And it was still going on.

About the time that Rawling and Guy were negotiating the jam-packed roads out through the suburbs of Colombo, His Majesty's two County-class cruisers, *Dorsetshire* and *Cornwall*, were alone in a wide open sea.

It was 1330 hours. Charlie Bilbow in *Dorsetshire*, taking his first stint as Officer of the Watch since being promoted to sub-lieutenant, lowered his binoculars and checked the ship's log. The speed of the two ships, which had been 23 knots for the first hour out of Colombo harbour, had gone up to 27½ knots, the maximum the slower *Cornwall* could do. They were pressing on at full Action Stations towards the rendezvous with the Eastern Fleet.

The sextant was steady. It was a fine tropical afternoon now, with a few light woolly clouds in the blue sky and the sun burning overhead. Nothing had been sighted since 11.30, when a black dot bobbing up and down on the distant horizon had been identified as an enemy aircraft. This caused a moment's consternation on the bridge. It meant either that Nagumo's Carrier Force was

100 miles closer than had been estimated, or else that the Japs had recce planes capable of a far greater range than any of them had bargained for.

Charlie heard Captain Agar discussing it in low tones with Commander Byas. The choice was either to alter course for a more westerly rendezvous, which would mean having to shift Admiral Somerville's striking force out of easy range of a night attack on the Jap fleet, or else to steam full ahead to the appointed R/V.

Agar must have decided to keep to the prearranged plan because Charlie saw no change on the gyro-compass from their course 185° SSE. But the Captain did break radio silence to send a message to Somerville via a shore station reporting the Jap shadower. There was a strict rule, Charlie knew, against reporting a single aircraft. It meant that Agar must be more worried than he let on.

A good radar screen in the ship's Transmitting Station would have picked up the recce plane even twenty miles away, from what Charlie Bilbow had heard. That was what *Dorsetshire* and *Cornwall* had been ordered back yesterday to Colombo to be fitted with, abandoning the relative safety of Addu Atoll. Charlie had seen the radar equipment, plus a couple of additional anti-aircraft guns, on the quayside when he was ferried ashore in the liberty boat. They were still on the quayside an hour and a half later when the general recall went out and Charlie came back on board. The whole point of returning to Colombo had been wasted.

Except for him. It had given him another hour with the girl he was going to marry. By the time he got to the Naval Office, Sylvia had already changed her watch with another cipherette. She came down the steps in her navy blue skirt, unpinning her hair and letting it flow in golden curls over the shoulders of her blouse. Drowsily she put her arms round his neck and lifted up her face for a kiss. She had been on two four-hour watches since midnight; her eyes were puffy from decoding numbers on pieces of paper under artificial light. Looking down at her, he had seen with a sudden pang of joy what it would be like to wake up in bed beside that soft milky drowsiness, not just once but always, letting her sleep there in glorious plump-breasted nakedness or teasing her awake and ready for love.

There was an absolute mass of things to arrange, as he'd told her. The wedding list was bound to be a stinker to work out because of the War and all the comings and goings (there would have to be a proper party with all their chums after the War was over). In fact they hadn't even fixed on a date with Archdeacon Hoathly for the plighting of troths yet, although they knew it would have to be soon, with the Japs about to start snapping at the Royal Navy's heels all over the Eastern oceans. . . .

But Sylvia was too tired to deal with all that just then, and it looked as if they would have the whole weekend together, so they went off instead, the pair of them in a rickshaw, to see a Laurel and Hardy film at the Majestic, *Hold That Ghost*. From which they were brought out into the hot light by an usherette with news of the general recall to the two cruisers, and had had to say a hurried goodbye at the landing jetty with a promise to settle all the wedding plans just as soon as the old tub was back in harbour, and with a hundred kisses to keep them going until then, and an extra long kiss to make him remember the ones that went before—

And Charlie Bilbow, on the bridge of *Dorsetshire*, staring out over the empty sea, summoned up the memory of Sylvia and held it like a shimmering bubble suspended for an instant in the rushing air, shimmering with all her beauty and the delicious things they would do together, when the metallic voice of Shaddick the Chief Telegraphist called up Captain Agar on the intercom.

"Streaks on the radar screen, sir. I can't make them out but I think there's something about!"

Agar spoke on the microphone, "Stand by! Stand by to open fire on hostile aircraft!" Without binoculars Charlie Bilbow could see them clearly now. Aircraft were streaming out of the sun, they were diving in waves of three. The second wave was making for *Dorsetshire*. He dropped the binoculars, turned. Agar was shouting. As the bombs arched down, bloody great bombs, thousand-pounders, Agar shouted "Hard over twenty-five degrees! Keep her turning!"

The first bomb hit the Walms catapult. Charlie saw a man with no legs leap in the air. Commander Byas left his station on the bridge: of course, he would be taking charge of the damage-control squads. As he disappeared, a bomb dropped right beside one of the paravanes.

The blast lifted Charlie off his feet and threw him hard against the deck. He lost consciousness. *That was a close shave, little goose*, he found himself murmuring to Sylvia when he came round – although he couldn't have blacked out for more than a moment because here was Captain Agar helping Byas, badly injured,

302

down the companionway and shouting over his shoulder, ''Bil-bow! Take the wheel!''

He took the wheel, seeing red through the shattered portholes and not wanting to think it was his own blood. Shells pumped vainly into the blue sky. Stretcher-parties ran through the smoke with morphia needles and tourniquets. He felt *Dorsetshire* buck and heave as more bombs exploded round her. At least one in the engine-room, surely, because dense black smoke and flames were pouring out of the deck and there was nothing the hoses could do.

The steering gear was jammed. *This isn't my day, little goose*. He spun the wheel but the ship kept turning to starboard, there was no way he could stop her, it wasn't his fault, she kept turning to starboard, heeling now, losing speed and heeling from the weight of water rushing in below.

Wave after wave of Japanese dive-bombers, and against them frail white tracers from the surviving oerlikons and pom-pom guns. The Main Wireless Office would be out of action. All communication from the bridge was gone. Charlie stood in the blast and concussion of the falling bombs, spinning the wheel of his first and last command, while the great ship paid him no attention but slewed in the water like a wounded thing, looking for a place to die.

The dense smoke made his eyes water and still the red kept streaming down. It was so difficult to breathe. He held on to the wheel, half to support himself, and kept his head low. The bombs fell with unbelievable accuracy; splinters of steel and twisted metal flew through the smoke. Machine-gun fire racked the superstructure and ricocheted round the bridge. He felt a fierce blow in his shoulder; he staggered back.

Captain Agar was there, he was beckoning him down the ladder. But what was he saying? This smoke was choking him. His captain was telling him something but a bullet had shot away the valve on the ship's siren and he couldn't hear it. Now he'd gone. The ship was listing over to port, she'd turn turtle soon.

Charlie couldn't hold on any more, he told Sylvia, *It's merry hell up here, old girl*. Slipping in his own blood he half-slid, half-fell down the ladder to the bedlam of the upper deck, his left arm strangely unhelpful, his legs not too bright either.

Men around him were running up the side of the listing deck. Agar must have given the order to abandon ship. Blinking back the blood Charlie saw a pillow of black smoke across the water – *Cornwall*, it must be sinking too. He saw a couple of men tie

303

lifebelts to Byas and throw him into the sea. The deck rose higher. Wheezing painfully he crawled up it towards the rail. Agar had gone back to the bridge. From high up on the masts men were falling into the sea or bouncing slowly off the side of the ship. Carley floats were in the water.

Giddy with loss of blood, Charlie saw the Indian Ocean mount towards him. It was no time to hang back, he'd be done for. Slipping and stumbling on the underside of *Dorsetshire* he ran to meet the sea he had played in all his life, the warm sea he had plunged through as a boy, carrying Sylvia on his back. It rushed to meet him, stinking, oily, foul, suffocating, and knocked the breath out of his body.

He came lazily to the surface, took a mouthful of fuel oil and sank again. This was no good. He was a strong swimmer, the best. But his left arm wouldn't work, and there was oil in his eyes and ears and lungs, and when Charlie Bilbow reached the surface a second time he never saw or knew that he was face upwards toward the sun.

It took them four hours to reach Kelani Lodge. They were the longest four hours of Guy Tancred's life. By the time they reached the outskirts of Colombo it was clear that the entire city had taken to its heels. The two Military Police jeeps bullied their way through as best they could, but it wasn't long before the second one was out of sight behind them. In Guy's jeep, the MP sitting next to the driver twice had to lift up the rifle on his knee and fire in the air. Each time the slowly moving throng in front of them scattered like frightened birds, falling into the paddy or down the riverbank in their haste to get away.

Guy Tancred sat in the back beside Rawling. He sat very still, with his hands folded in his lap. Rawling fidgeted continuously, flushed and sweating in the soft wet heat which was more suffocating than ever in this crush of bodies. He fretted, and looked at his watch, and several times tapped insect powder over himself from a small tin he kept in his pocket.

"Bicycles, bicycles everywhere," he complained. "Damned nuisances. They'll all have to go."

"Go where?"

"Don't be obtuse, Tancred. Go. Be destroyed. Broken up for scrap. In Malaya the Japs used every available bicycle to speed their advance. Each one of the bicycles you see around us is a secret weapon."

"You won't be popular," said Guy, as the jeep barged past the brown faces on either side.

"There's a hundred and forty years of loyalty to the British in Ceylon. You don't get rid of that in a hurry. The trick is to take them into your confidence, Tancred. I've been training up some of the local police in jungle sabotage and fifth-column work for after the Japs get here, and you'd be surprised how quickly they cotton on. You have a few bad apples; it's in the nature of things. The ones who've been dressing up as enemy agents in order to get the 5000-rupee reward. And the fanatics, of course, like your Kandasala chap—"

Guy interrupted. "What makes you think the Sama Samaj have got anything to do with the Japs?"

Rawling stopped fanning himself with his dark green beret long enough to look sharply at him. "My dear chap, what about the arms cache at Beruwala? Isn't that your landing beach? Not to mention yesterday's gaol break from the Kandy detention barracks!"

"What's that?"

"Didn't you know? It happened between midnight and six a.m. The four top Sama Samajists we held in custody, including Perera and Gunawardene. Escaped along with their guard. You're not going to tell me that was a coincidence."

Just as the snarl of traffic was easing, a commotion could be heard ahead. The MP went to investigate. When he came back, his face was grim.

"They say there's a dead pilot hanging from a parachute line in the trees," he reported to Rawling. "They think he's RAF."

They drove on in silence. Guy's shirt stuck to his back. Only his mouth was dry. What exactly had Harry meant when he said that the way to mastery was through surrender? It was his fault. He should have reported his brother's transmitter weeks ago.

They came at last to the dirt road leading to Kelani Lodge. Guy in a hoarse voice gave directions to the driver. When he sat back his hands were shaking. He clasped them together.

"What do you expect me to say to him?" he asked.

"Harry? You won't have to say anything," Rawling replied. "You've said what you had to say. If there's any unpleasantness, you can leave it to me to deal with."

"I feel this may turn out to be a wild goose chase."

"I hope so. For your sake." Rawling added, as an afterthought, "It's the religion, you know, the religion I'm afraid of."

The jeep rounded the steep bend, and Kelani Lodge lay before them in its familiar island of green, unchanged and as remotely beautiful as it had been six months ago when Guy first saw it. The War had been three thousand miles away then, in north Africa and the Ukraine. Now it had arrived at the front door, throwing up chips of gravel as the jeep skidded to a halt.

The MP leapt out and opened the rear door. Rawling clambered out, stiffly. A houseboy came flapping down the porch steps. The policeman unslung his rifle and prodded it in the petrified Boy's stomach.

"Is this Kandasala?" he called.

Guy flinched. "No."

"Where's the garden shed, Boy?"

"Hold on," Guy said hastily. "It's round the back, I'll—"

"That's all right, Tancred," said Rawling. He had his own pistol out. With a surprising fleetness of foot he raced up the steps and disappeared inside the house, the MP at his heels.

Guy followed them through the cool, shaded rooms with their familiar smells of Mansion polish . . . but another memory supervened, that of the gecko on his bathroom wall that first evening, beating out the brains of a defenceless moth.

He hurried out the back way, pattering feet behind him, into the heat of the sun. Rawling was at the garden shed. Rawling put his shoulder to it and barged in, followed by the MP. Guy sprinted across the grass.

Then the gun shot. A single shot. Over and done with. Crows rose in the air and settled back on the branches.

Guy burst in, and stopped still. Rawling had laid his swagger-stick down on the desk and was studying some papers. The MP was kneeling. He was examining with admiration Harry Tancred's transmitter, its dials and glass-cylinder valves which gave off a faint humming glow on the juice from the car batteries.

Behind them, on the floor, lay Michael Kandasala. For someone so recently shot dead, he looked disturbingly tranquil. Scarlet beads of blood were trickling from the corner of his mouth. His hand in a last compulsive gesture had pulled off his neck-chain and now lay palm upwards on the floor, a small silver crucifix tangled in its supplicating fingers. Above his brown eyes, gazing darkly upwards, Guy saw the neat, round hole in the centre of his forehead.

"Caught in the act," remarked Rawling. He handed a sheet of paper to Guy. "The little beggar was actually broadcasting this treason over the air as we broke in. Come on, it's time we went looking for your brother."

The Japanese phonetic spellings meant nothing to Guy. He could not take his eyes off Michael's body. An unobtrusive puddle of blood was forming under its right ear; a little funeral column of ants had already turned aside to investigate. . . .

The MP took him by the arm and led him outside.

They didn't have far to look for Harry Tancred. As they returned to the house he was coming through the dining room, bare-chested above his white sarong.

"What the devil—"

Rawling handed him a sheet of paper. "Do you recognise this?"

"Of course I do. I wrote it."

Rawling was momentarily silenced. Then he said, blinking rapidly behind his round spectacles, "Mr Tancred, do you know that treason carries the death sentence?"

"Treason be damned! This paper, do you know what it says?"

"It doesn't matter what—"

"Look. Roughly translated. 'Calling all Japanese servicemen in your ships at sea. This is the voice of your conscience. The conscience of all true followers of the Buddha Amitabha. The first Precept of the Buddha is to control the passion of anger, and not harm any living thing. As it is written in the Sutta Nipata and written again in The Eye of the True Law – *Whoever hurts or kills living creatures, who seek like him for happiness, he shall find no happiness after death.* We, the Buddhist people of Ceylon, entreat you—"

"That's enough!" Shaking with anger, Rawling snatched the document back. "Do you take me for a complete fool? You've been jamming our communications, broadcasting seditious material to the Japanese—"

"That's balderdash—"

"Undermining our own propaganda campaign by suing for peace with the enemy. Leaving a known extremist in control of your illegal transmitter—"

"Michael Kandasala? He's no such thing."

"He was. Not any longer, I'm glad to say."

"What's that?"

"We caught him at the microphone and we shot him. I pray to God we were not too late."

Harry's face went very red. "Is Michael dead?"

"He belonged to the Sama Samaj. He was in possession of highly secret and damaging information about the movements of our fleet."

"Did you kill him?"

"Yes."

There was a silence in the dining room. Guy became aware that Jill had come out of the bedroom and was standing at the open door. Harry Tancred stepped forward, his gaze very steady. Raising his fist he punched Rawling hard on the jaw.

Rawling's trouser creases buckled. He tottered, and collapsed in a heap on the carpet. As Guy watched in horror, the MP sprang at Harry and pinned his arms behind his back.

"Let him go!" It was Jill who cried out, she started forward. "Guy! Make them stop this!"

"No," said Harry calmly. "It was Guy who brought them here." He looked his brother in the face for the first time. "I fear he thought he was Doing his Duty."

Guy stared at him, through eyes which had filled with childish, humiliating tears. He shook his head. "You brought this on yourself, Harry," he said.

Rawling had got to his feet. He picked up his glasses and put them on. They heard a crackle of gravel as the second jeep drew up in the drive. The MP took out a pair of handcuffs. He fastened one to Harry's wrist, one to his own. "Take it easy now," he said.

"You can consider yourself under arrest, Tancred," Rawling said thickly, feeling his jaw. "We shall be taking some documents away. You can come out to the shed and identify them. Mrs Tancred, I believe that's my hat you've got there. Thank you."

Rawling, once more the soldier, led the way out of the dining room, followed by Harry Tancred and the MP walking in step. Guy was left in the drowning, sea-green shade. He raised his eyes to Jill. Her hands were clenched over her forehead. She drew them slowly down her cheeks with a long shuddering sigh.

Guy said, "They'll let him go. He didn't know what he was doing. The main thing is, you're safe."

She stared at him. He touched his itchy moustache. He said, "I'm sorry it had to happen this way."

"Sorry!" Her laugh veered suddenly upwards; she bit her hand to stop herself. "Oh, your politeness kills me," she hissed.

"Jill," he said, moving a step towards her.

"Don't touch me!"

"We've got to work something out. For God's sake!"

She had turned and run out of the room. He went after her, down the wide corridor and round the back of the verandah to the kitchen where a fat Tamil cook, oblivious of the drama, was rolling out pastry on his mountainous bare stomach with a rolling pin.

She fled into the garden. He went after her, calling out her name. She fled past the tennis-court and the servants' quarters and a grove of mangosteens, and began to climb the boulder-strewn hillside beyond.

"Jill!" he cried. "Jill!"

She would not stop. Panting he climbed after her in his Colombo shoes, slipping on the red gravelly soil, ripping his shirt on a thorn bush. Near the top he caught up with her. She was leaning, breathless, against a great grey rock that reared out of the earth. Her face was hidden from him.

"Leave me alone," she whispered.

"All right. I won't touch you. All I ask is that you look over there, right there, on the horizon. You see that dark haze? There was an attack on Colombo this morning. A clandestine transmitter blocked out the radar long enough for the Japs to take us by surprise. If I hadn't come here with Rawling, God knows what would have happened when they found out."

Jill was silent.

"It's not my fault," he went on with mounting exasperation. "You always used to say Harry had been out East too long."

"What has that got to do with it?"

"My darling. Jill. Don't you see? You can't go on living like this."

She turned her head and looked at him, splaying her fingers on the rock. "It was because of me, wasn't it?"

"What was?"

"Because of me that you blabbed about the transmitter."

"No!"

"You knew what Harry was doing. You knew it was just his harmless eccentricity. You blabbed because of me, because I said I wouldn't leave him."

"It was not harmless! Any more than what he's doing to you!"

She pushed away from the rock. She came up to him. Guy squinted in the painful sunlight.

"You say I can't go on living like this," she hissed at him. "How else am I expected to live? You still think that coming to Ceylon is like going out of London to the country. Well it's not. This isn't England, even when it pretends to be. It's a little tiny community, a long way from home, trying to keep the balance between East and West. People who can't do that don't belong out here. They mess things up—"

"Like Harry—"

"No! That just shows how little you know. Harry's a settler.

309

This is his country. He's like Bruce. He builds something and he sticks by it, and so what if he lets the rest of the world go hang! When I look at you, I see someone who's running so fast to keep up, you don't know what you want any more or what you believe in."

"You don't know . . . what are you saying?" He was inarticulate with the unfairness of this. He waved his arms at the shimmering horizons. "What about all this? You can't just sit here. It's not going to go on for ever, you know! What then?"

"Who cares? Australia, America, who cares? There's nothing for us in England any more. This stupid War . . . I used to laugh at Harry when he said that Eastern values were all that was left; that the codes he'd been brought up on had shattered. But he was right. You're an example of it. Look what you've just done to your own brother!"

In fury and frustration he made to strike her. Jill recoiled, lost her footing on the sloping ground and fell. Guy helped her up and saw she had cut her hand on a stone; pearls of blood welled from the graze. He tried to take her hand to his lips. She wrenched it away from him, her eyes full of tears.

"Why don't you go away!" she shouted. "Don't you see what you've done here? Haven't you drawn enough blood?"

"What kind of woman are you?" he cried out. "I thought you loved me."

"I never asked you to believe that."

Tears were rolling down her cheeks. He said, savagely, "What if you're pregnant? You might be pregnant. You've thought of that, haven't you?"

She did not answer. She walked a few steps down the hillside, covering her eyes. Below them stretched the Tancred estate. A dark green army of rubber trees, leaderless now.

"Tell me!"

"You can forget about all that," she said in a muffled voice. "Go back to England, Guy. Be a success. Make somebody proud of you. Harry used to be proud of you."

The sun that beat fiercely down on him merely touched her hair gold above the collar of her white blouse. Fire was her element, the one she was happiest in. He said, "I'm not going. I'm not. It'll be my child, not Harry's. I've had a cable from Dunlop Orient, you know, Jill. They want me back in London, they've got visions of me being captured by the Japanese. Well, I'm staying. You're going to need me now."

A horn sounded from way below them. Jill gave a cry, and started back down the hill.

310

"Wait! I'm coming with you," called Guy.

She stopped. When he reached her, she looked at him with a poignant, sad expression. He clasped her hand and tried to pull her into his arms, unable to bear the thought of losing her. She turned her face away.

He let her go.

"Please don't come down yet," she said. "I don't want you to be there when I talk to Harry."

"Why?"

She raised her arms and let them fall to her sides. "You may as well know. I was going to tell you anyway. That boy you saw at the native school, Harry's child, do you remember? Well, I'm adopting him. Harry doesn't know yet. But it's all going through. Peter is going to be my son. If you and I have made a baby . . . well I'm sorry, I won't be having it. I'm sorry, Guy. I've made up my mind."

Jill went away from him, down the hill. He stood as if rooted to the soil, along with the rocks and thorn bushes and all the dead, dry things that wouldn't grow out here. He saw below him the two Tamil Boys, Rasani and Kelamuttu, carrying Michael Kandasala's body out of the garden shed. From this distance they looked like small black insects struggling with their burden across the grass.

The sound of a horn again, impatient this time, brought him out of his stupor. He walked down and through the silent house to the drive. Rawling was waiting for him impatiently beside the remaining jeep.

"Where's Jill?" asked Guy. He looked across the forsaken lawn with its solitary flame tree. He looked back at the forsaken verandah.

"She went in the other jeep. With her husband. Couldn't stop her, I suppose. Hop in, Tancred. I have to get back before dark, you know. If we've been barking up the wrong tree, we'll just have to find the right one." He felt his jaw. "Sorry business though. About your brother, I mean."

It was a moment before Guy replied. "It's the East," he said then, getting into the jeep. "Things happen to people."

He sat very upright, as the jeep swept away from Kelani Lodge, and the rubber trees stood to attention on either side.

He woke up in the dark, with a headache. What the time was he had no idea. He reached out through levels of unconsciousness

311

for the clock on his bedside table. And rolled into the stream.

The cold water brought him to his senses. Gasping, he pulled himself from under the road-bridge, and up through the paddy to the side of the road. His left leg didn't want to go any further for the moment. He sat in the grass, shivering, slapping warmth and life back into his numbed body.

The jumble in David Gifford's brain assembled itself into coherent memory. His Hurricane had crashed somewhere... over there. He had come to in a heap of wreckage, with a Jap plane still circling overhead. It felt as if he had cracked his head open. His knee hurt. But he was in one piece. He remembered thinking – if he was to stay where he was, the Jap might go away. But he could smell fuel. It was leaking all over him. He unstrapped himself and half fell, half pushed himself out of the cockpit into the soft mud of a paddy-field.

The Zero had seen him. Spouts of mud and water skipped past him as the Zero came in, firing. He ran, limping, towards the edge of the paddy; then he fell into the mud as the Hurricane exploded behind him in a gust of flame. The Zero was circling for another run at him. With a fearful effort, he dragged himself under the road-bridge. He must have passed out almost immediately: he remembered nothing else at all.

It was a dirt road he had clambered up to. He might have to sit here all night to find someone to take him back towards Colombo. No sooner had this thought passed through his dazed mind than he thought he heard a clanking noise coming out of the darkness. Rubbing his eyes, he saw a faint firefly light which bobbed and swerved and grew brighter. Down the road came an old man on an even older bicycle.

David, pointing and gesturing, tried to get him to go for help. The old Sinhalese peasant would have none of it. With astonishing strength he got David to his feet and manoeuvred him on to his saddle, sitting backward, his injured leg off the ground. Pedalling upright, while his rescued airman held on with both hands to a black umbrella strapped to the rear luggage-carrier, the old man made unsteady progress to the main road.

Where they were, David had no means of knowing. The old peasant evidently knew, because at the main road he wobbled across it and stopped, considerately dismounting on the side of David's good leg. He took his umbrella, and began waving it at the Colombo-bound traffic. A couple of cars went by, too fast to have caught more than a glimpse of them in their muffled headlights. Then a lorry stopped. It reversed up to them on the narrow verge above the paddy. The old man negotiated David off the bike.

"Look, this is most awfully kind of you," muttered David through chattering teeth. He steadied himself against the side of the lorry and searched his pockets as if he expected to find a tip. The old man exposed betel-stained gums in a toothless grin.

"I'm afraid I don't seem . . .," David began. Then he remembered something; something he had no more use for. Reaching inside his vest he pulled out the Egyptian ankh, on its chain, and lifted it over his head. Even in the darkness it seemed to glow as if it had access to its own source of light.

"It's yours," he said, dropping it into the man's palm.

With several muttered exclamations, the old peasant salaamed and waggled his head. As the lorry-driver, a cleanly dressed Tamil, helped David into his cab, the man came back with his umbrella and pressed it into David's hand.

"*Botal arina yatura,*" he cried, waving the ankh. "*Bohoma istu-tiy!*"

"What was all that?" asked David as the lorry drove away.

"He said to you – 'Bottle-opener. Thank you greatly.' "

"Ah." David Gifford stretched out painfully in the seat. In the warmth of the cab his senses were returning. He began to realise what he must look like – although the lorry-driver, with customary Ceylonese reserve, had made no comment. His jacket had lost a sleeve. His shirt was ripped open. He was covered in mud and oil which in the dark he had taken for blood. His left leg was throbbing: he could see a deep gash above his knee, through the tattered trousers. His ankle was either sprained or broken.

But he was alive.

"What time is it?" he asked.

"Eight o'clock, sir."

"On Sunday night?"

"Yes, sir. This is Sunday." The man threw him a frightened glance.

He had been out cold for ten hours. To his amazement he felt in quite good shape, considering. His head was clear, even though it still hurt. Putting up his hand, he ran his fingers gingerly round a large bump above his left temple. The hair around it was sticky with blood.

"This is an evil day, sir," declared the lorry-driver. "An evil day." He dotted a cross on his chest. "You airmen, sir, you saved our bacon, no fear. I witnessed two planes in sky over Kotahena this morning. They were giving each other what for. It was a most

313

dangerous, unwatchable sight. Now I shall take you to General Hospital, sir. Is it?"

"Can you take me to Cinnamon Gardens?"

"Cinnamon Gardens? No trouble, sir. We will be there in a jiffy."

David gave him the address. Then he closed his eyes.

By the time they got there, his leg had stiffened up. But the throbbing had stopped. Balancing with the aid of the umbrella, he levered himself out of the cab.

"I think you should be in hospital, sir."

"No. I'm all right. Thank you. Thank you very much."

Alone, in the pitch dark, he opened the gate and limped up the drive. A wind had arisen. Trees he couldn't see clicked sharp tongues above his head. The bungalow was shuttered. Its front door opened into darkness. It all looked as deserted as the Colombo streets he had driven through.

For a moment, David was possessed by the wild idea that everybody had fled the bombed city; that he was the only living soul. Then, as he limped up the porch steps and hobbled into the Donaldsons' hall, he saw the music-room door ajar, and a triangle of light.

He hobbled towards the light – and stopped, rooted to the spot by the noise of someone crying their eyes out. And Maria's voice –

"Don't give up. Please, Sylvia. We mustn't give up hope!"

The crying eased, into long, sobbing breaths. He heard Sylvia say something about a silver brandy-flask. Then she wailed aloud, "Why couldn't he have gone to Dartmouth and been an officer like everyone else! It's not fair, it's not *fair*! Charlie's not the kind of person to die!"

David felt a wave of nausea come over him. With his umbrella he pushed open the door. Sylvia sat at her mother's old Dutch bureau, staring blindly into the tiny mirror inlaid between the cabinets. Maria de Vos, in a powder-blue dress rusted with smears of blood, stood behind her, brushing her hair, as David had seen ayahs do to comfort children. Sylvia's white hands clasped Maria's browner ones and pulled them down around her.

"Oh, Maria, hold me," she cried. "Oh, Maria, I know it's just as beastly for you!" She added in a broken voice, as Maria hugged her, "Do you know, Maria. When I came back here from England, I thought I was never going to feel so bitter cold again."

The two heads, blonde and dark, wept together for their dead.

David, at the doorway, fought down the sickness in his throat.

"Has the *Dorsetshire* gone down?" he said hoarsely.

Which of them shrieked he didn't know. A chair tumbled backwards. Maria took one swooning look at him and fainted to the carpet. Sylvia flew to him and held him tight.

"Oh, David!" She sobbed and hugged him, kissed him and hugged him again, her blonde hair against his torn and oily shirt. "Oh, David, I knew you'd be all right, I knew!"

David's head was whirling again. Charlie had always won the Swimming Cup. He waved his umbrella. "We must get water or something for Maria," he burst out. But Sylvia wouldn't let him go. She looked up at him through her tears; her eyes glistening; her lips parted in triumph.

"You see, I *believed* for you," she sobbed. "I believed in *us*."

FOUR

A LOUD bang. The cork sailed across the room, and landed in a wastepaper basket.

"Good shot, sir!" exclaimed the Governor of Ceylon, accepting a glass of champagne. "We could do with a few more like you on our capital ships."

J. P. Kandasala flushed with pleasure as he poured the precious champagne. His Excellency's remark was presumably jocular, but it set the seal on what had been a thoroughly top-notch day. The Civil Defence Underground Control Room had been J.P.'s baby almost from the start. In the present exalted company he would be the first to admit that his was a modest light – but there was no denying that it had come out from under its bushel and was shining brightly. Even the Civil Defence Commissioner himself, Mr Oliver Goonetilleke, had come up to him a few minutes ago and placed his hand familiarly on his shoulder and cried, "Well done, J.P.!"

His Excellency the Governor had taken a little longer to unbend. He had given a visible start when J.P. was introduced to him, as if the name Kandasala struck some disagreeable chord in his memory. His gaze had strayed, alighting finally on the Control Room roof.

"Not going to fall in on us, is it?"

"No, no, sir. No. Not without a palpable hit."

Which was true: although without having to look up, as he poured the last few drops of Mumm into his own glass on the table, J. P. Kandasala knew that the slab concrete was still wet in places, and bulged a bit over the door at the foot of the steps, and might possibly bulge in other parts which were concealed by the festoons of red and black wires, leads and copper pipes running directly underneath. But needs must. The bally job was completed, that was the main thing, and here they were, raising their glasses to His Excellency's toast –

"Ladies and gentlemen – to victory!"

"To victory!"

319

"Hear, hear, sir!"

"To victory!"

Glasses clinked. "And to your loyal Sinhalese workers who built this place!" toasted Oliver Goonetilleke silkily, to which the Governor led the Hear, hears!

Beaming with pleasure, J. P. Kandasala surveyed his cosy empire: the sparkling new telephone switchboards along the far wall which connected them with each ARP district and with all the major military and industrial installations in the Colombo area; and above them, his pride and joy, the enormous laminated map of the city, illuminated (his own idea) with twinkling Christmas-tree lights, red for military targets, green for civilian targets, blue marking the principal civic air-raid shelters. Between the doors to the storeroom and the WC, under a wall-clock salvaged from the wreckage of the Naval Stores after the Japanese air raid three days ago, hung another of J.P.'s inspirations. A placard, framed in passe-partout, it consists of just two words printed in large red letters – BE PREPARED.

Greatly daring, J.P. sidled up to the Governor. His Excellency had laid his tin hat down on the wide office table which stood in the middle of the room and was perusing some notes.

"Pardon me, Excellency. I have a sneaking hunch that both Buddha and your Sir Baden-Powell would concur with the efficacy of our injunction on the wall over there. Be Prepared is a message of universal application, would you not say?"

Sir Oliver Prescott was about to reply when there fell upon their ears a low, powerful rumbling noise, heading from the south. It died away. Immediately afterwards came a gigantic crash, directly overhead. The lights flickered. Two secretaries clung together. A switchboard operator screamed and clapped her hand over her mouth.

"Thunder! It's only thunder!" cried several voices. People began to laugh, rather loudly. Even J.P. could not resist smiling, though, really, the generator could have behaved better . . . but what on earth was this?

All around the corners of the ceiling beads of water were blossoming. As the rain drummed down, the beads formed necklaces; the necklaces formed pendants. Water, in little rivulets, began to run down the walls.

For a moment J. P. Kandasala stood paralysed with shock. Catching sight of one of the civil engineers from PWD, he pushed through a crowd of chattering civil defence workers and went to speak to him. When he returned, he was wringing his hands.

"I am most infernally sorry," he exclaimed to Goonetilleke and the Governor, his voice pitched higher in his distress. "The PWD fellow says damned if it isn't the guttering that's broken somewhere. We had guttering you know, to avoid this eventuality. I saw to it myself. I am most full of apologies." He looked down at his shoes. Already there was an inch of water on the floor. Raindrops were invading his laminated map of Colombo. At any moment he expected the Christmas-tree lights to fuse and plunge the city into darkness.

"Never mind, Mr Kandasala," returned Sir Oliver with a smile. "Experience teaches us to rise above disaster." So saying, with commendable presence of mind he hitched up his white ducks (the crisis had brought him out in long trousers) and sat himself on the table in the middle of the room, his feet well clear of the floor. As soon as he had been brought a chair for his feet, he raised his hand.

"Silence please!" shouted J. P. Kandasala.

The deferential hush was broken only by the rain on the roof and the soft throbbing of the generator next door.

"Thank you," said Sir Oliver, clearing his throat. "And thank you for inviting me to declare open this splendid new underground civil defence HQ. A remarkable civil engineering job by the PWD, if I may say so, although I'm sure you all hope we send the Japs packing before the monsoon rains begin!"

J. P. Kandasala led the laughter. Sir Oliver continued, his hands resting on his knees. "As you will all know by now, the Japs came over again yesterday and dropped a few bombs on Trinco before they turned tail and fled. Now I'm not going to sit here and tell you they didn't do any damage. Some of our harbour and aerodrome installations took a knocking. We lost a few aircraft I'm sorry to say. But the cheering news is, we gave the Japs a bloody nose. Six enemy aircraft destroyed. Six more probably destroyed, and two others damaged. It was time the Japs came in contact with bone. And by golly this time they did."

Sir Oliver paused, as if expecting a scattering of applause; although he could not help noticing that most of his audience were too preoccupied lifting first one foot then the other out of the rainwater, or finding chairs and typewriter cases to stand on, to take his news to heart. Perhaps it was for the best. He could not conceivably tell these people that the Japanese attack on Trincomalee had to all intents and purposes ended Ceylon's brief resistance; that the dockyards were still blazing; that China Bay had been virtually destroyed; that of the seventeen brave

321

Hurricanes which had taken to the air, outnumbered two to one, just nine crippled survivors had limped back to base; or that Japanese bombers were believed to have sent seven ships off the east coast to the bottom, including the aircraft-carrier *Hermes* with upwards of three hundred dead.

The lights flickered again. The generator next door sounded as if it was developing a bad chest. Rain might put the Control Room out of action before the Japanese could. Sitting to attention on the table, Sir Oliver groped for the right phrases.

"It is our view that the enemy won't be coming back in a hurry," he declared in a firm voice. "If they do . . . well, we've got one or two surprises up our sleeve. I can't tell you what they are. But you can take my word for it, the Japs aren't going to find us easy customers to deal with. . . ."

He hesitated again, suddenly at a loss, and surveyed the brown faces ranged around him in a half-circle, most of them politely smiling with that practised Indian smile which could encompass disbelief and suspicion as easily as encouragement – how passionately he wanted to reassure them, to speak mighty, stirring, heartfelt words which restored his place in their trust! *Let us be true to ourselves; let us be true to what history has made us.*

He cleared his throat. "As Governor of this island I have had occasion to observe that a close bond of friendship and common interest exists between the British and the Ceylonese. I intend to stay and see that link maintained and strengthened in the years ahead. I am proud of you, and what you have done, and you may like to know that my feelings are shared back home. A London newspaper wrote this week: 'The whole Empire will rejoice that this peaceful island of spicy breezes has shown what can be done against massed air assault when defences are well planned and the population inspiringly led –' "

"Hear! Hear!" interjected J. P. Kandasala.

" '– by a Commander like Admiral Sir Geoffrey Layton.' " With fingers which shook slightly, Sir Oliver took out of his shirt pocket a cutting from the *Ceylon Daily News*. From where J. P. Kandasala stood, ankle-deep in water, it looked like a piece of verse. "For my part, what I should like to offer up. . . ."

What, for his part, the Governor was going to offer up, J.P. and the others were never to discover. For at that moment, as the patter of rain died away, a new noise reached them, a growling noise, rapidly crescendoing to a full-throated roar. The lights flickered wildly. Switchboard operators, secretaries, messenger boys, with one accord dived under the Governor's table with shouts and screams and gesticulations of alarm.

Conscious of sitting on top of a heap of His Majesty's subjects, Sir Oliver Prescott drew in his legs and plucked fretfully at his trousers, hitching them higher and higher, and reciting something to himself in a low, disconsolate, muttering voice; while the lone Japanese recce plane flew on unmolested over the city, and all the Christmas lights on the map went out.

POSTSCRIPT

THE Japanese never came back; although it is unlikely that Harry Tancred's Buddhist messages of peace had any bearing on this strategic error. For nine more months, Ceylon returned to being, as Ovid had called it two thousand years earlier, the last outpost of the civilised world. And then, early the following year, the Australians drove the Japanese out of Papua, and the Americans defeated the Japanese in Guadalcanal, and the red sun began to set.

The slighting epithet used by the Malays about Singapore – *tarekh orang puteh lari*, "the time when the tuans ran" – never applied in Ceylon. But Miss Utteridge was right about the War. Win or lose, things would never be the same. For several weeks after the Easter Sunday raid, Colombo remained a deserted city. Trams and buses stopped running. Rickshaw coolies were as elusive as tree-monkeys. Sanitation fell into disrepair. Banks and hotels closed down or operated with skeleton staffs. Shops were abandoned and had to be taken over by government employees. In addition, Cargills and Elephant House were forced to announce the withdrawal of all credit facilities to their customers. Europeans not only had to do their own washing and shopping: they had to pay in cash.

One week after taking Harry Tancred into custody, Rawling tracked down the right transmitter. Housed in a Buddhist temple on the east coast, it had been used to transmit valuable information to a Japanese submarine offshore about the movement of Allied shipping in and out of Trincomalee. This success was soured for Rawling by the collapse of his entire secret counter-invasion strategy, based on the speed and performance of the Japanese bicycle. In the wreckage of a Jap bomber, brought down over Colombo, he discovered the remains of a revolutionary new kind of powerful light-weight motor-bike.

Major Rawling – he was never gazetted at the higher rank, allegedly on the grounds that it would focus undue attention on him – continued to mastermind Ceylon's intelligence operations

327

until the end of 1943 when his role was taken over by SOE. He was seconded back to Whitehall, and dropped out of sight, so successfully that no record of his post-War career has been made available.

Sea eagles still wheel on white-tipped wings over the grave of *Dorsetshire* and the men who went down in her. Charles Bilbow is not among them. His body was recovered from the sea, and buried in Kenatte cemetery in Colombo. On his tombstone are written the words given to the dying Sir Richard Grenville in Lord Alfred Tennyson's "The Revenge" –

> *I have fought for Queen and Faith like a valiant man and true;*
> *I have only done my duty as a man is bound to do.*

Bilbow's name is inscribed on Lutyens's Victory Column, along with that of Ingram Bywater who never recovered from the head wound he received on Easter Sunday in circumstances which remain mysterious to this day. The Victory Column was re-erected, with the added names of other Ceylon casualties of the Second World War, in Victoria Park in Cinnamon Gardens. It is now known plainly as the War Memorial; and the Park has been renamed Viharamahadevi after an ancient Sinhalese queen who was thrown overboard off Colombo and washed up near Yala. Enquiries have not disclosed the whereabouts of Michael Kandasala's grave.

The Colombo Club was taken over by the government in 1956 and is now a tourist bureau. Few of its erstwhile members survive, although when Mr Jayewardene ousted Mrs Bandaranaike's socialist coalition government in 1977, Tony Apple returned to buy himself a holiday home near Galle. Percy Buller resigned from the Club shortly after the Easter Sunday raid, and killed himself four months later after a scandal involving young Sinhalese girls in the Pettah. Sandy Duncannon died peacefully in bed, his latest dictionary asleep beside him.

Sebastian Clarke, his plans for destruction stillborn, was transferred to London in 1946 to work on the civil effects of atomic warfare. Kitty came with him. Deciding that he could have been inculpated in the Michael Kandasala fiasco, George Donaldson did the correct thing and tendered his resignation. The Governor refused to accept it; George Donaldson was transferred to other duties, and after the War returned to England where his brother found him a sinecure in his merchant bank. Elizabeth Donaldson, back in her element, reunited with her darling son, found a new lease of life, which happily has not yet expired.

Sir Oliver Prescott retired as soon as he decently could, after the War, loaded with honours and small grievances. Visitors to Castle Lodon in Hereford who look round the back of the church at the top of the street can see the half-profile of the tall brick rectory in which he spent the remaining fifteen years of his life. He married his housekeeper, who never ran out of marmalade, and became a local JP as well as a regular contributor of occasional verse to the parish magazine.

David Gifford ended the War with a DFC and the hand of Sylvia Donaldson. During his spell as a pilot for BOAC they lived in Maidenhead, where Sylvia brought up the son she had conceived in Ceylon some time around her twenty-first birthday. Andrew had blond hair and blue eyes: but their old Ceylon friends made a point of remarking that he had David's chin. Not long after the boy had finished school, David resigned from BOAC and bought the major share in a vineyard near Frant in Sussex. After two decades of hard labour this vineyard now produces a medium dry white wine good enough to be imported by the French – although they must surely be puzzled by the picture of a Model T on the label.

As for Maria de Vos, she went back to Mademoiselle Orliga's dance studio. After the War, she married her father's brightest Burgher law pupil, and for her wedding wore an old Dutch-period style wedding dress with a high neckline and a rounded collar edged with lace. When Independence came to Ceylon the following year, she emigrated with her husband to Australia. He gambled most of the proceeds of his law practice away on the horses, and died in his early fifties, but Maria herself is still a familiar voice on the end of the telephone for people reserving their Adelaide Festival tickets.

Guy Tancred never made it to China Bay. If he had heard the East a-callin', he never admitted it to Lydia. For a few weeks, until the Japanese threat had receded, he kicked his heels in Colombo, watching the statues of the Ceylon proconsuls shimmer and vanish in the pre-monsoon heat. Then, the recall papers from Dunlop Orient in his pocket, he returned to London.

Guy left Dunlop Orient some years before that company lost ground to its competitors overseas and was eventually bought up by Matsushida Industries of Japan. He used to speak of his brief time in Ceylon as exhilarating and adventuresome: and before long that was how it actually began to appear to him; although it always retained in his mind some of the quality of a hallucination, a transient, heightened, dreamlike interlude from which the awakening was always attended with sadness.

Nevertheless he got into the habit each year of sending a Christmas card to his brother and sister-in-law in Ceylon. Harry was not held for very long by the Colombo police. In the eyes of the authorities his chief crime was stupidity. He was a good planter; his pacifism was overlooked in the greater interests of the war effort.

Most of Kelani Lodge was requisitioned as a convalescent home for Australian soldiers. As soon as Harry was freed, Jill turned her back on Colombo and stayed up at Kelani to nurse the troops. When Bruce MacAlister died, they put in a request to leave Kelani and take over his rubber estate away in the Kitulgala hills. Guy pulled strings at Dunlop Orient, and the request was granted. The following year, Jill's Christmas card was addressed from Rubble House, Kitulgala Estate, Sabaragamuwa Province, Ceylon.

Life is what you make it!! Jill had written on the back of a photograph of Rubble House, the foundations already laid for an extension to MacAlister's bungalow. Guy put the card on the mantelpiece and took the dog out into the snow, so that the others never saw his unexpected tears.